Peder Victorious

A Tale of the Pioneers
Twenty Years Later

by

O. E. Rölvaag

Translated from the Norwegian
by Nora O. Solum & the Author

With an Introduction by Gudrun Hovde Gvåle

Translated from the Norwegian
& adapted by Einar Haugen

University of Nebraska Press
Lincoln and London

Manufactured in the United States of America

First Bison Book edition: 1982
Most recent printing indicated by the first digit below:
6   7   8   9   10

Library of Congress Cataloging in Publication Data
Rølvaag, Ole Edvart, 1876–1931.
  Peder victorious.

  Translation of: Peder Seier.
  Reprint. Originally published: New York : Harper & Row, 1929.
(Perennial classics)
  Bibliography: p.
  I. Title.
PT9150.R55P413   1982   839.8'2372   81–16402
ISBN 0–8032–8906–5 (pbk.)   AACR2

Published by arrangement with Harper & Row, Publishers,
Incorporated

Peder Victorious, a translation of *Peder Seier*, was first
published in Oslo, Norway, in 1928.

∞

Contents

Introduction*

Rölvaag's pioneer novel *Giants in the Earth* had no sooner made its successful appearance in Norway in 1925 than the author began to think of a sequel. It was going to require three full years, however, before he could complete the work that he himself as well as his readers awaited with impatience. They were eager to know how the spirit of Per Hansa was going to live on in Peder Victorious, the boy who was born with a victory cowl on the pioneers' first Christmas eve in Spring Creek. Even while he was at work on his great epic of pioneering, Rölvaag realized that he would have to write more books about the immigrants if he were to give a true and rounded picture of their lives. His letters from the year of publication show that he had two and even three volumes in mind, but also that he had no time for literary activity.

His leave of absence from St. Olaf College in 1923-24 had been no vacation, even though it had been an enriching, creative, and broadening experience. At the end of it he returned to head once more the Department of Norwegian, and he plunged into college life again in spite of his weariness. His classes were larger than ever, and he never spared himself in relation to his students. In 1925 he took an active part in preparing the great celebration of the Norse-American Centennial in Minneapolis, which resulted in his being made secretary of the newly founded Norwegian-American Historical Association. His literary

* From Gudrun Hovde Gvåle's *Ole Edvart Rølvaag: Nordmann og Amerikanar* (Oslo, 1962), pp. 372-385. Translated from the Norwegian and adapted for this edition by Einar Haugen.

work was limited to a few articles and to the preparation of the American version of *Giants*. He was also profoundly depressed over the indifference to his work on the part of his own countrymen in America: "Talk of crying in the wilderness!" he wrote to an old schoolmate in the winter of 1925.

Nevertheless, the theme of his next book had begun to take shape in his mind. He wrote to a friend in December of 1925: "I simply have to write another volume, one that will deal primarily with the second generation, to show those people over in Norway how inevitable it is that we have become Americans. But even this I don't have the time for. Art takes its whole man!" This focus on the problems of Americanization was an old one with Rölvaag, but his renewed residence in Norway had brought home to him the need for clarifying it for his countrymen there. In speeches and articles he pictured the emigrant's disillusionment at returning home and finding that he is a stranger to his own kin and that even highly educated people in the homeland imagine that Norwegians in America can remain "Norwegian" forever. In an interview with the Norwegian poet Nils Collett Vogt, who was a visitor to the Norse-American Centennial, Rölvaag had defended his students for writing their essays on Ibsen in English: "The young people are Americans. Don't forget that! They are going to live and work here. The crucial thing for us teachers is to give them an impression of Norwegian culture and to keep the contact alive as well as possible. We can't manage any more."

A major theme of the new book about the second generation would therefore be to show how the young people who grew up in America were shaped by their environment into real Americans, in spite of their Norwegian parents and their Norwegian heritage. A portrayal of the conflict between the generations would give him an opportunity to uncover ever-deeper layers of the tragedy of emigration, the basic motif to which Rölvaag's writing again and again returns.

Unhappily Rölvaag could not draw on his own experiences to the same extent that he could in his pioneer novel. To be sure, he had had intimate contact with the second generation ever since his immigration, above all in his teaching and also through his own children who were just

growing into the ranks of American youth. But it is clear
that he did not feel himself on nearly as safe ground in
dealing with Peder as with Beret and the others, where his
own intimate self-exhumation could provide the psychological groundwork. Just as he had turned to his father-
in-law as a "priceless source" of information about pioneer
days, so he now looked to his intelligent younger friends
for light on their problems. To Ruth Lima he wrote in
November of 1925: "You are a child of the second generation. I want you to give me the second-generation psychology. How did you feel at the very threshold of your
conscious life, as far back as you remember? How much
were you Norwegian, and how much were you American?
And when were you the one, when the other . . . ? Can
you relate some little incidents from your early youth that
tend to show how you felt at that time?"

The work did not proceed very expeditiously, however.
Not only was he hampered by his many duties, but the
heart disease that had long threatened him took a turn
for the worse and kept him from working most of the
summer of 1926. His health was shattered, but still he
never gave up. Most of *Peder Victorious* was written in
his cabin at Big Island Lake in the summer of 1927. The
publication was further delayed by his wish to have both
the English and the Norwegian version published simul-
taneously. The manuscript was sent to Aschehoug in Oslo
in the summer of 1928 and published that fall, while the
English translation by Nora Solum was published by
Harper & Brothers in New York on the 1st of January the
following year.

The background of the action in *Peder Victorious* is the
development of the American Midwest, which was then
considered the Northwest, and above all the transformation of the Dakota Territory into the states of North and
South Dakota in 1889. There are still echoes in this book
of the westward movement, stretching all the way to the
Pacific coast. Even in Spring Creek some of the settlers,
young and old, are carried along by the stream of westward
migration. Ole Holm, the oldest son of Beret and Per
Hansa, goes out to Montana to find himself a farm, and
his sister Anne Marie follows him. In South Dakota, society has begun to take shape, with institutions like school
and government being firmly established. The Norwegians

at Spring Creek also keep up with the times; as in other Norwegian communities, their churches are racked and split by doctrinal controversy. Spring Creek is a "mixed" settlement with a strong Irish-Catholic component, and the Norwegian language is therefore under strong pressures by the second generation.

In spite of the firm historical contours that are drawn up as a background for this story, there is not the same sweep, nor do we hear the same resounding echoes of man's greatest migration, that gave his pioneer story its glitter and grandeur. We do not see man silhouetted against the western skies in a gigantic battle with the trollish powers of nature. We are not witnesses to the drama of creation, only to the slow, unexciting process of the "mill of the gods" grinding out the materials for the building up of a new culture. The author conducts us down into the mazes of a youthful soul and holds us there a good deal of the time, in order to show us how "the roots grow down into the soil."

In this book that bears his name, Peder Victorious grows out of childhood into youth. "The theme of *Peder* is revolt," the author wrote to Lincoln Colcord, the translator of *Giants*. It was necessary, he felt, for the second generation to rebel against its elders if it were to win a foothold in American society. Peder's rebellion is made clear to us from the very first page.

In his school years, writes the author, Peder lives in three "rooms." In one of these rooms he is wholly by himself; he dreams about the future and all that he will take hold of when he is a grown man. Here everything is in English, and he is always happy. In the second room everything is in Norwegian, and there Peder is less content. He is accompanied by his mother and the family, but they understand little of all the adventures that could be waiting for all of them. They do their work routinely, and they take no interest in politics, which is Peder's passion. He is the youngest and the most American in the whole family. Least of all does he understand his mother, who neither can nor will talk English, the "easiest thing in the world!" And yet she could be so incredibly good and wise!

In the third room, too, everything is in Norwegian to begin with, for there his mother has been with him from the start. Later he is alone with God there in the dark, quiet room. In the first happy years when his father was still alive, Peder had always seen the Lord as a nice old grandpa. But when his father was lost in the snowstorm and was found dead on the western prairie, in spite of Peder's unwavering faith and his and his mother's fervent prayers, Peder's image of God changed completely. "God suddenly became a harsh, heartless creature one had to watch out for." After that time he felt rather a defiance when he entered the third room, and in the next years he is much affected by religious doubt. He finds it difficult to understand the goodness of a God who is also a vengeful God. Peder's intellect questions many of the Lutheran dogmas he meets in church and religious school.

His doubts about the church are strengthened through his frightening experience with the zealous pietism that drives the innocent little girl Oline Tuftan out of her mind and makes her hang herself. The quarreling and the gossip that accompanied the split in the congregation are also factors in young Peder's waning confidence in the church. He reaches the conclusion that this God who seems to hate life must be Norwegian. Even though his mother knows that she should try to see the good side of people, not just their sins, she is too afraid to let in the sunlight, too afraid of life for Peder to come to terms with her kind of Christianity. The Norwegian religious books, with their old-fashioned Danish language, do not promote a friendly attitude in Peder toward his religious heritage. Even so, he promises to read the Bible in order to please his mother, but he does not do so until the minister gives him a Bible in English.

The minister, Pastor Gabrielsen, has an eye for Peder's intelligence and tries to persuade him to read for the ministry. But in the face of Peder's growing interest in practical matters and his dawning love life the minister has to give in. The minister, however, is a factor in the growing Americanization, for he is convinced that "in twenty years there will not be heard a Norwegian word in all America." In the local district school the children are not allowed to use anything but English, even in the schoolyard. Miss Mahon warns Peder against speaking Norwegian at home, for he has "a bad accent," which he must get rid of. In this and other ways he is brought up to admire everything American. The author uses his opportu-

nity to air his distaste for the American common school
by drawing a thoroughly unsympathetic picture of this
young "Yankee" schoolma'am.

All the teaching in this school is exclusively concerned
with America and its life, a hymn to America as the
"home of the free." The immigrant children in particular
must learn to be grateful for their citizenship in a country
where everyone can aspire to wealth and the highest positions. The Declaration of Independence is Miss Mahon's
confession of faith and is read with solemn devotion every
morning and afternoon. It helps but little that Beret gets
Peder transferred to a more Norwegian school district the
last few years before confirmation. The language, the subjects, and the textbooks are the same there. The only thing
he finds about the country of his fathers is a drawing in a
geography book, which shows "a Norskie" wrestling with
a bear. In comparison with all the glorious things that he
has learned about American civilization this is so pitiful
that Peder wishes that he might go far away where he
would never again have to hear about Norwegians. His
heritage is an anachronism, rather like the old cow Rosie,
who came along into the new, modern barn on the Holm
farm.

This is the deep human tragedy of the book: the child
that slips into a world where his mother cannot go. She
can no longer make herself understood to her own children, while the child has its family roots cut. Rölvaag
wrote to the Norwegian-American editor Kristian Prest-
gard in 1928, "I think I have put my finger on the tragedy
of emigration, the true tragedy of the soul, more intensely
in this book than in any of my others."

In a long letter to Professor Percy Boynton in 1929, he
develops this theme of the conflict between generations:
"The break between the first and the second generations
of Americans of British descent may oftentimes be quite
violent, due to the difference in schooling and outlook and
the difference in traditions between the two countries. But
in the case of, for example, Scandinavian Americans, the
break is oftentimes brutal, though the human qualities
may be just as fine. You will agree with me, I think, that
it is a tragedy for mother and child not to be able to con-
verse intimately with each other. Her songs he cannot
understand. What her soul has found nourishment in, he

cannot comprehend. She seems to him a peculiar anachronism, a senseless, unreasonable being. Can you not feel the heartache of that mother as she sees the child slip away from her into another world? Thither she cannot follow, for she has not the key, and the magic password she does not know. Can you understand her utter helplessness? And can you understand, too, that the child suffers a loss which he can ill afford? There are tragedies in life for which language has no adequate expression—this is one of them."

Presumably because this was supposed to be the book about Peder, the author has kept Beret in the background. Only toward the middle of the book does he pick up the thread of her experiences since Per Hansa vanished in the snowstorm. He has not had a fortunate hand with this part of the book, the continuity of the story being interrupted by it. Beret represents so large a part of what Peder is revolting against that she dominates the scene even when Peder is in the foreground. No matter how great an understanding the author has developed of the inner problems of the younger generation, their lives are not his own right into the marrow of his bones in the same way as is Beret's. In spite of external differences, Rölvaag himself had wandered the heavy path of the emigrant and experienced the shepherd's grief at "the nine-and-ninety who were lost to us." Therefore Beret interests both author and reader more than Peder, and she remains the main character of the book.

In the first summer after Per's death Beret had more than once thought of picking up her effects and her children and going back to Nordland. But gradually it becomes clear to her that the children are more at home here than in Norway, that their opportunities are greater here, and, above all, that she cannot run away from all that Per Hansa had founded. It is as if he were lying over there in the graveyard and keeping an eye on her; she has to carry on, as the old minister had told her, try to bring his work to fruition, even though she does not feel up to it.

Beret picks up her burden and bears it honorably. She becomes the best farmer in the whole settlement; she and the children labor early and late and keep up with the latest methods of farming. The Holm farm becomes a model for the rest. When Beret builds a new barn, it fol-

lows the plans that Per had sketched for the boys before
he left, only with up-to-date improvements that were unknown in his time. It is as if some of Per's spirit has found
housing in Beret as well. She always thinks of what he
would have said when she is making a decision. She sits
in front of his picture on the bedroom wall and confers
with him, as it were, when she is in her deepest quan-
daries. Faithfulness to all that Per stood for becomes the
constructive force in Beret's life.

The religious crisis that followed Per's death has made
her more tolerant and understanding, but her life is one
long sacrifice. Her children depart one by one to make
their own futures. She finds herself surrounded by a youth
that departs from religion and tradition alike. Her children speak only English to one another, and with the
change of language come so many other changes. "When
we break down the fence," she says to the minister, "the
cows run away." She took Peder out of his first school to
keep him away from the Irish: "You can't have wheat and
potatoes in the same bin." She knows that the children
have to learn English, but just because a new language
comes in, the old one surely does not have to go out?
When the minister complains to Beret that "the world"
is about to swallow up Peder, she answers that surely this
only means that they have harvested as they had sown.
When young people forget their mother tongue and mix
with strangers, one cannot know where they will end.

When she first came to America, she had asked fearfully, "Are these plains to be peopled by having lives thrown
hopelessly away?" Now she sees that America demands
more than lives; it is asking for men's souls as well. Her
own children do not even keep their Norwegian names:
Store-Hans and Sophie call their oldest boy Henry Percival after the grandfathers Hans Olsa and Per Hansa;
Ole and Randi name themselves in having their son chris-
tened Randolph Osborne!

One of Rölvaag's central purposes in the book was to
give a detailed portrait of a young person on the threshold
of maturity. Contemporary literature showed a growing
interest in Freudian psychology, but Rölvaag was not
pleased with the new "realism," which tended to present
man as an animal in the grip of his own urges. For this
reason, and in keeping with the environment in which he

grew up, Peder's adolescence is dominated by the religious development and the social problems of his time. Rölvaag had an exalted view of love, including both the physical and spiritual basis for marriage. He found that in much contemporary literature this important and beautiful aspect of human life was either taboo or presented as something unworthy and unclean. Some even exploited it speculatively in order to titillate the senses. Rölvaag felt that the great writers of the past usually had a healthier view of sex, and none more so than the Bible. In the previously cited letter to Professor Boynton he spoke of the lies that surrounded sex in much of contemporary literature: "The poet of *The Song of Songs* refused to look at it that way; he glorified it, with the result that the poem has been handed down through the ages as one of the finest love songs ever written."

Rölvaag had something like this in mind when he set out to describe the dawning eros in Peder's life. In an undated letter of September, 1927, he wrote to Lincoln Colcord: "I want to do the psychology of youth in such a way, that intelligent young people who may happen to read it shall look upon themselves as children of Light rather than lost children of Darkness. I love mankind. Particularly youth. If it were not for that foolish feeling, I certainly would not be teaching this year!—And if I succeed in making the sex-urge beautiful instead of nasty, I shall perform a great service."

It is doubtful whether Rölvaag succeeded in giving his Peder "everlasting life" for this reason, but there are beautiful passages in the book which give unusually sensitive and lyrical glimpses of Peder's passage from boyhood to manhood. We see how he becomes aware of having a body of flesh and blood, and a sweet, restless longing for something soft and gentle to caress and protect with his youthful strength. There is the joy of feeling these powers rising in his body like the sap in a tree, of standing naked before the open window in one's bedroom in the evening, and letting the moonlight and the warm summer air play about one's young limbs. There are charmingly youthful love scenes, where a bashful glance or the light touch of a young cheek is enough to fill one's whole life with song and sunshine.

For a time Peder seems to be most delighted with the

latest girl he meets. Gradually there is one who emerges
as *the* girl, the nut-brown, kittenish Susie Doheny, sister
of his best friend and Irish schoolmate Charley. She is
vivaciously alive, with a pair of glittering blue eyes in
which yellow-brown spots drift "like fluffy good-weather
clouds under a deep afternoon sky."

Beret has watched Peder, the child of her heart, drifting
away from her bit by bit. First it was the school, then
confirmation, then politics, practical life, young America,
Whitman's song to "the Western youth":

> All the past we leave behind,
> We debouch upon a newer mightier world, varied world,
> Fresh and strong the world we seize, world of labor and
>   the march;
> Pioneers! O Pioneers!

Then comes the worst blow. When she discovers that
Peder is no longer running after girls in general, but has
settled upon this Irish lass, she is desperate. This surely
cannot be the will of the Lord! She makes futile attempts
to put an end to it. But then one night she dreams that
Per Hansa comes to her and asks her not to stand in
Peder's way: "Just let him have the girl when he's so fond
of her! Do you remember how I ran after you? And you
weren't much better; you didn't give a hoot what your
parents said, and I thank you for that." So it is Per Hansa's
spirit, young America, which wins its victory on this occasion also, and Beret drinks the last bitter drop of her
chalice. The book ends with her taking Peder over to the
Irish Dohenys in order to arrange for the wedding.

And so the book ends on a tragic note, which for Beret
is more poignant than the one which struck her at Per
Hansa's death, since she has now to resign herself to the
idea that "as things were shaping themselves now, it was
not just their bodies that America wanted!" The exchange
of languages, the changing of cultures, the mixture of peo-
ples, the whole process of Americanization moves inexor-
ably without regard to who resists it, or what it costs, or
what values are lost in this transformation.

Unsentimentally and objectively the author has drawn
his detailed, realistic picture of an age of vigorous conflict
in prairie society. Immigrants from many countries had

founded this kingdom, but the time had come when the national idiosyncracies had to be wiped out. This occurred earlier or later in the various settlements according to whether they were composed of several nationalities or of a homogeneous group. In the Spring Creek settlement the transition occurs in the second generation, in the 1880's and 1890's, something for which the book was criticized by many, since it generally took longer for the language change to occur in most Norwegian settlements of the Midwest. The time is defensible enough when one considers the strong Irish contingent in this settlement, but there was some justice in the criticism that Rölvaag was in fact describing the events of his own time. This explains also the somewhat chaotic impression which the book makes: the author stood in the midst of events and could not place them in a proper historical perspective. The picture has therefore not been drawn with the broad strokes that characterize the preceding book. It has its strength in the details, in the multifarious, pulsating life which throbs throughout the work. It stands like a Pompeii with its realistic insights into the vanishing Norwegian-American immigrant world in the midst of its transformation.

A conflict of generations that involves the break between two cultures and the "change of soul," as Rölvaag puts it, comes very near the limit of what men can bear. Rölvaag here uncovered a stratum of American life that had been overlooked up to this time. He had the right to exult just a little bit at having shaken the melting-pot optimism in certain circles, as he did when he wrote to Waldemar Ager, his close friend and fellow Norwegian-American author, in 1930: "I have actually succeeded in getting the 'Yankees' to see that the Norwegians are good people, and that the country has not lost anything in getting us here. Some write such touching letters to me about Peder and Beret. Americanization has suddenly acquired a different face: that which had been looked upon as a great blessing now begins to look like a tragedy!"

In spite of Beret's many defeats in her struggle against Americanization, the mood of the book is not pessimistic. Rölvaag's sober account does not leave one in doubt that his and our sympathies are with Beret, and if we look a little deeper, we find that even the second generation is

unmistakably Norwegian. One American reviewer declared, "These people on the Dakota prairies . . . are
spiritually and physically true descendants of the ancient
Norsemen of Sigrid Undset's stories." He noted particularly their quiet courage, their enterprise and individual-
ism, but also their deep feelings. Peder is marked by a
keen love of nature, with a touch of the artist in him.
And the pinchpenny politics of Gjermund Dahl are not
unknown in Norwegian life.

No matter how negatively Peder seems to react to the
views of his mother, we can see that he is fond of her and
understands that she is an unusually wise and good person. The seed she has sown in his youthful soul throughout the years will be able to sprout after wintering for
some years. The author repeatedly pointed out that this
was the book of Peder's "defiant period" though, of course,
he would some day find his way back to the paths of his
ancestors. "Wait until you see him at forty!" wrote Rölvaag to Colcord in 1929.

Another quality that has made the book so stimulating
is its typically Rölvaagian interest and faith in life. Everything that lives is worth being framed and reflected upon.
Everything has a divine origin and a divine purpose. The
portrayal of Peder's development fascinates with its strong,
healthy, refreshing joy of life. There is a delicate lyric
quality in the style, and there are many fine descriptions
of nature.

No one can be in doubt about the influence of Freud-
ianism in the study of Peder's development. One might
also mention Gustav Frenssen's *Jørn Uhl* (1901) as having
been influential, for there is something in its mood and in
the description of the link between man and soil that is
reminiscent of *Peder Victorious*. Rölvaag is known to have
admired this book very much. Any comparison with Tur-
genev's *Fathers and Sons*, however, serves only to bring
out Rölvaag's vigor and vitality.

Even though *Peder Victorious* was well received both
in Norway and the United States, it sold only about a
third as many copies as the pioneer novel, although it was
on the best-seller list for some months. There is little
drama connected with its reception, compared with that
of *Giants in the Earth*. Rölvaag chose to get along without
Anglo-American help in the translation, and even though

his colleague Nora Solum did a fine job of translation, which he himself revised, it is more of a Norwegian book translated into English than the preceding one. In the original the Norwegian style fits the contents more intimately, and the extensive use of dialect in the dialogues gives it a special mystique.

The criticisms that were most often made of the book, in Norway as in America, were that the construction was unclear and that the narration was too circumstantial. These are criticisms that one can level against much of Rölvaag's writing. To him all individuals and all phenomena in life were equally interesting; he enjoyed dwelling on each phenomenon and engrossing himself in it. His theme here had been the building up of a soul by exploiting "the innumerable impressions from its environment through which it broke its way into life." It is undeniable that now and then he may have needlessly multiplied his exemplification. But he was one of those who helped to bring psychological analysis and the close interpretation of life into American literature, a novelty to a public that had above all demanded action and entertainment.

Even if *Peder Victorious* was not the success that his previous book had been, Rölvaag had reason to be pleased with what he had achieved in his new work. He had secured his reputation as a Norwegian and an American author with a new book which combined Norwegian cultural heritage and literary tradition with an American theme and uncovered new areas of the literary continent he had discovered. He could be pleased with the bridge-building that he had accomplished: by clarifying the process whereby the emigrant in many ways becomes a stranger to his old homeland, as well as by giving the "Yankee" a deeper understanding of the problems facing the foreign-language immigrant.

GUDRUN HOVDE GVÅLE

Telemark College,
Norway

Peder Victorious

I. The Song of Life's Dismay

I

The moment the sun lifted his red face above the horizon, Peder was up; and in summer, just after the face had dropped out of sight, Peder was in bed again. . . . Strange old sun. . . . He often wondered what could make that face so red morning and evening. Perhaps weariness with shining so hard all the time. Since he himself often felt drowsy and full when evening came, Peder could very well understand this. . . . But how beautiful it was at sunup and sundown—especially at sundown. On evenings when God had remembered to hang out the clouds which betokened fair weather on the morrow, it was as if the world were enchanted, for that made the old sun so glad that he lay and laughed up at the clouds as he dropped off to sleep.

During his childhood Peder lived in three rooms. Moving freely among them, he scarcely realized when he left the one and went into the other. Yet only in the one did he feel really at home and dare to let himself go. Here he bustled about, doing just what he pleased; here he dreamed the future, built it; here he planned how he would do this thing and that, and how he would be the boss and set things to rights when he got to be a man. The place was like a treasure cave, stacked full of marvelous riches. What fun to play with them, to take things down and look at them, and to put them back again. And how jolly to find something new to put in—really the most fun of all. Many and remarkable indeed the adventures he had in here. In this room he lived everything in English.

1

The second room he shared with his mother, his two brothers, and his sister. Here he was not quite so happy, because all was so ordinary. As he grew older he felt an increasing desire to move things about and to rearrange them to suit himself. And he tried it, too, but he gave it up when he came to realize that it would be better not to say anything—not yet for a while, at least. Oh, how could grown people behave so stupidly! Here went Anna Marie, his sister, never giving so much as a thought to the future! Didn't she realize that she was almost grown up, and that she ought to get married and have a husband and children to look after? That's what happened to all women who were any good. Or, if she really wanted to learn to play, why didn't she ask Mother to give her a piano? Where would she get with that old organ into which she constantly sat pumping wind?

And now take his brothers, for example. They were even worse than Anna Marie, because they *were* grown up. Yet here they went—yes, here they went! Store-Hans, silent and poky, did nothing but wait on Mother. That was all right, of course—no harm in that. But couldn't he see all the fun he was missing? Peder was often puzzled about this brother, for at times, when he did cut loose, he might do such unexpected things.

And Ole—everlastingly dawdling! Why in the world didn't he get busy and buy a threshing rig, if he really wanted one? The very thought brought a gleam to Peder's eye. He wished he would get one, for then he, Peder, could hire out as bundle cutter, stay outdoors all fall and learn many useful things. And then he'd soon be grown up!

Simply good-for-nothings—that's what his brothers were! Why, here was Dakota Territory about to become a state—yessir, an inseparable part of the very Union itself. Everybody was excited about it. People held meetings, they talked meetings, they discussed politics until they got madder than blazes. Fairy tales and mighty deeds in all their talk. But here Store-Hans and Ole went about as calmly as though nothing were going on. They never even mentioned it, and they seldom attended any meetings. And when they did go he never could get leave to go with them. And do you suppose that Mother ever tried

to set them right? Peder got so angry that he had to spit
whenever he thought of these things.

Mother—yes! She was worse than all the rest. Look at
all the years she had lived in this country, and she couldn't
even talk decent English yet—English, 'the easiest language in the world to learn. And she wouldn't even try—
didn't care. "Talk Norwegian!" she would burst out all
of a sudden whenever any of them talked English at
home. She would even say it right out before people who
didn't understand Norwegian, so that Peder was often
ashamed when strangers came. . . . If only Mother had
been different, this second room might not have been so
bad. Mother was unusually smart in most things, for all
she was so queer. At times she knew exactly to a T what
he was thinking about . . . had a most uncanny insight. . . . Oh, well, wait till he was confirmed and
grown up and had something to say—then he'd change
things about and put them where they belonged. In this
room he lived everything in Norwegian.

And in the third room, too—a dim, shadowy place,
mysterious and secret, into which only God and he could
come. While Peder was yet a small boy he had been wont
to take his mother with him, but not now any more.

—God? Why, yes. In the room where He was, one had
to be very careful and not talk too loud, for there was no
telling what that Fellow might do. . . .

There had been a time when God was the most real
thing in Peder's life. He had never seen Him, to be sure,
but to Peder that only made the reality all the more real.
And for that matter Peder wasn't at all certain about
what he *might* have seen! One saw queer things after
dark. God's face was only eyes, eyes that spied everything.
They peered through the darkness . . . he knew they
were there. On rainy nights, when the water streamed
down the panes, Peder, on his knees, close up to the
window staring out into the dark, could see both the
white and the black in God's eye. Tears were flowing
from God's eyes because people would not behave as
He wanted them to. Peder felt sorry for God and tried
hard to be good after such a dismal evening. At night he
pulled the covers up over his head, so that the eyes
couldn't touch his face. . . . God's eyes were so cold
and wet! . . .

No one need worry that God wasn't present on this farm. As a little boy Peder used to tiptoe slowly around the corners of the house in order not to come upon Him too suddenly. These grown-ups were so skittish—no telling how God would take being startled. Moreover, Peder didn't want to scare anyone who was so kind. . . . God must be dreadfully old now! . . . He knew that Mother had said that God didn't have any age, but then, Mother didn't know everything either.

. . . Queer about God. He who could do all that He wanted, and wanted only that which was good, couldn't get people to do what He wanted? Peder simply couldn't understand it, and was so troubled that he finally went to his mother and asked her to explain it to him. But he always got the same answer: that God did these things just to try people.

The explanation satisfied him for a while. . . . Over in the cupboard stood a sugar-bowl, which Peder knew about. Whenever he was alone in the room and happened to remember the sugar, a most unreasoning desire to have a lump might come upon him. He was lucky indeed if he remembered God in time, for then he left the bowl untouched. Having resisted the temptation he would seat himself on a chair, and remaining seated for some time, would nod secretively as if to One who knew exactly what he was thinking about. And sometimes he would nod to that Other One as if to assure Him that He need never doubt his honor. Peder then felt very virtuous and his face brightened. On the other hand, it sometimes happened that Peder forgot and then his fingers went into the bowl and brought out not only one but even two lumps. Then suddenly sensing what he was doing, he would become much offended with God for not reminding him in time, or for not taking him by the arm and leading him away as Mother would have done.

Still, it was immeasurably pleasant to be on good terms with God, and to have Him always at his side. In a way— even better than to have Mother there, for God was so much stronger and wiser. Evenings Peder had long talks with God to remind Him of things He must not forget . . . old people were always so forgetful! At this time Peder believed implicitly that God would help him to the most wonderful thing that could ever be got by any human being. Father certainly knew what he was about when he named him *Victorious!* Just wait till he was big! Peder stuffed down all the food he could possibly eat, because he wanted to get on with this business of growing up.

II

But the intimate comradeship between God and Peder came to an end during the spring that Father was found dead over west on the prairie. Suddenly God changed; He became a hard, heartless monster, One that one must look out for.

Father was the most wonderful man that had ever lived—certainly Peder was the one to know that. Even God Himself didn't know much more than Father, and Father was every bit as ready to help . . . there was the man for you who could help! And so jolly and full of fun he was, and what things he could think of . . . Father was certainly a clever man!

Matters had gone very badly that winter four years ago when Peder's godfather, Hans Olsa, took sick with the cough. Fearing that the end had come he had wanted the minister, and so, in terrible weather Peder's father had set out to get him. Blizzard after blizzard was whipping heaven and earth into a milling whiteness. For days it had lasted. People thought that all the fury of hell had been unloosed. And night after night Peder had lain listening to his mother's burning prayers for Father. The very snowdrifts themselves must melt at such supplications, he thought. At times Peder became afraid of her . . . her face had such a strange look in it and her eyes were so unnaturally large and brilliant. Had it not been that she was so gentle with him in these days, he would have come to shun her. But that he could not, for the moment he was out of her sight, she would ask after him. She seemed to crave to have him near her; child though he was, he was the one in whom she sought comfort.

That winter he slept with his mother in the bedroom downstairs. Night after night Mother and he had a meeting with God. Night after night they importuned Him to return Father, Peder always joyously as one whose trust cannot falter. And this Peder knew, that more earnestly God had never been besought. This supernatural reality which his mother had, with such care, built up in him, stood firm when her own faith was tottering. Peder's logic was an armor from which everything rebounded. . . . God knew of course that they couldn't get along without Father; God was only love, and He was all powerful; Father was the finest man that ever lived and he was kinder than anyone else: It was as certain as the sun in the heavens that God would have to send Father back. Peder said it straight up into His face. And whenever he did Mother would look at him frightened and say that perhaps it was not God's will, and that he must be careful lest their prayer become blasphemy. Peder only laughed knowingly at her. Didn't God will only good to His children? And were not they His children? What nonsense she talked! Peder noticed that he had an influence over her, and was made the surer thereby.

Then the godfather died. Peder thought that now God certainly was acting strangely. What did He mean by taking Hans Olsa away in the dead of winter? Godmother Sörine almost cried herself to death. Didn't God know that Sörine was a good woman? Here He had left her all alone with two children; she had not even a hired man, and not a bit of food in the house! And Hans Olsa himself, the strongest man on the whole prairie—he was now lying out in the snowbank, in a coffin which Tönseten had made for him.

Peder could not understand such procedure on the part of One who was only goodness and who had all power in His hand and who did everything for the good of man. The revolt and bewilderment stirred up by such reflections soon subsided, however, probably because these tribulations lay outside the house in which he himself lived, and partly because it concerned other people. Moreover, there was enough to think about at home. . . . It might be, too, that Godfather hadn't taken the opportunity to talk to God every night and that God for that reason was offended with Hans Olsa, and so had let the cough take him. . . . It was hard to say.

Though Hans Olsa's death cut a deep wound in the

boy's faith, the wound was soon healed by the certainty that Father would return when the time came. For that matter, Father didn't need any help . . . he could do anything he set his mind to. The like of him had never lived. What stories he would have to tell when he came back! Peder thrilled in anticipation. Kneeling by the hour on a chair before the window, he would stare out over the bleak white reaches just to be the one to announce that now Father was coming. Every time he saw a person approaching the house he was certain that now they'd get news of Father. Each time the disappointment cut keener, yet he never despaired . . . it was only a question of time!

Days and weeks came and went. But no tidings. No one had seen anything of Father. In good weather people went out to search, and their search was always fruitless: they knew no more when they came back than when they went. Mother's anguish was working havoc with her. Peder saw it, yet his own faith remained unshaken. In his heart he knew that God couldn't take Father away like this. God couldn't be so contemptible. Peder's thoughts always traveled the same circle: God wanted to do only that which was good; God was almighty; no finer man than Father had ever lived; God could see that they couldn't get along without Father; consequently, he must come back! At times he cried for very impatience over the delay. Mother's anxiety only added fuel to the fire. Her lack of faith angered him. A grown woman, so well acquainted with God as Mother was, ought to be ashamed of herself. One night, their supplications being over, he summoned courage to speak to her. Looking straight at her, he asked her, as he knew Father would have done:

"What in the world is the matter with you? God will help Father to come back when the time comes . . . you know that!"

The mother did not say a word—only stared at him, frightened. Her manner did not disturb Peder in the least. He felt better now that he had spoken to her.

Then one day they brought Father home on a wagon, an ashy, stinking corpse, and they feared that Mother would lose her mind. From that moment God became a new being to Peder; He slipped farther and farther away —into utter remoteness; during the time immediately following He took on another shape . . . changed entirely.

One forenoon during their days of waiting, just as Peder woke up in the morning, the thought struck him that today Father would be coming. And wanting to be the first to meet him, he said nothing to anyone but put on a cap and quietly left the house while the others were out of doors, too busy with the morning's work to notice what he was doing; he made his way through the snow to the Indian Hill.* Here he remained standing a long time, staring out into the frost smoke. The day was bitter, the air popping with cold. When they had found him and brought him back into the house again, they discovered that one of his hands was frozen stiff. Then Mother had said:

"Now see what you've done . . . !"

The rebuke had filled him with fear, and he had begun to cry. These words he could not forget—again and again they'd come back, each time with greater force.

The father's terrible death and the mother's inconsolable grief were too much for Peder's faith. His sense of justice had been outraged, as if he had witnessed a bully in wanton rawness tear some precious object out of the hands of one who was too weak to defend himself, and run away with it. The first pangs of sorrow having assuaged themselves, Peder went about mumbling up into a face he could not see: "Now see what You've done!" . . . And hereafter, as soon as he entered the third room, there sat the defiance waiting for him.

And thus it happened that from now on God became to Peder another being. He was treacherous, sly, cunning, and because He was invisible and always lay in wait to pounce down on people and strike a blow at them, He was One you had to look out for. The first thing you knew, He would stretch out His hand and smite you. If the cough and other sickness didn't avail Him, He turned snowstorms loose and got people that way. . . . Disturbed and perplexed, Peder twice took his trouble to his mother, because he had to consult some grown person about it, and both times he got the old answer that

* A hill beyond the house, where they had found an Indian grave. Cf. *Giants In The Earth*, Part One.

it was punishment—punishment for sin they had committed. . . . After that he asked no more questions.
What was the use? Mother talked such nonsense at
times! Henceforth no power on earth could make him
believe that God, who had killed his father in this way,
could be only goodness.

Fortunately Peder's godmothers both lived so near that
he could visit them as often as Mother would permit him
to. And thereby he got himself many a tidbit, which he
otherwise would not have had. When only a little tot
he liked best to go to Godmother Kjersti's, because she
was always ready to bring out a piece of sugar or a piece
of cake. Besides, she knew so many funny stories, and
was always glad to tell them, though some of them made
both her and Peder cry.

Back on the clock-shelf at Kjersti's, hidden from view,
lay a curious old book. From it Kjersti often read to him,
and for a time after the treasure had been found, he had
to be permitted to see it whenever he came to visit her.
And Godmother Kjersti was never unwilling. With him in
her lap, his warm boy head close to her breast, her cheek
against his warm temple, there was at times more happiness in the old child than in the young. They had many
a jolly hour together over that book.

The title page had been lost, but happily all the others
were in good condition and in their proper places. The
pictures, constituting a series, revealed a strange tale, notwithstanding that the reading told them very little. Every
picture was made up, first of all, of a large heart. In the
middle of the first heart sat Jesus with a crown of thorns
on His head, looking very sad. Down in the corner of the
page, outside of the heart, Satan came tramping in on
horse's hoofs, pitchfork in hand. The series, continuing,
showed how by degrees Jesus slipped out of the heart
and Satan came in. But there was no fight! Peder wanted
to know how this displacement was possible without their
flying at each other, and asked Kjersti about it. Well,
didn't Peder understand that Jesus had to get out of the
way of that fork? . . . Later on in the series the situation
reversed, and by the time they neared the end Jesus once
more occupied the place where He first sat. On His face
there was now a pleased look, and tiny angels fluttered

and danced about in and out of the heart. Satan stalked out—in the opposite corner of the page.

—"Well now, don't you think that was remarkable?" Kjersti would say as she closed the book. "There he goes, the old scamp! If only you can live according to this now, Peder, you'll grow up to be a fine boy . . . you certainly will." . . . "But won't he come back?" Peder would ask. "Oh no, child, he'll have to stay home now!" . . . And then she would pat his head, and lift him up so high that his warm cheek came to lie against her wrinkled one. Peder always consented because he knew that a tidbit was sure to follow.

The reading wasn't very interesting, it seemed to Peder. When Kjersti read he always sat with his eyes closed, listening to the pictures tell the story. One thing he failed to understand, however: namely, that Jesus who was always so brave would get out of the way of that pitchfork. . . . Surely there must have been a fight? Wasn't it possible to draw pictures of fights? Since Kjersti could not explain these things it was no use to ask; and since it was this way in the book, it must be so. Everything in books was true—Peder knew that much!

When Peder was yet a little boy he knew for certain that Jesus lived in his heart. He could feel Him stir in there; was it from fear that the old fellow with the fork would come and chase Him out? But he comforted himself with the thought that it couldn't be so bad after all—since He came back on the last page! And the angels, too, were certainly here. Whenever he felt a flutter of happiness he knew it was all the little angels flying and dancing about. . . . Peder liked the angels almost better than he did Jesus.

All this was in those happy days when Peder was still on friendly terms with both God and Jesus. The pictures may have done their share toward making it impossible for him to think of God without seeing Him in human form. Since this was the way Jesus looked, God must look something like Him. Didn't people say that Peder looked like his father? . . . God might possibly be somewhat bigger than Jesus. And a great deal stronger? Jesus really didn't seem to be much bigger than any ordinary grown man. . . . Well, no matter—you might be certain that God wouldn't get out of the way of an ordinary pitchfork. . . . And

God certainly had a happier face than Jesus. Peder was confident that it was the happiest face in the world; for how could one go about managing things just as he pleased without being happy? It was only on dreary rain-nights that God had tears in His eyes.

After the father's death the image was no longer to be recognized. God grew until He took on huge proportions; His body rested on a mountain top out in the world somewhere; His head reached up among the stars. There He sat sweeping the heavens with His great arms. Beside Him lay an enormous fork with which He clawed out into the air whenever He wished to tear a storm loose. His face, bluish black . . . expressionless . . . His eyes seeking out someone to kill. This spring five Irish children had been tortured to death with scarlet fever. Mrs. Thompson, a neighbor, had died in childbed; last fall the bull had gored Ole Strandvold to death, and now the other day Peder Ness had killed himself while driving . . . people had said he was drunk. Peder found a special pleasure in enumerating all the calamities he heard about. Particularly all the deaths—for that too was God. God must be kept very busy collecting and sorting all the dead; that's why He had no time for anything else! Out there on the mountain top He sat, sorting dead men as fast as they came in. . . . He wore a black gown with a white ruff. The minister had worn just such a garb the day he came in and preached over Father before the neighbors carried him away. Peder was certain at this time that the old minister must be almost as strong as God. After the funeral the minister had stayed with them for three days, and had talked with Mother most of the time. Peder had stayed close by, but he hadn't heard much about God; the minister had talked mostly about the farm and about what Mother ought to do, now that all the responsibility rested on her; and in all his talk he had been like a father who knew everything, only he was even more kind. Peter had then thought a good deal about becoming a minister, if only he could avoid having anything to do with God, and just go about telling people how to manage so that they could make things go. But after God donned that black gown with the white ruff the image of the old minister was no longer so dear to Peder. And his earliest image of Jesus likewise underwent a noticeable change; it receded into distance and unreality. To think that He who was as mighty as the Father would get out of the way of that pitchfork! Now that he stopped to think of it that picture couldn't possibly be true. Why, that face had never known what joy is. And here He had saved the world, had rescued people from everlasting fire in hell, and yet He looked more mournful than one who had done something very wicked. . . . But Jesus' slipping away made Peder unhappy, for he had come to love Him on account of His great helplessness; now that He was gone, he felt the loss keenly. He had felt very sorry for Jesus . . . people had treated Him so cruelly. It happened that Peder would stand looking up a wall, wondering how it would feel to be nailed fast to it, hanging by the hands. The thought so overwhelmed him that he broke down and cried. What a licking they should have had for treating Jesus in this way!

Living in so many strange emotions made the boy look old for his age; at times he startled people by his almost uncanny insight into things. It would have been well had he had someone in whom he could confide and with whom he could have shared his thoughts. He pestered Mother with questions until she, wearily, assured him that he was the most stupid thing walking in two shoes. At times he almost scared the wits out of her; she would get angry and in the zeal of her great love chastise him severely; afterward, breaking into tears, she would implore him not to go thinking about such matters. . . . It was blasphemy! God's wrath would smite him. As for this last, well—he'd take a chance on that. . . . He knew the fists of his brothers . . . they weren't so soft either. . . . If only he could find out the truth of all this business about God! . . .

Terrible visions of how he would be burning in hell made him for a while almost frantic with fear. Gradually he became accustomed to that too, and tried in many ways to thrust fear away. Sometimes he found that singing helped; and working hard; helping Mother wasn't so bad either. Whenever he learned of anyone having committed a wrong he experienced a secret elation . . . he would not be alone *there!* He tried many schemes . . . but not prayer. Never would he ask that Fellow who had killed Father for help! If Mother insisted, he would rattle

off a práyer, thinking all the while of other things; or
else he would affect an innocent look and declare that he
had already said his prayers to himself. But saying grace
he could not escape, because he was the youngest in the
family.

During the summer of his eighth year he committed a
terrible sin, one which grew worse the longer he carried it
about with him:

Mother had bought a prize rooster, a regular show bird,
which she had named the Monarch. His jagged red comb
waved and sparkled as he strutted about in the yard. Peder
couldn't stand the sight of the rooster, because he was so
mean to the hens; every once in a while as he went about
picking corn, he would lift his head; and cocking it to one
side, his black eyes flashing fire, he would start chasing a
hen and treat her most shamefully. One day Peder decided
to punish him. Taking some oats in a cup, he coaxed the
chickens back of the barn and fed them; and then he took
a stick and, watching his chance, he hit the Monarch a
terrible crack on the head. He must have struck too hard,
for the rooster lay flat on the ground, kicking. The sight
was so horrible that Peder struck him a few more blows,
whereupon the rooster kicked no more. Peder hurried and
got the spade, and buried the fellow over in the grove.
. . . And now it came about that this sin brought many
in its wake, for Mother would ask Peder several times a
day if he hadn't seen the rooster, and Peder lied until he
shuddered with fear. . . . At night he would lie in his
bed, agonized and tortured, as he pictured himself being
consumed everlastingly.

III

Years came; years went. Life grew, and life withered.
It had always been thus; thus it would always be.

Strong June sun. Soft south wind. The prairie floated
in a sea of sun. Its existence had never been more delicious.
It had drunk light the whole outspread day. Satiated, lazy,
it wanted to lie down and sleep now that night was nearing . . . after the moon came, there would be other
things to think about! . . .

Peder was now in his eleventh year, and just at this

moment on his way home from parochial school. As he
trudged along, he struck at the tall grass by the wayside
with his lunch pail—his face clouded and angry, his step
slow. No need to hurry! School had begun two weeks ago.
Worse this year than ever. . . . The teacher was simply
impossible!

Today things had gone pretty rotten again. Nothing
unusual in that . . . only this was the worst ever. He
struck hard at the grass, stood still a moment, flew at it
again and cut it a blow with all his might. . . . Thus they
ought to have it. . . . Thus! And *thus!*

This is what had happened:

During the morning's session he had sat listening to the
older class being catechized in the story about Jesus walking on the water, and having become completely absorbed
in the remarkable episode he had blurted out in the broad
dialect of Nordland: "I'd like to know what kind of boots
He had on that time." This was neither unbelief nor
ridicule . . . the boy simply was so deeply absorbed in
the question of whether Jesus hadn't even got His feet wet.

The class had roared with laughter. But that wasn't the
worst of it. The teacher had placed a stick of wood end
up by his desk. On it Peder had been compelled to sit until
noon. Had not his anger kept him alive, he would surely
have fainted, for the stick was painfully uncomfortable.
But no one should have the satisfaction of knowing how
it had hurt him . . . don't you ever think it! Worse than
the torture were the words which the teacher had spoken
to him when he let him go: "If you were only half as smart
at getting your lessons as you are in thinking up all sorts
of mischief, you might turn out to be a pretty decent sort
of fellow . . . but it doesn't look as if there's much hope
for you!"

During the noon hour Peder had sneaked out on the
prairie, his body stiff and sore, his temper afire. . . . How
he hated the man! He gloried in the thought of it. Up
there on the stick facing the whole school alone, he had
felt a peculiar strength taking possession of him, and while
he sat there he had resolved to avenge himself. Some day
he would beat that fellow till he begged for mercy. Go
where he liked, he'd find him out!

As he walked along home, these thoughts were again
upon him. Every once in a while he went at it, striking

violently at the grass . . . oh! . . . Why didn't he answer
that question, the fool? Peder would bet his shirt that
when it came right down to it that fellow didn't understand a thing of what he was talking about. A smart aleck
and a dunce . . . that's what he was! The old fool
couldn't even talk English. Every other word he said was
wrong. But don't you suppose he had to jabber English
anyway—just to be on the good side of the kids, of course!
. . . He was always prating about how grand everything
was in old Norway—why didn't the fool go back there
then?

Peder walked and walked, hard of face and lost in
thought. Had there been a trace of righteousness in God,
He would have boxed this fellow's ears. But no. God
was probably too busy killing people!

Then suddenly, as he poked along hitting the grass,
something dawned on Peder. A bright light illuminated
what had hitherto been dark. Instantly an intense joy
surged through him. . . . Here he had found the solution
to the whole perplexing business: It was in Norway that
God was keeping himself! He knew it . . . distinctly and
clearly someone said it in his ear.

Mollified, he began to chuckle to himself . . . Mother
and the others were of course mistaken. God was undoubtedly being kept too busy over in Norway to have
time to come here. . . . And then, too—the Americans
were so much smarter than the Norwegians that they
didn't need so much help. America had men like Washington and Lincoln. The one had made the country and
the other had come and set all the slaves free. God himself could scarcely have done better even if He had been
here. . . . Besides America was a new land . . . only a
few years ago that Columbus found it! . . . Maybe it
wasn't a part of the world that the Bible history told
about? In that case—God had nothing to do with it at
all.

Peder felt a strange joy ripple through him. All of a
sudden another bright idea flashed upon him: If God lived
here, He must be an American. There you have it! . . .
What would they want of a Norwegian God in this country? Most likely that's just what these Norwegians didn't
understand and so things went wrong with them.

—Well, no one could make him believe that a really

American God would go about killing people with snow-storms and the like . . . just laying for people, watching His chance to sneak down on 'em. . . . People said it was contemptible to listen at a keyhole, and yet they tried to make him believe that God would listen to the thoughts which people kept in their innermost hearts and which they never told to anyone, though they couldn't help that they had them. And if the thoughts didn't please Him, He'd simply wallop the poor fellow who had 'em . . . such they called fair play of God! . . . Again Peder's face took on a preoccupied look. Today he had been thinking that he would marry Carrie Teigen as soon as he was grown up, and go straight out to the Black Hills and dig himself some gold. He had thought of Carrie because she had rosy cheeks and her throat was so beautiful! . . . Maybe it would be better to go West first, and then come back and marry her? . . . God would hardly approve of that, though. And Mother wouldn't like it either . . . Mother and God almost always thought alike! . . .

But just suppose now God didn't like their talking to Him in Norwegian? . . . When He was an American? Instantly the thoughtful boy face brightened, only to be-come as quickly clouded. The Bible history said, "Jacob's and Isaac's God." He must be a Jew! . . . The Jews had crucified Jesus—the history book said so. . . . Just the right kind of a God for such people!

Peder walked on, thinking hard for a long time. He couldn't remember that either Norway or America were mentioned in the Bible history. It gave him an immense satisfaction, nevertheless, to have discovered that God was a Jew. This made everything seem more reasonable to him, despite the fact that he knew nothing about the Jews. At the same time he couldn't get rid of the thought that it wasn't proper for an American to talk Norwegian to God.

That evening, as they were out in the barn yard milking, he maneuvered a cow close to where his mother sat, in order to get a chance to ask her a question or two. He wanted very much to know whether Father could talk much English; Peder couldn't remember. Whenever he thought of Father, of their jolly and pleasant companion-ship, words were unnecessary, for Father and he came so near to each other that they needed no speech.

—And why did Peder want to know that? The mother, sitting with her head against the cow's flank, pulled the teats more slowly in order the better to hear what he said.
—Well, he had just been wondering. . . . Could he?
—Oh, he was probably like the rest of 'em, who had come over here after they were grown up. Most of 'em blundered along as well as they could. Book learning, for that matter, was not Father's strong point.
—But he could talk English, could he? Peder couldn't conceal the anger he felt toward her, nor did he try either.
—Well, enough to get along . . . she s'posed.
—To be sure! Father could get along in everything. . . . Peder felt better. He thought hard for a while, and then suddenly demanded to know:
—Did he *pray* in English?
His mother was long in answering. When she did there was a hard ring in her voice, which Peder couldn't understand:
—Father didn't pray. And then as if to forestall another question, she added:
—He wasn't that kind!
To Peder this didn't seem strange at all. It only made him happier, gave him a feeling of greater security. . . . What would Father pray for? He could manage everything himself. This thought brought another question in its wake —one which hadn't occurred to Peder before:
—What did he go after, that time?
Again the mother was long in answering. She was very low-voiced and sad tonight; but Peder, occupied with his own thoughts, hardly noticed her spirits.
—He went to get the minister for Hans Olsa.
Unable to understand the reason, Peder straightway had to know why Hans Olsa wanted the minister. Again he waited a long time for the answer, meanwhile holding the teats in his hand without pulling them. Getting no answer, he looked up. And then he saw that she had finished milking, but that she still sat on the stool, the pail on the ground beside her; she held her apron up to her face, and shook with crying.
Peder felt so bad that he didn't know what to do—stood helpless; in a moment he too would burst out crying. . . . It was of course this about Father!
Burning with a desire to make right again the wrong he

had done, he began at once to carry in the milk; and he tried hard to think of some good thing to say. Not succeeding, he went to the woodpile and carried in a big armful of wood. He took his time about it, so that she might see how considerate he was . . . he knew she liked to have him remember this job.

In the window lay the book he had brought home from school. Taking it with him, he made his way to the cellar where she was already straining the milk, and holding the book up so that she could see it, said:

"Guess I'll have to study a spell, now. It's just terrible what lessons he gives us!" The mother made no reply, but Peder could feel how pleased she was.

He thrust the book under the bib of his overalls and ran up to the Indian Hill. Here stood a bench he himself had made of willow branches. He liked the place on evenings when the weather was fine, often finding something to do out here so that he could have an excuse for coming. The eye reached so far—from here he could count fourteen farms. Moreover, he was fascinated by the prairie quieting itself for the night.

He felt himself becoming one with the growing dusk and with everything around him. The mystic spell of the night, now fast nearing, whispered of pleasant things to him. He wondered why the prairie drew itself in at night? Godmother Sörine's house was only a stone's throw away; the hill down to Tönseten's disappeared. Perhaps it wasn't only people who were afraid in the dark? He, too, liked to curl up when he went to sleep.

He opened his book and paged through to where the lesson began. But he couldn't get started reading. Up from the barns at Godmother Sörine's the strains of a song came floating across the evening air Peder had to listen. . . . Hark! . . . It was Tambur-Ola singing his song as he went about tending the horses. . . . A queer tune, that. Peder knew it well himself, but he never sang it except when he wanted to sing tears away. The melody stirred many strange emotions

. . . All at once he was lost in thought. . . . Funny that grown people were not happy? . . . It seemed they were almost always ready to cry Before you knew it, it would overpower them . . An idea illuminated his face. The greatest thing on earth must be to make people happy

—so full of joy that they had to laugh . . . *that's what I want to do!*

Dusk continued to carry the melody up to him. As night closed in the sadness in the song seemed to deepen. The thought of Mother came back to him. He tucked the book under his bib and jumped up. If he didn't hurry home right away, he'd have to cry. As he walked down he began to shout the song which he had heard. . . . How alive the prairie tonight!

IV

The following spring—Peder was now twelve years old —something happened in the settlement which set the tongues awagging.

East on the prairie lived the widow Gunhild Tuftan with her stepdaughter, Oline. The widow managed so ably that by hiring help during the busy seasons she got along very well. In harvest especially many men would come to the place, mostly transients who stayed only for a few days and then were gone again. The talk about Gunhild herself was not of the best, she being often the subject of gossip. And people knew little or nothing about the stepdaughter since her confirmation a year or two back. She was supposed to be very beautiful of face; at least, that was the opinion of the young men who had been fortunate enough to see it. But those who saw her were not many, for she was so bashful that she turned away whenever anyone spoke to her. After she grew up she never came to meetings and never went to any of the places where people gathered. Talk had it that the two women didn't get along very well.

Now it happened the girl bore a child in secret that spring. Whether she had intended to do away with it no one could say; it was dead when the hired man found it over in a haystack. But since the authorities could find no evidence of violence when they came to investigate, they had to let the matter drop. It was a beautiful, well-shaped boy child.

No one but the minister was allowed to see the daughter. Gunhild gave the explanation that she feared all had not been right with Oline. They had had two hired men during the last harvest, both of whom had hung around the girl continually. One played a guitar and sang so heavenly that it was quite believable the girl had become infatuated with him—for she was very fond of music—and that he then had had his will with her. Gunhild, so she testified, had felt the matter too delicate to talk about. For one thing she wasn't certain; nor had she suspected the child was to come so soon. The day it happened Oline had gone out in the morning to cultivate the corn, had come home for dinner, but had eaten very little. When she returned in the evening she looked ill and had gone straight to bed. The next day the hired man had heard the crows cawing in the meadow; and having gone over to investigate had found the child in the haystack. Gunhild explained the whole matter very carefully to the minister and to all others who inquired. But she simply couldn't understand why Oline, who was so kind, both to folks and beasts, hadn't said anything to her.

The scandal threw the whole settlement into consternation. Everywhere the discussion raged. People maintained stoutly that something was wrong; if this had only happened to Gunhild herself, they might have believed it, for she was capable of almost anything. But as no more evidence came to light the talk gradually died down again.

Reverend Isaksen was new in the parish. He had been educated in the true faith of his fathers; and as soon as he had talked the matter over with Gunhild he knew exactly what must be done. Both mother and daughter were members of his congregation; and correct church polity, as it had been impressed upon him in the seminary, required that Oline be put under church discipline. Not only had she borne a child in secret, but circumstantial evidence pointed strongly to the fact that she had intended to let it die. Why had she said nothing to her mother? From the daughter herself he could learn little or nothing. The times he had been there to see her, she had only lain and stared at the wall, and could not be got to open her mouth except when he spoke sternly to her. Then he had been able to elicit a *yes* from her, but from the manner in which she answered he had got the impression that she only said it to be rid of him. Had it not been for Gunhild's clear testimony, he would hardly have known how to act in the matter. Now he called the deacons together, told them all he knew, and explained to them what order and propriety within a Christian congregation demanded in such extraordinary cases. And so it was decided that Oline Tuftan should be placed under church discipline the first Sunday of services, that is, on the fourth Sunday after Trinity.

The congregation had not yet succeeded in building a church. It held its services in the Tallaksen Schoolhouse, that being the largest and most central. At each meeting homemade benches were put in for more seating.

An unusual number of people came to church that Sunday; the schoolhouse was packed; the hall full; faces crowded in at every window; it seemed that every young person who could possibly get away was there.

After the sermon and baptism the minister came forward and explained in as charitable a manner as possible, though somewhat hesitatingly on account of all the talk which had drifted into the parsonage of late, the sin of which Oline Tuftan had made herself guilty, and what he in conference with the deacons had decided must be done about it. What they were now recommending was in accordance with God's Word and the precedent established by the church fathers in such cases. The fallen one was the child of the congregation; as Christians they could not let the matter pass. The girl, Oline Tuftan, was present here today; she was willing to confess her sin, and to ask the congregation to forgive her the awful offense which her ungodly conduct had brought upon them. The mercy which they hoped the Lord in His time would show unto them, they ought now grant to this poor, beguiled human being. The minister used many words and talked in great detail.

Thereupon he came down and spoke to someone up in front. A woman, clad in black from top to toe, got up. She walked forward, small, bent, and looking for all the world like a great, black bird which has been tamed sufficiently so that people can do what they like with it. Apparently she had tried to hide her face in the black kerchief she was wearing, for one could see only her eyes, nose, and chin. The deathly pallor of the girl's face was thrown into sharp relief against the kerchief. As she turned to face the audience a frightened look flew out across the room and came instantly back. She did not lift her eyes again.

The minister unfolded a paper and handed it to her. "Now read," he encouraged her kindly. Feebly, she took the document, and stood there fingering it. Intense silence followed. Each felt that all the others were finding it difficult to breathe; here and there a pent-up sigh escaped. Every window was crowded with eager faces.

. . . "Now read," the minister repeated mildly.

Her hands clutched the paper. Out from under the black kerchief came a childlike voice, trembling. It seemed to Peder that he had never heard anything quite so much like the cheeping of a frightened bird.

. . . "I, Oline Tuftan," faltered the voice (Peder sensed a storm of crying gather ominously in around it, crying which surged forward in swells, rose to a crest, and was forced back by superhuman effort; he himself wanted to cry, but couldn't, every nerve of him quivering to catch what was going on) "was forced to conceal my shame from men, and gave birth in secret . . ."

A hoarse voice broke in from the window at the rear: "Louder! louder! We can't hear back here!" . . . As if they had been waiting for this moment, a couple of men coughed loudly; another gave vent to a ponderous sigh, a horselike *tr-r-o*; a mother with an infant got up and walked out; several used the opportunity to shift to more comfortable positions; deathlike silence followed, disturbed only by depressed sighs which rose and fell like heavy billows.

Again came the voice, this time by starts and stops, like wheels of a mechanism whose spring has almost run down.

"But the arm of the Lord has . . . has . . . found me out, and brought . . . brought . . . both me . . . me and my sin . . . into the open."

Here the voice died out. The black figure swayed a couple of times, then sank down in a heap . . . a pair of worn black shoes sticking out underneath. A horrible sight, for it looked as though the spirit had deserted the body. People sat terror-struck.

Beret Holm was the first to come forward. "We must have help here right away," she said quietly. Immediately a couple of men rose; then more came; many stood up in order to see better; two men picked Oline up in their arms and carried her out. The minister followed and the crowd settled down again, an icy hand gripping their hearts. There were those in the audience who, remembering sins that they had themselves committed in secret, wondered if this was not the voice of the Lord, and felt oppressed at the thought.

When they came in again the minister and Gunhild were leading the girl between them. This time he let Oline sit down beside her mother. The kerchief having slipped down revealed a delicately shaped head with fair hair, which fell in waves and glittered like gold. The face, bent forward, was small and fine-featured; it would have been comely had it not been so distorted and ghastly white.

Again the minister got up, this time agitated and perplexed because of what had just happened. He began to repeat in detail what he had said before. The girl, and especially the mother (he now emphasized that it was particularly the mother) had confessed how it had all happened: A base fellow, who worked there last fall, had got Oline into his power, and had afterward left the country—perhaps a warning to all of them to be careful about whom they took into their houses. A master was responsible for his servant! No one knew where the man now was keeping himself. In judging her they ought to remember that she had had no father to watch over her, and ought also therefore to be charitable. Had her father been living, the misfortune would likely not have befallen her! Not only had she committed adultery, but the evidence, though circumstantial, indicated strongly that she had been contemplating that which was even worse! They were perhaps asking the very question he had had to ask himself: Why hadn't she told her mother about it? Such criticism, he felt, was just, but he could only answer by repeating what his wife had said to him: one might get into such circumstances that it was impossible to talk! . . . They ought to remember that Gunhild was not her right mother. Moreover, the girl could hardly be reckoned more than a child. Perhaps her mind wasn't as clear as it might be, either. He must admit that he had got that impression. What was written in this document the girl had both confessed to and signed; and though contrary to the rules of the church, he believed that it was their Christian duty not to compel her to read it herself, weak as she was; and for that matter, she had already read a part of it. If, then, there were no objections, he would read the confession himself. He coughed lightly, looked at the assembly, and paused.

Thereupon he read the confession which he himself had drawn up for her. And when he had finished he drew a sigh of relief—this was, by the help of God, so sensibly put together that it should excite no protest!

No sooner had the minister paused than old Tönseten was on his feet, red-faced and agitated; he leaned upon his stick, and let his eyes wander searchingly out over the crowd:

—St. Luke's was certainly blessed with a remarkable board of deacons, aye—that he must say! Here they were chasing around the prairies, poking their noses into all the filth of the whole settlement. And then they came dragging the stuff into congregational meetings! . . . Funny the minister didn't consider himself above such things. If this continued, they'd have to bring lunch with them to church, and bedding too—since they'd have to camp here most of the time to hold congregational meetings! . . . He was here to tell the deacons that this matter was none of their business. The law had already dealt with the case— he himself had once been an officer and knew what he was talking about! . . . How could the poor child help that this thing had happened to her just then, and that she hadn't been able to tell Gunhild about it? If the minister had known that old hussy, he would perhaps not have stuck his nose into the business! . . . Let him who knew himself guiltless cast the first stone! If he wasn't badly mistaken that's what the Scriptures said. He therefore proposed that they forgive the child, and that the congregation *strike* this thing off the records—Tönseten stressed the word emphatically—for it certainly would be cold comfort to their descendants to know that their forebears had been barbarians. . . . They'd have no popery in Dakota Territory!

Tönseten's temper relieved the tension of the crowd. The jocund voice of Aslak Tjöme, now running over with laughter, broke in as the other sat down:

"I second your motion, Syvert Tönseten, bet your life— I do!"

Many eyes sought the minister. . . . Certainly he could not let these words go unchallenged. Craning of necks in expectancy and excitement, among the young men; among the girls, quick glances darting up from hymn books; but most of the older people sat thoughtful and sober-faced.

The minister bit his lip as Tönseten talked. Without looking in that direction he said with great emphasis that those who wanted the floor must talk as was befitting in a Christian assembly, and confine themselves to the question. What he and the deacons had done they could answer for before both God and man . . . they had precepts enough to go by. There was now a motion before the house, which consisted of two parts: first that the girl, Oline Tuftan, had committed the sin of adultery . . .

"I said no such thing!" Tönseten flared up, angrily.

"But that's the meaning of your motion. And now you keep still—the floor is not yours!" The minister was pale; in a trembling voice he continued:

—The motion meant that the congregation grant her forgiveness for the offense which she had caused; and secondly, that all pertaining to this matter be stricken from the minutes—the motion was now open for discussion.

Down in the audience sat Nils Nilsen, a small, black-whiskered, brown-eyed man, reading his hymn book; his right hand, holding the page he was looking at, trembled violently. Now he rose slowly to his feet, fixed his brown eyes mildly upon the minister, and said deliberately: "According to the Law of Moses this woman must be led outside the city gates and stoned, if I understand Scriptures aright. I only want to call your attention to what God's Word says in the matter," he added gravely, and sat down.

The minister smiled at him disconcertedly and reminded him kindly that they were not living under the Old Dispensation, but in the New—not under the Law but by Grace, which said, that when your brother sins and repents, his sin shall be forgiven by men even as it is forgiven of God. "Judge not, that ye be not judged," were Christ's words.

The minister had not finished talking before Nils Nilsen was on his feet again:

—How did the minister and the deacons know for certain that God had forgiven Oline Tuftan? Had they sat in council with Him? This woman's sin was certainly grievous. Not only had she committed adultery, but she had deserted the child without saying a word to her mother; hence it was plain that she wanted the child to die . . . not only adultery, but murder! . . . Nils Nilsen paused, then continued still more calmly: Suppose now that God had not forgiven her, and that they went to work and for-

gave her, would not the curse then fall on them? . . . He
wanted to remind them that this congregation had had a
similar case before—six years ago this fall. That woman too
they had forgiven; punishment had fallen heavy upon them,
and not only on them but on the innocent as well. Did
they not understand that a winter like the one which followed, God did not send without provocation? He was
aware that people laughed at such old-fashioned ideas
nowadays, but he was compelled to speak them nevertheless!

Among the young people this interpretation of the cause
for the great snow winter was received with a fleer; old
Tönseten sat glowering, resting his head on his stick;
Aslak Tjöme chuckled at something he was thinking about;
but most of the audience sat silent and depressed. . . .
There might be some truth in what Nils had said. The
wrath of God might be near at times. Easy enough to sit
here and vote, but did they know what sort of lives these
women had led? Perhaps action had better be postponed?

The minister spoke again:—God would hardly punish
them when they acted in mercy, according to Christian
procedure and discipline, even if their charity were misguided and led them into wrong paths—"much shall be
forgiven him who loves much!"

Nils Nilsen seemed a bit vexed as he stood up and asked
if he might be allowed a word or two more. . . . In the
first place, he, an unlearned man, must ask the minister's
forgiveness for disputing him. But more than that, he must,
for the sake of his conscience, testify to the truth as he saw
it: This talk about love sounded beautiful enough—that
Satan knew too, for it was usually his first strategic move
against man. But the sweet feeling which they called love
might be of many kinds; for example, the soft mollycod-
dling of parents where a just God demanded stern righteousness. What if this woman, Oline Tuftan, would plead
love as her excuse? What was it she had felt as she played
with the sweet desires of sinful flesh? Had it really come
to this now, that young people could abandon themselves
to adultery and simply let the offspring perish, and still
remain members of a Christian congregation just by standing up and reading a few words which someone else had
written? *Then* the salt had certainly left the congregation
of the Lord! . . . He now wanted to propose as a sub-

stitute motion that they ask Gunhild to take her daughter
and leave the settlement; by dealing with the matter in that
way, the congregation would prevent these people from
becoming a source of offense and further temptation. In
order that no one should accuse them of acting unchar-
itably, he himself would offer to buy Gunhild's farm at the
price which the trustees of the congregation would fix. . . .
Nils Nilsen talked slowly and quietly, but underneath his
words burned a fire which threw sparks into minds easily
inflamed.

The minister was manifestly at a loss what to do. Here
he had presented the whole matter so clearly and had
planned the procedure for his parishioners so well that
action in the case would be only a matter of formality, and
now the whole business was snarling itself up into a tangle
which no one could unravel. Nothing was more dangerous
than to begin to argue publicly with religious fanatics . . .
he had had that impressed upon him during the years of
his training for the ministry! Faces watched him from all
parts of the room and inquired wonderingly what he intended to do with Nils Nilsen. Many were obviously
more interested now in the argument between him and
Nils than they were in the case which it concerned.

But then came the Lord in the guise of Aslak Tjöme and
rescued the minister from the embarrassing situation. Aslak
rose to his feet, and with laughter in every word said in a
droll voice, that if Nils Nilsen would undertake the erec-
tion of the city walls, then he'd get busy with his wheelbarrow and fetch all the stone necessary for the business
which was to take place outside. He'd be willing to begin
tomorrow, though perhaps there was no hurry until Nils
had got the walls decently plastered! . . . As for the substitute motion, he could see no sense in that. Nils had all
the land he could take care of; moreover, it seemed to him
more Christian that they keep their own sinners at home
rather than chase them out among innocent people! If he
hadn't known that Nils Nilsen was such a strict temper-
ance man, he would have suspected him of being a little
tipsy today. Midst an uproar of laughter Aslak moved the
question be put to a vote; he had no sooner sat down than
old Tönseten was on his feet. Pounding the floor with his
stick, he seconded the motion.

That stopped all further debate. The vote had to be

taken. Only one dissenting voice was heard. After the votes
had been counted, Nils Nilsen got up and asked in a quiet
manner that his vote be recorded in the minutes. Whereupon the meeting adjourned.

V

Beret and Peder sat in one of the seats near the front.
She felt, as the proceedings were about to begin, that perhaps she ought to take the boy and leave the room; but
then it occurred to her that being present at the trial
might impress upon him the fatal consequences of sin—
and so she stayed.

Peder sat there, glowing hot. A mysterious force had
hold of him and threatened to choke him—it was as
though he had never before understood what life meant.
A feeling of resentment welled up within him, surged back
and forth in his mind, gained force, and broke more
violently each time: This thing was wrong—God could not
want a human being treated in this way!

His eyes were riveted upon the black figure before him;
as he beheld the face from which Death himself peered
out, and heard the scared voice begin to read, he threw
back his head and looked about, his eyes burning, his
tongue cleaving to the roof of his mouth, his clammy hands
opening and clenching convulsively: now a miracle must
happen! That voice can't have done anything so terribly
wrong . . . now God must come! . . . His mother got
up to help and he wanted to go with her; but no—this was
only for the grown-ups, and so he had to remain where he
was. . . . Could she be dead already? He didn't wonder at
that in the least . . . he himself had felt times when his
heart had threatened to stop. And that for lesser reasons
than this . . . They wouldn't bury her today, would they?
Perhaps Jesus might come and wake her up again? The
Bible history told about such cases. But as he realized
more clearly how impossible it all was he shook with anger,
his hands opening and closing. When he grew up, he
would . . . he would. . . . Furious, he tried to think
of what he would do to the minister and the deacons, and
to all who had had to do with this outrage, but nothing

quite terrible enough would come to him. Oh, he would—
he *would!* . . .

After they had brought her in again and Nils Nilsen had
spoken so touchingly about stoning her, Peder never
doubted that it would take place. In order not to scream he
put his arm up to his mouth and bit at his coat sleeve. . . .
Everything that was wrong and terrible always happened.
. . . But there'd be more dead ones—he'd throw rocks
right in their faces! If he'd only had time to run home
after his gun! So intense was his emotion that he burst
into tears as soon as Aslak Tjöme had finished talking.
For in the bright light of the man's droll logic, Peder saw
at once how utterly impossible this stoning business was.
. . . It can not happen—no, it can not happen! He
would have liked to get up and shout hurray for Aslak
Tjöme and Tönseten for being such bully fellows. . . .
Peder felt certain that someday he too would get people
to laugh at their own stupidity!

The relief from the terrible tension under which he had
been brought with it a pleasant calm. He looked about to
see what people were thinking. Once more he sensed in
the others the feeling of shame which he himself had felt
earlier; he seemed to detect it even in his mother.

What did this strange grin on the faces of the men
mean? And why were the girls so red and shamefaced—
why did they keep looking down? . . . What were the
people ashamed of anyway?

As his mother and he walked along over to the wagon
they passed a group of men who stood talking. One of
them was saying in low tones: "A fellow can't fool with
the girls over here—in the old country a brat or two didn't
make much difference!" Laughing, another added: "Well,
you've got to be smarter about it here, you see." . . . At
that the whole group guffawed. His mother took him by
the arm and dragged him hurriedly away. . . . What did
it all mean?

On the way home no one spoke. The brothers put up
the horses without a word. His sister kept out of his way.
Peder noticed these things; and the secretiveness about
it all added to the mystery of it. Stealing upstairs to his
room, he took his Epitome, read everything in it on adultery, without getting any the wiser.

And now as the excitement died down, he felt sick and

wanted to vomit. He didn't let on, however; but when dinner time came and he smelled the food cooking, he could stand it no longer and had to go to bed. All afternoon he lay perspiring and thinking of many things.

In the evening when his mother was in the cellar straining the milk, he got up and began to move about. It occurred to him that a cup of warm, fresh milk would taste good; besides, he needed a chance to talk to her. . . . If only that Anna Marie would stay away! He looked about, then stole down to the cellar.

. . . Dusky and cool down here, and easy to talk. He waited till his mother turned her back to him; after a little while he asked what wrong Oline had done. The mother filled the pan before she answered:

"You heard that today, didn't you? Pray God that you never bring a woman into such misery!" The last seemed to come out of many thoughts—as if she had been a long way after it.

"Wasn't she married?"

"No."

"Is it adultery to have children when you aren't married?" . . . He felt his throat getting dry, and gulped down another swallow of milk.

The mother did not answer immediately, for which Peder was glad. She bent down over a milk pan, moving it farther in on the shelf. . . . "So the Book says." Her voice had a tired sound in it now, but Peder paid no attention to that.

"Well—is that so wrong then?"

The mother filled another pan. She stood as if she hesitated about where to set it. Her voice seemed to come from far away and carried so much sadness that he was touched:

"You'd better take your Catechism and read the Seventh Commandment. That'll tell you plain enough, I'm sure!"

Peder saw a new thought coming, and seized it instantly:

"Does it say the same thing in English?" He had no sooner uttered the words than he felt that this thing could not possibly be so obscure in his language . . . everything was plainer in English.

"I suppose it does," she said resignedly.

Peder stood awhile and thought hard:

"Do you think God wanted her to do what they made her do today—when He has forgiven her? . . . It doesn't matter to anybody else, does it?"

She paused before answering:

"It isn't always easy to know His will." She turned toward him. "You'd better go up now and study your lesson for tomorrow—that I'm certain will be pleasing in His sight."

But then another thought struck Peder, one which he could not keep back; it was so easy to say it to her now that she was standing there in the dark:

"Why can't I learn my lessons in English?"

She set the pail down and came over to the cellar way:

"How you talk, Permand!" she said kindly. "Study your lessons in English?" she added, in order to show him how absurd the idea was.

"It's much easier!"

"For anyone as smart in Norwegian as you are?"

"But I can't understand the words!" he insisted stubbornly.

"Well, then you'll have to learn them," she said firmly.

He could tell by the sound of her voice that it was no use to argue any more. And here he had gone to work and spoiled everything for himself, so that now he couldn't even ask about this other matter either. Then, as if in self-defense, he answered:

"Others do it!"

"We can't pay attention to what others do!" . . . When she spoke again, her voice was milder: "You wouldn't put me to shame like that, would you, Permand?" She came nearer him.

"Shame?" he repeated, as he stepped higher up in the cellar way.

"Aye—indeed!"

"That such a shame?"

"Certainly! The idea of a Norwegian boy wanting to talk to God in a language his own mother can't understand. . . . Go right along now and get at your lessons."

Peder came out into the evening, boiling with anger. Now Mother saw no further than her nose—as usual. *He* . . . a Norwegian boy . . . huh! . . . *The idea!*

Over near the cow barn stood a team and a rig. Weren't those Sam Solum's horses? The loud talk of men came

from the buggy; cautiously, Peder circled nearer and nearer
. . . it might be interesting to hear what they were talking
about. *Sh—sh*—he must be careful not to come so near
that they'd discover him and chase him away! . . . Yes,
sure enough—it was Sam. Chris Tallaksen was with him.
Ole stood with one foot on the front hub; Store-Hans on
the other side the same way. Sam did the talking . . .
his speech had gusto in it, the others laughing noisily and
thrusting in a remark now and then. It was all about
Gunhild Tuftan, how she would chase around when she
was man-crazy, how often she got the spells, who had
been over there, and the like; many names were mentioned. Strange and dark words, these, to Peder. They
stirred about in and among hidden things, things which
he had vaguely sensed as in a dream he couldn't remember clearly. He was ashamed that his brothers knew so
much about such matters. Sam accused Ole too of having
been there, even naming the evening. Peder looked up
toward the house—Mother must not hear this . . . not
for all the world!

The buggy rolled away, and Peder went in to his books.
But it was not long before other company came, Godmother Sörine and her whole family. She and Vesle-Hans
in the lead, Sofie and Tambur-Ola* following close.

The latter's real name was Ole Tönaas. As a half-grown
boy he had come from Norway with his parents; the
family had settled in Wisconsin, where they managed to
get forty acres of cut-over land on easy payments; here
they had started life anew; but they were not long in dis-
covering that they had not yet reached paradise.

And when the boy was twenty-two the great war had
broken out, and so the draft had claimed him together
with many others. He had been assigned to the drum
corps, which post gave him the nickname that stuck to
him ever after. Possibly he had been born with great
musical talent; the sense of rhythm was still strong in
him, for every once in a while he would strike up a tune
and beat time to it. And when he sang he put so much
into the singing that people hearing him had to stop and
listen.

A remarkable fellow in many ways. At times he might
be so jolly and full of life that he made people laugh them-

* Tambur, equivalent to the English *drummer*.

selves sick at all the nonsense he talked, and then again—
he would get a spell in which he went about gloomy and
silent for days at a time.

As Sörine little by little learned to know him better, she
could predict when a spell would be coming on; for it
always began by his going about humming a certain melody, singular because of the many variations he introduced into it, and because of its plaintive melancholy. In
mood it was much like some drear November evening out
on a bleak prairie. It really consisted of two melodies—
a soldier's song coupled to a Norwegian folk song by some
drawn-out *hum-ums*, both in the minor mode. He had
now hummed this tune so long that all in the house knew
it, and others too. Sörine had asked him once what the
name of that song was; and then he had made a terrible
grimace and said that it was the song of life's dismay.
Thereupon he had grinned sardonically, and had left the
room. After that, the people in Sörine's house had called
it Tambur-Ola's Killdeer-song; it was Sofie who thought
of that name because she always wanted to cry when she
heard anyone humming it.

And then, too, there was this peculiarity about the man
that he would always laugh at and make fun of everything pertaining to religion. Whenever people broached
the subject in his presence, he either got up and left immediately or began to ridicule their opinions; and so some
insisted that he wasn't in his right mind.

There were those who claimed that he had got that
way from the half year's imprisonment in Andersonville;
others said it had begun in those ill-fated days when he
served in the war . . . when he lost both his sweetheart
and his parents. As for his parents, poverty and toil down
there in the cut-over country had made them an easy prey
to the cough when it ravaged the settlement one spring.
And after he went to the war his sweetheart, never hearing from him, concluded that he was dead and, rather
than mourn alone all her life, sought a man to help her.
When Ole one fine day bobbed up to claim her he found
her a married woman with two children—that was the end
of that romance.

And so he had drifted West. Despite his oddities one
would have had to hunt through many counties for a
steadier and more faithful workman; he had been at Mrs.

Waag's now going on three years; there were those who whispered that he was courting the widow. Be that as it may, she was the only one who was permitted to peep behind the curtain of his past, and now he went about as if he were one of the family. There was not a person on the whole prairie whom Peder esteemed more highly than he did Tambur-Ola. He thought him about equal to Abraham Lincoln himself, and for a time went about trying to imitate him in speech and manners. But he was, for that matter, not the only one in that household who admired Tambur-Ola. Beret had heard his story from Sörine. At times she would sit and look at the face upon which life had engraved such deep furrows, until she felt a desire to go over and to touch it lovingly; his many eccentricities went by her almost unnoticed.

After the company came, both of the brothers, who were upstairs—where they nearly always spent their Sunday evenings at home—came down in a hurry. Tonight, as usual, the mother and the godmother sat in the kitchen and talked; the others went into the living room; Peder tagged along, in order to be near Tambur-Ola, and to observe Store-Hans and Sofie. This spring Peder had noticed a strange expression come into his brother's eyes every time he looked at the girl. . . . He wondered what her eyes were like when she looked at Store-Hans. Peder liked her very well . . . there was such a warm luxuriance about her person, almost like rich prairie on balmy spring nights. And now his attention was drawn to her throat, to the soft, supple curve of it; he'd like to chuck his hand in . . . and let it follow down over those two little bumps just beneath.

Otherwise he could detect nothing unusual in her, except that now and then she would glance at Store-Hans; and each time she looked at him her eyes laughed, and there was a mild, warm glow in them. The glow usually brightened whenever Tambur-Ola said something very funny. But the brother looked at Sofie so much that Peder felt embarrassed on account of him. . . . Mother ought to have seen this!

Then he forgot both of them, because he had to listen to Tambur-Ola. Last year, at the Fourth of July celebration, Peder had had the thrilling adventure of seeing fireworks; and he was reminded of it now—here sat this man amusing himself by sending off rockets! As soon as he began, Store-Hans closed the door between the kitchen and the living room.

This evening Tambur-Ola was delivering a sort of lecture on Nils Nilsen and the structure he would have to build before Dakota Territory would be habitable. . . . He had talked to Nils today, he said, and had immediately hired himself out to him. A shame not to help a man with an undertaking so important. And Nils had entrusted him with the position of centurion . . . oh, yes, someday he'd be sitting high! He had come here this evening to engage a couple of able-bodied men. Old Tönseten had already hired himself out for a year. . . . But pity poor Aslak with the wheelbarrow! Had they heard that as soon as Mrs. Tjöme came home today she began to boil ointment for Aslak's back?—a thoughtful wife that of Aslak's. . . . Oh, yes, this would be a noble structure, all right . . . nothing else like it in all the world. Nils had described it in detail. Listen: Twelve ells high and twelve ells wide the wall; twelve gates in it, with twelve doors in each gate—in case there'd be much business with stoning and the like; above each gate twelve towers; each tower a place for twelve watchmen; each watchman armed with twelve carbines; for each carbine enough ammunition for twice twelve rounds of powder and shot—yessir! Every time a boy steals away to fool with a girl, every watchman shall fire twelve rounds of powder; if then the sinner doesn't right about-face, every watchman in all the twelve towers shall fire twelve rounds of shot, all at the same time and as fast as the fingers can make the trigger go—this all in order that the heart of Nils Nilsen may be kept free from evil thoughts. . . . Yes indeed—Store-Hans had better be careful hereafter!

One of Tambur-Ola's feet beat rhythmically upon the other, as to music. He sat as sober as a judge, waiting for the others to stop laughing. Then he continued in a low, gentle voice, but coaxed into the ironic story a sort of grim frightfulness; the bitter expression which he always wore upon his face intensified the feeling:

"On each tower shall be built a black turret, to the glory of the city and to the delight of the eyes of Nils Nilsen. In each turret there shall be twelve chambers, each as black as night itself; under each chamber there shall stand twelve boiling caldrons, abubble night and day; in every chamber shall be stationed twelve hags—only those with very sharp eyes are eligible for the office; every hag shall be provided with twelve huge poles, each having at the end a good gaff-hook. Every time a hag sees a farmer girl who she thinks is about to think of some boy, she shall hook the girl, haul her in and boil her twelve days in each of the twelve caldrons" (Tambur-Ola made a grim pause before he continued), "only then will the rottenness be boiled out of them sufficiently so that the carcasses can be served as a hot dish to the watchmen in the towers . . . for nothing unclean must come into them! . . . Oh, yes, when Nils Nilsen once gets this city well started, it won't be easy to be a girl!" he added gloomily. He would therefore advise every maiden to marry early, for old married men and women could sin to their heart's desire, just as Nils Nilsen himself did, because for them there was no punishment either within or without the city walls. . . . Well—he thought he'd better go straight home now and go to bed before the toil began! . . . Tambur-Ola yawned and stretched himself like a man greatly fatigued.

"O-o-h, how terrible you talk!" Sofie shuddered, and got up.

"I s'pose so," Tambur-Ola replied wearily. "But it is as the hen said: One must cackle with the beak one has."

Peder felt compelled to go over to him; in a low excited voice he asked:

"Why were there twelve of everything?"

"Oh, that," said Tambur-Ola, carelessly, "that is in honor of the twelve tribes of Israel. You'll find all of it in that book of yours. Is it possible there can be such igorance in a Christian congregation?"

Just as they were about to leave Sofie came over to Peder, and putting her arm around his neck, drew him close to her; then she put her hand under his chin and lifted his face. "What a handsome boy you will be, Permand! I'd better take you before all that nastiness of Tambur-Ola's gets us." . . . A soft warm hand stroked his cheek. Suddenly she was gone. Peder found himself alone in the living room, blushing, but strangely happy.

He went upstairs and undressed, taking plenty of time. The words which Sofie had spoken continued to ring in his ear. He wondered if it were true that he was handsome? Was he, really? Then it would be still more jolly to be grown up. . . . He took off his clothes, sat down on the edge of the bed and stroked his body, patted himself, and found it pleasant. At last he got into bed, and then drifted away into an unreasonably sweet longing for someone to love—for someone to whom he could be kind. . . . From now on this longing came upon him every time he entered the room in which he busied himself building the future.

VI

The following night Peder nearly scared the wits out of both his mother and himself; and the next day he went about laughing at it all . . . it certainly must be true as Mother said that he was the biggest dunce in the world . . . though he could hardly believe that either.

At the head of the stairs at Mrs. Holm's one came into a narrow hallway; on each side of it there were two rooms, separated by thin partitions. One of these rooms belonged to Anna Marie; here she lived with her things; adjoining it on the same side was the best room, used only when company came to the house and stayed overnight. The farthermost room on the opposite side was Ole's and Store-Hans'; and next to it, nearest the stairway, was Peder's. Until a year ago he had slept downstairs with his mother; but then she had moved him up here. She had thought that perhaps it wasn't good for him to share a bed with her—he seemed to be developing very fast physically, and was thinking so many queer things.

This evening he went up to go to bed as usual. A big green moon stood high in the heaven, staring right into the room and over onto the bed. He undressed completely, went directly into the flood of light and remained there stroking and petting his body just as he had done the evening before. He felt a vague uneasiness and a strange, joyous quickening within himself; but he also was half afraid. He let his night clothes lie awhile, went to the window and looked out. It was pleasant to stand here, this way, in such a flood of light.

In his imagination he began pretending that he was one of the fairies his Reader told about. If only he could stand quite still now and think of something very beautiful, perhaps one of them would come dancing down on the moonbeams. . . . On such moon-nights they frolicked and flitted about, he knew. If only she would come now, he would dance with her! Then he'd go home to her castle and see where she lived. Perhaps she would want him to marry her? . . . Strange that Sofie who was herself so beautiful should say that of him!

The night came toward him, soft and caressing; the green-blue dimness lowered itself listening over all that had life, stroked it . . . and exulted. Over in the grove shadows of many forms moved mysteriously . . . some bulky, others tiny—scarcely discernible in the dimness. . . . Hush, did someone step on a twig? He laid his ear close to the screen. Felt a thumping through his head. Outside there was someone whispering: *Si-i, su-i, su-i, si-i.* . . . There must be many of them; he could hear them from every direction; and now they came right into his ear. He wished that she who was to come for him would be soft-skinned and full-bosomed like Sofie. . . . He'd tuck his hand in and tickle a little. . . . Not so big, of course, but grown up—he didn't care to play that way with children.

. . . A peculiar shadow, that—over yonder? Didn't it stretch up on tiptoe to listen? Perhaps it heard human voices from the kitchen and was afraid of the light from the window? *There* . . . he certainly heard something whisper? Just wait till the house is quiet, then we'll see! . . . Eerie green light peeping in through the branches . . . shadows stretching themselves in it . . . withdrawing . . . coming back again . . . nearer each time—a queer shadow that! Then he saw the head and one arm. Oh, she would come all right, when it got quiet enough downstairs. A strange ripple passed through him.

All of a sudden Peder heard Ole talking loudly in the next room. Cautiously, he tiptoed across the floor, put on his night-shirt, climbed into bed, and sat upright listening. The brother was loud-voiced tonight. Peder became so absorbed in what was being said in the next room that he forgot the one who stood down in the grove and wanted to come up to him. . . . What terrible things he was hearing!

Ole had been to town that afternoon; he had just come home; as the brothers undressed, Ole told Store-Hans what he had heard:

—Oline had killed herself last night, he related. Yessir, when they came to the cow barn this morning to do the milking, there she hung dangling. . . . Some sight all right! She had on the church clothes of yesterday. Neither the hired man nor Gunhild herself had dared to cut her down . . . oh, no, they were too scared, and so they had gone to the neighbors. . . . They'd sure have excitement now! According to what people said the child might not be hers at all; Gunhild was not above that job herself. Nils Rognaldsen, who had stood sponsor to Oline, declared that a more innocent person never had walked in two shoes—that he'd swear to. But Gunhild herself was man-crazy all the time; that too Nils had said. The hired man over there must be a devil of a fellow; most likely Gunhild knew just how to get him to swear to everything she pointed at. Nils Rognaldsen had talked about getting people together and driving her out of the country. Others had said that both the deacons and the minister ought to be fired for meddling in the matter. Ole laughed jocosely: Tönseten was going about roaring like a mad bull, and swearing that he'd write the President of the Synod and get him to come out; he declared up and down that it was on account of the circus yesterday that she had killed herself. Now they'd certainly have a merry time! Ole concluded.

Store-Hans had listened to his brother without interrupting him. But now his deep voice, too, came through the partition:

"They ought to chase that preacher to Jericho; the fool could have talked to her privately! . . . Mother thinks so too."

"Well, if it wasn't for Mother," said Ole disgustedly, flinging a garment over on the chair, "I'd have nothing to do with the congregation; then they could jabber all they pleased for me . . . there are other things to do in America!"

"Well, that would hardly do either, I s'pose," said Store-Hans soberly.

"We'll just see about that when the time comes!"

After that there was no more talk on the other side of the partition. The brothers went to bed; Peder could hear the breathing.

After a little he forgot about them. Suddenly he lay shivering. A stream of greenish light flooded the room, as if someone were lighting in through the window with a lantern. In order not to see it, he pulled the covers up over his head. But that did not help, for now the whole scene of yesterday was upon him, only more vivid, more terrible. Everything came so near, and he alone with it all—the little pale face peeping out of the black kerchief; the look of utter helplessness over the whole figure; the child voice full of terror . . . now he heard it even more distinctly than yesterday. And then that hunted look . . . and the eyes—oh, those eyes, how they implored in terror! . . .

There she hung because they had treated her so shamefully and because no one would come to her rescue!

All at once a thought overpowered him—made him sit up in bed: The strange shadow down in the grove, perhaps that was Oline? Godmother Kjersti knew about ghosts who haunted places because they wanted people to do something for them in order to get peace. . . . And now, and now . . . this was Oline who stood there begging him to stand forth and witness before men that she was innocent!

The stillness opened wide and listened throughout the whole house, and asked him what he intended to do about it. Outside the window stood someone waiting for the answer. . . . There—she tapped on the window!

Peder lay in a cold sweat, trembling; he must get up at once, or this thing clutching his heart would choke the life out of him; he jumped out of bed and dashed to the window, his eyes sucking in everything down there. Since he last stood here the moon had stolen forward between two branches; at the right side of the living shadow it had found a wee twig with tender foliage which trembled beneath the caresses of the night breeze; wanting to look at the twig a little closer, the moon took beam after beam of sifted light and lay down upon it, and there came a whitish green spot. Peder saw the spot and screamed, but could make only a hoarse sound . . . there stood Oline big as life. In her hand she still held the paper she had read from yesterday—now she beckoned with it!

Peder tore across the room, tumbled down the stairs, and into his mother's bedroom; there he threw himself into her bed, and pulled the covers over his head. He was so beside himself with terror, that he didn't know where he was; but the moment he felt the warmth of her body, he burst into tears. . . . Beret was startled by his strange behavior; she sat up, spoke sternly to him, and tried to push him away . . . she was embarrassed, being so scantily clad now during the hot season. But the head he burrowed into her would not budge.

"Oline has killed herself," he whispered, hoarse and terrified. . . . "She is standing over in the grove and wants us to help her!"

Upon hearing what the matter was Beret stroked his head soothingly. Many thoughts about this child over whom she had watched with such tender care came and went. Her mind was like the heavens over which dark clouds drive in conflict with a sun that wants to come out and shine. Now it cleared; his sympathy with all who were in trouble was a constant comfort to her. After a little she freed herself from his arms, got up, dressed, lit the lamp—giving herself plenty of time. But she said nothing.

Peder, having lifted the edge of the cover, lay watching her until he forgot himself and asked:

"What are you going to do now?"

At first Beret didn't answer; she went out into the kitchen after the lantern, brought it in and lit it. Then she came over to the bed:

"If it is true that Oline has come, I suppose we'd better go out and help her. Jump up now and show me where she is . . . we will help her right away."

Peder tried to plunge himself down into the terror again, but couldn't. On the table both the lamp and the lantern stood burning; all in the room looked homey and safe; Mother was teasing him. Pulling the quilt over his head he tried to recover the terror, and found nothing but a feeling of shame. . . . A good thing that Mother was the only one who knew about this!

Beret waited a moment, then took hold of the quilt to pull it off:

"Come now and go with me. We must find out what scared you."

Peder turned away in disgust. Then her voice grew firmer; and taking him by the arm so hard that it hurt, she said:

"Hurry now, we want peace here tonight." And then she added more gently: "I can't have a big boy like you around scaring the wits out of both himself and the rest of us. What do you think will become of such a fellow?"

"Aw, I s'pose it was just my foolishness again," Peder admitted meekly, hoping thereby to escape.

"Come on now!"

Peder crept slowly out of bed and went with her. But not until he stood outside in the dewy grass and felt the coolness of the night about him did he really sense how utterly absurd it was for two grown people to run around with a lantern hunting for a shadow. He could, for that matter, point to the identical tree from which the shadow had come . . . how silly of Mother!

"Well, where was it?" asked Beret.

"Where it *was*?"

"Yes . . . that you saw her?"

Peder dropped her hand and ran in among the trees.

"Right *here* she stood! The paper she read out of yesterday she held in her hand . . . she motioned to me with it . . . *that's as true as I'm standing here!*"

The mother came up to him. "Can you see now how foolish you are?" In order to convince him the more she threw the light of the lantern in among the trees.

"Now you stand there scaring her with the lantern!" Peder said reproachfully.

At that Beret had to laugh:

"Oh, Permand, Permand!" . . .

"Well—yes—I do think of a lot of funny things," he admitted cheerfully.

When they returned to the house he went directly to the stairway to go up; Beret, speaking gently, stopped him:

"Perhaps you'd better stay down here with me tonight— then you'll sleep better."

The proposal seemed sensible to Peder. And a little later he felt safe, as he snuggled close, his arm about his mother. . . . If his sister should find out that he slept here tonight, she'd be calling him names . . . well, shucks! . . . He'd

get up as soon as Mother stirred in the morning. They lay
quiet for a long while.

. . . Was she awake yet? he wondered. Peder stirred.

"What is it, Permand?"

"Yes, I . . . well, you see, I was wondering how God
could let anything so terrible happen to Oline."

—It wasn't God!

—Who then?

—Satan.

—Was *he* the strongest?

—No.

—He was *too!* Peter raised himself on his elbow.

—He mustn't talk so wickedly. Beret took a firm hold
of the arm which lay about her.

—Yes, he was, because he always got things the way he
wanted them! God couldn't do a thing against him!
Peder's voice sounded firm and confident.

Beret turned toward him.

"Tell me, Peder, where do you get all those ideas?" she
asked in grave concern.

"I can see it!" he said confidently. "All God can do is
to get people to pray . . . and read the Bible . . . and
go to church . . . and then He counts all the dead ones."

"You musn't talk that way!"

"I will too! Because the other fellow, he gets people to
fight . . . to commit adultery . . . to kill each other . . .
he gets everything to be wrong—there's nothing but wrong
here!" Peder's voice was cheerful and bright; here in the
dark it was easy to talk, and now he felt the need of
speaking his mind.

Beret sat up in bed. The boy's words affected her so
much the more terribly because they had been spoken
with such conviction and warmth. In the voice of one
who pleads for the dearest thing on earth, she told him
about the sin he was committing in harboring such
thoughts. She began to admonish him; anxiety, and then
tears, came into her voice. . . . He must pray unceasingly,
pray God's angels to be near him! . . . For only in that
way could he keep his heart pure. It was with evil thoughts
as with weeds: If once they were let into the heart and
allowed to root there, they would choke out all that was
good! . . . She moaned, sobbed in anguish, implored him
to be obedient and go the ways she pointed! . . . At last

crying got the better of her, and throwing herself down over him, she crushed him to her. She kept it up until Peder had to cry too, though for the life of him he couldn't imagine what wrong he had done now. Neither of them could say a word. But she petted him and stroked him; and he snuggled closer to her, sank down into something wonderfully soft and pleasant—suddenly he forgot all because it felt so luxuriously sweet to lie here.

. . . The next day he found no peace, because that Kill-deer-song of Tambur-Ola's haunted him; now loud and near, now soft and distant, but never so faint but that he could hear it. He had to sing it, and kept the singing up until he was happy again.

VII

A period of storm and disruption broke loose over St. Luke's Norwegian Evangelical Congregation. The boat keeled perilously, with no one to calm the troubled waters. The worst of it was that Reverend Isaksen wanted the steady hand and the clear eye of his predecessor, and was, therefore, but ill-fitted to stand at the helm in the terrific tempest which now began to rage.

Oline Tuftan's tragic death had the effect of a violent shock upon the whole congregation; she, who during her few days on earth had been so shy and retiring, now walked in at every man's door, demanding to know what he thought, became insistent, and refused to leave before she got an answer.

And none were more profoundly affected by her death than the quickened ones. Here they saw plainly what happened to a congregation over which the World had got the upper hand. Sin and unspeakable wickedness! And the watchmen in Zion slumbering peacefully, thinking that all was well indeed! . . . The dissatisfaction which hitherto had only lain smoldering now suddenly burst into a roaring flame.

There was among the converted a small group of people—three or four families in all—known as the Prayer Circle; these met every other Sunday afternoon and edified themselves by the singing of hymns, by prayer, and by listening to the testimony of some brother who had aught on his heart which he felt the need of unburdening. What had happened in their midst was so terrible that neither prayer nor song could banish it from their minds, and the result was that the meetings became little better than gossip fests; one had heard this; another had heard that; and all pointed to the same thing: the end was near—yea, verily, the end was now drawing nigh!

The trouble began by Nils Nilsen's making a long journey, the object of which none other than his wife was permitted to know. An old friend in Marshalltown, Iowa, wrote to him that they in that city expected a visit from an ambassador of the Lord, a man singularly endowed with the power of leading people to God; could not Nils Nilsen come to their city and take part in the Pentecost which they were certain would now descend upon them? He himself knew, of course, that the more gifts of grace they could bring together, the more abundant would be the harvest.

After receiving the invitation Nils Nilsen went about his work, more thoughtful and taciturn than usual. When he had finished cultivating the corn, he packed two newly starched shirts into a valise, told Elise, his wife, to keep quiet as to why and where he had gone—people had enough to talk about for a while anyway—and left.

Elise was happy the day he went. The Lord in His mercy had indeed given her a good and pious husband. This she knew and was thankful for it; yet a feeling of relief came over her at the prospect of having the children and the farm to herself for a time. No one knew better than she that Nils meant well; but he was hard handed in his treatment of the children; it seemed to her that he worked them pitilessly and was too quick to seize the rod. She had often worried about Miriam, the next to the youngest; the girl was so high-spirited and full of life, and had been chastised both in and out of season; yet her mother knew that the Lord had never given a warmer heart to any human being. During her married life Elise had learned not to remonstrate; it seemed better to try to mend matters in some other way.

On this particular occasion it would have been better had she said just a little bit more. Whenever anyone asked her where Nils was keeping himself these days she either scarcely answered at all, or spoke in such an ambiguous

way that people began to wonder. . . . Strange that Nils
Nilsen had time to be away from the farm at this season
of the year! Why had he gone? Where was he? And then
all of a sudden a rumor was abroad that Nils Nilsen had
deserted his family; some said they had seen him down
in Sioux City, and that he was then in the company of
a strange woman.

But after a month's absence people saw Nils Nilsen on
his farm, going about his work as usual. To persons who
were inquisitive and asked him outright he only answered
quietly that he had been away and had had a meeting
with the Lord. More he would not say and that was all
anyone ever found out.

At the first meeting which the Prayer Circle held after
his return, he got up and spoke in beautiful, entreating
terms about how important it was to work at one's own
regeneration on the one hand, and to cleanse the Lord's
Vineyard on the other; for now wickedness was spreading
by leaps and bounds; the last days were swiftly drawing
near; soon the night would come—the deep, brooding
darkness in which no one could work. This they had
heard both themselves and him say before, but today a
new glow was emanating from his testimony. It was good
to hear him, his friends thought; they experienced a
quickening of the spirit as does sprouting life on a balmy
spring night when the rain mizzles warmly. The best of
all came at the end; for when he had finished his talk,
he proposed that hereafter they meet every Sunday afternoon. It must be very discouraging for the Lord to sit up
there in His heaven and watch His children down below.
Though He was offering them the Bread of Life, they
felt no need of coming to Him oftener than twice a
month! Was it not the express command of the Saviour
to His disciples that they should pray without ceasing?
Did they try to follow that command? Did they feel the
need of it? Or had they become lukewarm and altogether
indifferent because of all the sin around about them?
Small wonder then that wickedness was spreading as it
did in the days of Sodom and Gomorrah! They remembered, did they not, that there, too, an immigrant people
had become contaminated, and that many were destroyed
by the fire of God's wrath? After the meeting he had very

little to say to those of his brethren who wanted to talk to him, and left early.

However it came about, new life was injected into the Sunday afternoon meetings. Testimonial followed testimonial, the one enkindling the other. The flame which burned fattened, and seemed to have an irresistible power; several of the lukewarm were drawn in; every meeting saw a larger group; the testimonials became more frequent; the joy, more courageous; and with it came an increasing zeal for winning new souls for the Lord—soon "the night cometh, when no man can work!"

This last strain, recurring again and again, became like the motif of a funeral march.

Reverend Isaksen did not attend the meetings; this was fanaticism; and they seemed indeed not to need his presence—they might at least have shown him the courtesy of inviting him!

A few of the young people, looking for escape, were caught by the fervor of the revival. Of these some had been excluded from the Singing Society because they had no voice; others had too much pride to seek the pleasures of the village saloon; none of them were old enough yet to enter politics but all were filled with an indefinable longing after greater human happiness, and to do deeds that might stir the world. These now began to attend the meetings. Here they beheld strange pictures, painted in gorgeous colors. Some of the scenes cast an enchanting spell because of their sweet sadness, and told of wondrous things—about the journey through the Wilderness of the World; about the desire of sinful flesh and the bright light of the Spirit; or about the struggle, the eternal warfare between the Mighty Hosts of the Lord and the Forces of Darkness; or again about the Blood of the Lamb with its miraculous power to cleanse from all sin, yea, even though it be as red as crimson. Now and then there came sweet, sensuous dream pictures which held them spellbound because they were so sad and yet so beautiful; they told of the Immaculate Bridegroom, who must sorrow as long as time lasts, because the Bride has not arrayed herself in the Wedding Garment, that which had been washed white in the Blood of the Lamb. And then again, the pictures would take on still more supernatural colors: yonder, on the other side of the Valley of Death, shone the Golden City where joy was never dimmed by sorrow nor by care nor by any toil whatsoever; these things the Lord God had hidden forever under the Mantle of His Love. What then mattered this short sojourn in the Vale of Tears when compared with eternal bliss at the Bosom of the Bridegroom, there tasting that God is good? The pictures were often broken and described incoherently, but reflected, nevertheless, so much of the speaker's personal experience that the whole series left an impression of vital reality.

The leaven was working. A people's soul had begun to stir. That which the mind in some hidden cove of a Norwegian fjord, or on some lonely island—far out where the mighty sea booms eternally—through centuries had conceived of religious mysticism, and there shaped so as to fit the conditions of life, now sought a natural expression on the open reaches of the prairies. New forces, forces which they themselves did not understand, were at work here. The lure of the unknown and the restless, roving spirit of the race had torn them loose from their ancient moorings, from home and kindred and fatherland, and from all that hitherto had given them a sense of security and a feeling of safety, and had led them into this strange and faraway land. Now the tide bore back again; their imagination was busily at work, painting enchanting pictures of the old home which they never more could regain; on evenings when the weather was fair, they might stand on the prairie and sense its presence in the gloaming as a sunken Atlantis. With these people the feeling of strangeness in this alien land and the utter impossibility of striking new roots here gave to their testimony the tone of deep, rich spiritual experience. Two newcomers were the most eloquent whenever they arose to testify.

It happened that young people, sitting at the meetings, looked at the pictures until they imagined they, too, caught glimpses of new plains on which it would be pleasant to rove—saw them, and gave themselves over. But there were other young people also, shame-smitten by a secret sin, the sin which may not be mentioned among men, who, not knowing what to do with themselves, took to these revivals as the last resort for restoring their self-respect. And so they likewise surrendered. When the great miracle happened that a youth got up and testified that now he, too, saw the Saviour, old men and women wept for joy over the new Pentecost which was sweeping the prairies. Had anyone ever seen the like? It was almost as if the days of Hauge* had come again!

The desirability of a congregation consisting exclusively of confessing Christians arose out of the turmoil. And no sooner had the idea found utterance than it began to gain followers. Several of the brethren saw it at once: there was but one thing to do—they must withdraw from St. Luke's and set up a church of their own! To be a member of a congregation in which the children of this world were in complete control was as good as surrendering themselves to the power of the devil. All warfare against Satan would be futile. How could the Kingdom of God flourish under such conditions? That was the opinion of some. Others readily agreed, and added that Soldiers of God would certainly have to proceed differently. A congregation wherein God's Word was preached only by the regenerated would shine like a city built on a hill, and draw like a powerful magnet. For was not the Word of God life? Did they not have ample proof of that right now? . . . In the old days God founded His Kingdom with twelve common workmen—didn't they remember that? What if now a few simple farmers set themselves the task of extending it? The new history they were making out here, and the pioneer's unfaltering faith in the future, told them that of course it would be possible! Suppose that the Lord God had led them here into the very heart of America to be a pillar of light unto all His people? They would discuss the idea until their faces beamed joyously.

No one could make out where Nils Nilsen stood in the matter. He never spoke when it was mentioned in his presence. But if anyone questioned him, he would answer allegorically that he who intended to build a tower would do well first to estimate the cost thereof. The brethren did not understand him and wondered what he might mean.

Then one Sunday afternoon just at the close of a blessed meeting in Nilsen's grove—so many came to the meetings

* Hans Nielsen Hauge, Norway's great revivalist (1771-1824).

now that the houses could not hold them all—a young man (he couldn't be much over twenty) by the name of Andrew Holte got up and publicly proposed the forming of a congregation of their own. There was something likable about his personality; and for being so young, he spoke with much ease and great assurance. He had been thinking about the matter all summer, he said, and now he would like to hear the opinion of the older brethren. They all saw, he felt sure, that St. Luke's had become a house divided against itself, and he need not remind them what the Lord said concerning such a structure! Would it not be better then for those who were of one mind and one heart to band themselves together, in order the better to carry on the great work of salvation? They ought not forget how good God had been to them and to their fathers! Had He not set them free from the thraldom of the State Church of Norway and given them liberty abundantly? Why not make use of the freedom which He in His great mercy had given them? Here, out on these wide prairies, was opportunity enough for the people of God to build further. What if they were singled out to be the instrument in His hand? Who could tell? He hoped they would forgive him, the youngest and most inexperienced among them, for getting up and testifying in this matter. But he would remind them that even asses could talk when they had something to say! Here Andrew Holte looked around and smiled kindly into the faces: perhaps that explained why so many these days suddenly became endowed with the gift of speech! . . . A joyous restlessness passed through the crowd as Andrew Holte sat down.

Nils Nilsen sat silent, looking out over the audience. He perceived clearly how intently they were bent on the same thing—how deeply they felt that this was the only right course to pursue. The mood of the crowd gave him a feeling of safety, as fair weather reassures the traveler who is about to cross dangerous seas. All eyes were focused expectantly on him. So far, he had led the revival, and now they wanted an answer to the question. Nils Nilsen bowed his head; everyone felt that he was having a meeting with God. A deep silence settled upon the audience.

Deeply moved by the seriousness of the situation, yet fully master of himself, he arose and began to speak:

"The ways of Zion do mourn, because none come to the solemn feasts; all her gates are desolate: her priests sigh, her virgins are afflicted, and she *is* in bitterness." Using those holy words as an introduction he began to reason with them about what must be done. . . . That he had not ventured to express himself sooner in this matter was not because he was in doubt, but rather because he had deemed it wise to let the Lord's leaven work undisturbed as long as possible. Whether this was the will of God or only a notion of man, would soon manifest itself. It might indeed be that he had made flesh his arm, he would not deny it, for he had trembled at the thought of the sacrifice which the Lord would demand of them. If they were to organize a congregation of their own, there would be only two courses open to them: either they must call a servant of the Lord according to their own heart, or else they must form a congregation after the manner of the Apostles. Were they to choose the former, they would have to shoulder heavy burdens. Yet the other course, though undoubtedly right, would scarcely be any easier, for then they would have to elect a leader from their midst, in other words, have no regular pastor. The early Christian churches had carried on their work in that way—undoubtedly. Which would mean that they must be prepared to meet all the persecution which Satan would send against them . . . the burden of the Cross was inescapable for all true followers of Christ. Now that the matter had come up he would advise that they consider it earnestly, and in prayer.

From down on one of the benches a cheerful voice interrupted him:

"We'll do our own preaching—don't worry about that!"

The crowd laughed good-naturedly at the remark. All were happy at the prospect that at last they might get a chance to work for the Kindom of God unhampered.

God's own cheerfulness lay in the warm autumn breeze which touched caressingly everything that it found upon its way. It was good to sit here in the company of the brethren; too early, moreover, to go home and begin the chores. And so one got up and asked if it were not possible to organize the congregation right now. Why delay when they were agreed? And was it not better to arm themselves for battle at once? People nodded in assent;

no one opposed. And thus it came about that Bethel
Evangelical Lutheran Church was founded on the six-
teenth Sunday after Trinity. A heated discussion sprang
up concerning the name. Nils Nilsen moved the name
Bethel Norwegian Lutheran Church, which would have
been adopted at once had not Andrew Holte protested.
He thought of the young people and of the future, he
explained; they were now thousands of miles away from
Norway, so why call it *Norwegian?* He moved to substitute
the word *evangelical* for *Norwegian,* since it was as an
evangelist that the church should work. A couple of the
older men raised objections to his proposal, one of them
talking himself into a heat, but finally yielding to Nils
Nilsen's sane counsel, that they must not permit anything so trivial to stand in the way of the cause of the
Lord. For if disagreement arose over so unimportant a
matter, what would happen when tribulations came
upon them? His remark was so sensible that all saw the
reasonableness of it at once—thus amity was again established. A committee was elected to draft a plan of
work, and to go to Reverend Isaksen, on behalf of all the
signers, and inform him that they thereby resigned from
St. Luke's. For this important commission John Baardsen,
Knut Veum, and Hans Lykken were chosen. They further
agreed to meet here at Nils Nilsen's again next Sunday at
the regular hour for morning service—it was just as well
to begin at once. Before they disbanded Nils Nilsen
admonished them to live quietly now for a while; the seed
must get a chance to take root. They must pray without
ceasing, pray for the outpouring of the spirit upon the
work which they had undertaken; for the power of prayer
was as mighty now as in the days of old. . . . That
evening people went away, satisfied and happy. Now for
the first time in the Spring Creek settlement the work in
the Lord's Vineyard would be done right!

VIII

But the following Sunday when the minister called a
congregational meeting immediately after the close of
services for the purpose of presenting a matter which

could not be deferred, storm clouds began to gather over St. Luke's.

The committee from the newly organized Bethel had met a couple of times during the week and had found themselves confronted with a number of perplexing problems. Not until yesterday afternoon had they got around to informing Reverend Isaksen of their withdrawal, and then they had intruded themselves upon him just as he was in the midst of preparing his sermon for the morrow. Up to that moment he had not had the slightest inkling of the trouble which was brewing.

And it had not taken the committee long to realize what a Jonah mission was theirs. They had handed the minister the paper on which it was written that sixteen families and about as many single persons—all names attached—thereby resigned from the congregation, and he had taken the paper and looked at it, without understanding what it was all about. When it had finally dawned on him what this meant, that fully one-fourth of his main congregation was now leaving him, he had become deeply offended and had come to say more than he really ought. All of which might have been remediable; but he had not talked long to the committee before the feeling of being insulted changed into anger—and then things had gone very badly indeed. He had talked until he became so incensed that he jumped up from his chair and demanded if they were crazy. Had the Evil One so blinded them that they no longer knew what they were about? . . . All of John Baardsen's explanations about their now having been given the light to see the Way, and about their having resolved to go the Lord's errands while it was yet day, had only added fuel to the fire. . . . So, it was in order to break up the congregation, was it, that they had been holding secret meetings around the country? he raged at them. He'd tell them what they had been about: they had used the holy Sabbath to sow the seed of dissension in a Christian congregation—they had done the Devil's own errands! They had let themselves be tricked by a fanatic, obsessed with the lust for power. And now they might go straight to Nils Nilsen and tell him so. . . . But as long as there was law in the land, neither they nor Nils Nilsen need think for one moment that they would be allowed to destroy his congregation. After this outburst John Baardsen, meekly and humbly, had endeavored to explain to the minister that they were only trying to do what was right in the sight of the Lord; wickedness was spreading fearfully—all could see that, and night would soon be upon them. . . .

At this point the minister had interrupted him. Trembling with indignation he jumped up, and pointing to the door, ordered them out. "Go! Go!" he raged: "I'll not stand for your coming in here to insult me while I'm meditating upon the Word of God which I'm to preach to you tomorrow. Get out, I say!" He stamped the floor and looked so menacing that he frightened them.

Whereupon they had left. Once outside, they had stopped and tried to collect their senses. John Baardsen, being completely bewildered, had begun to talk biblically: "An unclean spirit possesseth him!" Brother Veum, having found the explanation altogether reasonable, had added with great certitude that in his opinion this kind of spirit would hardly let itself be driven out either by prayer or by fasting—that he would wager! But Hans Lykken, the third member of the committee, had ambled, thoughtful and stooped, over to the wagon; there he had stopped to find his plug of tobacco. . . . Why on earth had he not acted on his first impulse and refused to be a member of the committee? This looked like murder and bloodshed—no doubt about it!

Later the minister had regained his calm, but the outlook was very sad to him indeed. He had not been able to concentrate his thoughts on the text which he must expound on the morrow. He foresaw nothing but shame and disgrace; soon the scandal would be talked about throughout the whole Synod; perhaps even written about in the papers! His fellow clergymen would look down on him with scorn and contempt—he who had won the praise of all the professors at the seminary because he had taken the work of preparing his sermons so seriously! The praise was deserved too, that he felt sure of; he knew that he could build up a sermon so as to bring out a beautiful harmony between the different parts. . . . That the calamity had its origin in the slovenly work of his predecessor, that uneducated old fogy, who had done naught else but gad about and drink coffee with the women, that, of course, no outsider would understand. . . . The parishioners were even apotheosizing the old fool; now they were about to begin collecting funds for erecting a big monument on his grave! As Reverend Isaksen sat with a copy of the pericope before him, he saw all the injustice in the world heaping itself upon him. Finally it had all become so terrible that he laid his head down on the table and wept. That evening his wife had found him a crushed and bewildered man when she came in to tell him that his buttermilk porridge was ready, his favorite dish every Sabbath eve because it made his mind so clear for the day following. . . . All that night he had wandered in the wilderness, forth and back on the parlor floor. . . . How was he to arm himself against the onslaught of malice now threatening him?

The congregation sat staring at the minister, wondering what might be up. Some of the members guessed at this and that; a few of them had been hearing strange rumors these last days. As they looked at the minister they noticed an air of definiteness about him. He unfolded the paper which the committee had handed him yesterday, and read it ceremoniously: thereupon he read all the signatures, pausing after each name, which made the list seem appallingly long. When he finally stopped reading, a depressing silence followed, relieved shortly by a laugh from somewhere back in the audience; the laugh was good-natured—it must have come from Aslak Tjöme. Several looked back and smiled.

But then the minister spoke again:

—He hereby laid the matter before the congregation. Before they took it up, however, he begged leave to read to them Article VI of the Constitution, concerning resignations. Here is what the Article said: "A member may not resign from the congregation so long as he remains in residence in this place, unless, however, it can be proved that the minister is teaching false doctrine, in which case the President of the Synod ought to be summoned." The question thus became, he continued, whether or not it could clearly be proved that he was preaching false doctrine. If it could not, these people had no right to withdraw. Since the matter concerned him personally, it would not be in accordance with the best church polity

for him to preside over the meeting. Would they therefore elect another chairman? . . . He looked out over the
audience, offended and mortified, all worn out after his
night's wandering in the desert.

The congregation was suddenly in a flurry of excitement; a babble of discussion arose, each talking to the
one that happened to sit nearest him. Some wanted a
committee elected; others demanded that the President
be sent for at once—the matter was too serious for ordinary folks to meddle with! One rejoiced to think that
they finally were rid of these people; a couple of men fell
to quarreling about what ought to be done to Nils Nilsen
and that gang of his. A droll voice rose above the turmoil:
"If this business is to be threshed out today, we'd better
send the women folks home after our supper!" At that
someone laughed, a gleeful chuckle; people had to turn
around to look; and there sat Tambur-Ola—he had come
to the meeting today and was now apparently enjoying
himself immensely.

After some discussion Tom Helgesen was elected chairman, and the meeting was called to order. At once all
seemed stricken with dumbness.

Tom looked at the crowd for a while. At last he said,
smiling, "Seeing that none of you have anything to say,
we might as well adjourn and go home." At that remark,
signs of life began to manifest themselves. One got up,
wondering if they hadn't better elect a committee to
go and talk to Nils Nilsen. Another gave as his opinion
that the trustees ought to consider the case first, and
then report to the congregation. No, not the trustees but
the deacons, corrected a third. Then another got up and
said with great feeling, that if they were to lose so many
members now, prospects didn't look very bright for the
church which they had talked about building; but he
had no motion to make. The moment he sat down a new
speaker arose and held forth at length about the necessity
of getting the church built; for if Nils Nilsen had had a
church in which to hold his meetings, he would hardly
have done this thing; St. Luke's was certainly in need of
evangelical preaching—then all might have gone to hear
him. Instantly a new speaker was on his feet, moving a
committee to see what could be done about getting a
church. The motion caused Tom Helgesen to scratch his

head; he had his doubts as to the last two speakers being in order, because they had not, strictly speaking, adhered to the question under consideration. Tom's remark touched the honor of the last speaker too closely, and so this one began hotly to defend himself, making it clear as the sun that his motion concerned the question; if they had had a church, both he and Nils and the others would have been so busy getting it paid for that they wouldn't have had time to make trouble. A man, slow and ponderous of speech, wondered what their former pastor would have done in this case . . . well, what did they think? *He* would have gone straight to Nils Nilsen and talked to him privately—that's all! Personally, he was of the opinion that they ought to ask Reverend Isaksen to do just that. At last Gjermund Dahl managed to get the floor and made the motion that they hold a special meeting Friday night at 7:30 for the purpose of considering the matter. In case they did not finish then, they could continue next Sunday, after the services. The motion was seconded at once and passed without debate.

Throughout the discussion Tönseten had sat up in front, listening to all the speeches, resting his chin on his stick. Now he jumped up, demanding that he be given the floor.

"My good people, what's all this nonsense about anyway? I am certainly surprised at you! Do you really propose to hold meetings about such nonsense?" With that introduction Tönseten went on to make a real speech, which fortunately neither Nils Nilsen nor any of his followers got the benefit of. Looking like the very god of thunder, he wanted to know if they had forgotten that they had fought a Civil War in America. What had they fought about? Well—he'd tell 'em. Some rebels down South had sulked because they couldn't have their own way, and so they had hit upon the idea of going out of the church to start up by themselves. Had they been permitted to do it? *No, siree!* They'd got a lusty licking, that's what they had. They had to stay where they were and be good! And then and there it had been settled once and for all, that a minority could not get up and walk out of the room any old time they felt like it, just because they didn't like the paint on the walls! If Nils and his gang insisted on sulking, there was, God be praised, law and right in the country! Before Tönseten sat down again he looked about with a mien which plainly asked: Now isn't this so? . . . It was obvious that some agreed with him, for they applauded as he sat down.

Tom Helgesen threw a helpless look out over the crowd: "I think we stand adjourned, though that's a good idea you brought out there, Syvert—it won't hurt us to take it to heart!"

IX

The controversy in St. Luke's raged like a devastating, destructive storm. It tore into everything in the settlement, ripped it up, passed on, turned about and came back, only to augment in fury with each turn. This matter of what was right according to the will of God was so serious that people quarreled about it until they became hoarse of voice and dark of mien, and the hand unconsciously sought a weapon.

The bitterly disputed issue was: Should the "rebels," as Tönseten had dubbed Nils Nilsen and his followers, be allowed to leave the congregation? To sanction such an act required a spirit of brotherhood and good will beyond human power; for if a new congregation were to be organized in the same place, among the same people— both old and new confessing the same faith—the one must necessarily get in the way of the other. Sensible people foresaw what would happen: strife and dissensions as long as time should last. The church edifice which they had hoped soon to see rearing itself, now lay hopelessly in ruins.

Some action must be taken at once. They tried first what seemed the easiest: they summoned the President of the Synod. He came out on the one mission of settling the controversy, holding meetings with the people throughout three whole days; he questioned and advised, talked and persuaded, rebuked severely and then again tried gentle words. But all to no purpose. Matters got worse instead of better. The longer people argued, the hotter waxed their temper. That which at the outset some of them had gone into just for the sport of it—an insane notion only to be laughed at—soon became a question of conscience, and then a matter of salvation. Everyone was, in some way, drawn into the turmoil; individuals who formerly had cared about neither church nor religion, now sought membership. Even Tambur-Ola joined the congregation. Those best acquainted with him knew that he did it just to have the satisfaction of voting against Nils Nilsen. . . . Some of the younger wags were having great sport these days!

The majority, a very considerable one, would not listen to any proposal letting the dissenters secede; they had taken their stand and remained adamant. All attempts, even the most level-headed, at winning members of this group over to the other side were as futile as arguing against the north wind. No use to try! Never would the majority be a party to the act of tearing down what they had had such pleasure in building up, just to pacify a few opinionated fools. Otherwise the majority showed a conciliatory spirit: Let Nils Nilsen hold as many prayer meetings as he liked and in other ways do just as he pleased, nothing in the world to prevent him; only he could not secede from St. Luke's and start a new congregation. He had signed the Constitution and would have to abide by it, he as well as the rest—that's all there was to *that!* In all democratic organizations the majority ruled; it had to be so, or there would be anarchy. . . . All the awful ungodliness which the others talked so much about, only infuriated the majority the more and made them see red; the holiness that had to hide itself in order to thrive smelled of skunk. Don't ever mention such Christianity to us!

The Bethel people were not so loud-spoken, neither did they talk so fast; but they were just as immovable: They *had* already left St. Luke's! . . . It would indeed be stranger than strange if any power on earth could compel them to remain in a congregation which their conscience told them plainly it was sinful to have dealings with. They'd just show them whether they could leave or not! "Shun the council of the wicked," so the Scriptures said. "Beware of the leaven of the Pharisees." "Obey God before man." The last days would be full of tribulations for the little flock—yes, they realized that. . . . But did not the Saviour break with the Pharisees? Did He ask permission to leave the congregation? Did not He incite people

against the church to which He belonged? Well, well,
the world is wise in many ways! . . . Just take Luther,
for example. Didn't he break with his own church and
set up a new? Did he ask permission of anybody? Dear
brethren, let's not be terrified by the world! And what
about Hans Nielsen Hauge? Did he ask the State Church
of Norway for permission to go the way the Lord pointed
out to him? . . . All of a sudden, a new line of arguments seemed to spring out of their very being—their
racial consciousness was astir: Full freedom in all matters
of faith, that's the inalienable right of a free people! Oh,
ho—so that was the idea: St. Luke's intended to set up a
state church and coerce people by force? Look out now!
Don't go too far! Did not the constitution of the land
grant them full liberty? Did they not pay taxes to the
government in order to have protection? Ought they con-
sent to being shackled like slaves, out here in the kingdom which they themselves had wrested from the wilderness? Look out, good folk, lest you go too far! . . .
Never before had their own meetings seen so much
zeal. The fire which before had only given light and cast
a pleasant warmth, now suddenly leaped into flames that
roared devastatingly. Curiosity seekers came to attend the
meetings; it did actually happen that now one and then
another were caught by the fire and drawn in. . . . Again
and again the name of Oline Tuftan was mentioned,
every speaker using it as a battle cry. Adultery, murder,
suicide . . . there they had the fruit of the tree! Did
people repent? No. They hardened themselves. Let us
flee this monstrous iniquity and not look back! . . . "How
blessed the little flock!" They found comfort both in the
fewness of their number and in the fact that they were
made to bear new tribulations. For was it not better to
suffer persecution here, for a little while, than to be cast
into hell? . . . Fear not, thou little band! . . . The
blood of the Lamb of God was shed for you. Now what
will you do for Him? . . .
The storm raged and tore asunder. Neighbors who formerly had lived peacefully together, and had exchanged
work whenever convenient, finding much pleasure therein,
would not now look at one another. The threshing seemed
so odd that fall: one's nearest neighbor might be working
just across the road, and never so much as look up. The

ill will abroad changed into hatred; even families were torn asunder. It was soon noised abroad that old Lars Holte had given his son the choice either of saying good-bye to Nils Nilsen and his crowd or of leaving home; Andrew chose the latter. He went to Mrs. Tuftan and rented her farm, and was never again seen at services in St. Luke's. But the mother took sides with the son . . . that, too, people knew, even though the Holtes themselves never mentioned the matter.

Over at Joe Lund's matters were, in a way, even worse; there husband and wife quarreled until she finally joined with the Bethel people; and she, being the stronger of the two, took the children with her. Whenever Joe, with his best horse hitched to the new buggy, drove to services in St. Luke's, she would put the children into the lumber wagon and set out for Bethel. "I s'pose it's free people in a free country? I'll not have Joe bossing me in this matter—I don't care who knows it!" People listened to both of them and had much fun about Joe and his wife.

During that fall and throughout the whole winter the controversy continued unabated; meetings were held; committees were busily at work; neighboring pastors came in to give wise counsel, and the situation remained unchanged. "We *have* gone out, can't you understand?" the Bethel people would say. . . . "What nonsense— that's the one thing in the world you cannot do!" St. Luke's would answer. And there the matter stood. All through the settlement that winter people sat poring over the Bible to find arguments; one must arm oneself. It might happen that a farmer woman would fling right into her neighbor's face, "It is written," and thereupon quote a passage from Scripture for which her sister had not yet found an answer.

With the coming on of spring and fine days, just as the outdoor work was beginning, the events came thick and fast. First Reverend Isaksen resigned, without even laying the matter before the congregation. Neither side had paid much attention to him, to tell the truth. He had gone about almost like a child whom the grown-ups take with them to work and then turn loose to putter by himself, because they are too busy to look after him. Through days and sleepless nights he had sorrowed over being thus set aside. The whole matter was personal, one which concerned him alone, and yet he wasn't even being consulted—and he a Lord's anointed and duly elected by the congregation! . . . His resignation had the effect of a sudden puff of wind in a sultry calm. Now see what you have done, said the people of St. Luke's; there you have driven the minister away! To which the other side merely shrugged its shoulders derisively: Then we must have done you a good turn—you certainly didn't care much for him!

Shortly after the resignation, the incredible happened: the Dissenters began building a church! The thing was so preposterous, that at first people refused to believe it; how could it be possible? Dumbfounded by the unheard-of brazenness, they began to inquire. . . . The very devil himself must have been turned loose among Nils Nilsen and his followers!

But it was true nevertheless. On a site exactly three-quarters of a mile from where St. Luke's intended to build its church, the others now began to erect theirs. Rumors about all sorts of unbelievable things were being circulated; Nils Nilsen was said to have given a thousand dollars toward the project; several were said to have subscribed five hundred each; some two. It was even reported that the Bethel people intended to call a minister from another synod!

There was only one course open. A congregational meeting was called in St. Luke's and the trustees were given full power to act, which they did. They went to town at once, engaged a lawyer and had an injunction served on Nils Nilsen. A lawsuit followed, into which practically the whole settlement was drawn.

People went about silent and depressed, as if speech were dangerous. This thing was terrible. . . . Now and then strange gleams would leap into the eyes; a back would straighten itself; a hand would reach out after a pitchfork. . . . Wasn't it possible to put a stop to this madness? If people persisted in their lunacy, they'd have to take the consequences! . . .

X

Every Sunday during summer Beret had attended the meetings of the Prayer Circle. At first she had taken her whole family with her. Then one Sunday, just as they were about to leave, Ole had announced that he expected company later in the afternoon, and so couldn't go. Beret only looked at him and said nothing, but it was plain to all that she didn't like it. During the whole of the week following she went about very silent, as was her habit whenever anything displeased her.

On the Sunday after, Ole pretended that he was sick; as soon as dinner was over he went to his room and lay down and the others had to leave without him. Store-Hans drove. Beret sat in the front seat with him. After they were well on their way, she turned to him:

"I guess you don't care very much about going either, do you?"

The boy did not answer right away. "To tell you the truth," he confessed openly, "I know of things I like better. . . . But there is nothing else to do Sunday afternoons," he added.

Nothing more was said about the matter that day, nor during the week either. But the next Sunday, just as they were about to leave (Ole had taken one of the horses and had ridden away without saying a word) Beret turned to Store-Hans:

"You'd better stay home today; someone might come; and it isn't necessary for all of us to leave the farm."

The boy looked at his mother astonished. The very friendliness in her voice made him want to go. As he was about to step up into the wagon her voice sounded still friendlier·

"You better do as I say; you need to rest up for tomorrow; never mind the chores until we come home."

Store-Hans yielded to what seemed to be her wish. And thus it came about that thereafter only she and the two youngest children attended the meetings. The new arrangement suited Peder very well, for it meant that now he would be doing the driving. So many people came to the meetings; the yard would be full of vehicles and horses; his own would be restless, but he'd show people how easily he could manage 'em.

On the Sunday Bethel was organized Beret had been in no hurry to leave after the meeting was over. She waited until the yard was almost empty of people; then she went over to Nils Nilsen, and after greeting him, said:

"What a blessed summer this has been. You shouldn't have let that Holte boy spoil things for us. . . . *You* know that the tares and the wheat must grow together until harvest time. . . . But we had it too pleasant, I suppose."

Nils Nilsen looked at her in great kindness and handed her the paper to which the others had signed their names:

"We want you with us, Beret Holm; you, I have been counting on all the time."

"You better not," she answered slowly. "That kind of Christianity which must go off by itself in order to thrive may have a hard time of it when it gets to heaven. . . . I know I'm only an old woman, and don't understand much, but I really can't see any harm in calling the congregation *Norwegian*. It's among the Norwegians that you intend to work, isn't it?"

"Don't let that worry you, Mrs. Holm." Instantly, a great zeal was upon him: "Do you know, I think this is the happiest moment of my life. By the grace of God, we shall make this thing go!"

Beret looked down; a couple of straws had fastened themselves to her skirt; she picked them off, and then pulled her skirt around to see if there were more. Straightening herself, she looked right into his eyes:

"With His help, yes—that's one thing! But now you are putting your trust in that son of Lars Holte's."

"*In the beauties of holiness from the womb of the morning: thou hast the dew of thy youth*"—he quoted with a quiet warmth in his voice. "The spirit of youth is accomplishing wonders in America! . . . But you we must have with us; I have prayed God to give us you and all of yours. God's children must stand together in this hour!" he pleaded with her.

A short silence followed during which both looked down; from the other side of the yard a man called to Nils Nilsen; neither of the two heard him. Then Beret answered slowly:

"You'll have to do without me, I guess. . . . I can't take part in tearing down what our old pastor with so much care built up!" Gazing into the distance, she added soberly: "I don't see how you can, either. . . . Now I want to bid you good-bye and tell you that I'm thankful for the summer." She was about to offer him her hand, but the man who had called to Nils stood there beside him and asked if he might speak with him privately, and so Nils turned away from her. But just as he left he said: "Some other time I want to see you about this, Beret Holm!"

Anna Marie now came to look for her mother. Peder had got the horses out long ago and was sitting in the wagon, impatient and excited. . . . Here everybody was leaving without his getting a chance to show them how well he could handle his horses! What in the world was Mother up to anyway? Did it take her all this time to say that she would join, and to write her name? . . . Not that he was angry. Fun to sit here. All who passed his wagon looked at him and nodded pleasantly. Two men came up and inquired whose boy he was. They told him how nice it was of him to come here with his mother— God liked such boys! Peder listened to them with only half an ear; he was too busy looking for his mother and thinking about what a great speech Andrew Holte had made. There was the man for you! . . . Peder had listened intently while Andrew spoke. A joyous feeling had surged through him, and so he had nodded yes and amen to everything Andrew said; he had felt like clapping his hands.

He would have liked to talk to his mother about Andrew and that speech of his, but all the way home she sat in deep silence, as if her thoughts were busy with serious things; her face looked leaden in the glow of the evening sun; Peder understood that she was displeased about something. He s'posed that she was feeling bad because the brothers hadn't come to the meeting today, and such a fine meeting, too. He wanted to talk to her about it, but before he could find the right thing to say, she began humming a melody to herself, soft and low. Listening, he recognized Tambur-Ola's song. He would never have believed that she knew it! He forgot both his horses and his driving. Never before had he heard so many mysterious things in that melody. . . . Thereafter, he often heard her humming it as she went about her work.

Among the converted was a certain man, Simon Simonsen by name, who read his Bible diligently, lived much by himself, and got at times rather queer notions; he had lately had an inspiration, the carrying out of which was attracting considerable attention.

St. Luke's Congregation had plotted a cemetery for itself on the site where its church was to stand, and had assigned each family its lot. And now Simon had gone a step or two further in his preparation: he had hired a carpenter to make him two coffins, the one for his wife and the other for himself. Both of these now stood in the granary, waiting. The preparation, however, didn't seem quite sufficient; and so this last week he had had a huge monument put up on his lot, bearing the names and the dates of birth of both himself and his wife. Underneath each name was chiseled: *Died* A. D. And below the dates: *Rest in Peace!* On the top of the monument stood two angels with wings outstretched and with a light garment tied about the loins. Now Mr. and Mrs. Simonsen could safely lie down and die any day; the monument dealer would be responsible for putting in the dates—that was a part of the contract.

It didn't take long for people to find out what Simon was doing over in the cemetery. Curiosity had to be satisfied, and so, when anyone happened to pass that way, he'd go in and have a look at the wonder. The idea was positively uncanny! The worst cut-ups among the young people made great sport of the poor angels who, thinly clad as they were, had to stand out in the cemetery waiting for Simon and his wife.

That evening Ole did not come home until after the others had sat down to supper. Then he was talkative and noisy. He and several others had been over to have a look at the monument. No sooner had he taken his seat at the table than he began to describe it, in a manner as if he yet couldn't believe it himself; he gave a detailed, picturesque account and laughed boisterously over how silly people could become. His mood had contagion in it; Store-Hans caught it and doubled up laughing. But Anna Marie refused to believe the story, and so Ole had to tell it all over again, this time still more picturesquely; then she too fell into a fit of laughter. Peder wanted to know if it was Simon's intention to have himself buried right away—when he wasn't *dead?* And this made the thing so irresistibly funny that even Beret had to join in the laugh.

Peder, realizing that he had talked stupidly again, straightway tried to redeem himself. As soon as it was quiet enough for him to be heard he launched into a description of the afternoon's meeting. He talked grown-up, and tried to make his story as interesting as that of his brother, depicting the events in the same fantastic glow as he himself had experienced them. . . . Now there'd be something doing around here, he assured them. They just ought to have been along this afternoon and heard how Andrew Holte had got Nils Nilsen to start a new congregation!

"What d'you say?" cried Ole.

"Bet your life!" exclaimed Peder. 'Twould be great fun to be along there! Andrew himself was to be the minister, Peder had heard several men say so; but Andrew, he would have nothing to do with Norwegian! Two old codgers had got up on their ears about the Norwegian business, but Andrew, he had downed them just like *that!* There was the boy who could preach!

Ole stared at him in amazement.

"Some more of your fibbing!"

"Fibbing?" Peder repeated enthusiastically. Hadn't they just come from there? Mother had signed them all up and everything. Next Sunday they'd begin in real earnest.

Store-Hans smiled knowingly. . . . So *that* was the reason Mother didn't want him along!

The mother spoke sternly to Peder:

"What is all this nonsense you are telling, Peder? Are you out of your head?"

Ole rose abruptly from the table and shoved his chair back into place; his face had a hard and angry look:

"This is the craziest thing I ever heard!" He stopped in his stride across the floor and turning toward his mother, snarled, "You'll not catch me going with that crowd, that I can tell you now!" He grabbed his hat and rushed out of the room.

. . . "I suppose it's true," remarked Beret after a while, "that the worst must come from one's own. . . . You'd better say grace now, Permand."

Nothing more was said about the new congregation. That night Ole didn't come home until after midnight.

XI

Low, woolly-gray sky. Dismal November day. A northwest wind, chill-laden, wintry, sang out across a lifeless landscape; hurried on. No use to linger in these open reaches. Were the low sky to come still nearer earth, it would surely crush the prairie flatter than it already was. Human habitations lay far apart upon the open stretches. Miles apart in places. One could not borrow warmth from the other here. Through the cold grayness they seemed to huddle up, to crouch low over something, as if jealously guarding it. Though it was not yet two o'clock, it looked as though day were nearly spent. If anyone stood outdoors and heard a dog baying in the distance, he could not tell whether the sound came from above the earth or from some cavern underneath. Now and then the wind filched sticky flakes from out of the interminable gloom and flung them before itself. They came with such speed that they left a sting in their wake. . . . No doubt the night would bring snow.

The first stormy congregational meeting of St. Luke's was just over. By an overwhelming majority the members had denied Nils Nilsen and his followers the right to withdraw. Whoever heard of such a silly notion? If they went too far with their nonsense—well, there was law and justice in the land. . . . They had better look out and not say any more.

On both sides statements had been made which would not soon be forgotten. Defiant words, full of threat. Indignation had boiled over. During the debate some had experienced a peculiar joy, an unknown power welling up out of their being and filling every word with a strange exultation. The more forceful and pointed the expression, the keener it would cut—that's the way to treat such stubbornness. . . . Let no one dare to call this a just demand; Don't try it! Some, on the other hand, had been made speechless by the malignity of the debate. If the Lord should come upon them this night, how then would St. Luke's fare? The Book of Revelation spoke of The Great Whore. Worse things than they had heard here today could scarcely be said. . . . It was terrible!

And now Beret Holm and her whole family were on their way home from the meeting. On and on into the raw grayness the wagon bore them. The mood of the occupants was even grayer than that of the oncoming winter. The girl, hidden within a shawl, had tried to hum a tune to herself; her humming had irritated Peder; he had asked her to shut up; they had fallen to quarreling. Store-Hans had threatened to throw them both out of the wagon if they didn't stop immediately. Ole drove; the mother shared the front seat with him; neither of them was in a mood to interfere with what was going on behind them.

Ole was, as yet, the only one in the family who had the right to vote; and today he had cast his vote with the majority, in spite of the fact that he knew that in so doing he was acting directly contrary to his mother's wishes. The others knew it, too. The reckoning would be difficult, but they would have to face it.

Yet that wasn't the worst of it:

Today the vote had been taken by roll call; thus each had heard where the others stood. The voting was no sooner over than the debate had broken loose afresh, and now with a more sinister growling from the minority. Then the incredible had happened: Beret Holm had risen and asked for permission to say a word or two. The audience had stared at her. Never before had a woman talked at a congregational meeting. . . . A *woman* mixing up in this business—and *publicly!* Some were so embarrassed that they didn't know where to look.

Without waiting for the chairman to recover from his astonishment, she had begun to tell them how ill-advised, in her opinion, their action was. Did they really think they were doing the Lord's will now? She had spoken slowly, falteringly at first; the words which she had found had been full of fear; there had been tears in her voice. But as she went on, the fear had seemed to leave her. She saw only the great sin that was being committed. Finally, she had stood there admonishing them like a devoted mother who, sorrowfully, tries to correct her erring child. Some of the women looked at her and wept—had she now become queer again? . . . Here sat some of their own neighbors, she had said, asking for permission to part company with them in order the better to please

God. Could that be so very wrong? Why not give them leave to try it? Not all people were alike. In some the life of the Spirit needed a tending that might seem odd to others. If Nils Nilsen's plan should work out the way he thought, it would prove a blessing to all of them. If, on the contrary, he was being led astray by his own vanity, then the congregation would be all the better off for having let him go. Only with living stones could the Lord build—a mystery that no mind could fathom! Even though He summoned all His omnipotence He could build with none other. . . . Whatever they did they must not stand in the way of anyone who wanted to come closer to God! "Whoso shall offend one of these little ones which believe in me, it were better for him that a millstone were hanged about his neck and that he were drowned in the depth of the sea," these were the words of Jesus in Matthew. "Woe unto the world because of offenses! For it must needs be that the offenses come; but woe to that man by whom the offense cometh!" that, too, the Gospel said. In the Day of Judgment it would not matter how large St. Luke's had been, but rather how many would be permitted to stand at the Lord's right hand. God grant that they all inherit everlasting life!

The deathly silence prevailing as Beret sat down had been shattered by a man shouting indignantly: "Are the women too turning preachers these days?" Thereupon the storm had begun to rage as violently as ever. . . . Peder could have walked over and struck the man. While the mother was speaking Ole's face had had an ugly look.

At last the wagon rumbled into the yard at home. Not a word had been said about the meeting. Beret stepped down, and turning to the boys as though nothing out of the ordinary had happened, told them to hurry up and do the chores; supper would soon be ready—Permand must not forget the pigs!

Peder wanted to help his brother unhitch the horses before he went. They'd have something to say now, he felt pretty sure. But then he got in Ole's way, and was pushed aside. "Get out of here and mind your own business!"

And so Peder sauntered off down to the corn crib. There was something invigorating about the northwest wind today; soon the snow would be here—then he could take his skis to school. A merry tune which one of the threshers this fall had sung incessantly, now came back to him:

A kiss I got and two I gave,
Ha, ha, tra la—
And two I gave.
Were greater store
I'd take some more
Ha, ha, tra la—
I'd take some more!

The song had a jolly lilt to it. He could hear it tra-la-ing gaily and began to whistle it.

Having entered the crib, he stood there awhile, scoop in hand, kicking into the corn . . . she certainly had spoken well, that he must say. And true every bit of it, too . . . though only a woman, she had held them spellbound. How had she dared it? Right into their very faces she had flung the words. Even the minister himself had sat there listening. . . . Peder took a scoopful and threw it into the pen. 'Twasn't a bit heavy today! He went back into the crib, and having filled the scoop heaping full, he carried it out and flung it into the pen . . . when he was grown up he would preach so . . . so . . . well, so that every mother's son of them would have to go the way he pointed!

The northwest wind was getting headier. It drove the sleet before it so fiercely that it stung the face. Peder swung past the barn to hear what his brothers were talking about. Store-Hans stood leaning up against the door on the inside. Peder did not notice him at first; all his attention focused itself upon Ole, who, having put the bridle on one of the horses and having led it out into the passage, was speaking. It sounded as if there had been a quarrel.

". . . She's been crazy before, you know that as well as I; such things often come back again. You'd better get her off to the asylum!" Ole paused, and then continued: "But she needn't have put us to shame before the whole settlement—that wasn't craziness only!" Ole buckled the bridle strap; his eyes had a hard look in them.

Peder had stopped in the doorway.

"Where are you going?" he asked, frightened.

"Get out of the way there!"

Peder did not move immediately, and so Ole came around in front of the horse:

"Didn't you hear what I said?"

Store-Hans stepped over to his brother and spoke to him earnestly, in low tones:

"Listen to me now, this thing will straighten itself out, in some way."

"Sounded that way!"

"Behave yourself!" the other pleaded, as if in great fear. "She's our mother, you know!"

"Did she remember today that we were her children?" Ole's face was pale; the hand which held the reins shook; he lifted it as if to strike his brother. "If she says anything, you can just tell her that from me!" Thereupon he led the horse out, swung himself up and rode down the yard.

Store-Hans looked toward the house, and went over to the cow barn to clean the calf stall, a job left from the morning. Peder tagged after him, his throat so dry that he could scarcely get the words out:

"Where's Ole going?"

The brother didn't seem to be aware of his presence, but went into the stall, took the pitchfork, and began to clean out.

"Fetch me some straw, so that we can get done," he said to Peder.

Peder had to look at his brother, for his voice sounded far away, and that made it all the more difficult to go on:

"Where did he go?"

"Down to Tönseten . . . fetch that straw."

"What was he mad about?"

"Ask him yourself!"

Peder hurried after a couple of armfuls of bedding, considered that sufficient, and forced himself to ask:

"Isn't he coming back?"

"Shut up with your nonsense!" The brother struck at a calf's muzzle which poked into him, wanting to suck.

" 'Tisn't nonsense—I could tell on him!"

The brother straightened up, glared menacingly at Peder and said in a harsh voice:

"Don't you dare breathe a word about it to Mother, do you hear me?" Immediately his voice became gentler, and petting the calf he had struck he looked up: "Fetch me another armful, then I guess we'll call it good."

Peder returned with the straw, threw it in, and stood waiting:

"What was he so mad about?"

"It's none of our business. And now you listen to me: Don't you dare mention this to Mother!" His brother's warning made Peder's heart still heavier—did Store-Hans really consider him as stupid as all that?

Shortly afterward both went into the house, Peder a little behind his brother. He had wanted to remain outside awhile, had, in fact, decided to do so, but was drawn in by a demoniacal force. He felt as if his mother was about to be butchered, and that his own brother must do the job.

In the kitchen the fire burned cheerily; his mother was standing by the stove, stirring a kettle from which rose a delicious odor; she had a white apron on, with crocheted lace at the bottom—all reminding him of Sabbath and the good things which she always prepared on such days. Beret looked calm, almost happy. In order to master the feeling which was threatening to choke him, Peder went to the wood box to see if it would hold another armful. Store-Hans was washing himself. Then the mother spoke:

"What has become of Ole?" She lifted the kettle from the fire and set it to one side.

Store-Hans waited, an interminably long time it seemed to Peder, before answering. All that Ole had said kept buzzing through his ear.

"He went down to Syvert's."

"What's that?" Beret stood staring at him. "What was he going there for now?"

"To find out if he might rent Syvert's farm," Store-Hans informed her very quietly, his voice so strange that Peder had to look at him. His face was ashen, his features were contorted.

With head bent forward to hear better, the mother came toward him, her face relaxed, imploring, like one about to look on tragedy. But then it set again, in impenetrable dismay.

"That's what he said!" the brother reiterated hoarsely.

The mother walked over to the window facing the yard. Stood there and looked out. She seemed to have forgotten everything about her.

The room became deathly silent. Anna Marie had retreated to the chimney corner, and picking up a stick now sat digging into the cracks, poking it in and pulling it out. Store-Hans leaned against the wall. Peder had just finished washing and had hung the towel away; he took it down once more and began rubbing his face assiduously.

Beret turned away from the window and looked about her, like one just awakening from a heavy sleep in which she has suffered bad dreams.

"I believe we are forgetting our dinner," she said dazed, and went to the stove and began to dish it up. "Come now and sit down."

When she had set the food on the table, she asked them to begin and not to wait for her, went into the bedroom and closed the door. But after a little she was standing in the doorway:

"Now you must be sure to eat enough . . . I don't feel just right today . . . I think I'll lie down awhile."

Thereupon she went back into her room. No one dared to look that way. Peder ate until the tears streamed down into his food.

A little later Beret came out again and took the chair nearest Store-Hans:

"Do you know—I just happened to think that Syvert and Kjersti haven't been to our place for a decent meal all fall. And now we have plenty of everything on hand." She stopped, and looking at him pleadingly like a dog that begs its master, she added: "I think you'd better go and ask them to come over. Tell them to do the chores before they come, then they'll not have to hurry home so soon. . . . What do you think about it?"

Store-Hans did not answer. Nor did he look up. Suddenly he rose, pushed his chair back, went to the wall where his coat hung; there he stood still a moment before taking it down.

"I'll go right away," he said, and tore open the door.

Out on the steps he stopped and put on his coat. . . . Was there ever the like of Mother! . . . The wind cut his face so savagely that he had to wipe his eyes. . . . If only he could find his brother! . . . His fits of temper never lasted long—that was one good thing about Ole! The mother had gone into the bedroom again. Peder wasn't equal to being alone in the room with his sister just now. She sniffled so easily, poor thing! He hurried to get his coat on, went out into the yard, and stood there looking down the road. Strains of a melody hummed disturbingly in his head. He caught them and began singing, not realizing that it was the Killdeer-song of Tambur-Ola. An irritating restlessness compelled him to action; he ran down to the barn and into the calf stall. There he coaxed up to him the poor beast which Store-Hans had treated so badly a while ago. The calf had a white arrow in its forehead and a white tuft at the end of its tail; its nose felt warm and soft and silken. A great need to love some living thing was upon Peder. Before he knew it, he was petting the calf. But being unable to love it enough without at the same time speaking affectionate words, he had to stop his singing.

Again Peder was walking in the yard, driven on by an unexplainable restlessness. Today it felt so strange to be alive; he wanted to laugh; then again he felt the need of crying. How he would have liked to do something big and wonderfully grown up! He thought and pondered on it until he felt utterly exhausted by his own helplessness. He went into the kitchen and looked around; there, on the shelf, lay the Bible. Taking it down and placing it on the table, he sat down to read. He'd just begin at the very beginning and never give up before he had reached the end! . . . He'd show Mother that there was at least one in this house who was good!

II. The Mill of the Gods

I

The drowsy November sun was nearing the prairie. Now lingering for a moment, it waited for the creatures in that curious mound down on the plain to come crawling out of their hiding place, so that it could light the last one on its way before it went to bed—there wasn't much else to look after at this season of the year. Its face became big and puffy and red from waiting so long.

But inside the schoolhouse there were as yet no signs of closing for the day. A languid glow was filling the room, tingeing cheeks aslant over books and lessons, and firing the imagination of young minds eager for adventure until eyes kindled and heads stood erect; or the glow might become so stupefying that some big clodhopper of a boy who had no dreams at all yawned wearily from sheer deadness. . . . Good Lord, would this day never end!

Up in the front seat to the left the heads of two boys were bending close together: the one brown and curly; the other blond, its heavy hair falling back in even waves. Both heads looked as hard as gnarled chopping blocks. Every now and then the brown would butt into the other, only to withdraw as quickly; at each butt the blond would try to get out of the way, but forgetting itself, immediately would spring back to its former position.

The boys were of the same size, both about twelve years old. So seriously, however, had they taken the business of growing up that they actually looked a couple of years older; the blond one was slightly shorter, but by way of compensation, somewhat more solidly knit together.

At present they were busy drawing pictures. The brown

one had begun, and so the blond had to try also. The latter was just now completing a large encampment: in the background tents, before which blazed great fires; on the hillsides artillery; in the foreground regiments in battle formation (in the picture these became indistinct and resembled tall grass waving in the wind), and officers on horse, whom the artist had taken much pains to make stately looking. The picture was one of many details. When it was finished the boy studied it critically, and began to touch it up here and there. Underneath he printed in bold letters: WASHINGTON AT VALLEY FORGE.

The other boy first sketched the façade of a colonial mansion; in front of it he drew a garden, in the middle of which he planted a large tree loaded with a small, round fruit; close to the tree he drew a bareheaded boy who, hatchet in hand, was chopping away at the trunk. Judging by the expression on his face, the boy in the picture must be in a raging temper, for every detail seemed to conspire in making him look as angry as possible—his hair straight on end, his features awry. But the real ingeniousness of the figure lay principally in the posture of the boy. As he stood there swinging his hatchet, he was the very embodiment of fury, chips flying about him in all directions. Every time the artist put in a new chip, he lunged a little to the side—hence the butting. At last he, too, had finished, and sat a long time scrutinizing his work, so completely absorbed in it that he was oblivious of everything about him. Suddenly his face lighted with inspiration, and he hastened to write above the last chip: *"Damn it!"* making the letters as bold as possible. Once more he studied his creation, and finding nothing more to be done to it, printed underneath: WASHINGTON AND HIS HATCHET. After a final look he thrust it over in front of his companion, his face questioning, his eyes sparkling with life and deviltry.

The blond boy took the whole picture in at a glance, let slip an abrupt *huh*, which he as quickly coughed away again in order not to attract the attention of the teacher sitting up at the desk. Directly he began to examine it in detail. His eyes rounded in wonder; at sight of the expression above the chip, a shudder of admiration over such unheard-of recklessness ran through him. He glanced at his chum: How did you dare? Without further ado he grabbed his pen, wrote his name: *Peder Victorious Holm,* and carefully placed the drawing in a book he was taking home for tonight. His pal's face smiled gleefully at this undisguised compliment; picking up the pen he wrote his own name under Peder's picture: *Charley Doheny,* and stuck it in his pocket.

Only the quiet breathing of children, in a half stupor, with now and then the escape of a long drawn-out sigh, and an occasional rustling of paper disturbed the drowsy stillness of the room; here and there a foot shuffled, or a book was thrust aside, but these sounds were too much a part of the place to attract notice. The late afternoon, immense and reddening, creeping in through the window on the west, mingled imperceptibly with the torpor.

Back of the desk up on the little platform in front sat Miss Clarabelle Mahon, the teacher, industriously preparing her notes for tomorrow's history lesson. The slight flush from the history period, recently over, still lingered on her cheeks, rendering inconspicuous the soft wrinkles under her eyes. The thoughts which she was now arranging into the form of a lecture, heightened the flush and gave to her delicate face, dangerously old-maidish at times, a look almost young and pretty.

The flush had come naturally enough. Her country's history was the subject she cherished above all others; nowhere had she felt the call of apostleship quite so urgently as out here in Spring Creek, where she had in her charge all these children of immigrants from foreign lands. The very thought of it excited her. It remained to be seen whether she had sufficient strength to instil in them the very spirit of America—that mighty force which had brought their parents out of bondage in the Old World, had flung wide the doors to this great land, and thereupon had invited the poor and the downtrodden to come and be happy in the beauty and promise of the New World. And hither they had come, all the unfortunate and the oppressed of the earth. Here they bought, without pay, wine and milk; here they had built, happily confident of the perfect existence to come! All previous history was finished, worn out like an old garment and discarded because no longer usable.

The beat of her kind schoolma'am heart quickened as she pored over her notes; the flush in her cheeks deepened.

All that which was heterogeneous and foreign must here be molded together so as to make one heart and one mind, seeing only the highest and wanting only the best. These immigrant children were the clay, she the potter, her country's history the pattern after which she must fashion them. Miss Mahon, Miss Clarabelle Mahon, to be exact, derived inspiration from that history in very much the same manner as the pious-minded draws sustenance from the sacred stories of the Bible. Whenever the textbook, in her judgment, treated any episode insufficiently, she would at once draw upon the inexhaustible storehouse of her own romantic imagination. This particular afternoon as she had listened to the eighth-graders reciting about Washington at Valley Forge, she had become deeply moved by this great figure and his mighty achievements; she had forgotten the lesson and had asked the class to listen while she related incidents from his youth and early manhood. His purity of mind and loftiness of purpose, even as a mere child, were nothing short of marvelous! On the boy's eighth birthday his father had given him a beautiful little hatchet, in order that he might early learn the use of weapons—those were turbulent days, they must remember! The gift had made the boy so happy that he was beside himself with joy. He took the hatchet, ran out and began playing with it. But then something very unfortunate happened: In the orchard his father had planted a cherry tree, one of a very rare variety, bearing very choice fruit; his father had imported it from England, and had tended it with the greatest of care. As little George ran about playing with his hatchet, trying it now on one thing, now on another, he also came to the cherry tree. The tree was of just the right size, he thought, for him to test his strength; and so in his thoughtlessness, he chopped it down! When the father, a very austere man, shortly afterward chanced to come out into the orchard and discovered the evil deed, his righteous indignation knew no bounds; he called his whole household together and demanded to know who the culprit was. One must remember, explained Miss Mahon, that these were stern times—a right-thinking master regarded it as his duty both to try and to chastise. "What was young George to do now? What would one of you, my young friends, have done in his place? Listen carefully now Our young hero steps courageously up to his enraged parent and says: 'Dear Father, I can not tell a lie; it was I who chopped down the tree! Punish me as I have deserved!' How nobly done of the boy! What an ideal to pattern your own lives after! This heroic deed has inspired thousands upon thousands of young American boys to become great men!" But Miss Mahon did not have time for extended comments; she had to hurry on and relate other incidents from Washington's early life—fantastic, incredible stories which would have sounded like the wildest fairy tales had it not been for the goodness and the intense zealousness of her who told them. Despite her great zeal there were Thomases who found it hard to believe all she said.

At last she had finished her preparations for tomorrow. She rose from her chair, and fingering the gold chain which hung about her neck and down over her bosom, hemmed kindly to indicate that she now desired the attention of the whole school. Her face took on a deeper red from what she was about to do, even though it was the same as what she had done last night, and every other night before.

"Charles Doheny, come forward, please!" Her voice, though commanding, had a soft, mild quality which one could not very well oppose.

The brown-haired boy in the front seat to the left gave his pal a kick in the leg, rose immediately, and came forward. As he stood facing the room his eyes twinkled mischievously; otherwise his features looked grave as a statue.

"All stand, please! Not so much noise," she requested mildly.

Nevertheless there was noise; books had to be chucked away; papers had to be hidden; a couple of seats fell down; small feet shuffled uneasily; wraps were put on, which act caused considerable disturbance; one boy hurriedly thrust a book into his pocket, making use of the opportunity to poke his seatmate in the side, and that, of course, brought a jab in return, and suppressed snickerings from those in the seat just behind.

The kind voice grew firmer:

"Now we are through for today. During the few hours that we have been here, we have learned many good and useful lessons, which will help us to become great men

and women. Education is our only weapon against igno-
rance and against the inherited customs we have brought
with us from the old country. We shall close the day by
reminding ourselves of the many blessings we enjoy, we
who have been given the right of citizenship in this beloved land of liberty! Whether we be poor or rich, we may
all drink freely of the life-giving waters of the fountain of
knowledge and thereby learn how to become gentlemen
and ladies" (Miss Mahon always mentioned *ladies* last)
"so that we may gain admittance to the highest positions
in the land even though we are only the children of poor
immigrants. Remember Lincoln! The humblest of log
cabins was his boyhood home, and yet he attained the
highest position on earth! Every one of you may advance to
the same position, provided that you have the courage to
follow the ideal!" Charley, drawing his head well into his
shoulders, turned slowly toward the girls' side of the room,
and cast furtive glances in that direction. . . . "Now
we shall close the day by calling to mind one of the most
precious inheritances which the fathers of our country have
bequeathed to us and have asked us to preserve. Charles,
you may now recite the Declaration of Independence for
us. Speak slowly and distinctly, please, so that the rest
of us can follow you. You must all listen carefully to
Charles, because his accent is so pure. It's really too bad
the way some of you speak the language of our country!
One might think you had just come across!" she added
good-naturedly. "One, two, three, ready!"

The boy raised his head, and took the lead, the whole
school reciting in unison. The scholars had been so well
trained, that once started there was no stopping them until
they had reached the end. During the reciting Peder Holm
leaned his head as far forward and as much to the side as
propriety would allow, in order to ascertain whether Miss
Mahon knew the Declaration today, for Charley had
sworn that he saw her look in the book last night!

As soon as they had disposed of Jefferson's immortal
document, Miss Mahon turned to the girls' side and said,
with a motherly smile:

"Tomorrow one of my little girls" (all children were
hers) "shall be the leader. I'm not going to tell you now
who it will be. But take your books home and practice

diligently, all of you! . . . Charles, let's see whether you can walk back to your seat as becomes a gentleman . . . and now, Peder Holm, you may come forward."

All eyes followed the two boys. Some laughed. Charley's face wore an indescribable grin as he passed his friend. Miss Mahon waited patiently until Peder had come into position just in front of her desk.

"Now let me hear how well you can give the *Gettysburg Address*—you stumbled last night, you remember!" Her voice was unusually mild and importuning. . . . "You must all repeat it with him, so that we can learn this beautiful speech. One, two, three, ready!"

With a deep, clear voice, religious in its earnestness, Peder launched into the speech. And this time, it was Charley who leaned forward to see if the teacher had to look in her book.

"And now we shall sing 'America'; all of you remain standing for a moment, please, after we have finished—I have something to tell you which I want you to mention as soon as you come home tonight." She didn't say what it was but began singing immediately.

As soon as the last line had been sung, impatient feet moved restlessly, eager to be gone; the older boys wanted to be off and took no pains to conceal the fact. She never could get ready. She would always think up some nonsense to pester them with just as they were ready to leave!

Miss Mahon came forward to the very edge of the platform, and teetering on her heels and toes, announced:

"There will be a meeting here at 8 o'clock tonight. You must be sure to tell your parents about it. A speaker is coming all the way from Sioux Falls. Matters of momentous importance will be discussed. This district is to agree upon instructions to be sent to the legislature in Huron next month. The question of the division of this vast Territory will be debated. As many as can possibly come must do so. It wouldn't hurt if many of the women attended the meeting, for they, too, stand in need of being enlightened concerning the affairs of our dear country. You may tell your mothers that I said so! . . . And now I want you, Peder Holm, and you, Charles Doheny, to be here tonight. You two big boys of mine speak beautifully. Maybe I can arrange to have both of you on the program. Of course, I can't promise that, though I can scarcely imagine anything more fitting with which to begin a program of this kind than just those two selections which you give so nicely. You must therefore be sure to be here!" Miss Mahon made these announcements in a tone as if she herself were planning the whole meeting and had the management of it all.

In a twinkling the schoolroom was empty. Peder tumbled out of his seat and up to the teacher, his comrade following him somewhat reluctantly.

"Am I—am I—going to speak that piece at the meeting tonight?" he stammered, joyous suspense almost taking the breath away from him. The thing seemed incredible. *He* to speak here, before a house packed full of grown people?

"Yes, both you and Charles!" The schoolroom was now empty; Miss Clarabelle Mahon came down from the platform, put her arm about the shoulder of each boy, and continued, "You must hurry home, now, and study your selections carefully, so that you won't disgrace me tonight, I who am working so patiently with you! You, Peder, have a bad accent; you ought not talk anything but your country's language for a while, though your speech will do very well out here. Don't speak quite so loud, then your beautiful voice will show off to better advantage." She leaned toward Peder; and with her thumb and forefinger she toyed with the lobe of his ear; her hand, delicate and warm, touched his cheek. This so embarrassed the boy that he drew himself away, and mumbling a low good night, hurried out.

II

The boys stood out in the schoolyard pulling on their overcoats, Charley laughing, but Peder so serious that he looked almost angry. He turned to his pal and asked in a low voice:

"Are you coming tonight?"

"Bet your neck! Father is bringing the speaker from Sioux Falls. Aren't you?"

Peder did not answer for a moment. "If my mother will let me," he said hesitatingly, without looking up.

"Let you?—When you're to be Lincoln?"

Peder made no reply, but turned and started to walk

off, his eyes blurring as he looked out into the evening; he buttoned his coat tight, his hands trembling.

"You got to come!" said the other, following him. "He's a great speaker, I tell you. The place is going to be jammed full. Everybody is coming. They'll quarrel and everything, and get awfully mad! It's going to be a lot of fun!"

Peder, continuing silent, trudged on a little ahead of his companion. He soon reached the main road, where he was to turn off; there he stopped:

"Are you going to give that piece?"

"Sure, if they want me to."

"Just the thing," nodded Peder decisively, "it's just the thing, I tell you!" And as if he couldn't make the assertion strong enough, he added: "Just what they need to hear!"

"So's yours!"

Peder made no answer; he was thinking intently—he scowled:

"Was your father at the convention this fall?"*

" 'Course he was!"

"Has he told you about it?"

"Sure! He's going to Huron next month; there they'll settle the whole business—division and all!"

"Bet you, they'll settle it!" A sigh of relief escaped Peder; his eyes brightened and his face relaxed. "Does he think Huron will be the capital?"

"He don't know—he only talks about the division."

"Is he in favor of it?"

"Bet you, he is—he says they'll do it or *bust!*"

"Say," Peder grabbed Charley's arm, excitedly, "what does your father think of those fellows who set a legislature of their own up at Bismarck, many hundreds of miles away, where there's only a great wilderness?" The boy had to stop to recover his breath. . . . "Huh, nothing but Indians and buffaloes and barbarism out there!" Peder's face flamed as he stood there giving vent to his pent-up thoughts.

"Ought to hang 'em!" pronounced Charley decisively; he had heard the verdict often enough.

"Hang 'em!—bet you! They'll never make a state up

* The convention here referred to is the Constitutional Convention held in Sioux Falls, S. Dak., in September, 1885.

there . . . not one that'll amount to anything anyway."

"*There?*" Charley spoke with an air of finality, "why there's nothing but Indians and foreigners up there! But now the Territory will be divided; then they can just stay up there and see how they like it. Good enough for 'em, the fools!"

"You know what," proposed Peder eagerly, "if they don't divide this time either, then somebody just ought to take and move the government right back again! Hasn't your father said anything about *that?*"

"Huh, said anything about it? Father is always talking politics!"

To Peder this sounded so wonderful that he had to think about it awhile. No wonder Charley knew so much and could be so smart when he had a father like that to talk to all the time. Here *he* had to be alone with everything.

The boys had come to the fork in the road, where each must go his own way. None of the other scholars could now be seen.

"Come on home with me," suggested Charley, "then I'll go back with you and ask for you . . . much easier that way!"

Peder was kicking at the dust in the road. A voice within him was saying, "That you must not!" And at once there flashed before him, plain as could be, a picture of his mother going about waiting for him at home; every once in a while she came to the window and looked out toward the west. The picture cautioned still more distinctly, "No, you must not!"

Charley burst into an uproarious ha, ha, ha. "Now you look just like Miss Mahon when she's getting ready to make a speech. No wonder she likes you so well!"

"It's *you* she likes!" Peder's face had flushed crimson.

"Huh, haven't I seen it?"

"I've seen about you too!"

" 'Bout me?"

"Yes, you. 'Cause it's you she likes!"

"Aw, you're crazy!" Charley swung round and ran. Peder after. He had to discuss the subject further with his pal . . . much easier if Charley came and asked for him. Then Mother would understand. And it wouldn't take long to go over to Doheny's either. Peder caught up with his friend, and walked so fast that the other had to hurry to keep pace with him.

"Say," Charley thrust his glowing brown face right up into Peder's, "she didn't know your piece tonight either. I saw her look in the book three times!"

Peder walked on, smiling to himself. Then his mouth opened; he was about to say something, but changed his mind. He began to walk faster; not until they found themselves racing did they slacken their pace.

"Did she know mine?" Charley demanded.

"Don't know."

"Didn't you see it?"

"She—well, she did look in the book," Peter admitted reluctantly; immediately regretting what he had said, he tried to change the subject by asking:

"Do you think that's all nonsense, that story about the tree?"

"What tree?"

"That story about Washington."

"Nonsense every bit of it!" There wasn't a shadow of doubt in Charley's mind. "Washington was no old hen. It's only in schoolma'am stories boys do such things!"

The amazing recklessness of his chum once more made Peder's eyes glow with admiration: but his feelings were strangely mingled; he felt uncomfortable over talking so disrespectfully about the very Father of America, just as whenever he had tried to make himself manly and had used bad words and had cussed. For a while he walked on in silence. Then he said retractingly: "He became a soldier . . . even a general!"

"Yes siree," Charley asserted emphatically, "he stabbed people to death, chopped their heads off, blew 'em to smithereens with cannons—to sausage meat, man! Oh no, he was no chicken, Washington wasn't!" Charley braced his shoulders and quickened his gait; now his face was puckering. "I tell you something," he confided, "she's a *nut*, that's what she is!"

"Well, yes—she is a little funny," Peder conceded thoughtfully.

"Funny, huh! The way she paws all over people and wants to be sweet—ish, ish, I just hate her. I'll run away from the whole school and all her old pawing!"

"Aw no, you won't"

"Yes siree!"

"Where?" asked Peder, a little skeptical.

"Aw, out to the Black Hills. The Indians are getting funny again; maybe there'll be war and everything." Charley's words had such joyous faith that Peder was quite carried away by them. But then he remembered something which he must tell Charley right away; it was very important too:

"In the Civil War it was almost only boys; lots of 'em not any older'n us; it says so in a book we have at home. They certainly could use us if war broke out."

"Bet you! And if there isn't war, we can begin to dig gold; terrible how they're carrying on out in Deadwood; the paper is all full of it."

All of a sudden Peder broke into a bright, rippling laugh. "Listen: Let's go to Bismarck, and take the whole shebang and move it back again. Those fellows can't set up any state—we'll just show 'em they can't!"

"That would mean war, boy!"

"Lincoln didn't care about that the time the South tried to act smart and break away. Those fellows up at Bismarck certainly need to be shown a thing or two!" Peder spoke with deep earnestness; one might think that the wrong had been done him personally, which struck Charley as so funny that he had to look at him—was he trying to act grown up? But Peder's crimson face was at the moment the very expression of righteous indignation; his deep blue eyes flashed; his face looked angrier than that of any grown person Charley had ever seen quarreling over politics. And then he smiled admiringly at him:

"That would be some racket, all right!"

III

The boys were completely absorbed in what they were talking about; before they knew it they were standing in the yard at Doheny's. The dog Shep brought them to; coming out from his hiding place under the porch, he ran to meet them, wagging his tail, and jumping up and down begging to be petted and played with.

"Hello there, Shep, old boy, here we are!" Charley had

the dog in his arms and went romping across the yard with him; for the moment he forgot his pal.

Meanwhile Peder was looking around. The buildings lay in a semi-circle: to the right the living house, a squat two-story structure, which looked lower than it actually was because of the high border of manure and straw banked up along the sills, as a protection against the winter. The sod huts, in the center of the circle, crouched low as if shivering with cold despite the fact that they were well covered with straw. Right next to the huts the new granary reared itself, freshly painted and rather imposing. Farthest to the left stood the new barn, dominating the whole yard because of its colossal dimensions; even the new granary dwindled into insignificance beside it.

"Come on in and have a slice of bread!" called Charley. "It won't take long."

"You go; I want to see the barn. Hurry up!"

"Look all you please, only don't scare the cows—they ain't used to Norwegians!"

Presently Peder was standing inside the barn. No sign of life anywhere. Stalls lined both sides, harnesses hanging at each; at the far end of the horse barn ran a partition, the doors to which stood open. Peder walked slowly down the aisle, passed through the door and found himself in a square room; on the one side a stair led up to the hayloft; opposite was an open hay chute. Beyond the room lay the cow barn, down both sides of which a row of stalls stretched themselves. Peder sauntered in through the place, stood still awhile and looked about. This certainly was a fine barn; there must be room for at least twenty cows in here.

Peder's reflections came to an abrupt end: A tightly twisted bundle of straw came flying from out of the dusk and struck him square in the neck. He jumped high, but was so startled that he could not move and stood there hot and dazed. Not a sound nor a sign of life anywhere. The half-dark gathered in around him and helped him listen. So tense was the grip of the silence that it threatened to choke him, and he had to cough. . . . Charley must be up to one of his tricks again. Peder took a few cautious steps, looked first into one stall and then into another, his mouth half open with suspense. Suddenly a girl shot out of the stall next to him, snickers and broken ripples of laughter trailing her. Like an arrow she darted out through the light, flew up the hayloft stairs and disappeared. . . . Deathlike silence filled the barn as before.

Recovering the use of his legs Peder ran after her. Just what he intended to do he didn't know, but he felt hot and ashamed to think that a girl should dare to make a fool of him in this way. He reached the top of the stairs. A mysterious quiet lay across the hay in the loft; a queer half-sleeping dusk filled the place; straws were rustling and snapping, and raising themselves. He ran up in the hay, stumbled, stood still, listened breathlessly. The air seemed full of sounds, about to awaken; yet no life to be seen. . . . Was it there? . . . No, it must be there! Again he was choking; he trembled so violently that he could scarcely stand up; his arms felt as though they would drop from his shoulders; his mouth was dry. . . . What had she done with herself? She couldn't have run very far in. He stood stock still, straining to hear where she might be hiding. . . . Peder gasped for breath. . . . *There!* In the wink of an eye he was on the spot. From under some loose hay, the toe of a shoe stuck out; Peder made one circling sweep with his hand and threw himself straight down; in the next instant he held within his arms a trembling body, crushing it to him. Soft and living warm it lay there, for a while—entirely still. But presently it began to heave; short choppy billows beat violently; frightened, warm life surged into his. Momentarily he was dazed . . . did not know what he was doing. He wanted to let go, but dared not; if he released his hold now, some calamity would happen.

"Let me go!" a voice whispered.

Peder loosened his grip a little.

"Let me go!" it panted, hotly and excitedly right into his ear.

Trembling he raised his head to get up. The body he was clasping began to wriggle, a cheek touched his, and he was aware of it at once—he had never felt anything so silken and soft. His chin sank down into the warm hollow of her throat, his cheek pressing close. Then there was a patter of quick footsteps below; someone came into the barn, and stood listening. . . . A voice called out; uncannily loud and hollow, the call sounded in the silence of the great empty barn:

"Peder!"

Terror-stricken, the two sank together, for the moment merged into one; held their breath and dared not let it go; when finally it escaped them it broke like a peal of thunder.

"Pe—der!"

Tip-tap, tip-tap, ran the footsteps the whole length of the barn.

"Peder . . . hoi oi!" And then at the other end:

"Susie . . . *Susie!*"

The call rent the air. And suddenly it came from out in the yard, making it worse than ever, because there it called upon everything between heaven and earth.

Waves coursed through the body which Peder held in his arms; they heaped themselves up, gathered strength, and grew into breakers—great heavy ones that heaved themselves forward and broke across all barriers. He felt her crying against his face, hot breath accompanying tears, and now she clung to him helplessly. . . . The calling in the yard faded away. At length Peder found sufficient strength to tear loose. Trembling and bewildered, he got up and managed to reach the stairs, his whole body shaking so violently that he had to support himself against the wall. Down in the barn he stopped to listen, like a criminal who knows that he is being pursued. Only one thing was clear to him: he must get away unseen!

Charley was out in the yard playing with Shep; as soon as he spied Peder slip out through the door, he came running. And so there began a wild chase around the barn, Peder ahead, his jaws set, Charley following, yelling and whooping. The dog found it impossible to stand idly by and look at all this fun; he, too, his tongue hanging out of his mouth, joined the chase, now at the side of one, letting out a jubilant woof that set the whole place afire, then more woofs and off to the other boy; but the dog soon sensed that the boy ahead was the one who must be caught, and set out in pursuit of him. In so doing he got in Peder's way and hindered his pace. That finally gave Charley a chance to throw himself upon Peder's neck, sending both boys headlong to the ground—with the dog standing triumphant, his forelegs on the topmost.

"Now you . . . be . . . Washington, *th—ere!*" This came from Charley, who was on top.

The boys closed harder, Charley good-naturedly, despite the fact that he grappled with all the strength he possessed. Every now and then some teasing remark would escape him; from Peder came only hot pantings. As soon as he felt that he was getting the upper hand, he would loosen his grip just enough to permit Charley to get on top again, and then he would go at it as hard as before. He let it happen over and over again. After a while Peder gave up entirely, lay still until the other boy straddled his back, and then said quietly:

"Now you quit. I got to go home!"

"Golly, you're strong!" said Charley admiringly and remained sitting. . . . "Where were you?"

"Do you think so?" Peder began to wriggle and raised himself up with the other on his back. Shep, thinking that now they were going to start up again, commenced barking, and danced joyfully around the boys.

But the fight was over. Charley let go his hold. Peder stood red and breathless, scraping the ground with the toe of his shoe, unable to look at his friend; he wanted to run away from him, to get home, but could not tear himself loose. He felt, somehow, that he must have Charley's permission to leave the place. Mechanically he turned his head and looked at the barn. There it stood, silent and mysterious as before.

"Where were you?" demanded Charley.

"Up in the hayloft," confessed Peder, his face getting blood red.

"Pretty fine, eh?"

"It's—it's big!" Peder stole a glance at his friend, and perceiving a way of escape, took it: "Must cost a lot. . . . We, too, got to build pretty soon."

"Over two thousand. We had twelve men working at it. Lots of fun, I tell you!" explained Charley proudly. "I helped with the hauling every day. Went to Sioux Falls all alone—what do you think about that?"

"Uh huh!" nodded Peder admiringly, but added lamely that he s'posed he'd better be going now.

"Oh no, you aren't. Got to come in and have some lunch first. It's all ready!" said Charley. And when he saw the other still hesitating, he added: "Father isn't home yet. It won't take us long."

"Well . . . all right, but I got to be home and help with the chores."

"The lunch is ready. It's on the table and everything."

Peder pretended not to hear what Charley was saying, began to walk slowly away, but feeling that he could not leave just yet, he turned and came back. "Let's hurry then!" he said quickly and low, and followed into the kitchen.

Dusk was settling inside. The room was untidy; garments of all sorts hung around on the walls; pails and pans of many kinds littered the floor. On the table stood bread and butter and two glasses of milk; the table was clean and the food looked appetizing.

A fire crackling cheerily in the stove threw a wavering light across the room. In an easy chair drawn close to the stove an old, old woman knitting a sock sat rocking to and fro. There was that about her which compelled one to look twice: On her head was perched a black cap, the top of which nodded pleasantly down upon her knitting. The countless wrinkles in her face seemed to have sought after more space, but to have found none; and having long since wearied of their vain search now lay fixed like the lines and curves of some ancient piece of woodcarving. The whole face seemed petrified. But the knitting hands, the constant motion of the lips, the two dark eyes peering out of their deep caverns, testified that the life spark still lingered within. In spite of its innumerable furrows the face looked benignantly kind. Down over the front of her dress hung a long string of large glass beads, in the loop of which was fastened a crucifix; now and then the hands dropped the needles and fingered one of the beads. A dark brown clay pipe with a black bowl lay on top of the stove; judging by the odor of strong tobacco hanging heavy in the air, the pipe must just have been laid aside.

The sibyl head turned toward the boys as they entered; faint quavering words came, as if from far within a mysterious passage; but the old woman seemed to have forgotten them instantly. Peder had stopped in front of her, fascinated by the sight. Was this actually a human being?

Charley gave him a push in the back. "You sit there," he said pointing to the other side of the table; he himself took the nearest chair.

Peder walked around the table and sat down. He took

a slice of bread and was trying to butter it, but couldn't get it done because every once in a while he had to look at the figure by the stove.

"Don't look at her," said Charley calmly, " 'cause then she'll think we're talking about her; she doesn't like that. But you can say all you want to; she can't hear."

"Can't she hear at all?" asked Peder in a low voice; in spite of Charley's warning Peder had to look at her—he just couldn't help himself.

"Not a thing, except when there's a heavy fog and we holler right in her ear. But she understands very well."

"Gee, she must be old!"

"Hundred years, Father thinks. She's his grandmother."

"Can she talk?"

Charley laughed heartily at this stupidity.

"Sure she can talk; you just ought to hear her tell stories."

"Wish I could." Peder's face brightened. "What does she tell about?"

"Aw, old stories from Ireland. About love and fighting and everything. She knows a lot of others too. One is about some seed wheat that came falling right down from heaven into a church bell; there had been several bad years, and then there was a famine, and the priests prayed, and the nuns sang in the churches at night and everything. It's an awfully good story. Father says it's true, too."

"What's she talking about now?"

"She ain't talking!"

"But her mouth's going, can't you hear?" asked Peder dubiously, stealing another glance at the withered face.

"Aw, that—she's only praying now!"

This made Peder marvel still more. But his wonder was suddenly cut short by the door being flung upon; in came a girl carrying an armful of wood, which she threw into the wood box in the corner by the stove. She stopped to brush her dress, a job which seemed to take her a long time.

Charley talked over his shoulder to her; "Just wait till I catch you, Susie—I'll fix you!" Then in a more conciliatory tone: "Where do you keep yourself all day?"

The girl appeared not to take her brother's threat very seriously. She snickered teasingly: "Is that so?" Then added, "Let's see you try it!"

The brother ignored her challenge.

"Where were you?"

"Aw, slaving as usual." And suddenly she took the offensive, "Now you'd better get a hustle on yourself! Father said you should let the cows in, and do the milking till he got home. Serves you right, the way you've been loafing all day! What does Miss Mahon do to such lazy fellows anyway?" The words came by spurts, in a voice soft and full of laughter. Peder sat chuckling without knowing it. The girl unfastened the kerchief she was wearing and hung it on the wall. Intrenching herself behind the black cap she rested her arms on the back of the chair and began to stroke gently the furrowed cheeks. So situated, she could at any moment hide her face behind the head in front of her. The deep dusk which lay upon the room shaded off into near dark in the far corner, rendering the objects barely discernible. Yet off and on, a sudden flare of light bursting from the stove door lit the corner and revealed the two figures. Peder shot a glance in the direction of the stove and met a face, brown and laughing, at which he turned burning hot. He didn't look that way again.

The girl was Charley's twin sister. They were as alike as two peas in a pod, she slightly smaller and more delicately built than he, but if one saw both faces at the same time, he would scarcely notice the difference because she looked the more mature of the two. Susie was not going to school this year; the mother having died of consumption early in the summer, the girl was needed at home to keep house.

Pedar hurried to get the slice of bread down, and sent the glass of milk after it; then he got up and came around the table.

"You don't have to come with me. Be sure to be early tomorrow morning!" he said as he took hold of the door knob. An irresistible force turned his head toward the stove; in the next flare of light she met his eyes, only to disappear instantly behind the black cap. . . . The instant afterward Peder was out on the porch, took the steps in one jump and was gone like a shot.

IV

Almost dark now. A dull glow lingered in the western sky and showed where day had gone. The air grew noticeably colder. . . . We're pretty sure to have a heavy frost tonight, thought Peder.

He had a good two miles' walk home. Half of the first mile he ran; then he slackened his speed, took time to get his breath—by and by he was only poking along.

A welter of strange thoughts came out of nowhere and laid hold of him; they surged through him, unloosed feelings so new and wonderful that he almost forgot to walk. And the slower his gait, the more completely this mysterious thing took possession of him. But that he did not notice, because he had begun to sing to himself. When he discovered that he was singing, he stopped at once. Not for anything in the world must he be caught singing now! Within him he was conscious of an upwelling of something soft and warm and very pleasant; it suffused his whole body. He felt himself reddening, turned and looked around. There wasn't anybody here who could see him, was there? All about him lay the night—intense, quiet, and alert. He became aware of how distinctly one could hear the smallest sound; the tramp of his shoes in the road echoed loudly; he stepped more lightly as he proceeded. Somewhere lurked a wee fear, watching its chance to get him. No . . . not fear either, exactly. Uneasiness rather, a trembling wonder, a force unknown—no, a great happiness it was! Instantly his arms shot out and he began rowing with them. They were wings, and could easily carry him. On and on past the glow of dying day and way into the bright light beyond, he'd like to fly, for there great marvels lay waiting for him. He laughed at the thought of it and rowed on!

He felt hot and wished he could take off his clothes. Suddenly he knew he had a body of flesh and blood . . . was this the way it felt to be grown up?

The experience in the hayloft was upon him. His walk became slow as a snail's. Had anyone ever felt anything so soft and living? Peder laughed to himself. . . . Her heart had lain right in his hand; he could still feel how it beat. . . . And she had cried—that was just the remarkable thing about it! He hadn't wanted to do her any harm, only punish her a little because she had almost scared the life out of him. . . . Why had she cried? Yes, *why* had she cried? . . . His throat felt dry; the landscape about him blurred because the dark sent whiffs of cold into his eyes, filling them with water. Slight chills ran through his body even though he was warm and perspiring. . . . A jag of hay lay in the road waiting for the first puff of wind, not caring whither it would be blown. Peder gave it a kick. . . . Here lay another. Must have been hauling hay here today. They ought to be more careful in loading! There were more jags. Peder had to take a kick at all of them.

. . . But that she had cried, and that it had been all his fault, and still she hadn't been angry with him! . . . No, she hadn't been angry—he felt sure of it; at least it didn't sound that way when she came in. Suddenly a thought confronted him; he had to stop and examine it more closely: Were he and Susie engaged now? The question frightened him. But after it came another idea which gave him courage: If he was engaged, then it could only mean that he was getting grown up. Peder straightened as he stood there on the deserted prairie—kids didn't get themselves engaged! Somewhere over west in the dark, a dog began barking, short, angry yelps. . . . Must be Shep. Perhaps Doheny was just coming home from Sioux Falls. Far off toward the southeast rose the light from a straw-stack fire; successive sheets of light leaped skyward; he thought he could hear the roaring and sensed the power coming from it. The feeling did him good. Suddenly he broke into a run; the whirring of the air against his face soothed him; he slowed down just enough to allow him to thrust his arms out into the darkness and row awhile again. . . . And once more he gave a laugh.

Deep darkness reigned when at last he ran into the yard at home. Then he stopped running and walked hesitatingly. From the kitchen window a light blinked out into the night; it seemed to be on the lookout for him, and asked as soon as it caught sight of him: So you've come at last? He didn't like the question and struck off in the direction of the barns, which in the dark resembled a row of straw stacks. From out of one of them came the sharp voice of a man. . . . That's Ole, thought Peder; now he's talking to one of the horses. Just then the kitchen door opened, letting a light fall across the yard. His mother came out and set a pail on the porch, went in again, leaving the door slightly ajar. . . . There is Mother; now she's going out to feed the pigs, and that's my job! He nerved himself, ran across the yard, and stepped into the kitchen.

The light was so bright that he had to turn away from it. Anna Marie was already setting the table for supper; the mother stood bending low over a pail near the stove; she had her outdoor clothes on, an old overcoat and a homeknit stocking cap.

"I'll feed the pigs," he said quietly. This was his first utterance in Norwegian since he had left home early this morning; the sound of the words, the sight of his sister and his mother going about doing the work—as they had every day of his life—the sight of this room with all its secrets, obliterated in an instant the whole world in which he had lived so intensely during the day. Here was another world altogether. He had had the same feeling before, but to-night it brought with it such wonder that he had to stop to collect himself. Was it here he belonged, or was it out there in the other world?

"You are very late tonight. I was going out to hunt for you," said his mother without turning around to look at him. The rebuke cut all the more keenly because her words were spoken so quietly. They made him feel how worried she had been about him. . . . He shouldn't have gone with Charley—he knew he shouldn't!

The sister turned toward him:

"Did you have to stay after school?"

"Stay after school?" he repeated scornfully, and without paying any attention to her, walked over to his mother and was about to take her pail.

"There's going to be a great meeting in the schoolhouse tonight, there'll be a speaker from Sioux Falls, Miss Mahon says I have to be on the program, and she wants you to come too," announced Peder hurriedly and with much bluster, but realized at once that it sounded out of place in here.

"You'll have to empty both pails in the south pen," said his mother, straightening herself and looking straight into his eyes. "The others have got theirs."

"Corn too?" Peder tried to avoid her eyes.

"No, you must give them corn. Take the pail that's out on the porch with you, and don't spill!" His mother said nothing more, and that Peder could not understand.

By the pig pen he set the swill-pails down, took the scoop and began throwing in corn. Instantly a terrible racket flared up among the black devils out there in the dark; the first scoopful started it: prolonged squeals, shuf-flings, angry grunts, infuriated snorts. This evening Peder laughed as he threw scoopful after scoopful right into their snouts. That's the way to give it to 'em! . . . Now take that! And when he poured the swill into the troughs the black fury became satanical; for then all were bound to drink at the same time and in exactly the same place. He leaned over the fence and pulled the ears he could reach. . . . Lot of fun to feed the pigs tonight! But he supposed he'd better hurry to the barn and help Store-Hans with the milking.

Up under the ceiling near the middle of the cow barn hung a sooty lantern. Peder could hear where his brother sat, took one of the pails and a stool, and uttering a care-less "hello," picked out a cow farther in.

Store-Hans did not answer until after he had finished his cow and had been out in the entry to empty his pail, but when he returned he stopped in front of Peder:

"About time you got home. Better not try that trick again. Mother shouldn't have to run around the prairies hunting for you!" There was more of serious concern than of real anger in his brother's words. But he wasn't through yet: "What have you been up to all day?"

"All day?" snorted Peder.

"I want to know what you've been up to." His brother came dangerously close.

"Up to?"

"Yes—up to."

"Nothing."

"I want to know!" Store-Hans put down his pail.

Peder knew that now there was no escape, his brother being in that frame of mind. "Oh, I just went with

Charley, and then we had to have lunch—if you got to know it."

"You needn't run around to the neighbors for something to eat; it's the second time you've been late, and now it's got to stop—remember I have told you!" Having given his brother this warning, Store-Hans picked up his pail and sat down to milk the next cow.

Peder quivered with anger. They could just hold their horses awhile! Here four of 'em went watching him. Even Anna Marie, that old fool of a girl, had to play guardian angel! If she didn't, some of the rest of 'em would. And that poky Store-Hans, always so serious, had to stick his nose into everything. . . . And Mother—well, of course, that was different. But, well, they could just wait awhile!

His feeling of anger soon subsided. It was pleasant to sit here with his forehead pressed close against the warm flank and to feel the quiet rise and fall of the beast's breathing. The constant chewing of the cud by a whole barnful of drowsy cows sounded like friendly chatting which he could readily understand. . . . Hurry?—no, not tonight. His brother could bluster as much as he liked.

V

Supper was on the table when they came in from the milking. Ole, sitting directly in the light of the lamp on the clock shelf, was reading *The Sioux Falls Press*; Peder was looking over his shoulder while he waited for Store-Hans to finish washing.

"Got a new paper? What does it say about politics?" His voice was needlessly loud. Upon getting no answer he began reading to the others:

"Legislature convenes in Huron next month." . . . "Many meetings being held." . . . "People gather to agree upon instructions." . . . "Meetings in every school district." . . . "Bismarck insists on division . . . believes northern will be admitted first." . . . Peder forgot himself; his eyes grew large and bright. . . . "They ought to be hanged!"—There were a couple of other words which Charley had used that Peder now felt the need of employing but caught himself in time.

The rest paid no attention to him. Now he had to wash. His brother put the paper away. Soon after, all were seated at the table and Peder said grace.

No one had a word to say tonight either. Peder was so used to the silence at the table that he would scarcely have noticed it, were it not that he detected something ominous in it. It lay in the air, asking for utterance, became insistent and annoying. He stole a glance now at one, now at another. He was aware how all sat waiting—demanding to know what he and Susie had been up to in the hayloft. Every moment the silence threatened to break open and disclose it all. . . . That shall never happen! thought Peder. He saw words drift past his eyes, grabbed recklessly after them and began to speak. He told about the meeting to be held in the schoolhouse tonight, loudly, in a chanting tone; the words poured in a steady stream:

A great speaker, the one who was coming; Doheny had gone all the way to Sioux Falls after him. Peder took his time talking about Doheny, left him and came back to him again: Yessir, Doheny had made the trip just to get him; he came back only a little while ago, and had the speaker with him. Doheny was going to the legislature in Huron; he thought maybe Huron would be the capital; that's all they talked about over at Doheny's. It occurred to Peder that perhaps all this talking about Doheny might sound a bit suspicious, and so he immediately asked them to pass him the potatoes. Having taken a helping he went on about Miss Mahon:

She had told him to come; she had just gone ahead and put him on the program, without his knowing anything about it, because his piece was so fitting. Miss Mahon sure was a good teacher. A lot of the kids couldn't get along with her though. Peder chuckled at something the others could not possibly know, and then went on telling about her father, who had been killed in the Battle of Stone River. Her mother had died of grief. . . . Miss Mahon had said that he must be sure to bring Mother along tonight. . . . Couldn't they take the lumber wagon and go, all of them? Anna Marie needn't stay home alone!

Peder talked for dear life. Everyone looked at him, and then at the mother, as if asking her to stop him.

"Why so much noise, Permand? We have heard that

now," the mother said calmly. After that he quieted down and they were left to eat their supper in peace.

The mother finished first; after a little, Anna Marie. The brothers ate a long time. Store-Hans was always the last to get through. But finally he, too, had finished, so that Peder could say grace. All sat waiting, with their hands folded. And then the mother began singing a stanza of a hymn; her voice was soft and frail, like that of one who has borne a heavy burden and has become tired and worn out:

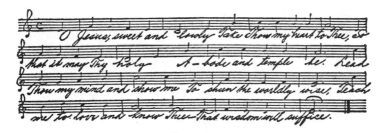

The sister joined in the singing; the others listened. As soon as the stanza was ended all got up from the table and a sense of calm and safety descended upon Peder—now he too could have sung a snatch! The mother went over to the stove and began tending a kettle which stood warming; Ole took the newspaper down from the clock shelf; Anna Marie started to wash the supper dishes; Store-Hans began examining a husking pin which had given him trouble during the afternoon. Peder fussed about, hunting for a book with the *Gettysburg Address* in it. . . . He wondered what they intended to do about the meeting tonight . . . Well, he'd better wait a little—it wasn't more than half past six yet; it wouldn't take him long to get there!

Beret spoke from over by the stove:

"You better come and carry the pail for me, Permand; my arms are so tired tonight."

All looked up at the same time. His mother was only asking him a small favor; yet her words, because of the irresistible kindness in them, commanded instant obedience. Peder immediately began hunting for his cap; his face had turned red. All knew, and he himself best of all, that now a reckoning was at hand. Store-Hans examined the pin more closely—he wondered if there ever were the like of Mother. Thus she had planned it just to spare the kid! He wished, though, that she had let Peder go this time, because he had given the culprit all he needed for a while.

The boy crossed the yard with his mother, he ahead, she following with the lantern. Huge shadows swayed in front of them, and to the side, mobile, fantastic monsters; they plunged forward into the dark; Peder thought his own the longer. The ground underneath their feet seemed to give way mysteriously; it was almost as if it sank beneath them. Neither said anything.

They went to the barn.

In one of the middle stalls stood an old scarecrow of a cow that had been given this place because Beret Holm considered it the warmest spot in the barn. Once upon a time the critter had been a cow and her name had been Rosie. The name still clung to her, the last vestige of her beauty. Now she was only old age and shag and bald spots. She gave no milk, had ceased to rut; her teeth had long since dropped out. When she came outside she would stare dumbly upon a world to which she no longer belonged; and then would begin to poke around among the barns and sheds, carefully, until she found the warmest spot of sun. There she would lie down with her head close to her side, quite unmindful of the flies. She need never worry about her nourishment because she was fed warm gruel morning and evening, and in addition, as much fine cornmeal as she could manage to lap up. The cow had made the journey the time the family moved here from Fillmore County—almost thirteen years ago that was. To sell or to butcher Rosie was as far removed from Beret Holm's thoughts as to kill one of her own children. And she would permit no one else to tend her either. The feeling seemed to be mutual, for if Rosie felt another hand touching her, she became irritable and wanted to hook. Last winter she had gone blind, too, whether from age or from having stood so long in the dark straw barn it was hard to say.

Beret fussed long over Rosie tonight, stood scratching her as she noisily slobbered about in the gruel, fetched more straw for bedding, and then went and got a horse-blanket, which she tied around her.

Peder had never been able to understand his mother's

concern about a dead cow, and had said as much on several occasions; he saw no use in caring for that which no longer belonged to this life; no amount of tending would do any good anyway. But as he let the light from his lantern fall on the bald hide, a fascinating picture flashed before him—of a laughing girl who stood back of a chair petting an old, old, wrinkled cheek. The picture was so jolly to look at that he was on the point of forgetting the unpleasant business which he was about to face.

At last it seemed that the mother was through with the cow. Peder stood in the adjoining stall, resting the lantern on the partition. His mother went in to Rosie, took the lantern out of his hand, and held it so that the light fell directly on his face.

"There is much you don't understand yet, Permand, but you will by and by, I suppose. We have to be good to Rosie, poor thing, even though she is old! . . . Tell me now how it happened that you didn't come home on time today." The voice was very friendly and kind; she continued to let the light fall on his face.

Peder's throat constricted, forcing him to swallow; he spoke with difficulty:

"I went home with Charley."

"Did that take so long?"

"We had to have lunch," Peder confessed stammering.

"Why, Peder! Do you need to go to those people for lunch?"

"Charley asked me to!"

"What if he did? There are many things people will offer you that you'll have to learn to say no to. Didn't it occur to you I might be worrying about you?"

"Well, no—not exactly." Peder was trying hard to face it like a man. "I guess maybe it did—a little."

A long silence ensued, the weight of which became too much for Peder; his head bent forward under it. But his mother only moved the lantern farther down on the partition so that the light could flood his face; unable to endure the scrutiny, Peder turned away. . . . Rosie was uneasy and prepared to lie down; hearing her mistress' voice, she stopped in the middle of her preparations:

"What did you and Charley talk about?"

"Aw—we just looked at their new barn. You just ought

to see it; it's awfully big! . . . Charley is a fine fellow, I tell you!" Peder put much emphasis into the statement. There was a pause in the conversation. When the mother spoke again her voice was low and intense in its earnestness:

"You will have to find another playmate, Peder!"

"Why?"

"Because you are Norwegian and they are Irish! . . . But likely you don't understand that yet, and I couldn't expect you to."

"They are *people* just the same," objected Peder sagely, in the utmost candor.

The mother smiled ever so little.

"But they are of another kind. They have another faith. And that is dangerous. For it is with such things as with weeds. The authorities made a terrible mistake when they threw us in with those people. And it is no better for them than it is for us. We should never have had the school together—you can't mix wheat and potatoes in the same bin. The authorities ought to have known as much."

But Peder didn't understand her reasoning, and so did not know what to answer her.

Then she began again:

"I ask one thing of you, Permand"—she came one step nearer so that she could put her hand on his shoulder, "don't do this again! Come home as soon as school lets out! I go here worrying all day long; I just can't help it. And it hurts me so. From the time you leave until you come home, I think of nothing else. I feel like a bird that isn't able to look after its own brood. . . . I don't understand what God means with it all!" She talked low, with difficulty; there was a deep plaintive seriousness in her voice, which cut right into the heart of the boy. He had to step back into the dark; great heavings surged through him. Beret did not hurry him. After a while she said, fully composed, as if nothing had happened between them:

"Here we're wasting our time and poor Rosie can't go to rest." She waited until he had calmed himself, then took the lantern and went out of the barn; there she was standing when he finally came out. As she shut the door tightly after them she said kindly:

"You go and get me an armful of wood, so I won't have to."

Her request smote Peder worse than anything she had said before, because bringing in wood was the job he was responsible for during the corn husking. Now he himself could see how reprehensible his conduct had been. But he s'posed the other things she had said were true too. . . . Peder was on his knees in the woodpile, rubbing his eyes with his coat sleeve; deliberately, he piled stick after stick up on his arm.

Beret hung away her barn clothes and went into the bedroom. Returning to the kitchen a while later she had her hair combed and was wearing a Sunday dress. She looked at Store-Hans as if to ask his advice, but when her question came, it was directed to all of them:

"What do you think? Had we better go? . . . It's just this, that it isn't nice of me not to go as long as the teacher has invited me . . . you better go and hitch up the horses, boys!"

VI

All during the eighties, one fruitful season followed another. They were years of plenty. From eternity the prairie had lain here lapping sun and drinking moisture, and had peered up into an endless blue day, brimful to running over. At evening it had listened to strange tales told by the twilight breeze. But now other concerns had come to occupy the thoughts of the Great Plain, giving it not so much as a moment of rest.

The sod huts crumbled and merged again with the earth out of which they had come. Sod is but sod, after all, and was never meant to shelter human beings so long as they can stand on their legs. Large dwellings and huge barns sprang up all over. Summers the Great Plain tried tornadoes; in spring and autumn, prairie fires, until heaven and earth roared in one blaze; during the winters she would let loose all the deviltry she could think of, by way of raging blizzards, spewing out a horror of snow and cold. But all in vain; the houses reared themselves faster than she could destroy them. Even the elements were to learn that the power of man had to be respected, especially when energized by a great joy.

New settlers swarmed out over the vast expanses of prairie. Some in large flocks, others in small. By day and night they would pass. Wherever the railroad thundered on ahead, the westward-moving bands would follow after, like seagulls in the wake of a ship. The old settlers could never have imagined such a landslide of humanity. They looked at it in amazement, and laughed joyously at visions which they saw being fulfilled—endless reaches of golden grain! One new settler after the other put his plow into the ground, until there waved fields from skyline to skyline. . . . Ought not people settle here where everything that was stuck into the ground grew so one could hear it? Risky to dig corpses into such soil! Just suppose that they too should begin to grow? Then we should be in a hell of a fix, said the land agents. We all know, don't we, that the Lord is constantly creating more people, but whoever heard of Him creating more land? Be careful, good people, about what you put into the ground! . . . Banner years all through the eighties. The locust plague was now an incredible event in a dim past—so much had taken place since those days.

From horizon to horizon highways were worming their way across the prairie, out of one small town and into the next; this decade was the first great period of road-building in the Territory.

County and townships were organized; schools and churches; offices in countless numbers for which incumbents had to be elected; committees and commissions and church governments—all had to be provided for. It might happen that the man who, in the old country, had been nothing but a scurvy rat of a cottager, here became centurion over hundreds, yea, even over thousands. No questions were asked about a man's past—that might be embarrassing to many; but did he have his head in the right place? And was there anything in it? And could he express himself? A confusion of tongues far worse than at the time of Babel set in; neither before nor since have such liberties been taken with English speech; and the language which the people had brought with them, fared not one whit better.

Rumors and stories of all sorts threw ferment into the minds these days:

In the Black Hills gold was being dug right out of the ground. Tales of lawlessness and of terrible murders came from out there. Man's might was man's right. Farming was after all only farming; it would take a long time to get rich that way. Many a poor devil, trusting to luck and selling what little he owned for what he could get at the moment, struck out for the West, perhaps never to be heard from again.

And along the railway routes towns popped up like gopher mounds—well, that is to say, people called them towns! Oftentimes the towns would anticipate the railway, for there were always some who knew exactly where the line would run, even long before it had been surveyed; and these simply went to work and plotted the town, staking out the main street and setting aside lots for post office, schoolhouse, bank, church, and a saloon or two. Then the selling began. People gambled for big pots. A man might stake all he owned on one throw, only to go out the next day and begin all over again. The air fairly buzzed with predictions of unbelievable things, like the prophecies concerning the Last Day: Now it was at hand, and *now!* Here it would strike for certain; no—not here, but *there!* And then it was in yet another place, *now they were absolutely sure!* He who seized time by the forelock and bought up the lots would get rich over night, no doubt about it! In the saloons the faces glowed in anticipation of the glory to come. . . . Just wait now, I say! Men talked with such conviction that even the most obdurate skeptic was knocked cold. A man was never so poor in those days that he couldn't afford a drink. . . . A feverish time, full of great plans and the talk of strong men. Folk would listen eagerly until they raved in drunken joy. The enchanted land which they beheld bound them in a spell, like the haze of some fair evening in high summer.

But most remarkable of all—there was to be a state out here; these vast prairies were actually to become an indissoluble part of the Union itself! And the capital might come to be located right at one's very door! In any event it could not be placed farther west then Pierre. People hereabout were betting on Huron; and several predicted

Sioux Falls. . . . Well, they'd take a chance on that.
They would now be admitted to statehood, so much was
certain. . . . Then they would be as good as the rest of
them. . . . Just you wait, boys, and see!

It got to be a little late before Beret Holm with her
family reached the schoolhouse. A welter of horses and
vehicles outside. A houseful of men within. A curious
scene indeed: Two heavily clad, bewhiskered men jammed
into each seat; a stockade of young people along the
walls; tightly packed rows of people in the aisles; some
sat insecurely on the corner of a desk; here and there a
man who had been so fortunate as to secure a seat stuck
out a knee, laughed up into the nearest face, with the
result that the other accepted the offer and sat down.

Obviously the women had paid little attention to Miss
Mahon's invitation, except for a few of the roving kind
who take to their wings as soon as they sense excitement.
There was not an elderly woman to be seen in the whole
crowd.

Beret Holm stepped into the packed room, caught the
full force of it instantly, and stood dazed. . . . This is
no place for me! . . . All eyes and faces seemed to agree
with her; she saw smiles which questioned, wonderings
which demanded answers; faces leaned toward each other
and whispered.

But Miss Mahon came floating across the floor and
took charge of her. She beamed so benignantly that Beret
was more embarrassed by her than by all the rest. Miss
Mahon led her up to the front seat in the middle row, and
said to the man who sat there: "Let this lady sit down
here, please"; and then to Beret: "I'm so glad you left
your work and came—I don't think we women are more
stupid than the men!" Beret sank down on the edge of
the seat, beside a strange man. He nodded and smiled
good-naturedly at her, cast a triumphant look to the other
side as much as to say: Here sit I, fellows, the only
favored among men.

Miss Mahon tripped nervously about in the little space
up in front still unoccupied; she smiled graciously to faces
she knew, talked now and then to a tall and very handsome man, who everyone could see was a stranger, and to
Michael Doheny, standing beside him.

Presently she tripped up onto the platform, turned to the assembly, which immediately settled down expectantly, and cleared her throat ever so slightly; her left hand toyed with her gold chain. In a voice trembling with emotion she bade them all welcome to her school. A very great honor, indeed, for her to have the whole district assembled here tonight. But she was absolutely convinced, she went on, that if the beautiful promises which the future held out to this land were to be realized, the school must play its part in the realization. For the public school was the bulwark and the guardian of the nation—the throbbing heart from which its lifeblood was to flow. Nay, she would put it even stronger than that: The school was the hearth of the nation; the place from which everything great and beautiful must come. She had come to the Territory this fall, from an old and well-established community in the East; with their kind permission she would now like to give them a glimpse of what she was endeavoring to do for them. Her face was radiating goodness and romantic schoolma'am emotion—she knew she had made a beautiful speech! . . . She beckoned Charley to come forward.

The boy edged his way out of one of the rows and stepped reluctantly up on the platform. Smiling affectionately upon him she put her hand on his shoulder, and let it lie there while she whispered something into his ear. His shirt collar wasn't just right, it seemed, one corner of it having turned itself up, but fortunately she discovered the irregularity and straightened it out for him. After giving him a motherly pat she stepped down and took a place beside those in front, from which vantage point she could watch her boy.

No sooner did Charley have the platform to himself, than he dashed into the Declaration of Independence and began reeling it off furiously. The boy was so boiling mad that he would have flown in the face of the first person who dared to come near him—here she had been pawing him all over with the whole settlement looking on! When he finally came to the last paragraph and was sure of reaching the end he let himself go completely; the words poured out of his mouth in a torrent; the classic sentences vibrated under the speed which he gave them. Just as he was finishing he cast his eyes to the floor, half in anger, and half in shame, and in the instant saw the two words at the end of the piece in the book: "John Hancock." On the floor in front of him lay a wad of paper which someone had rolled up and thrown there before the audience had quieted itself—that, too, he saw, and giving it a mighty kick, sent the two words flying after: *John Hancock!* The audience applauded violently; several laughed; a couple of young fellows yelled *hurray*; But Miss Mahon, much moved by the praise her boy had won both for himself and for her too, wiped the tears from her eyes. Then she looked about for Peder and motioned to him to come up!—

Once more she stepped up on the rostrum and made a little speech. . . . Now they were about to hear the most beautiful words which God had ever put into the mouth of an American citizen—the words of none other than *Abraham Lincoln* himself. . . . These were indeed momentous days. It was her fervent prayer that his beautiful thoughts might sink deep into every heart!

As soon as they had come in Peder had hidden himself in the crowd by the left wall. A peculiar tremor was making him uneasy tonight. Mother was here! Suddenly, he had to look to where she sat. . . . Mother in this place! The incredible had actually happened—she had stepped out of her own world and had accompanied him into his. There she was sitting beside Pat Murphy, just as though she, too, belonged here. And the sky wasn't falling because of it! . . . He stole a glance at the audience, and a feeling of awe came upon him. The extreme nearness of the great crowd almost took his breath away; he fell into the rhythm of its heavy breathing. He was aware of how furiously his heart pounded, and had to look about to see if others could hear it. Over in the row to the right, a freckled, brown face, full of laughter, peered out from behind the shoulder of a tall man. He had seen it there after he came in. Well, he had better not look in that direction again—not for a while, at least.

Peder heard Charley speaking and forgot himself—what was the matter with Charley tonight? Was he angry? He certainly was going much too fast! A feeling of self-confidence came over Peder—he knew he could give his piece better than that.

Miss Mahon was on the platform waiting for him.

With him, too, she found something wrong and had to whisper in his ear.

What it was he never heard, for a living monster confronted him; all those questioning eyes, glowing in the half-dark, suddenly overwhelmed him. Mother—where was Mother? There, directly in front of him, she sat. He caught her face at a glance, and beheld in it a stranger he had never seen before. Her eyes, wide and kind, had a solemn look, as if she were praying; her sadness, which once earlier in the evening had undone him, encircled her face, as the frame a picture. Now he would show her how beautiful his world really was!

"*Four score and seven years ago,*" he began joyously. The words struck home, he felt; their echo came back to him, just as when he leaned over the edge of the well at home and dropped pebbles down—a deep, reverberating sound, full of many secrets. A little below him was his mother's face, her eyes so lucent that he seemed to see far into them. He did not know her like this. And so, with intense earnestness, he spoke Lincoln's words to her. He dared not encounter the look of the monster in front of him, for it lay there ready to pounce upon him; Mother alone was to hear how beautiful it was. When he came to

But in a larger sense we cannot dedicate, we cannot consecrate, we cannot hallow this ground

he had reached that part of the speech which he liked best of all, and straightway forgot the monster threatening him. He looked out upon the crowd and felt no fear whatsoever . . . only a warm, throbbing joy, filling him with a peculiar power, remained. The faces before him met his with kindness, wishing him only well; and so he launched into the last portion of the speech with such passionate fervor that the crowd sat spellbound:

that this nation, under God, shall have a new birth of freedom; and that government of the people, by the people, for the people shall not perish from the earth.

Peder came down amid a roar of applause, but was scarcely aware of it. A strange weariness came over him; his knees shook—he wished he could have gone home now!

. . . He found himself on the side of the room he had come from, and so near the front that he could see his mother's face. Her eyes met his instantly. She seemed disturbed yet happy, as one who doesn't know whether to laugh or to cry, her whole face asking plainly: What is this anyway, Permand? . . . Did he see tears in her eyes? What could be the trouble . . . now that all was just as it ought to be? . . . But suddenly there were other matters to think about—the meeting began in real earnest.

VII

The crowd sat waiting for the fun it had come to enjoy. The moment quiet prevailed Michael Doheny stepped up on the platform and said facetiously that since one of his own family had already in so thorough and so orthodox a fashion explained to them exactly how they must conduct themselves both for the present and in the future, there remained nothing for him to do but go home and go to bed. Which was a bit provoking to him, inasmuch as he had made a special trip to Sioux Falls today in order to provide entertainment for them. Here sat Senator McGregor fairly burning up with a desire to talk to them. If there was anyone in the audience who wanted to leave without hearing him, he had better go right now! . . . As soon as the applause had died down he introduced the Senator.

As Senator McGregor mounted the platform a voice called out loudly from the back of the room, "There, boys, you see the fellow who is to be the first real governor of Dakota—take a look at him!" Rounds of hand-clapping and stamping of feet greeted the prophecy.

McGregor, handsome and well-groomed, seemed to be enjoying himself as he stood there looking into the expectant faces in front of him, a serene self-confidence emanating from his person, his face radiating intelligence. Then he began speaking, in a jocular vein at first.

—The proposal about going home and going to bed was not a bad idea at all. In fact, he felt strongly inclined to second the motion; nothing would suit him better than to draw the covers well up over his ears and go to sleep.

But to be able to do so one must have quiet and peace round about. Just at present things of such great historic consequence were taking place here, that it was difficult for anyone wanting to keep abreast of them to get rest, either by dark or by dawn; he himself at times found it necessary to get up in the middle of the night to ascertain what was happening.

"Yessiree, there you said it!" several voices broke in.

—But once, he continued, they had settled everything and had got the whole machinery running smoothly, they'd have plenty of time for resting, provided, of course, any of them were still alive! . . . First of all he would like to thank the two boys who tonight had read the articles of faith to them, and not least her who had taught them to speak the selections so beautifully—the Senator bowed graciously to Miss Mahon. By listening to the boys he had been inspired by the hope that the great work which the older generation had worn themselves out in carrying forward would be taken up and brought to completion by the younger. They certainly had the stuff in them!

Thereupon he turned to the speech he had come to make. Nonchalantly and easily he flung ideas into the face of the crowd; the clarity and the good-natured humor with which he spoke made his reasoning take hold of the mind and stick there.

During the course of his address he argued in favor of two points: They must now stand shoulder to shoulder and insist that the Territory be divided. Second, Dakota must be admitted to the Union at the next session of Congress. Until these two things had been accomplished, no man would be master in his own house—they realized that, of course. For as long as their officers were appointed from Washington, they themselves having nothing to say about it but to accept and be grateful, they would have to put up with what they got, even though it be ever so scabby a sheep!

But could one really call that liberty? Was that Jefferson's conception of it? Was it what Lincoln had meant by government *of* the people, *by* the people, *for* the people? Most certainly not! Guardianship, no matter how well exercised, could never be freedom! . . . The room thundered approval. Yet here and there glowered a face, saying

plainly: Just wait till you've finished, then we will talk
some more about this division business. . . . As soon as
the volley had subsided, he went on:

—He knew that some opposition to division still persisted out here. Nothing to be done about that, for there
would always be those who did not understand their own
best interests. There were, for example, people whom it
was simply impossible to get into heaven, even though
St. Peter himself stood holding the gate wide open for
them, and beckoning until his arm fell off! . . . And why
were they opposed to division? Because they feared higher
taxes. They figured that obviously it would be cheaper for
two men to own one pair of trousers between them, than
for each to have his own pair. Perhaps that was sound
calculation. But in that case why not only one pair of
boots and one wife? That would undeniably be cheaper.
But pity the poor woman; he reckoned she would have a
tough time of it. . . . No, he asserted emphatically,
those who agitated against division had no vision at all
of the future that lay before the country in which they
were living. When the day came that land cultivation out
here on these great prairies began to approach the high-
water mark, and they had a government of their own,
chosen by the people and responsible directly to them,
taxes would be lower than they were at present, and their
ability to bear them manifoldly increased!

Angry mutterings of protest from a couple of places
down in the audience greeted the assertion. But McGregor
only smiled affably and continued: They did understand,
did they not, that Dakota Territory was much too vast an
empire for only one state? Almighty Providence had hidden
this portion of the world away from man until he should
have made such progress in enlightenment, and in the
knowledge of self-government and brotherhood, that he
could make use of, to the fullest, the great opportunities
that here lay awaiting him. Was there really anyone in this
audience who doubted that Dakota Territory was destined
to be the largest and most productive grain country in the
world? Nothing less did the radiant dawn now gilding
these prairies betoken. But did they not realize at the same
time, that this mighty empire with its many special interests needed all the representation in Washington which it
could get? There was the South with its cotton standing

solidly together as one man. And there was the East with
its industry and commerce, its many states, too, uniting on
all great common interests. And now came the Middle
West, more important than either of the other two, with
interests entirely different—what would happen to it?
If the whole Territory was made one state, it would
have only two senators in Washington; if it became two
states, it would have four! Did they not comprehend what
that meant whenever vital issues came up? It had been
estimated that in time probably 6,000,000 people would
be living out here; some predicted even more; and these
6,000,000 were to have only two seats in the Senate! But
Rhode Island with its handful also had two; out here
under these wide heavens one could tuck away a hundred
Rhode Islands so easily that not one of them would know
where the others lay. Yet had any one heard that Rhode
Island considered uniting with Massachusetts or Connecti-
cut on account of the taxes? Oh no, no American would
sell his birthright for so paltry a price! That would be to
renounce the very principle upon which this country had
been built. . . .

Senator McGregor concluded by proposing a resolution
to the legislature, to the effect that immediately upon
convening next month, it should send a delegation to
Bismarck for the purpose of trying to induce the Ter-
ritorial Legislature up there to make division its main
issue. He added, laughingly, that if they tugged hard
enough at both ends, there would have to be a split somewhere! What portion was admitted to the Union first
didn't affect his conscience in any way. But to be master
on his own premises, and to know that his neighbor was
as free as he himself, were matters which concerned him
vitally—not until all that had been brought about could
he afford to go home and sleep!

No sooner had McGregor left the platform than the
crowd was in a furor of excitement. The resolution was
now to be discussed and then voted upon. All knew that
several of those present were fanatically opposed to division
—the real fun was about to begin!

The moment Doheny had taken the chair three men
jumped up demanding the floor. People craned their necks
in order to see and hear better; the two rows swayed like
an alley of trees in a storm.

The most impatient of the three was an old square-shouldered man, badly crippled with rheumatism; his bristling whiskers, which once upon a time had been red, had long since been whitened by the years. Without waiting to be recognized by the chairman, he thrust both his thumbs inside his trouser band and burst out in such righteous indignation at the government in Washington that everyone had to laugh. Doheny saw no way of silencing the man and so had to let him go on; but Miss Mahon sat burning with mortification because of the awful English he used. The man who had taken the floor was old Syvert Tönseten.

—Well, division or no division was all the same to him. The Lord had certainly given them enough land to make two or even four states! . . . As if to demonstrate the fact Tönseten's right hand let go of the trouser band and described an arc in the air. . . . Not that he objected to trying out this business of one wife and one pair of pants. He remembered the time when he couldn't afford even that much. They ought to have been here in the grasshopper days when people sat sucking their thumbs for something to eat, and patching the only pair of pants they owned! Nowadays it was easy enough to talk big and brag about both pants and wives! . . . Well, he didn't intend to make any speech this evening; plenty here who were sick to talk! But he did have a question which he'd like someone to answer for him: Why the deuce had they got nowhere at Washington? They had tried one wife, coaxed and fooled in all sorts of ways, and still were as stuck as ever. Now for some time they had been trying to get two wives, and the thing looked as confoundedly hopeless as when they began! He would therefore propose to the legislature that they get their dander up and try getting along without either wife or pants and see what they would look like! . . . He would also like to ask McGregor, who had been to Washington, what the devil they were monkeying with down there, and why they couldn't get anywhere. They had been back and forth with this division question for as long as he could remember; they had had meetings and held conventions, and so help him, hadn't they turned the world topsy-turvy; and still, they were no further than the a, b, c's! Tönseten grew more excited and his voice more angry as he went on:

They had discovered this kingdom without the aid of either preacher or policeman; they had settled here, a self-governing people; they had cultivated millions of acres of wilderness; they had built churches and schools; they had elected officers and set things going so that all ran as fine as any clock. But—and here he touched on what remained a mystery to him—when they went to Washington and offered Uncle Sam the whole business on a silver platter, he simply flapped his coattails and didn't know whether to answer yes or no; he must be terribly old and muddleheaded, poor fellow! . . . As for him, he was getting sick and tired of everlastingly courting and never getting a straightforward answer. Had they asked for a thing that the Constitution didn't give them a perfect right to? People out here were no longer children who had to have the minister's blessing before they could act for themselves! He would let them know that the Norwegians had ruled themselves a thousand years without asking either kaiser or pope which pants leg to pull on first, and he supposed that the same thing was just about true of the Irish too. He himself had been the first to venture into Canaan's land, the first one to put down his claim stakes! No one could blame him for wanting to see what was going to happen to these parts before he went to his grave. And so he proposed a resolution that they should not so much as mention this matter of statehood, not for a while at least! Had they not this fall elected both a governor and a legislature, and neither moon nor stars had fallen on that account? What they ought to do now was to continue managing their own affairs and not so much as say a word to Washington—let Old Coattails look at that move for a while!

Tönseten seemed to be greatly offended because the Territory hadn't been admitted to statehood long ago, and didn't care who knew it either. His face was red when he seated himself, but he looked pleased, for he knew he had told them the truth! . . . Some applauded violently; some stamped the floor, many laughed, and one called out to Tönseten to go on. . . . This was great fun—let's have more of it!

Peder's eyes had been riveted on Senator McGregor from the moment he began to speak until he left the platform. So absorbed had he been in what the man was saying that he had stared open-mouthed. Never had he heard such wonderful speaking! And this man had been in Washington; he had sat in the Senate and represented Dakota Territory; he had associated with the greatest people in the country, even though he lived down in Sioux Falls—next door, so to speak!

At first it was the personality of the man which had most fascinated Peder, his fine, elegant clothes, his easy, unembarrassed manner; he stood there as if he were playing an interesting game. And the way he could talk! Peder had actually seen the thoughts before they were uttered. There was nothing new in them except that they were clothed with the same elegance as McGregor himself. He had listened in rapt attention. Words and phrases which in Miss Mahon's mouth seemed so sugary sweet and sticky, had taken on a manly nobility that was perfection itself. That's how English sounds when spoken correctly! Involuntarily Peder's fists clenched; he vowed then and there that he would learn to speak English as beautifully as McGregor. Miss Mahon was right about all—he mustn't talk so much Norwegian at home, because, if he did, English could never be more than a foreign language to him. . . . Well, he knew what to do about that—hereafter he would talk no Norwegian except to his mother. That idea was soon forgotten because he had begun to repeat to himself certain of McGregor's expressions, trying them again and again until he was satisfied that he could say them just right. He was brought to with a start by a man's nudging him in the side and whispering:

"Are you going to make another speech?" Ashamed of himself, he moved away immediately.

Then Tönseten had begun speaking and Peder simply couldn't look up, for it sounded so terrible; every other word mispronounced; the sentences topsy-turvy; the grammar all wrong. Peder fell to wondering if all the Norwegians talked English so wretchedly. . . . No, he didn't think so. Anna Marie really spoke it very well.

Tönseten stood down in the crowd while he talked. All in front of him turned his way in order to see him. Peder, standing on the same side of the room as Tönseten, felt so annoyed by all the eyes coming his way, that he dared scarcely lift his own. But in a certain place in the aisle opposite was a pair of eyes that would not leave him alone.

That's Susie, he thought, and colored furiously. How could he return her look with the wall of faces confronting him? . . . Suddenly raising his eyes he let them wander in her direction just for an instant in order to make sure that it was she. As his eyes reached the spot, Susie, with perfect naturalness, turned her head away, as though she hadn't been looking at him at all. That trick of hers struck Peder as being very clever; it made him smile—he simply could not help himself. A feeling of warm happiness filled him; he quite forgot Tönseten and the faces. . . . Now that she was looking in another direction, he supposed it would be safe for him to steal over to her for a moment—he had to keep his eyes somewhere! If she should come back, he'd get away in time, all right. The dim light in the room softened the brownness of her complexion. . . . She had on another dress, he noticed; this one had lace around the neck; her cheek curved delicately about the lace. Peder had to look twice at that cheek; it had touched his own only a while ago; then it had been so warm and downy, and so frightened! He should have liked to tell her that he hadn't meant to do her any harm. . . . His eyes had an eager look. He saw she was getting uneasy; she shifted to the other foot and pretended to be listening hard to Tönseten's speech. Did she really sense that he was looking at her, and dared not meet him? How strange! . . . He fixed his eyes on her, and putting his whole soul into the act, stared intently. . . . Aha, she was shifting back to the other foot! Suddenly she turned her head and looked up; he got away just in time. . . . Then he hit upon a very ingenious scheme: He began letting his eyes wander from one person to another, casually, as if he were tired of listening; coming close enough to see her through the corner of one eye he glanced down while he passed, and then opened up to catch her in the corner of the other. There he held her for a while. . . . Now she was looking straight at him, and that look he had to return, smiling broadly as he hurried on to Tönseten. . . . After a little he faced her squarely, his eyes down, his heart thumping madly—this was almost as hard as holding one's breath. . . . Now I won't look at her, he decided, until Tönseten finishes; then I'll risk it, because then there is certain to be great commotion and nobody will see me. Just as he was reaching the decision, she coughed; he detected plainly that she coughed on purpose; but that she should think of doing it at this moment struck him as being so clever that he had to find out what she was up to. There she was standing in the half-dark aisle waiting for him, her soft brown eyes sparkling with merriment. Why can't you leave me alone? they asked teasingly. . . . It's you who won't leave *me* alone! he answered in open innocence. She seemed to concede the point, for smiling, she tossed her head and wandered back to Tönseten. . . . What was she fooling with anyway—now that everything was so jolly? . . . He had a lot of things he would have liked to tell her!

In the general stir which followed he lost her entirely. Tönseten, finishing his speech, sat down; the farther row swayed; Dennis Gilligan took one step forward and to the side, thereby hiding Susie from him. Peder couldn't catch her eye again and didn't have time to try either, for he became very much absorbed in what was going on.

A very tall, light-complexioned man made his way to the front of the room; without stepping up on the platform the man turned toward the audience, rested one elbow on the edge of the desk and crossed his left leg over his right; there was an indefinable twinkle in his eye. Slowly and deliberately, he began picking his way among many ideas, getting on only by stops and starts; at times he almost gave the impression of talking to himself.

The man was Gjermund Dahl. He had the reputation of being one of the most sensible men in the settlement, had been a member of the Constitutional Convention two years ago and again this fall, and was, moreover, at present holding many positions of trust.

"Let's look at these calculations of the Senator's," Gjermund began, making a long pause as if he were scrutinizing them himself. . . . They had been told that it wouldn't cost more to have two states rather than one. Well—he wondered about that. Did the calculation sound reasonable to them? . . . Two legislatures? Two governors? Two sets of judiciary officers? Two departments of education? Everything doubled—and the cost would remain the same? . . . If a man could now go to Sioux Falls and get two portions of everything at the price of one, he would want to go down tonight, and he'd say that Sioux Falls ought to become the capital of Dakota!

Gjermund took his elbow off the desk and straightened himself ever so little, a faint smile playing upon his face. He continued asking questions, short ones, each followed by a quick projecting of the lower lip; each question threw a greater clarity upon the whole problem, like a light moving along a row of faces. Perhaps McGregor had slipped in his figuring? That sometimes happened to politicians! As a matter of fact, the cost would actually be doubled. . . . And the gain? They might stop to consider that a moment. . . . Four senators in Washington instead of two—how much gained? Well, two more chances for office seekers. Gjermund could see no more. If these four were to stand alone against the conservative democratic South as well as against the industrially dominated East, the situation would be pretty hopeless for the four. . . . Even though they divided the Territory into ten states, they would still be helpless against the two other groups. . . . Perhaps they ought to take the time to look yet more closely at the Senator's calculations:

—Suppose now that they did make two states and did get two senators for each. Was there anything to guarantee that these four would always stand together? Or was it reasonable to suppose that there might be rivalry between the two states? Gjermund wondered if perhaps there might not have been some miscalculation here too. . . . On the other hand, if it were true that Dakota Territory was destined to become the richest grain country in the world—really a beautiful idea, he liked to believe in it —then it was hardly reasonable that either the South or the East could afford to destroy such an empire. Didn't they agree with him? Wouldn't the opposite be more likely to happen? For he was willing to eat snuff that, no matter whether people labored with cotton, or dug in mines, or sold shirts, they'd all have to have *bread!* Wasn't that true? Who then would try to destroy things for them? . . . No! Rather than to carve that which in itself was magnificent into pieces, they ought to build it stronger, for only then would the great be really beautiful! . . .

—By a wise Destiny the Territory had come to be occupied throughout by people of like race, Irish, Germans, Scandinavians—all cousins, so to speak. And it had the same kind of agriculture from one end of it to the other. One people; the same interests; common aspirations. . . .

This empire they would now carve up for the sake of providing more chances for politicians! What—would they take a fine watch to pieces and barter away its parts? . . . Gjermund raised himself to his full height, and now for the first time one saw how tall the man really was. . . . No, he continued calmly, he had a resolution to propose which had some sense in it: They should ask the legislature to send a delegation to Bismarck to try to effect an agreement with the people up there to have only one state —which he still thought possible since they had not drifted so far apart but that they could be brought together again.

Gjermund had not reached his seat before the crowd was in a turmoil. The heated agitation for and against division which had been going on for nearly five years, had made people's minds so touchy that the slightest spark struck fire. Three resolutions were before the house, or rather two, for no one paid any attention to Tönseten's except himself; it was about the other two that the controversy raged. It soon became evident, however, that McGregor's had the most adherents, which fact was offset to some extent by the recklessness and the fearless courage of the anti-divisionists, as they were called. When Michael Doheny thought it was getting so late that they'd have to adjourn, the vote was taken, and the first resolution received 47 votes, the second only 12. Gjermund Dahl then rose and flung a threat at the crowd—next Saturday night the anti-divisionists would hold a meeting in Tallaksen's Schoolhouse and would there agree upon a resolution with some sense in it!

VIII

At length the meeting broke up. Hubbub followed, a pushing, noisy milling confusion; people gathered in small groups; here and there the sound of angry words rose above the din.

Charley elbowed his way through the crowd until he reached Peder's side; Susie, seeing her brother there, joined them. Here the three, caught in the jam, were shoved back and forth by the moving crowd, and pressed so close together that they couldn't even talk; but it was all such great fun that they laughed heartily.

Peder's hand touched Susie's, though he hadn't intended that it should. Thinking that he ought to beg her pardon, he grasped it; it felt very warm, and so small that he was immediately seized with a desire to hide it within his own big one. There the hand lay and made no effort to free itself. The longer he held it the softer and more pleasant it felt, and the more meaning he could put into his clasp.

Suddenly Peder made a discovery so astonishing that he stared in open-mouthed wonder: Catching her eyes at a certain slant, he observed—would you believe it?—that they changed color. They were not brown at all, as he had thought, but blue, deep blue. And how they sparkled! On their surface floated a few brown specks, adrift, like dainty clouds on a serene evening sky. Peder was so taken with the marvel that he was about to exclaim, "Look here, are you trying to fool me?" But then she laughed and remarked that he was a good speaker. The blue lying underneath the brown shone so brightly as she spoke that he burst into a hearty laugh—only this time he looked at Charley!

The press around them became terrific, some forcing their way through the throng in order to get out, others returning to join those still arguing. And then who should come but Miss Mahon! The crowd fell back like furrows to let her through. She made straight for the boys and hauled them up in front. What—were her two boys going to leave without shaking hands with the Senator? Oh, how proud she was of them tonight! She took them in tow through the crowd, and presented them to McGregor. The fine, distinguished-looking gentleman talked to them exactly as if they were grown-ups and in every respect his equals. Two such bright boys would certainly make a name for themselves in the state of Dakota. How fortunate for them that they could begin where its history began! This empire their own fathers had discovered and founded, and now it remained for just such boys as they to build it up!—Senator McGregor made the boys a real speech, saying it all so beautifully, and looking so handsome that Miss Mahon had tears in her eyes. Oh, the great things in life, how glorious they were!

In some way or other Peder, dazed, made his way out to the wagon and climbed in. Ole drove; the mother sat beside him; Store-Hans stood in the wagon box holding

on to the back of the seat. Peder had the whole back part
of the wagon to himself—tonight he didn't need support.
Just as a vessel, filled to the brim, spills over at the slightest
jolt, so Peder had to give vent to all the wonderful feelings
within him. He began a tune, hummed it in sheer ecstasy,
wholly unconscious of what he was doing. Over in the
eastern sky stood a big star blinking glints of gold right
into his eye. Every time the wagon hove over some bump
in the road he thrust his arms out—not to steady himself,
to be sure, for that he did not need, but as if to fly; his
body felt so eerily light and it was such fun to try with
his arms!

His mother's voice brought him to: "Must you sing at
this hour of the night?" Not until then did he know that
he had uttered a sound. Sensing her displeasure, he
stopped at once.

An easy matter for him to be obedient now. He would
be willing to do anything they asked him to, no matter
how unreasonable it might be. But he should have liked
to sing out with his whole soul! Had he only been alone
he would have flung joyous song against the sky just to
hear it ring in the blue vault up there. . . . Peder broke
into a laugh—there wasn't any vault! Miss Mahon had
said so the other day. At the time he had been puzzled
by the statement and had sat a long time wondering about
it because he could not figure it out: Nothing at all but
golden pinheads from here to—to—to *where?* How he
would like to find out what was beyond—beyond—yes,
beyond where the end was. Well—but—there was no end.
Peder peered in among the stars and chuckled to himself:
Man alive, it must be fun to be grown up!

That night Beret Holm spent another of her sleepless
nights. They had reached home at about eleven o'clock;
the boys had put up the horses and had gone upstairs immediately. They had quarreled out in the yard, and they
had no sooner reached their room than they broke out
again. Peder's voice, youthful, and as yet too thin when it
became high-pitched with excitement, could be heard
above the heavier voices of his brothers. Wanting to find
out what the trouble was, Beret went over to the stairs, listening. Only this everlasting politics again! It sounded as if

both of the older boys agreed with Gjermund, and that Peder was trying to convince them of their error; he had to talk fast—hence the shrillness of his voice. An emphatic *shut-your-mouth* and *go-on* and *go-to-bed* from Store-Hans finally brought silence upstairs. She noticed the boys were talking English again. . . . Getting to be a good deal of that about the house now!

Beret busied herself about various tasks in the kitchen. There was the oatmeal to be got ready for breakfast; she might as well set the table at the same time. They needed to be in the cornfield early tomorrow, for winter would soon be upon them. She wondered if there was a large enough supply of whole mitts. Taking a great heap of them from a basket she sat down near the lamp to mend. All she had lived through during the evening came and stood by her, demanding reconsideration. Once she had begun looking at it, there came other matters as well. . . .

Beret had sat in the schoolroom and listened to all that was being said. Most of it had passed her by as unintelligible sound; the questions were of no concern to her; their content she knew from before. What it was all about she had, moreover, seen in the countenances of those who spoke; the air was full of it; she sensed it in the mood of the crowd. And people talked nothing but politics these days. She marveled that they could get worked up over such unimportant affairs; whether there were two states or one would hardly make life any easier.

. . . And there was Permand, yes, Permand—what a boy! . . . He had talked to a room packed full of people . . . beautifully as if he had done nothing else in his life! . . . She had felt how completely he lost himself in what he was doing, how intensely he had been absorbed in it, and it had made her happy, in a way. Yet, uneasy. . . . What one really gives himself up to is sure to take him. . . . Her hand began to tremble; never could she get him so interested in anything. . . . Were strange forces at work, conspiring to lure him away from her? She had feared it all last year and especially this fall after he had started school. . . . Now she knew it unmistakably! . . . As she sat thus pondering the seriousness in her mood deepened; her features became swollen like a vein when stemmed.

Something which had angered her had happened at the

schoolhouse. Now it came drifting into her reflections, making her hands shake so violently that she had to rest them on her work. Most of the people had gone, the boys were outside hitching up the horses, she had put on her coat and was waiting. Meanwhile this silly thing of a teacher, coming up and sitting down beside her, had put both her hands on Beret's knee, thrust her face close to hers, and begun to talk with such intimacy that Beret had not known what to do with herself for sheer embarrassment. And it was all about Peder—about how bright he was, what wonderful talents he had, and how proud they could both be of him. She too felt a mother's interest in him, she assured Beret. Hadn't he spoken well tonight? She *must* send him to college, without question—for he was destined to do something great. Oh, what a privilege it was for a teacher to have some pupils entrusted to her care! . . . Making herself still sweeter, she lowered her voice: She had something very confidential to say about Peder, and now Beret, as his mother, must try to help him out of the difficulty. It was this, that Peder spoke English with a foreign accent. He must by all means get rid of that accent! It would be a calamity for an American, especially for one which such rare talents, not to be able to speak perfect English! If he didn't get rid of his foreignism now, it might stay with him for life. . . . Finally, Beret had become disgusted at the honeyed maternal solicitude of this total stranger. Some of it she had understood, some of it not. She had arisen and said, in broken English, that she considered it more important that the boy should learn to understand his own mother than that he should learn to talk nice! If Store-Hans hadn't happened to come in at that moment, announcing that they were ready to leave, she didn't know what terrible things she would have said.

Beret picked up a mitt and fitted a patch to it. . . . The mitt was hardly worth mending, was it? Removing the patch she looked at the hole. . . . A terrible misfortune that they should have come to belong to the school district west of the creek. . . . How could the authorities act so senselessly? . . . Here they had mixed people as though they were of no more consequence than the swill they slopped together for their pigs. . . . No one need tell

her that such government was instituted by God. . . .
Oh no—it was man who ruled here. The Lord did not have
much to say!

Beside the clock hung an enlarged picture of Beret's
deceased husband, its massive frame draped with black
crêpe. The original had been taken during the market fair
the year previous to their leaving Norway. Per Hansa must
have been in a jolly mood at the sitting, for when the
light fell on the picture from a certain angle, he seemed
to be laughing. Beret did tonight what she had often
done before when she could see no way out of her difficulties: She looked up at the picture as if to ask her husband's advice.

. . . Permand didn't talk nice enough? Huh . . . and
so his own mother must make herself ridiculous by trying
to use a language which would always be foreign to her,
in order that he might speak better English! . . . She
heard only English all day long; the children would speak
nothing else among themselves. . . . There isn't very
much left of us now, she told the picture. Soon we can't
even talk! . . .

The face up in the shadows seemed to smile at her and
to ask what all this nonsense was about, anyway. . . .
The hour was long past midnight. Beret continued to
mend.

Every day, both forenoon and afternoon, Beret helped
with the husking. During the morning she husked with
Store-Hans, since it took him the longest to wake up; in
the afternoon she worked with Ole because he tired the
soonest, and would leave so much standing after him.
Thus she had a good opportunity to chat with each of the
boys separately.

The following morning the load was nearly half full before either she or Store-Hans spoke. He had gained considerable on her. Straightening to rest his back a little he
began examining his mitt. The mother glanced up for a
moment, and went on working.

"I believe I'm beating you today," he said, pulling on
his mitt.

"Looks that way."

Mother must be tired today, he thought, and husked

down her row until they met. When the wagon had got well into the corn again and they were working side by side, she asked:

"What do you think of that teacher?"

"I don't know what to make of her. Strikes me she isn't all there." He looked at the cob he had stripped, threw it into the wagon, and hastened to add, "They say, though, she's a good teacher. She certainly has taught Permand a lot."

Beret made no reply, and so Store-Hans resumed the conversation:

"Did you talk to her last night?"

"I did—and I'm afraid that things are going wrong over there."

"How so?"

"Oh, she has a notion that we talk too much Norwegian at home." Beret flung a cob. "Such nonsense can do a lot of harm to a youngster who isn't old enough to know better."

"Did she say that?" Store-Hans had stopped to examine his husking pin closely.

"Yes, she did."

"How do you suppose she found that out?"

Beret laughed, bitterly:

"She can tell it the way Permand speaks—just imagine! Fools do think up queer things!"

Store-Hans' face colored, he spoke sharply to the horses, telling them to move on. He had snapped off a cob, to which clung considerable husk; now he began stripping it, taking plenty of time. . . . He didn't wonder at all that she could tell it by their speech; that seemed likely enough. . . . And now gossip had a hold on that too—they couldn't talk English decently! "She said so, did she?" he repeated in a low voice, as he began husking again.

"That's what she did. . . . Do you know—I have been thinking that we'd better try to get the boy in at the Tallaksen School; it isn't right that he should be thrown in with all those Irish!"

"Well, no—but we are living in America!" said Store-Hans darkly, and began working hard.

The sun was already high in the heavens; the day promised to be warm for this season of the year; Beret removed the kerchief from her head and hung it on the wagon box. When she answered there was an unusual mildness in her voice:

"But we'll have to live like human beings for all that! . . . And now it seems to me we can hardly justify ourselves in letting this go any longer." The next cob she took hold of sat hard; she had to pause while she broke it off. . . . "You and I better go over after chore-time and see about it. I was thinking of it all night. . . . While the weather is nice he can ride horseback. Later he can stay at Johannes Mörstad's—they are kind folks, both he and she. . . . You will have to help me, Store-Hans." Her voice had become pleading and affectionate; it sounded as though she were trying to persuade a good friend to do something which she knew beforehand he was opposed to, but for which she must at all costs get his assistance.

"Then they'll have that, too, to gossip about all over the settlement!" protested Store-Hans; without looking at his mother he jerked out cob after cob and flung them into the wagon.

"Oh, we can stand that all right!" she said reassuringly. She looked at him but couldn't catch his face; for now he worked furiously, and was fast gaining on her.

The matter was not mentioned again that morning. But in the evening they drove over east to see about getting Peder in at the Tallaksen School.

IX

On the evening of the meeting in the schoolhouse, it so happened that John Bolgen occupied the front seat to the right. Because he was a quiet, reticent man, slow of thought, he had to examine carefully everything presenting itself to him. For that reason he was always just a little behind time, whether in speech or in action; people had often been disgusted with him and had fastened a nickname to him, calling him "Tag."

Tom Erickson shared the seat with him. The meeting had not yet begun; and John Bolgen, having exhausted all his resources for talk, sat there not knowing what to do with himself because he could find no more to say. But fortunately he discovered the book which Peder had intended to take home with him (it had lain right under his nose all the time) and was saved, for here was something to look at. Immediately he began reading, a few words here, a few there, and looking at the pictures. As he sat thus paging through the book he came upon the drawing which Peder had put there; taking the paper out and unfolding it, he studied it a long time, profoundly absorbed. That children should be doing such things in school caused him to forget his reticence. Nudging Tom in the ribs and thrusting the drawing in front of him, he asked him if he could explain what this meant. Tom knew enough American history to recognize the famous story about the cherry tree, and had to laugh heartily at George Washington standing there chopping away for dear life. He, too, thought it rather odd that the scholars should be set to making drawings of that nature, and handed the picture to Ole Hegg sitting in the seat just behind. Ole Hegg looked at the masterpiece awhile, and concluded that it might as well be passed on. From him it went from one to the other down the whole row, was looked at and commented upon; an Irishman in the back of the room exclaimed in a loud voice when the drawing reached him, "Sure and here you can see what it is these terrible Norwegians be up to!" After a while the picture came traveling up the next row, until it reached Pat Murphy; he caught himself just in time and didn't show it to Beret Holm, who sat beside him, for Pat was a kind-hearted soul and pitied the mother having a son so bad that he found pleasure in making pictures like that. Murphy handed the sheet of paper back to John Bolgen. John fingered it awhile, spread it out, then folded it together again; he thought a long time before he put it back into the book. But when the meeting was over and he was ready to go, he took the paper with him and placed it on the teacher's desk. An idea had dawned on him, gradually—school children ought not swear! There was enough sin and wickedness in the world anyway. . . . Others who had seen the picture were of the same opinion. Some even went farther: Mrs. Holm, pious as she always wanted to be, had better look after her own family, and they didn't in the least mind saying it.

In just about as beatific a state of mind as it is possible
for one to reach in this earthly existence Miss Mahon
went tripping along on her way to school the next morning. The low, indolent autumn day shed its benediction
upon her. High up in the haze sat the sun, lazy as could
be. The slight rustle of leaves in the dry cornfields along
the road sounded like a song to her.

This morning she had arisen in the exalted mood of
last evening. It was still upon her. The tremendous sig-
nificance of last night's meeting to the people out here,
she never so much as sensed. The firm purpose of strong
men, intently bent upon building a great future, had
passed her by entirely. The boys she herself had taught
had outdone themselves. Peder's English had not sounded
impossible—not at all; she'd get that foreign accent out of
him yet.

The picture of the boys was crowded out by another,
which took all her attention—a vision of Senator Mc-
Gregor standing before her very eyes. As her musings centered upon the distinguished gentleman who had talked to
her in so cultured a manner last night, her mood grew more
tender and caressing. He had held her hand a long time.
Actually fondled it! It was a soft, genteel hand. . . . In
an unguarded moment at breakfast she had betrayed herself by asking Mrs. Murphy if she knew whether Senator
McGregor was married. The question had made Mrs.
Murphy laugh long and heartily and Miss Mahon had
been compelled to join in. These country women were so
vulgar! Why shouldn't she wonder whether he was married? . . . It would—well, it would be nice if he were not!
The thought filled her with hope. She went along,
chuckling to herself. All of a sudden, seized with an impulse to divine the future, she began to count the but-
tons on her coat: Eni, meni, mini, moe. . . . Oh pshaw,
he was married! But one count could hardly be relied
upon. She counted again—and then he wasn't married at
all! Miss Mahon dared not risk a third count. For now
she knew exactly what to do: She would write the Senator
and ask him to lend her some books! He would readily
understand how little there was from which one could de-
rive inspiration out here in the wilderness, and how lonely
and unhappy she must be among these poor immigrants.
And then she would thank him for the many beautiful

thoughts he had given her last night. Such things could be so much more perfectly expressed in writing; she knew exactly how she would formulate her sentences. There would come a letter in return to which she'd have to reply; the exchange would go on; many letters would come—just like a beautiful romance!

She reached the schoolhouse and hung up her wraps, opened the window and set things in order. None of the scholars had arrived yet; she sat down at her desk to work out some difficult problems in the arithmetic lesson of the eighth grade. She sighed despairingly—oh, this horrid arithmetic!

On the desk lay a paper with a drawing on it; picking it up, she looked at it abstractedly, her thoughts far away. A smile broke over her face, only to die down instantly; her features took on a strange expression; her eyes became unnaturally bright, like glass; hectic spots leaped into her cheeks. She craned forward to examine the drawing closer. When at last she understood the awful truth fully, a rude hand struck out, demolishing mercilessly all her castles in the air. She burst into tears; great tempestuous sobs shook her; she was wounded, hysterical; all the beauty of life had been shattered wantonly—smashed to smithereens!

At first the shock paralyzed her. Then the revulsion set in; righteous indignation seized her, her features hardened; she jumped up, stamped the floor, clenched her hands convulsively. . . . Oh, the contemptible brat . . . the offspring of that immigrant woman! To think that he dared, that he dared to ridicule sacred things in her school! Getting down off the platform, she paced angrily back and forth across the floor:

. . . She ought to send for the officers of the law and have *them* take charge of him; but where were they to be found in these barbarian surroundings? No, she'd summon the School Board; oh, she'd lay the whole matter before them, she'd force them to act; she'd get him out of here, she'd not tolerate such a Benedict Arnold in her presence! She fumed and raged, but could think of no punishment severe enough for the heinous crime. . . . This was the blackest ingratitude . . . the depravity of a degenerate heart . . . plain rebellion . . . treachery . . . sedition, deadly sin! Oh, oh, oh! . . .

The children began coming but she scarcely noticed them. She sat down and she got up, went out and came in again; finally the clock passed the hour of nine, and so school had to begin today too.

Though not in the customary manner. They had always closed the day's work by the singing of "America"; today they began with it. But when they had got well into the third stanza the singing died out in an uncanny silence. One after the other had looked at the teacher, and stopped. At last the whole school was staring at her in terrified wonder. What could be the matter? Miss Mahon, having come to the third stanza, could bear it no longer. The thought that here stood a traitor singing this song in her school and in her presence, was too much for her. She took out her handkerchief; as soon as it touched her eyes, the floodgates burst open in real earnest. She turned toward the blackboard; great waves of crying threw her body into convulsions, her back arching like a bow. It was so painful to look at that some of the younger children began to cry hysterically; the others sat like statues in the unbearable silence which had settled upon the school.

Miss Mahon stood thus a long while. Then the sorrow seemed to subside, and she turned to face the room. Over on the far wall was a bare spot, the paint having flaked off; her eyes found it and rested there. Shortly, she began to talk, brokenly, pausing often:

—She was hurt . . . crushed. . . . There was only one thing for her to do—to resign and get away from here, to a place where no one knew her. . . . To be allowed to die quietly would be a great blessing. What had happened was too terrible for any human being to bear—such sorrow, such shame! . . .

Relieved by the confession and noticing how intently all were listening to her, she felt her strength return. Her eyes let go of the spot on the wall, to wander around among those occupying the back seats.

. . . Something terrible had happened here, she continued darkly, making a long pause which weighed heavily upon the pupils. Many sat thinking of things they wouldn't care to have announced in church. The toughest among the bigger boys wondered how much she really knew and where she could possibly have found it out.

Charley glanced at Peder. Had he tattled? He wasn't a bit better himself! . . . Peder stared hard at the wall—so, Susie had told on him last night! . . . Belle Flannagen, the biggest girl in the room, had had a letter from Mike O'Hara during recess yesterday, and it was about . . . Belle blushed hotly and put her hand to her bosom where her answer lay hidden safely. . . . Seven-year-old Arnold Solum cried as if his heart would break because he had sicked the dog on the cat last night. But most of them sat dumb, not thinking at all.

. . . The seed which had been sown in the hearts of the children, Miss Mahon went on, must indeed have been corrupt since it could bear fruits of wickedness thus early in life! If these things were allowed to flourish, her beloved land, the country which Washington had founded, and for whose defense Lincoln and her own father had died a martyr's death, would soon be transformed into a stinking slough of iniquity! Should such a catastrophe befall, darkness would again brood over the world and humanity be enslaved as before. It must not happen; it should never be permitted to happen as long as she and the great sisterhood of teachers throughout the country were able to stand guard! . . . Miss Mahon became strangely conscious of the beauty of what she was saying; all eyes were staring at her in terrified attention; and again she felt like the potter who can mold the clay in his hand as he wills—the thought gave her confidence and courage.

Her head moved until her eyes rested between the heads of two boys in the front seat to the right; letting it remain there, she raised her voice:

"And now, Peder Holm, I shall have a few words to say to you! You have betrayed your country! Oh, it is shameful—shameful, I say! You have ridiculed the Father of our Country by making a miserable clown of him, an object of contempt and scorn, you whose mother can't talk English so that people can understand her! In trying to help you I have nourished a viper at my breast, and this is how you reward me! The punishment you deserve, I, a frail woman, cannot administer, the authorities will have to do that, but such things shall not pass in my school; I'll not have your offense upon my head—take your history book and come forward!"

Peder sat petrified. Hot waves rushed to his face, flooded

his cheeks, then receded as quickly to give way to deathly pallor. He remained immovable as a statue.

"I command you to come!"

Peder did not move.

"Do you dare to defy me?" Her neat schoolma'am foot stamped the floor peremptorily.

Peder saw darkness floating before his eyes; within it raged a fearful monster threatening to tear him to pieces. And it had to happen! He stumbled out of his seat, stood still, put the back of his hand over his eyes to shield himself against the terrible thing he sensed coming.

"Take your book . . . you won't obey me . . . what?" Miss Mahon's body shot forward, the words hissing out of her mouth. Some of the smaller children cried aloud and dared not look on any longer.

One thing was clear to Peder: If he didn't obey immediately, she would be upon him in an instant. The thought flashed before him—now I must die! . . . He dragged himself back to his desk, took the book which lay there, then returned, and shutting his eyes, handed it to her. But no blow falling, he had to look up.

Miss Mahon ran down and grabbed a chair standing in the corner; placing it with its back to the blackboard, she stationed herself beside it. "There!" her hand pointing dramatically, "*Take that seat!* You are to memorize all about Washington, *everything*, I say! And from now on you will recite one portion every morning and one every evening. That shall be your punishment until I can turn you over to the law!"

Even before she had finished the last tirade Peder had scrambled to the platform and had sunk down on the chair.

Like a flash a new inspiration came to Miss Mahon; she lifted her head, carried away by the power within her; she looked out over the room, her eyes blazing, a gleam of white in them.

"In order that no one may accuse me of being unjust I shall now show you what this Benedict Arnold has done. Come forward, all of you!" She waited a moment, and feeling annoyed because she was not being obeyed quickly enough, she repeated sternly, "Come at once, I say!" Thereupon she snatched up the drawing, and with a pin fastened it to the blackboard molding directly above

Peder's head. Turning to face the scholars now gathered around the platform, she pointed to the picture:

"There you see what kind of thoughts this foreigner carries in his heart about him—him," it sounded as if she were about to choke, "about him who founded America!"

"Can you see it?" she asked, pointing to the words above the chip. "Mike O'Hara, say it!"

Mike, frightened, cleared his throat, and said "damn it!" But thinking he hadn't succeeded in saying it distinctly enough to suit her, furious as she was, he repeated it—this time so loudly that he felt sure she must be satisfied. Obviously Mike had satisfied her, for she cried out immediately: "What do you think of it? Doesn't it sound nice? That's the kind of language he puts into the mouth of George Washington, the beloved Father of our Country, across whose lips no unclean word ever passed—now judge for yourselves!"

Miss Mahon straightened herself up and stood like an outraged goddess of righteousness pronouncing sentence. Had the scholars that instant fallen upon Peder and torn him to pieces, she would only have felt thankful that justice had been meted out so expeditiously.

But that didn't happen at all. On the contrary something wholly different; suddenly, unexpectedly, it came, blinding like lightning, and throwing the whole school topsy-turvy, Miss Mahon along with the rest:

Down on the floor Charley Doheny was standing among the others. At her command he had risen with the rest, but had taken his time about coming forward. Now he broke through the group, jumped up on the platform, and began kicking at the chair on which Peder sat, yelling furiously:

"Get down from here!"

Without further ado he tore the picture from the wall and waved it menacingly at Miss Mahon, "This is *mine*, and it's none of your business, if you want to know it!"

With this berserker rage upon him he'd have to have more room or he'd bust. He glared wildly about. In front of the desk, the scholars, terrified, crowded into a knot; here sat Peder voiceless, half dead, with Miss Mahon, that old hen, heaping abuse upon him! Charley simply had to have more room. Grabbing hold of the chair and tipping it forward, he forced Peder to his feet. "Get down, I say!"

He gave the chair a mighty kick, which sent it flying down from the platform.

. . . "Charley Doheny!"

"Yes'm!"

"How dare you ——?"

"Dare?" He raised his arm to give her a whack, but at the sight of her, dropped it as quickly, his fury running off him like water off a duck's back. Why, there she was standing as helpless and bewildered as a wet hen! Instead of the blow, his curly head came threateningly near to her:

"Aren't we going to have school today?"

Without waiting for an answer Charley marched off to his seat and sat down; Peder followed; the others, seeing them leave, gathered their wits sufficiently to troop back to their places.

Miss Mahon sank down on her chair, her face buried in her crossed arms; she was again in a paroxysm of crying. The hour for the arithmetic lesson passed. The time for the reading period came. She got up, went out and was gone for some time. Upon her return they could detect nothing particularly wrong with her, except that her face was red and swollen.

X

About an hour before school time the following Monday morning Peder was down in the barn busily currying a gray mare which the boys used as a saddle horse whenever one of them had an errand to run. Today Peder did the currying with meticulous care. He worked with the mane until it fell like silk down over the neck. At last he seemed satisfied with the job. Leading the horse out he swung himself upon it and rode across the yard to the kitchen steps. There he stopped and waited for someone to bring him his lunch pail.

Today his mother brought it herself. But she didn't hand him the pail right away. Thrusting her hand under the horse's mane she patted the neck of the horse. The light, falling full on her face, revealed innumerable tiny wrinkles under her eyes. Peder thought she looked old and worn. She has something on her mind, he concluded. Eager to be off he reached for the pail.

She pretended not to notice it. Presently she said quietly: "Today I am very happy. I have prayed to God that this might happen. His ways are strange, but that is not for us to question." She let go of the mane and put her hand on Peder's knee; there were tears in her eyes, he noticed, her voice low and entreating: "I lay awake last night praying Him to be with you, now that you are to begin over there, and that I am certain He will. Here is your lunch," she said, handing him the pail. "Try to be a good boy now!"

Peder took the pail without answering. He dared not look at his mother. He felt heavy of heart as he rode down the yard. He would have liked to cry, but held back because he was a grown man; nevertheless he did have to wipe his eyes. Then he took heart—'twasn't everyone who could ride to school! He looked up into the day and laughed, struck his horse and rode faster. But the thought of the ridiculousness of his situation continued to disturb him.

Here he was off to *English* school among the *Norwegians* because Mother was afraid . . . well, just what did she fear might happen to him among the Irish? . . . Queer about Mother. At times she could see clearer than anyone else; there wasn't a thing she couldn't understand. Yet the world that was his and all the promise it held in store for him, its greatness and many wonders—she simply was not aware of its existence. How could it be possible? And his brothers hadn't put in a word for him this time . . . surely they must understand! Now people certainly would believe all the terrible things Miss Mahon had accused him of . . . when he ran away like this! . . . Charley and Susie would laugh and poke fun at him because he had to go to school among the Norwegians in order to become a Norwegian—he who couldn't talk English decently!

He crossed the creek at Tönseten's and struck off east on the four-mile stretch to the Tallaksen Schoolhouse. When a little better than halfway, he overtook a girl and a boy trudging along in the road. The boy he knew; he was Joseph Granem; the girl he took to be the sister; her name was Agnes.

Peder said *hello*; Joseph glanced up at him and returned the greeting. Peder thought he detected a grin on Joseph's

face; the girl walked along with her eyes fastened on the
road. Peder slackened the reins and asked in English:
"Going to school?"
"Yep." Nothing more from Joseph.
"So'm I." Peder affected an air of carefree confidence.
"To ours?"
"Yep!"
"Huh—that so?" . . .
Peder would have liked to join them; but both the boy
and the girl walked along and continued to stare at the
road, Joseph saying nothing, and his sister just as mum.
Their silence became embarrassing to Peder; he lashed his
horse and rode on. . . . He wasn't going to force his
company upon anyone!

When Peder reached Nils Rognaldsen's cornfield he was
forced to stop awhile. Nils was out husking; he had just
come to the end of the field and had driven his wagon out
into the road to turn. Seeing Peder coming, he seated himself on the wagon box to wait for him. Nils was a talkative
man, who never let an opportunity for a good gossip pass
by; moreover, it was almost time for the forenoon lunch
to be brought out and he needed to rest a little. He had
heard about the rumpus over in the Murphy School, and
when he recognized Peder, he thought he'd better find out
exactly what had happened. Rognaldsen was most inquisitive, asking all sorts of questions. Peder thought he detected a malicious joy in them. He wanted to get by, but
the wagon blocked the road. The man talked Norwegian,
too, which only made matters so much the worse for Peder,
because he couldn't answer just the way he wanted, nor
find the right words; besides, in Norwegian, the story
sounded so terrible.

. . . Oho—so that was the way it happened? Well,
well . . . why hadn't he got the boys together and strung
up the old hag? And why didn't the School Board chase
her out of the county? . . . Let's see—just what was it
she had called him? Benedict Arnold, eh? Well, who was
he? Oho . . . so . . . well, well! . . . But was it true
that Peder had told her to go to hell, and that she had
fainted, and that she had threatened to kill herself, and
that there was going to be a lawsuit? . . . That so? Well,
well, that was a terrible story, all right! . . . And now he
was on his way to their school? Well, he'd find something

different over here! That Nellie Quam she was a dandy, she was! . . . But what did his mother say? . . . You don't say? Well, well. . . . Were his brothers soon through with the corn? All the while Rognaldsen quizzed Peder, he sat picking kernels of corn out of a large cob. When he seemed satisfied he got up and drove his wagon into the field again.

Peder rode eastward, straight into the wide-spreading sun-filled day, scarcely seeing the road ahead of him. . . . A stranger had stripped him naked, and looked him over, then flayed him without mercy.

The road to Mörstad's ran right by the schoolhouse. Peder glanced up as he passed; the door was open; a group of girls stood in a knot on the porch; a few boys lolled along the wall on the sunny side. He took in the whole scene, and his spirits sank still lower. He whipped up the horse and whizzed by.

The Mörstad children had already gone when he reached the farm. He took his time about putting up the horse and giving it hay. That done, he went in and said good morning to Mrs. Mörstad, but didn't linger long because he knew she was the talkative kind—she might have questions to ask. The three-quarters of a mile back to the school he was in no hurry to cover; he didn't want to arrive until all should have gone in.

And he had figured right. When he reached the schoolhouse not a soul was to be seen outside. He walked into the entry and set his pail down. Then he debated a moment if he hadn't better put it in some other place, picked it up and moved it. He couldn't understand what made his knees so weak. He waited awhile before he rapped at the door.

A matronly-looking woman in a blue dress with white lace collar came to the door; her features were rather masculine; the expression in her deep-set gray eyes was one of cool composure. She knew him at once, it seemed.

"Oh—here you are! I began to fear that your mother had changed her mind. You aren't in the habit of coming late, I hope? That will not do here. Now we must hurry, the others are hard at work already." She spoke calmly, without effort; her voice was full and pleasant. She led him in as she talked.

"This is Peder Holm," she announced, presenting him to a whole roomful of staring eyes, some knowing, some questioning. A couple of the biggest boys grinned maliciously at him. "He got tired of the Irish and now he is going to try here," the teacher explained. She ushered him to the front desk in the center row. "Jim, you let him sit here with Nils, and we'll find another seat for you."— Then she turned to Peder again, "In this school we begin at the front and move back according to how well we get our lessons and how well we behave; we don't know you yet. Nils, you'll have to help him along for the present."

He found it hard to stand up against all the inquisitive eyes confronting him. Defiance flared up in him; he flung his head back, his brows knit—now look all you please! But try as he might, he was powerless against all this curiosity asking him, What do you want here? He turned pale and looked straight down.

A lanky gawk of a boy, fair-haired like himself, was occupying the left half of the seat in which Peder had been told to sit. The boy was cross-eyed. He squinted at Peder with one eye; there was appraisal in it: Can't say that I care much about having you here. Peder did not look at the face, but noticed how dirty one hand was at the wrist; not having seen him before he wondered where he came from.

Depressed and heart-sore Peder had dropped into the seat. He felt utterly sick and weary of everything. All the eyes back of him pricked his neck like pins. Directly in front of him hung the blackboard; at the top of it was written in a beautiful hand, "*This is an American school; in work and play alike we speak English only!*" He read the commandment twice; a feeling of shame came over him and he slunk even lower in his seat. He couldn't look to the side, because there were the eyes, watching for him; he tried to look straight ahead, but there were the words on the blackboard, which he didn't care to read a third time, and so he had to confine his eyes to the top of his desk and the dirty wrist of his seatmate. The other boy had a bad breath.

On the desk lay a few books. Mechanically, he picked up the top one and began turning the pages. It was a geography book containing many illustrations. After a while he came upon a picture which he had to look at more closely: that of a combat between a man and an infuriated bear. The beast already had both its front paws on the man's shoulder; but the man looked undaunted; in his hand he held a sheath-knife, his arm drawn back; in a moment the steel would be buried in the breast of the bear. The title of the paragraph accompanying the picture was the single word: *Norway.* Under the picture someone had written in pencil: "A Norskie." Slowly and deliberately Peder read the short paragraph about the land of his ancestors. Throughout the whole process of his education in the public school, this was the only information he ever got about the land from which his people had come. . . . His feeling of being ill increased. He closed the book and put it back. An idea which he found comfort in, took possession of him: When I am grown up I am going to go so far away that I'll never hear the word *Norwegian* again! He felt so sore of heart that he could have lain right down and bawled.

During recess he stayed inside and talked to the teacher. She had to find out to what grade he belonged, which books he had used, and how well he had done in the various subjects. And now that she had him all alone, it wouldn't hurt to ascertain just what had happened between him and Miss Mahon. She questioned him long and in detail. Peder found it easy enough to tell the story to her; her big, kind face met him understandingly. When he had finished she laughed and assured him that they would, no doubt, be good friends by and by, and thereupon assigned him his lessons. There were other things Peder would have liked to confide in her, but didn't quite dare—she might not understand.

After what seemed an interminably long time, the noon hour came. Peder, following the example of the rest, brought in his lunch pail and ate in his seat. And now it wasn't at all crowded; Nils had found another place to eat, which puzzled Peder. He kept thinking about it until it became difficult for him to swallow. . . . Nils wouldn't sit with him unless he had to; Joseph Granem hadn't cared to talk to him, wouldn't even have him in his company; the sister hadn't dared to look at him; and Rognaldsen had talked as if he were the blackest criminal on earth. . . . I s'pose people think I've done something terrible, he mused . . . and found it increasingly difficult to get the food down.

Most of them finished their eating in a hurry. As soon as one was through he took his pail and went out. All turned to look at Peder before leaving the room, most of them eyeing him curiously. At last it became so embarrassing that he pretended not to notice them as they passed.

Sounds of noisy merriment came in from the schoolground; individual voices could be heard above the din; laughter rippled loud and infectiously. Peder listened but couldn't hear the voices of the bigger boys. . . . If I stay inside, he concluded, they'll think I'm scared of 'em. They're back of the schoolhouse, talking about me. As soon as I come out I'll walk up to them and show 'em that I'm not scared. I'll stick my hands in my pockets and stand right among them, just as though I belonged here. . . . I guess I can think of something to say, all right, because I'm not really scared! This about not being scared, he had to repeat to himself, and added that shucks—they are only *boys!* Out in the entry he stopped a moment and with great deliberation picked a place for his pail.

The smaller children were playing "Last Couple Out"; two groups of the larger girls were sitting in the sun playing jacks; down in the road a number of boys were running a race; a few scouted about on the prairie for gopher holes; six of the biggest boys were leaning up against the wall in the sun. As he came around the corner Peder saw them and sauntered over. Feeling that something had to be said, he ventured manfully:

"Here you are, fellows."

No one answered at first. A silly grin passed over the faces. The one nearest Peder crossed his legs, looked knowingly out into the air and spat. Finally one of those at the other end of the row found his voice and said in Norwegian:

"Yep, so we are!"

Thereupon the grin broke into a laugh. Lloyd Bolgen, a long gandershanks of a boy standing in the middle, hee-hawed in the same language:

"You're damn right we are!" The remark was so comical that the laughter became uproarious.

Peder tried to smile but couldn't make it; he walked slowly to the other end of the row, saw Nils standing there, and since they were supposed to be seatmates, took a place beside him. Nils straightway edged over to the next boy, as near as he could get, thereby making a great gap between Peder and the row.

Peder felt the insult of the move but could not make himself leave—no, not now!

Soon Lloyd's voice sang out again, this time, too, in Norwegian:

"Better look out, Nils!"

Lloyd's companion on the right evidently felt compelled to join in the conversation and asked, also in Norwegian:

"Say, what kind of fellow was that Benedict Arnold?" Without waiting for an answer, he looked at his pal: "Did you say he was a Nordlænding?" *

A deep, jubilant gurgle passed down the line. Nils had to turn toward Peder to note the effect of the sally, his crossed eye fixed laughingly on him, asking if it was true, and his other eye looking straight into space.

Peder paid no attention to him. A cold, indifferent calm possessed him; chills coursed through his body; he felt deathly pale; his lips were so dry that he had to wet them with his tongue. . . . This has got to stop, no matter how badly I get licked, he thought. He stepped out from the wall, stood for a moment looking at the two in the middle, his eyes searching for the speaker; then going straight up to them, he thrust his elbows defiantly between them and said in broad Nordland dialect:

"Move over, boys, this is my place right here!"

He crowded himself in; and as if to give more force to his command he crossed his arms over his breast, letting his elbows stick well out. . . . In a second I'll have the whole gang on top of me, he thought; the shivers made the muscles of his face contract—to the two nearest it looked as though he were grinning at them.

Nils left the wall first; he had to walk over a few steps in order to see what would happen; the boy at the other end of the row felt constrained to do likewise; the one next to him followed suit, and thereupon the one who

* Peder's parents had come from Nordland in Norway. Nordlænding, a person from Nordland.

had stood nearest to Nils. The four grinned mockingly at the three by the wall.

Peder heard words singing in the air, and repeated them:

"Seems to be plenty of room here now!"

The next instant Lloyd darted out to join the four, put his arms about the necks of two of them, and said something, but in so low a voice that Peder couldn't hear it; and then the remaining boy, hitting upon an idea, which he must impart to the others, hurried over to them. There all six now stood in a tight knot, their arms about each other, talking low and excitedly; off and on a head turned around to look at Peder.

Peder was still leaning against the wall; the chills increased; his throat was so tight and dry that he kept smacking his lips; he felt a peculiar faintness come over him; his limbs grew strangely heavy; there was a gnawing in the pit of his stomach—a hand (it must be a big hand) groped around among his innards; his eyes were riveted on the group in front of him; the seconds dragged themselves by, endless as years.

. . . too bad I have to kill someone here today, but it can't be helped. 'Twill be worst for poor Mother! And Susie will think me bad. . . . He sighed wearily.

Finally, he could endure it no longer; if he remained here another minute, he'd have to scream. All of a sudden he found himself approaching the group, then stopping near them, and saying in a cheerful voice:

"Can't you get ready, fellows?" But to him it sounded indistinct, a fact which he couldn't understand; and he had said it in English, which perhaps was wrong, in spite of what he had read on the blackboard. He waited for them yet awhile. He wasn't so sure but that he was laughing. . . .

It was that neck of Lloyd's which caused him to wait. He had to study it so that he'd know just where to grab hold. Oh, but how he would choke him! He'd strangle him—right *there* he'd take a hold! . . . Deliberately, he thrust his hands into his pockets and began to walk slowly down the yard without looking back. If they didn't come right now, he'd go straight home . . . well, here he was going!

XI

In the group playing jacks, nearest the wall, squatted a girl watching the game. She was brown-eyed and dark-haired, every nerve of her vibrant with life, large for her age, too old to care much about the game, yet enough of a child to want to look on; she reminded one of a full peony bud ready to burst open at the first touch of the sun.

In her emotional life she was too close to womanhood to have many chums among the other girls in the school. She had heard the whole story about Peder and the trouble over in the Spring Creek School. The injustice he had suffered had enraged her. Today she had watched him as he came in; she had caught some of the whispered remarks of the older boys, had seen him left alone with his lunch, had noted the malicious grins given him by many in passing; and it had made her so furious that she had all she could do to keep herself from taking her lunch and going over to sit down beside him.

The moment Peder came out she forgot the game, and began watching the group by the wall to see what would happen. She sat near enough to hear every word. Seeing him leave the wall and approach the group, she sprang to her feet, hastened across the yard and went in. In the entry she hesitated, turned and slipped quietly out on the steps again; there she remained standing, straining forward and listening to catch the slightest sound.

When Peder went by she made as if to jump down; but the set expression in his face frightened her. In a few moments three boys came running past the other corner, stopping long enough in front of the porch to cast a hasty glance in through the door. In the same instant the three others came around from the opposite side of the school-house and did the same thing. She waited till she saw them close in on Peder, just as he reached the main road to go westward.

Yet a moment she seemed undecided. But then indignation got the better of her; in one leap she made the ground and started on a dead run after the boys. She reached the scene just as Lloyd was about to spring at Peder and heard his singsong voice shout:

"By God, boy, now you'll get a licking!" Lloyd bore down on the last words in order to give them greater emphasis.

The threat had no sooner escaped his mouth than the girl was confronting him; she gasped for breath:

"So you dare now—you coward! Shame on you! You just wait!"

The attack was as sudden as it was unexpected.

"Aw, go to ——!" Lloyd lifted his foot to kick her, but realizing in time that he couldn't do that to a girl, dropped it and drew back a couple of steps; he fought with his arms to ward off her blows.

But the girl followed, furiously as before, just as threatening: "If you dare touch him, I'll call teacher—oh, but you'll catch it!"

The group had split into three, Lloyd and the two who had followed him standing to the left; the other three to the right, the girl and Peder in between—Peder as dazed as one who, having fallen asleep in his own bed, suddenly awakens to find himself in a strange place.

Then Jim, one of the three to the right, volunteered the information, teasingly, in Norwegian:

"Aw, he's her fellow, Lloyd; they're going to get married Thanksgiving!"

The girl turned around and gave him a look, her eyes gleaming and narrow. "Say it again, will you?" As if to hear better, she stepped close to him. The leer on Jim's face became unbearable to her; instantaneously her hand shot out and fetched him a ringing blow square on the ear.

"Do you hit people?" shouted Jim angrily.

"No," she panted. "Not *people!*"

Chagrin over having their ingeniously planned attack frustrated by this snip of a girl made Lloyd see red; he leaped at her and grabbed her by the arm:

"This is none of your business! If you don't get out of here this minute, you'll be ——!" Finding no word emphatic enough and sufficiently threatening, he could only stammer: "You'll be—you'll be ——!" Nils, his crossed eye discerning in the air the penalty Lloyd wanted to inflict, came at once to his rescue, roaring out:

"*Scalped!*"

The girl strove to wrench her arm loose, but couldn't. She threw her head back defiantly; her brown eyes flashed fire at Lloyd. The next moment she saw Peder approaching him from behind, the fearful expression still on his face, only more set and ominous—she had never seen a face like it. Now something terrible will happen! Instantly she sent out a ringing cry, "Miss Quam!" and noticing that Peder heard and wavered—his face changing perceptibly, the dark cloud in it seeming to lift—she called again with all her might, "Miss Quam! Miss Qu-*am!*"

All looked at her terrified. Was she crazy? How did she dare? Didn't she know any better than to yell for the teacher *now?*

The storm center had broken up. The onlookers, upon this unexpected turn of affairs, stood waiting sheepishly for what would happen next. Just as the fight had been about to start, a couple of the smaller boys, tired from racing, had perched themselves on two of the stoutest fence posts, where they sat basking in the sun while they recovered their breath; no sooner did they perceive that a fight was brewing down in the road than they began to shout jubilantly: "A *fight—hurray!*" jumped down and came running. Their shouts and the cries of the girl set the whole prairie afire; every soul looked about and started for the scene. Miss Quam last; like a hen who follows her brood, she came waddling after, without haste, without the slightest trace of excitement.

As soon as Miriam had called Lloyd had let go of her arm; she had spoiled everything, damn her! He began to elbow his way out of the crowd; the largest boys found it expedient to follow his example; the appearance of Miss Quam made the boys decide that there was no hurry and so they took their time about leaving.

Lloyd was the first to meet the teacher—he'd show 'em that he wasn't one to sneak away! He bent over to pull up a straw while he waited for her to pass.

But Miss Quam took it into her head not to pass; she stepped right up to him, her calm eyes surveying him from top to toe.

"What are you boys up to now?"

"Only me and that Peder." He straightened himself indifferently and started to walk past.

Miss Quam did exactly what Lloyd for all the world wouldn't have had her do: She locked arms with him; and this time it was he who couldn't wrench loose.

"Oh, it was you two?"

"Yes."

"We say *yes ma'am*, here," she corrected him. "And it was you who started it?"

"Well ——"

"I heard how you welcomed him when he came out. That was unpardonable of you, Lloyd! Peder has done nothing wrong."

"Aw, is that so? I guess my father saw the picture with his own eyes!" Lloyd's eyes gleamed white; his voice hissed resentment.

"When?"

"The night of the meeting over there!"

"That may be; but people sometimes see wrong, and that's what you don't realize." Quietly and briefly she related what had happened that night, adding, "Now there's only one thing for you to do—you will have to make friends with Peder. And it's up to you to do it! Let's see, I'll give you till tomorrow night; then both of you are to come to me, after school is out. If everything isn't all right then, I shall have to see your father about it and you'll have to leave this school. Remember, it's tomorrow night, and both of you are to come! You realize, of course, that this is a serious matter?" Near the steps she stopped and let go of his arm; the matronly in her personality was as unruffled as ever. Lloyd could not move because her sober gray eyes continued to hold him.

For a while the others remained in the road, dumbfounded. What kind of performance was this anyway? Wasn't there going to be a fight? Who had been fighting? . . . There was a tenseness in the air, a deathly stillness as after an unexpected explosion. . . . Must be that Irish boy who had tried to pick a fight with Lloyd. Worse devils for fighting than the Irish were not to be found on the whole prairie! All stared at Peder, the girls open-mouthed, their heads slightly tilted; the boys trembling in jubilant excitement over the prospect of many fights—they'd have rows aplenty from now on! For Lloyd wasn't the fellow to stand for much; he usually paid back with interest. Bet-

ter find out from him how it had started. . . . By pairs
and in knots the boys trotted off toward the schoolhouse;
the girls saw them going, and so they followed.

Peder noticed the others leave. The terrible strain which
had threatened to suffocate him gave way. Once more it
was pleasant to be alive and to breathe the sunshine. The
prairie and all that it contained floated about him delecta-
bly as on a balmy spring evening. . . . He liked this place.
He'd just as soon be here as at the Murphy School. . . .
If only Charley had been with him now, he would have
gone after those fellows and teased 'em a bit. Charley was
a dandy at such things!

He became aware of someone standing near him. What
could he want? Huh—why, it was that girl! What a neat
blow she had given that face of Jim's! Peder was chuckling
to himself: "Guess I just missed getting a licking," he said,
speaking Norwegian. Concluding that he had made a mistake he repeated the remark in English. The girl had
turned away from him. Was she crying? How could that be
now? And she had cuffed Jim so admirably. . . . He must
think of something wherewith to console her; and still in
the same happy frame of mind he ventured cheerfully,
"Good thing you came!" Wanting to thank her heartily,
he took hold of the arm she was holding up to her eyes,
but at his touch she flung herself down on the grass in the
roadside and went into a fit of crying. He stared at her,
struck dumb with amazement—well, I never saw the like
of that!

Peder watched her body rise and fall under the convulsions. . . . A full, round body, supple and graceful in its
curves. Her face was buried in the crook of her arm. What
a glorious mass of hair. . . . Now she's feeling bad, poor
girl! Maybe if I leave her awhile she'll get over it quicker;
that's the way with me. I know. Peder walked off toward
the east a little way. . . . Was that anything to cry about?
Girls certainly were funny fellows! An image, vague and
far away, struggled for supremacy in his consciousness but
didn't come out distinctly. A lovely image known to no
soul but himself—of a wet cheek pressed to his own, of a
heart panicky with fear beating against his; an image of
eyes blue as heaven itself with soft evening clouds floating
lazily . . . man alive, what eyes! . . . I can't be thinking
of such pleasant things now when this girl here is feeling so

bad and crying her eyes out! . . . Why do the girls cry
as soon as I come near them? Peder felt himself trembling,
and yet he was happy. . . . He s'posed she felt bad because she had hit Jim. Not nice for girls to fight. . . .
Let's see—what was it Jim had said? A new image popped
up before his eyes, clear and near by. Peder could hear the
words distinctly and laughed outright at them. . . . He
would go to her and tell her not to cry about *that!*

He walked back. The girl was sitting by the roadside
waiting for him. Over her brown eyes lay a thin, wet veil,
softening them and giving a peculiar expression to the
smile which stole out to meet him. In fact, her whole face
radiated the smile, cheek and mouth, chin and throat, particularly the mouth—softly and shyly, as from one bringing a gift which he is eager to give but feels timid about
offering. Peder looked at her until he completely forgot
what he had come to say. He was conscious of a sweet
weariness taking possession of him. Suddenly he threw
himself down beside her.

She arose instantly:

"Are you going to go to school here?"

"Maybe." He had taken his time about answering; his
voice sounded a bit peevish.

"Aren't you sure?" Now she looked at him and laughed.
"But then you mustn't fight!"

"I'll do as I please about that."

" 'Tisn't nice to fight."

"Two of 'em are going to catch it!" he nodded determined. . . . "Maybe three. Jim's probably got to have a
little more."

"Oh, you mustn't!"

Peder hunted for an answer; before he found it, the bell
rang.

He jumped up, and they began walking side by side up
the road. In her gait was a swinging rhythm, as if she were
keeping step to a merry tune. He kept looking at her all
the time.

"What's your name?" he asked.

"Miriam—Miriam Nilsen."

"Nils Nilsen's daughter?"

"Yes."

Peder looked at her in utter astonishment, almost falling out of step. A wave of sympathy swept over him; he

felt sorry for her. What would her father say when he heard of the fight? He had some questions he would like to ask her.

"Just where does the road go from here to your place?"

"Two miles north and one east."

"That's easy to remember."

"How so?"

"Because then I only have to walk straight ahead and turn to the right! . . . Are there many going your way?"

"Just the first mile."

"Only the first?"

"The others turn east there. . . . Don't fight any more!"

"I haven't been fighting!" he laughed at her.

"You were going to!" Then she, too, laughed but deeper and more melodiously than he. "What would you have done if I hadn't come and helped you?"

"Done—huh!" They were so near the steps now that he was spared the necessity of stating just what he would have done.

XII

O you youths, Western youths,
So impatient; full of action, full of manly pride and
*   friendship,*
Plain I see you Western youths, see you tramping with
*   the foremost,*
Pioneers! O pioneers!

Have the elder races halted?
Do they droop and end their lesson, wearied over there
*   beyond the seas?*
We take up the task eternal, and the burden and the
*   lesson,*
Pioneers! O pioneers!

All the past we leave behind,
We debouch upon a newer mightier world, varied world,
Fresh and strong the world we seize, world of labor and
*   the march,*
Pioneers! O pioneers!

Peder had been delayed. Just before school was out Miss Quam had written these three stanzas on the blackboard and had asked the two upper grades to copy them in order to take them home and learn them by heart for tomorrow. The school had said them in unison several times, Miss Quam leading. She had seemed to change perceptibly under the reading, her matronly body swaying rhythmically, her gray eyes sparkling joyously. The ponderousness of her person had become light and comely. Peder, holding his paper in one hand, had looked from it to her as he pronounced the words ringingly and with much emphasis. But during the reading he had discovered that he had made a mistake in copying the last stanza and so he had to recopy all of it. Hence his delay.

He was now standing down by the barn at Johannes Mörstad's, bridling his horse. He was impatient to be off and talked sharply to the mare about holding her head still. One of the little girls had been out and asked him in for lunch, which invitation he had declined. No time for that now! Before he got the rein buckled Mrs. Mörstad herself was standing out on the porch calling to him. Without answering he swung himself up on the horse, got himself seated and rode in a trot up the yard. The vibrant life of the living flesh underneath him passed into his own body, animating him with an impatient strength. Sitting thus high, he could speed away on the wings of the wind. *"Fresh and strong the world we seize"*—heigh, ho! heigh, ho! . . . He drew up for a moment in front of the porch, talked fast about having to get home early to help with the chores, for all the folks were in the cornfield, even Mother; he thanked her just the same—another time perhaps—he liked lunches all right—fine weather this, for husking! He said it all in one breath, excitedly, and was on his way before the woman could get in a word. . . . That's a boy any mother can be proud of, thought Mrs. Mörstad as she went into the house.

An eager restlessness was upon Peder. "Fresh and strong the world we seize!" it sang within him. There were a couple of other lines too that had such a dandy lilt to them, but he didn't remember them and couldn't bother about looking at his paper now. He urged the horse on till he reached the crossroads east of the schoolhouse; here he slackened up a bit to look around. . . . Ought to be possible to go north here, he debated. I haven't been over this road before and it won't hurt to get acquainted. . . . He headed his horse northward; but the mare evidently disapproved; she snorted and dropped into a walk. . . . Ever see such an obstinate beast! Peder lashed the mare several times before he got her into a gallop again; and then he shook so that he had to take a firm hold in order to steady himself. The air he cleaved pressed against his cheeks and forced water to his eyes. As he raced on he was scanning the prairie in every direction, breathlessly alert for any sound.

The first mile ahead of him lay straight as a rod. Not a sign of life upon it. He was now riding as fast as the horse could go. Just as he passed the road running to the right, he caught glimpses of figures far off to the east.

Just a little way north of this crossroad the landscape became somewhat irregular. Once upon a time the prairie must have conceived the notion that perhaps it didn't look well for her to lie here so flat and spread out. She had stirred ever so little, but had soon been alarmed over the small swellings forming under her skin. She had stretched out to get herself smooth again, but all to no purpose; the lumps had come to stay and were still reminding her of her vanity. In the depressions the ground, spring and fall, was too wet to allow a road across it. The first one who crossed this stretch had kept to the hillsides; the next had followed in his wake. Thus it happened that in time their wagon tracks had become a road which for a half-mile wound in and out among many hillocks.

Up ahead in one of the curves Peder detected a lone figure trudging along swinging a pail. . . . Did you ever see the like! Was he going to meet people here? Who might that be? He wiped the water from his eyes and slowed up; his heart beat so turbulently that he was sure the thud of it could be heard all over the prairie.

When he reached her Miriam would not look up; he thought he detected a tremble in her voice as she spoke:

"Do you go this way?"

Peder was stung by the rebuke of her words and found it difficult to answer:

"I go west at the next corner. I ride fast, you see!" Being conscious of how inadequate his explanation must seem to her, he tried hard to find another that would sound more reasonable. And finding none, he began to wait for her to speak again. But she only walked on as before. The silence began to ask why he had come. He could feel distinctly how hard it listened—the insistency of it only increasing his mortification. Soon it became unbearable. . . . She continued to walk. He sat high above her and looked straight down at her neck. The road was so deep and narrow that it was impossible to get up alongside of her. . . . Couldn't she understand that he had something he must say to her? . . . Couldn't she stop? In a little while they would be at the corner!

"Wait!" he said hoarsely, slipping down from the horse and twisting the reins around his arms as he hurried after her.

But she neither stopped nor turned around.

He came up beside her and looked intently at her face. The flush under the tan had deepened. Did he see a smile in it? She surely wasn't going to cry again?

Then the horse blew a long *tr-r-o-o*, which shattered the silence, like bits of glass jingling down the wall of a precipice. Peder let go of his breath and recovered his voice: "I just wanted to find out how far it was by this road!"

"You have to turn west at the corner!" An intense excitement was upon her. She walked fast; she still had not looked at him.

Can it be that she is afraid of me? Peder was breathing heavily:

"If I'm not good enough company, I can leave you! I only wanted to thank you for the way you helped me," he said haughtily and stopped to climb up on the horse. . . . He wasn't going to thrust himself on anybody!

Miriam, too, had stopped; she set her pail down and turned to him:

"Are you mad again?" The words seemed to come out of a deep blush, and were so kind in tone that he forgot his peevishness. He stepped close to her.

"That was fine of you!"

"What?"

"That you smashed Jim's face for him!"

"Do you think so?"

"Of course I do!" Peder assured her cheerfully.

She could find nothing to answer and her great helplessness became pathetic. After a while she said timidly—it sounded almost as if she were entreating him: "I am glad you came!" Suddenly something unexpected happened, frightening both of them: She grabbed his hands, drew him toward her, and pleaded: "You must go now!"

"Certainly, of course!" Peder's laugh was unnaturally loud.

"Go, I say!" she panted beseechingly. But the mysterious richness of her being opened wide and begged him to stay. Peder stood bewildered. He tried to laugh but could only make a grimace because of the joy he felt pulsating within him. The spell of an unknown force was upon him; it made him quiver and feel afraid of himself; all his strength seemed to desert him. . . . That she should be afraid of him! . . . What did she fear?

Freeing his hand he began to stroke her cheek. The cheek was warm and silken; underneath lay a life just awakening. How rude and awkward I am, he thought! . . . Feeling that he must do it better he used the other hand too. . . . About him and within him whirred a mighty storm. He could hear naught else. . . . They came very close . . . had to come closer still. All the while her blurred dark eyes looked right into his. Do you mean this? they pleaded.

Suddenly a terrible cry rent the silence. An angry caw, pursued by one still angrier, blared right into their ears— the air was filled with irate scoldings: *Caw, caw, caw!* over and over again.

The cries came from a pair of old crows that had tarried too long in the big woods surrounding one of the lakes far up in northern Minnesota. This morning, having been awakened early by the biting of the frost, they had got an inkling as to what time of the year it might be and had immediately set out upon their flight to the south. But gradually the day had grown milder; they had flown into balmy sunshine and soft autumn hazes, and so the old man who had led the way had taken to wondering if he might not have been dreaming this morning. As he remembered all the tasty carrion up there in the north he had detoured far westerly, constantly on the lookout for quiet woods and new lakes. Not until he cleaved the first cool whiffs of evening did he change his mind and steer southerly again. After a long flight he spied some small tucked-away hills sticking up ahead of him. Perhaps he could snooze here for the night? In the cornfields round about there would be plenty of food for an empty stomach, that is, if he weren't too hungry for fresh meat. He flew low, heading straight for the place. All at once he shot upward, so suddenly that his feathers whirred; directly below him, right where he intended to alight, stood two figures, the one a horse, the other. . . ? His eyes blazed red with anger; he let out an infuriated *caw* to the old woman, warning her that here she'd better watch her tack. No sooner had she answered than the one figure became two!

The exasperated screams rent the quiet evening, calling on the whole prairie to listen sharply, for here something very improper was going on.

Seized with terror Peder and Miriam jumped apart. The bewildering mystery in which they, drunk with joy, had lost themselves, vanished completely, irrecoverably. Only a few pale hillocks remained. The whole landscape lay barren and desolate, but so intensely alert that it was almost impossible to breathe. Across the prairie from the west the sun, blood red and puffy-faced, sought them out and demanded to know what they were up to. . . . The silence round about them was terribly alive.

Before Peder could recover his senses, Miriam had grabbed her pail and was gone. His eyes caught her and followed her—gosh how skittish these girls were! Feeling weak and worn out, he led the mare so close to the roadside that he could climb up. . . . The air must have grown cooler, he had to clench his teeth to keep them from chattering.

As he sat there swaying rhythmically to the movement of the galloping horse he became conscious of a great satisfaction with himself and with all the world. Now he was getting to be a man. . . . Bet you! The feeling of exultation mounted within him. Thrusting his hand under his coat he pulled out a paper and glanced at it. . . . What marvelous lines these—they were swelling with song.

> *All the past we leave behind,*
> *We debauch upon a newer mightier world, varied world,*
> *Fresh and strong the world we seize, world of labor and*
> *   the march,*
> *Pioneers! O pioneers!*

He would surely read this poem to Mother! Lashing his horse he raced away to the rhythm of the verse: *Fresh and strong the world we seize!*

In the cornfields along the road the leaves nodded in agreement to what the line said. The sun was already down, but a deep glow lingered in the western sky. It smiled at him, inviting him to come on! . . .

III. The Eyes That Did Not See

I

It was often heard said of Beret Holm that she was the ablest farmer in the town of Spring Creek. Small thanks to her, folks would usually add; she ought to get on, considering all the help she had. If one spoke thus in her presence Beret would look to see if he were trying to be spiteful.

For Beret herself knew that she was not equal to the tasks life now had set her. Never having been aught but a helpless creature who needed to lean on others for support, how was she to lead where no way was? No, that she could not. At times it seemed to her that what she did here was merely make-believe. It could not be reality. . . . Oh no, the founding of kingdoms was not for her!

That fatal winter, after her husband disappeared and she was left alone with all the responsibility resting on her, she felt at once how utterly helpless she was to cope with the situation. Difficulties, however, had a way of paying small heed to what she thought: They only continued to heap themselves up at her door, giving her little leisure to worry. Every day the boys, wanting to know what to do, beseiged her with questions; and if she didn't stand ready to answer on the spot, they would rush ahead, solving the problems in their own way—those fellows had no moments to waste! Ole, always impulsive, never had time to wait. Frequently things went wrong for the boys, so that she had to step in and take hold herself in order to prevent disaster.

The moment the fury of the storm in which Per Hansa was lost had spent itself and people had dug themselves out of their lairs, they set strenuously to work to save what might still be alive. One morning the boys came storming into the kitchen to inform their mother that they had to go slaughter a calf—they must do it right away, the critter was as good as dead already! Ole took the butcher knife and began whetting it; Store-Hans wanted a pail in which to catch the blood; both tore about excitedly and had no time to wait for their mother. Beret put on some wraps and followed.

During the night the storm had swept the roof off the shed which sheltered the young cattle; one of the summer calves, having caught itself between the poles, had broken both its front legs, and now lay there shivering, unable to get up. Lifting the calf onto a sled, they hauled it up to the house and brought it into the kitchen, where Beret put splints on its legs—she could remember their doing that in Norway for both animals and people. The calf had recovered and had been allowed to remain in the kitchen until the snow disappeared in the spring. By that time the poor beast had become one of the family.

One morning Hans Olsa had died. Sörine, his wife, had been left sitting alone in the snowdrifts, with a half-grown girl and an infant, and with two herds needing care, one of them a couple of miles away. Little help could be had from neighbors; they had enough to do looking after themselves; Kjersti had hurt herself so badly that she could not get out of bed; moreover, people didn't run about the country unless compelled by the direst necessity.

During the forenoon, Ole came home and informed them that today Hans Olsa had died: Yessir, now he was dead all right! He had just come from there. The boy related the news noisily, as if something great had happened. Beret listened to him awhile, then went to the window and stood there, staring at an endless wilderness of snow. All the awfulness out there rose up like the flood tide of a mighty sea. She had to grasp the window sill to steady herself. . . . God had not found pleasure in her ways after all, even though she had seen them so clearly. Oh, no—He would not permit any human being to sit in on His counsel of mercy! . . . Five days already since Per Hansa had left. Where could he be? Surely God could not take his life just because she had wanted him to do what seemed right? Fear began to seize hold of her and finally overpowered her, bewildering her thoughts. The billowing sea of white outside rolled on in icy calm, into an eternity of snow. Strange sparks danced before her eyes, black and yellow ones, dazzling her sight; they blinked out of nowhere, stood there, and were gone as mysteriously as they had come. The air was alive with them.

Ole's talk aroused her: Someone ought to go over and help Sörine; terrible over there; Sörine only walked the floor, moaning, not knowing what to do with herself; Sofie couldn't talk; the cows were bellowing something awful; and Hans Olsa himself——"Come on, Hansey, let's you and me go!" . . .

Beret went into her bedroom, put on men's clothing, and coming back into the kitchen, said that she would go herself. Before leaving she gave instructions: Ole was to stay at home to look after things here; Anna Marie must get the meals and take care of Permand; Store-Hans would come with her, they'd need someone to go and get help.

Ole, disappointed, remonstrated against such a senseless arrangement. This was a fine business indeed! What earthly use could she be over there? Could she take care of the cattle? Could she make a coffin, get people together and carry Hans Olsa out?

Beret gave him a cuff on the ear and commanded him to stop his everlasting bluster.

Taking the other boy with her and stepping into Ole's skis, she set out, but found it difficult to make any headway. The boy, impatient because she was so slow, left her as the gull the boat it doesn't care to follow any longer. She struggled up to the top of a drift; careening over its ridge she skimmed down so fast that the wind took her breath away; before she knew it she lay floundering in the snow. That happened many times. At last she began to cry. Just why was she going? Perhaps Ole was right after all? Again the feeling of unreality possessed her. Was it really she who was walking here? How could she have driven her husband into death—and only more misery have come of it? She must be dreaming again. . . . Nearing the farm, she heard the pitiful bellowing of the cattle, from down in the snowdrifts, and came to. Here, at least, was reality enough!

At her neighbor's house she found a distress more hopeless than her own. The house was cold and disorderly. In the living room lay the corpse, unwashed, with a cloth thrown over its face; by the stove stood the girl, lost in one of her father's coats—her child's face ashen, and distraught from the agony of grief; on a chair in front of the bed sat Sörine moaning, Little-Hans asleep on her lap; all three were dressed as if ready to go out.

Beret saw it all, and the ache within her gave way to a feeling of pity for her neighbor. Instinctively, she did what first needed to be done. She told Store-Hans to go fetch some hay for the stove, set him and Sofie to twisting faggots, and started the fire; if they didn't get the house warmed up right away, they'd all freeze to death. Because the gloom hung heavier in the kitchen than anywhere else she began putting things in order there first. She brought out the coffee-pot, set it on the stove, and looked about for things she needed. Finding that she could not go on without the aid of someone acquainted with the house, she went into the living room and asked Sörine to come and help her; Sörine, putting the child away, began assisting Beret as if she were a servant working under her direction.

Little by little, as the room became warmer, the gloom lifted. Soon all were sitting around the table, trying to eat, Beret spreading the bread for them. This slice was for Sörine; here was one for Sofie, she said, as she handed the slices about. She had taken charge exactly as though she were at home portioning out the food to her own children. And now Sörine must put on some wraps and go out with Store-Hans to look after the cattle, for the boy couldn't manage alone; Sofie must put on her skis and go over to tell Tönseten what had happened. He must go at once and get menfolk to watch here tonight! Beret spoke very calmly, and with forethought. No one objected to her counsel because what she advised was apparently the only thing that could be done.

She stayed until late afternoon. She set herself to straightening up the house; she cleaned, and did all that she saw must be done; she hunted in cupboard and drawers for whatever she needed. First of all, she took care of the dead man. She poured lukewarm water into a basin and washed him carefully with soap and water. That done, she went after a comb and dressed his hair and beard. Unable to get the hair to lie as she wanted it to, because it persisted in curling up at the temples, she found the scissors and trimmed it a bit. She took great pains with this work. Hans Olsa had been a handsome man, very cleanly and neat—they must not forget that, and now he was coming into the presence of God. . . . It seemed as though she couldn't do enough for him, and so she found a hymn book which she placed between his hands. One eyelid didn't close entirely; she put dead weights on both eyes. Finally, taking a clean sheet she covered the corpse with it, leaving the face bare. Now Hans Olsa was comely to look at. There he lay sleeping, the contentment of childhood resting upon his great, rugged countenance, making it appear almost as though he were ready to break into a smile. Beret looked at him. . . . God grant that you are as contented as you seem to be! she thought. A feeling akin to happiness stole over her at the thought of what she had been able to do for her old neighbor.

She left Hans Olsa and began to work in the kitchen. But he would give her no peace—she kept thinking of him all the while. Leaving her work, she went into the bedroom where she had seen a bottle of camphor. She took the bottle, and going back to the dead man, poured a few drops on his beard, and combed it again until it looked like the softest silk. Still the odor of death persisted in the room. Beret wondered how she could get rid of it. In the kitchen she had seen a large iron kettle which Hans Olsa had brought with him from Norway; putting some faggots of hay into it, she carried it out to the living room, where she touched a match to the faggots. Thereupon she took a few bits of stick cinnamon out of a bag in the kitchen cupboard and threw them on the fire in the kettle. Thinking that this might not be enough she put a couple of pieces on the stove also. . . . I don't see that there is anything more I can do for you, Hans Olsa, and now you must leave me alone; there is much for me to do here. After that she was able to work in peace.

It was late afternoon when Sörine came in. Beret sat holding Little-Hans in her lap, and tending a kettle of sweet milk simmering on the stove. She had fed the child all he could eat, and was now crooning to him as he smiled contentedly up into her face. How cozy and comfortable it seems in here, thought Sörine. The delicious, sweet odor coming from the kettle made her hungry. She couldn't wait, but brought a cup, which Beret filled for her.

Beret got up and asked Sörine to come into the living room with her. At the head of the bed burned a candle. "I have laid out your husband as well as I could. He looks nice now, though he has always done that." Beret spoke quietly. Sörine began to cry. Turning toward Beret and putting her head on her shoulder she broke down under her grief. Feeling how well the other understood her affliction she clung to Beret as if she were the only person in the world on whom she could rely for help. Beret did not utter a word. . . . If she can really cry herself out now, she thought, it will be easier for her later. I can well understand how she feels!

Toward evening Henry Solum came up and offered to watch that night, and so Beret felt she could leave Sörine. The going home seemed easier; she could manage the skis better; and now she was less disturbed by fear. Store-Hans waited for her. . . . She would never see Per Hansa alive again . . . knew it now for a certainty. Yet that night she fell asleep almost as soon as she had gone to bed.

Time and again that winter Beret said to herself that her situation had become impossible. How could she manage it all? She simply was not equal to it. But her husband did not return; the work out of doors became harder and more imperative as the season grew. Despite the conviction of her own inability she soon came to realize that the difficulties solved themselves better if she worked with the boys than when she let them manage alone. And yet, as soon as the troubles began piling up and the demands called insistently, she was straightway ready to answer: This I am not able to do. It would be better, in fact, much better, to give up altogether, for then my failures would come to an end! But at these moments it would happen that she saw a door somewhere swing slowly open into a room where was revealed a picture, indistinct, and shadowy, in a dim half-light—of a plan she might give a trial; and because she could see no other way out, she would try the plan, more often in pretense than in real seriousness.

The weeks went by. The blizzards kept on raging. The struggle changed into endless toil. The fuel was gone; the supply of oil long since exhausted; the salt likewise; not a grain of flour in the house except what they could grind in the coffee-mill; coffee and sugar were luxuries scarcely remembered anymore.

And it was hard on the clothes for the boys, worst of all on the footwear. Often she would sit patching until late into the night; then she would let the light burn in the window—in case he should come tonight! . . . One evening, taking a pair of heavy wool socks Per Hansa had brought with him from Norway, she began sewing rags on them, layer upon layer, stitching them firmly together. These would make good, warm footgear, she thought. After she had finished making the socks she felt disgusted with herself for not having thought of it sooner. . . . Just what she had known all along: She was no good!

But most unbearable of all was the suffering of the animals, famine grinning with glistening teeth from cow and horse stall alike, and the haystacks two miles away, the snow eight feet deep on the level. Day in and day out she and the boys slaved with the fodder; they carried it home; they dragged it home on skis and sleds; and yet, throughout the whole day, the poor beasts would not cease their pitiful crying for more.

On a warm, sunshiny day toward the end of March as they were struggling to get hay home, they beheld a strange apparition. Across the billowing reaches of snow, in the distant southeast, it moved across the sky; two fantastic figures pulling a long low house, a dwarf bringing up the rear. Up in the sky it passed, seeming at times to stand on its head. Beret turned pale at the sight, and stared like one rooted to the ground until the phantom had vanished. It must be her husband's wraith? Now someone would soon find his body and bring it home! . . . Later they heard that it was a coffin on a sled; Gjermund Dahl's mother had died of the cough, and Gjermund himself together with his oldest son and one of the younger children had been at the neighbor's to have a coffin made.

Every morning Beret put men's clothes on and went out with the boys to help with the work. Evenings she often sat down to talk with them about how they might best proceed with this task or that, more for the sake of clarifying matters in her own mind than getting counsel from them. Later it became a habit with her. Hence her thoughtful look; particularly when talking with people about serious things did she give the impression that she was feeling her way across a rough and impassable country. . . . Oh no, Beret could not cope with her difficulties —she saw it only too clearly.

Spring was late in coming that year. But when at length it did break through it set to work with a will to compensate for its tardiness. Warm breezes out of the south began tonguing the prairie; the sun quivered the whole day long, from the moment it gilded the sky at dawn until it dozed off in lazy, lukewarm evening. All the flat lowlands became a sea of water, lying there for a day to be hidden by an impenetrable fog at dusk; as the next sun sank, the sea was gone and the fields were dry. One day the sun set to work in real earnest. The smell of wet earth and of growing vegetation became so strong that all life breathed in sheer giddiness! Balmy day lay bright and beaming under the blue firmament as if it had been there from the beginning of eternity. . . . Never before had folks felt such need of bestirring themselves.

Things went black before the eyes of Beret the day the men brought Per Hansa home. For three whole days the minister sat with her. Gently and cautiously he tried to lead her, taking her by the hand, moving very slowly, coming back and going over the same road again and again. . . . In the wisdom and paternal care of Almighty God there were no accidents! When the clear light of Resurrection Morn dispelled the darkness of sorrow, she would see that all had been done in the goodness of love. The minister grappled with her as if she had been a man. And all to no purpose. For a while she would listen silently to his talk, only to become so disgusted with him that she walked away. . . . He simply did not fathom what she was struggling with!

The evening of the last night the minister was there, the children had already gone to bed and he sat by the table smoking his pipe. Beret came and took the place opposite him:

"Now I am going to explain the whole matter to you," she began, "so that you may know just how bad I am." The lamp was on the table between them; its light seemed to annoy her, and she turned it down so low that it barely kept alive; her face was strong with purpose.

And so she began to confess, slowly and circumstantially, going back and repeating as if she were afraid she wasn't including all. It took her a long time. The minister smoked in silence. After a while he began interrupting her, asking a question occasionally; at length he became stern and questioned her closer. Finally he lapsed into silence. He forgot to smoke and his pipe went out.

Beret admitted frankly that it was she who had driven Per Hansa to his death; she omitted no detail of what had happened between them the day he went. There had been angry words, she had nagged him, he had left in a terrible temper! . . . Beret had lived through the scene many times, but never until now that she sat telling it, in bare words to another, had she seen it in all its awfulness.

The minister jumped up but sank down again as quickly, asking in a husky voice, "What's this you say?"

—It was as true as that she sat here telling it, Beret confirmed, moaning. Then like the good child who, having received his punishment, must present all the excuses he has in order not to appear worse than he is, she described her conversation with Hans Olsa the night she watched at his bedside. Never had the Lord's way been clearer to her. And she had been as the clay in His hands! She depicted the indescribable fear she had seen in the face of the dying man—the nameless terror which came upon him because he was not ready to meet God. Was it wrong of her that she had *had* to send someone for help? And there had been no one to ask but Per Hansa —whom else could she have asked? . . . Why had God let this happen? Had He chosen her to be a curse? Throwing herself down over the table, she implored him to give her an answer.

Unconsciously, the minister drew away from her. For a while he sat pondering, not saying a word, not even looking up. At length he asked her a couple of questions, which she answered carefully and honestly, feeling that she was now standing before the face of God and that her day of judgment was at hand. . . . The minister, however, had more questions to ask, about things she scarcely had taken thought of. And little by little, the picture began to assume another color, which she couldn't understand, for now it seemed that it was she who had needed God's forgiveness and not Hans Olsa. This vexed her— why, she had been with Hans Olsa herself and knew what condition he was in! . . . Bethinking herself, she sat silent for a while. But the minister would not leave her alone; he continued asking questions about matters which took her farther back in time, to the marriage relation of her husband and herself during the last years; he became personal and vulgar, she thought, kept prying into affairs that made her blush hotly with shame. . . . Never had she imagined that she would come to discuss these things with any human being!

Presently the minister rose and began to walk back and forth across the floor, fitfully, his step uncertain, like a man who staggers in drunkenness.

Beret looked at him, unable to understand what was the matter. Was he getting ill? Ought she offer him something with which to strengthen himself? There was a bottle of whisky left standing by Per Hansa. She turned up the lamp, wanting to see him better. What could be ailing him?

When the minister came back he spoke very quietly; even though he sat right here at the table his voice sounded tired and seemed to come from far away. Yet so intently did she hang on every word he uttered that she scarcely noticed his manner. She was to receive her sentence, for now he knew all!

The minister talked on, making frequent pauses. . . . "That your husband's days were over I believe for a certainty, for it is the Lord God who measures out the span of life for every human being. And it is as the old saying has it, 'Death must always have some cause.'" . . . Here he fell silent again, his face taking on a preoccupied look.

"But since He let it happen in just this way, it must have been for our sakes, for yours and mine." He seemed overcome, his voice threatening to stop. "I see now what a poor shepherd I have been. May the Lord forgive me for having forsaken two of His children in a great wilderness."

For a while he stopped talking altogether. Taking his pipe, he filled it, but held it without lighting it. . . . "For your sake," he resumed, "this was necessary, that I can clearly see. You have permitted a great sin to blind your sight; you have forgotten that it is God who causes all life to flower and who has put both good and evil into the hearts of men. I don't think I have known two better men than your husband and the friend he gave his life for. It is hardly possible that God didn't find them good enough for a place of honor in His heaven, no—hardly! . . . From what your neighbor tells me it is altogether likely that your husband would have undertaken the trip even though nothing had come up between you and him, of that I think I can assure you!"

Again the minister was lost in thought; it was a long time before he spoke. When he did his words sounded very strange to Beret:

"No, your worst sin does not consist in what you did to your husband that day; rather it lies in your discontent with God's special creatures, with your fellow men. For that reason you can experience no real happiness. . . . That is a grievous sin, Beret Holm!"

The minister got up and paced back and forth. Beret sat looking into what he had said, trying to understand the meaning of it. . . . He can hardly believe it himself, a man so well versed in God's Word. But it is kind of him to speak so well of Hans Olsa and Per Hansa!

At length, coming over to her and standing right in front of her, he said quietly:

"I'm tired now, and I'd like to go to bed. But before I leave, I want to say this to you, Beret Holm: It is you who must carry on the great work which your husband has begun out here—it is yours to do with as you will. But one thing you must keep in mind—if you are to prosper and all is to go well with you, you must learn to find the good in your fellow man. Remember that God created him, *Satan did not do that job!*"

The next day the minister left the settlement. He returned often that spring and whenever he came back he stayed at Beret Holm's. His visits were so frequent that people began to wonder, and it was not altogether certain that the tongues didn't wag. Surely Beret Holm wasn't the first woman to be left a widow! What about Mrs. Waag? . . . Enough of those who needed comfort. . . . This certainly looked strange.

II

All that summer thoughts of Norway bore more strongly in upon the mind of Beret than at any time since her coming to America. Not that she longed greatly for her fatherland, but Norway was beautiful and now she was her own master. Nothing could compare with summer in Nordland, for that was enchantment itself—she had heard many people say so. On warm nights, when she found it difficult to sleep, she would sometimes get up and go out to sit on the porch in order to let the night air soothe her mind and body. Then old scenes would come back to her, the mood of the prairie night round about her being strangely reminiscent of them. It might happen that she would sit here on her own porch and watch a lazy sea billowing listlessly into a quiet cove, washing up against kelp-covered rocks. . . . Clear, quiescent night. Drowsy, sated light upon heathery hills. Purple inland mountains dozing in a hazy sun. She could hear the call of the gull in the meadows. Down on the bay floated flocks of eider ducks, dreaming, their bills tucked under their wings. . . . A boat paddled its way toward shore. Put in at the landing. A man in heavy sea boots ascended the rocky path. That was Father. Tonight he had been out coal fishing.

Her memory became trancelike; she would see all as clearly as if she were standing by the corner of the cottage at home. . . . Yes, there came Father! Who took care of the house for him after Mother had gone? He never wrote to her, and it seemed she never could make herself write to him. How could she write to people who didn't understand how things were over here? . . . She could sell, to be sure, and go back to Norway. . . . Wondered if that might not be wise? For then the children would regain race and fatherland and their mother tongue. . . . Was it possible to atone for sin that way? In old times people made long pilgrimages to distant lands, she had heard. . . . It would not be easy for her. . . . No. . . . Over in the churchyard yonder lay Per Hansa watching every move she made. Ought she leave him to lie here alone in this alien land? . . . Whenever these thoughts came she would feel like a traitor. He had had such great dreams about how things were to be in the New Kingdom, had talked about a royal mansion and many other wonders. Were she to get up and leave it all, how would she account to him if they ever met again? He would surely want to know how she had carried on the work. . . . No, the move would not be easy for her. And the children —what would they say? . . .

But the thought of Norway would not give her peace. One Sunday, when on a visit to Sörine, she mentioned the idea to her. What did she think? Ought they sell and move back to Norway?

Sörine sat playing with the child. "If it weren't for the children," she answered as though she had thought a great deal about the matter, "I'd be on my way now. With the money you and I would get if we sold, we could live very comfortably there."

"What makes you think it wouldn't be all right for the children?"

"Oh, you know that as well as I. You surely don't wish that they should be strangers in Norway, the way we've been here? . . . That would be terrible!"

"But that could never happen," Beret objected . . . "they'd be coming back to their own people!"

"Well, I wonder now? Sofie doesn't remember much of Norway, and the baby was born here, you know. Besides, you wouldn't want your boys to slave on the sea for a living, would you? . . . Here we have plenty both to eat and to drink."

To which Beret made no reply. After that the subject was never discussed between them.

That summer Beret tried several times to write to her father, each effort to end only by her burning the letter. She never could say what she wished to, it seemed; either she would tell altogether too little, and thereby make the whole picture untrue, or she would have to include so much that she never could finish.

Moreover, she scarcely had time to think of more than what each day demanded. The moment dawn crimsoned her bedroom window she was up; and never went to bed until long after dark. In her work outside she wore men's clothing, a habit she continued until she discovered that the children didn't like it.

Duties multiplied and made increasing demands on her time. The days were always too short. The weariness at night gave pleasant relief. More than anything else she enjoyed taking care of the cattle; every creature on the farm responded to her voice. How good to feel that all life was fond of her! The first spring and summer she let every creature born on the farm live. Not until late in the fall did she sell any cattle, and then only because the boys compelled her to. Just suppose now, they argued, that they had another winter like the last one; what would she do with all the stock? They certainly didn't intend to slave the way they did last year!

On warm evenings that summer, as soon as the children had gone to bed, Beret would heat water, and undressing in her bedroom and putting out the light, she would go back of the house and bathe her whole body. Then, with only her night clothes on, she would often sit on the porch to rest awhile before going to bed. On such nights it frequently happened that an intense longing for her husband came upon her; she actually ached to feel masculine strength embrace her. All the endearing terms Per Hansa had used, the many kinds of caresses he could think of when he was in the mood, now came back to her with all the poignancy of actuality. . . . One thing she realized more and more clearly as time went on: She and her husband had not lived together as they ought during the last years, and it was, she thought, mostly her fault. And never could it be done over again! . . . Gnawing remorse filled her mind—it might have been heaven between her and Per Hansa, and instead it had become hell. Now she lived in bereavement, a strong, healthy woman in her best years!

That these balmy moon-nights, burning a verdigris green, were dangerous to her, she did not realize! It often happened that Tambur-Ola's face, springing out of nowhere, would stand gazing at her, the expression of his face changing from ironic mockery to a quiet peacefulness—the whole man a poor wounded creature begging for kindness from hearts that could understand. She didn't wonder that he begged! Strange feelings stole over her. She let herself be carried away by them . . . liked them. But the next day she would go about feeling so ashamed of herself that she did not dare look at the children. Nevertheless, she couldn't banish the man from her thoughts; and truth to tell, she didn't want to either. And so she must go about dreading that sin too.

. . . Could she only have known how many of her troubles had been ordained by God! . . . Assuredly, His ways were unsearchable. Never had truer words been spoken by human tongue. Here he had worked the greatest of miracles with her, had restored full understanding and reason to her. Had it been done only that she might do yet greater wrongs? . . . Why had He let Tambur-Ola come into her life?

. . . "You must learn to find the good in your fellow man."

The words would keep ringing in Beret's ears. Perhaps the minister was right? There was more goodness in the world than she had seen. Could it be that she was still stricken with blindness? . . . Folks had been remarkably kind to her since Per Hansa died. The neighbors had banded together and helped her with the work during both the spring and the harvest season that first year. Even the hardest labor had been nothing but fun. Those who had helped had enjoyed it like children playing a game. Not that she had needed help, for she could afford to hire, and they were three grown persons themselves. Nevertheless, the neighbors' kindness had been of great comfort to her. It felt pleasant, as though someone, after a hard day's toil, had pushed an armchair up to her and invited her to sit down.

It might be that the minister was right. There were the children, for example. At times she didn't know what to do with them because they had the notion that they must carry her on their hands. Their eagerness often became embarrassing. Did they actually think she was helpless? Surely they weren't guarding her? Beret laughed outright at the thought. The idea—couldn't they understand that she must be both first and last herself? . . . And Ole, so impulsive by nature—never before had she known what a heart there was in the boy. He would look out for her continually. Had she permitted it, he would have worked nights too in order to spare her. He and his brother literally competed to see who could be the more diligent and the more manly. . . . And here toddled Permand, that dear ridiculous little youngster, always asking questions and always wanting to help. Tears would come into her eyes when she thought of the child. Well, him at least she would take good care of! . . . A more difficult matter with the older ones. Not so easy to know just what they might be up to the moment she wasn't around; children were, after all, only children. . . . Once while the boys were busy patching up the barn for the winter, Store-Hans had run a rusty nail through his foot. But they had kept the accident a secret until several days later. Ole had simply ordered his brother to pull off his shoe and sock, and had lain down to suck the blood out. After supper they had had an errand to Tönseten's and had driven over. That night they had gone to Crazy-Brita's west on the prairie to get ointment for the foot. . . . Always thus with anything which might cause her to worry. Merciful heaven, could it be that they feared there was something wrong with her?

. . . Queer this—about the good in people. There it was, and then again it would be gone, like an object bobbing up and down in the sea over on the horizon. If one looked hard it would disappear altogether. . . . No one saw things as she saw them. People talked politics until they got drunk with excitement; the discussion only made her still more aloof and silent. She saw how, by it, good will and neighborliness were being blighted, like beautiful wheat by rust. Abominableness and hatred, and a futile chasing after wind were all the fruits they harvested! What difference would it make whether they had two states or one? What for all this hate? Did quarreling and bitter wrangling make for sweeter temper? . . . Supposing they spent all that energy in trying to live peaceably together and in helping one another? . . . It really was possible to make life pleasant out here.

Was she so different from all others? . . . She craved to be understood but found no response. If she spoke her thoughts, she was sure to be greeted with laughter, just as if she had been a child trying to talk grown-up. . . . She had tried to talk but had learned to keep silent.

This summer the minister had died of a stroke. Beret, mourning his death as though he had been her own father, felt the need of being alone, that in solitude she might thank God for what He, through this man, had done for her. No one seemed to share her feeling. The whole con-

gregation was soon in a stew as to whom they should call
to succeed him. And so they had gone to work and called
that dolt of a man! Then Beret had had to protest because she must prevent a calamity, and had said more than
was proper for an ignorant farmer woman. . . . That
Simple Simon to explain the mysterious workings of God
with man! . . . No one had listened to her; people had
seemed stricken with blindness. He looked so nice in the
pulpit; he had the best of recommendations; he was very
well educated; he was so tactful in his associations; he came
of good family; and he didn't use tobacco, they had argued.
Sörine, in her amiable way, had laughed at her and said
they surely weren't going to marry the man! . . . Now
they were lying in the bed they had made for themselves.
But where a people are being stunted by spiritual starva-
tion, the knowledge that they are themselves to blame
gives small comfort. That, too, was in Beret's mind.

III

How could it be that she always seemed to see things
that others scarcely noticed? Was she really more stupid
than anyone else?

One evening, the first winter after Per Hansa died,
Kjersti was sitting in the kitchen at Beret's knitting a sock,
and bubbling over with gossip.

A terrible rumpus in the settlement now! Hadn't Beret
heard about it? Really? Could it be possible? Why, people
weren't talking about anything else! Ole Tallaksen had
gone off and got married to Rose Mary. Awful commotion
on account of it. Reverend Isaksen had refused to marry
them unless Rose Mary turned Lutheran and joined the
church. Tallaksen himself was on a terrible rampage;
fierce the way he was cussing and carrying on; he declared
that before he'd let any of his marry a Catholic he'd see
him buried alive! Foolish of Tallaksen to talk that way.
Two young people loving each other in that manner didn't
stop to consider their faith—she certainly could remember
what happened summers in Nordland when the herring
fishers came! . . . Kjersti had dropped a stitch, necessitat-
ing that she unravel to pick it up. . . . Let's see now,
what was she saying? Oh, yes, well—the boy wasn't so

slow; nor the girl either, you bet! They had run away and got themselves squared; things had probably gone a bit too far with them, 'cording to what people said! Young folks will be thoughtless, you know. And now the Catholic priest was maintaining that they weren't married at all, but that they were living in sin and adultery! She wondered about that though. *Her* husband said that 'cording to law it was right enough, no doubt about that, just so it was done properly and in a Christian way; but of course it depended on how the Lord would look at it! Well, that's what *he* said, and he ought to know, for it was Syvert who had married Johannes Mörstad and Josie, and with them it had turned out just fine! . . . A lot going on these days. Much jollier now than the first years when they saw nothing but gophers and Indians. . . .

A faraway look came over Beret's face as she listened to the story. Back in her mind a Scripture passage strove to come out into the light, something about the sons of God going in to the daughters of men, and wickedness increasing fearfully on account of it. . . . The second marriage of the kind in less than two years. Out here people seemed no longer to care with whom they mixed and whored. Had the like of it ever been known before among either humans or beasts? It was terrible! . . . But He who reigns in heaven laughs.

During the winter of the terrible snow the school had fared badly; for weeks it had been closed altogether, the pupils attending irregularly the time it was in session; none of Beret's had been there after the memorable February blizzards.

But the following winter she sent the three youngest. Permand had teased and fussed so long that she had finally let him go also. Store-Hans was still attending and could look after him; it probably wasn't so easy for a little tot the first year. Later she came to regret having let the child start so early.

The school seemed to exert an influence that Beret could not understand. The children, once started, would think of nothing else. Evenings as soon as they had swallowed the last bite, they would clear the kitchen table and sit down to their books. In a moment they were off in a world where she could not follow. And they would act as if possessed;

they neither heard nor saw. Never had she seen the like of it, for it was school, school, school all the time; as far as they were concerned nothing else seemed to exist.

At first, she had not realized what was taking place, feeling contented because she had the children at home, right here by the kitchen table; Ole, too, having subscribed for an English farm paper, sat here with the others. At times she would think of questions to ask just to make them come out of their world. What were they doing now? What was the lesson about? Yes, but couldn't they say it in Norwegian? . . . Well, was that anything for grown folks to learn? Either she would be ignored altogether, or she would get an answer so nonsensical that it vexed her. They could at least listen to what she asked, could they not? If the two younger were called upon to explain, they would stammer or stumble over the words, and immediately switch into English; then they weren't stuck for words!

Peder had not attended many weeks before he would talk nothing but English. He had started school knowing only a few English words, such as were used daily in the Norwegian speech at home. Returning one day he had left behind him the language he had spoken all his life. The mother talked to him in Norwegian; Peder answered her in English; his voice loud and boisterous, the boy seemed almost beside himself. The others had to join in the laugh, which only emboldened him so that he went on with still greater swagger, talking nothing but English. Finally his mother stopped talking to him altogether. That same evening, taking the Norwegian primer, she sat down to teach him from it; then all ambition and joy vanished. But he didn't escape for all that, either that night or later.

Henceforth a peculiar uneasiness hovered about Beret. At times she wasn't particularly aware of it; but it never quite disappeared; it merely lay there, existing, enjoying itself until an opportunity should come. Suddenly, stirring, it would rise up and breathe apprehension, making her sensibilities painfully acute.

For a long time she couldn't quite comprehend the nature of her uneasiness. Nor did she want to think about it either. Nevertheless, it was there, would come stealing upon her at intervals, throwing shadows, uncertain, fleeting—yet shadows which persisted; they approached and passed on, might move so far that she thought they were gone; before she was aware, they were upon her again, threatening like black clouds, and now nearer than ever. As time passed the dread of impending evil grew. Turn where she might she saw no escape. And though realizing more and more clearly the inevitableness of what she was facing, she could not make herself believe it—no, not altogether. Merciful God! was it possible that a people could disappear utterly and yet continue to exist? Was this retributive justice for having torn themselves loose from kindred and fatherland? If so, then there would be many in America that would be brought low! . . . There had been many in Noah's day too—God hadn't hesitated on that account! . . . No, she could not fathom it. Perhaps it was with the Norwegians in this country as with the fertilizer she scattered on the fields in spring? She spread it there that it might give strength and virility to the growth which was to come. . . .

The dread would paint pictures for her, especially on sleepless nights when she wasn't able to get up and read it away. One picture often returned. She saw herself sitting on a lone rock far out at sea. The surf sucked and boomed. There must be a terrible storm brewing. The tide had begun to rise. Never had it risen more circumstantially. She watched it come. Little by little the surf began sucking her feet. A skua kept circling about the rock. That bird hacked rapaciously at dead bodies floating on the surface—always the eyes first. She remembered her father telling her that once. . . . She might lie and look at the picture so long that she would involuntarily draw her feet up under her and in suspense raise herself from the pillow. . . . Oh, no, America would not be satisfied with getting their bodies only!

Hidden forces were taking the children away from her —Beret saw it clearly. And strangely enough, they were enticing the youngest first. Permand and Anna Marie would watch every opportunity to talk English to each other, surreptitiously; the two older boys, she felt sure, did the same the moment she was out of their sight. Nor would they talk anything but English when youngsters of their own age came to the farm. And never did she hear them so much as mention what pertained to

them as Norwegians. . . . Here was a people going away
from itself, and not realizing it!

Fairy tales she had heard in childhood and now only
vaguely remembered came back to her, stories about sor-
cerers—Lapps skilled in the black art, her mother had
said—who, slipping out of their human integument, would
roam about in the guise of animals; if anyone in the meantime chanced upon their forms and touched them, their
owners could never again become human; forever and ever
they must wander about as evil spirits. Was that what was
happening to the children now? . . . At times, as she
listened to their talk she would fall to wondering whether
she actually was their mother—their language was not
hers. Here, so it seemed, each did not bring forth after
its own kind as the Lord had ordained. Wheat did not
yield wheat; nor cattle beget cattle. . . . Had nature's
laws been annulled altogether in this land?

One evening while she was sitting by the kitchen table
reading the *Skandinaven*,* the two youngest, opposite
her, were poring over their books. Peder, now in the third
year of school, had already reached the fourth grade.
Coming upon an awfully good story, he straightway
wanted to read it to Anna Marie. His sister, remembering
the selection from the year before, showed no interest.
But Peder, undismayed, launched into the reading at once,
loudly throwing himself into it with all the enthusiasm
and vim he possessed—he'd make them listen all right!

Beret looked up and waited till he had finished the
story; then she asked him to come and sit down beside
her—here she had found an interesting story.

At first he pretended not to have heard her. But after
a little, slowly and unwillingly, he came shuffling around
the table and plumped himself down next to her.

"What is it then?" he asked apathetically.

"You read this to me, my eyes bother me so."

"Huh!" he grunted and was silent.

"You can do that much for your mother, can't you?"

Peder bethought himself long, his whole figure indifferent and miserably bored. When at length he began to
read, his voice sounded resentful and was husky with

* A Norwegian newspaper, published in Chicago.

tears. Every other word he hacked to pieces or carelessly mispronounced. The boy acted as though he were being tortured, slowly.

Beret listened to him awhile. Unable to endure his behavior any longer she grabbed him by the arm and shook him.

"Now you read decently!"

Silence.

"Don't you hear me?"

Peder put his fists to his eyes and rubbed.

"Ain't I reading?" he whined.

His obstinacy infuriated her. Springing up, she boxed his ear, then seized him by the shoulders and shook him violently; letting go of his shoulders, she grabbed hold of one ear, and held while she beat the other unmercifully.

"Now will you read?" she panted hoarsely.

It was deathly quiet in the room. Store-Hans, repairing a harness, looked up and coughed lightly. Ole jumped up, seized his cap, and went out. The sister, realizing how this would end, had retreated to the living room. After a little, sounds of the organ began coming from there—subdued, hesitating. Suddenly Store-Hans, too, got up, put the harness on his arm and walked toward the door. Before he reached it, he stopped.

"If you two are going to keep this up, the rest of us better move to the barn."

"Might as well. Soon we'll be like the beasts anyway!"

Store-Hans fingered a strap, cast a look at his mother, and left, slamming the door hard.

That wasn't the only set-to between the mother and Peder. But the winter he read the Bible through Beret experienced serene peace. Perhaps the Lord had listened to her supplications and was ordaining all for the best? Her own Bible, a family heirloom, was difficult to read because it was written in the Danish language of two hundred years ago. And so she sent after a new one for the boy, a beautiful book with clear type, bound in leather, and gilt-edged. Elated over the gift, Peder went at his reading with still greater diligence.

Until the fall she had him transferred to the Tallaksen School, things seemed to go tolerably well. But she soon realized that that move had been a mistake; from now on she found it increasingly difficult to keep him to his

Norwegian lessons; and because the farm constantly demanded more of her attention she had little time to help him.

IV

"All right—now we're off!"

Confirmation class was out, and the pupils had already left the church. Reverend Gabrielsen had just emerged from the vestry and was locking the door. The instant he turned to go down the steps the sun caught his yellow beard, making the whole of his reddish face still more ruddy.

At a little distance beyond the steps stood Peder Holm, solemn-faced and impatient to be gone. He had to make a trip to town after a load of material for their new barn this afternoon, and so had no time to waste. Here it was nearly noon already, and he must take the minister home first. This business of driving the minister to and from church every Saturday Peder liked only moderately, though —well, never mind, there he was coming!

"What's that you said?" the minister laughed, as he came up to Peder, and thrust an arm into his. "You ought to get out of the habit of always being in such a hurry. Give God's blessed sun a chance to shine on you; that'll bring you a good coat of tan, which is excellent for the health!" In his youth Reverend Gabrielsen had been a sailor and still retained a slight lilt in his walk; swaying a little with every step he tugged at Peder, thereby making it awkward for the boy, who was trying hard to adapt himself to the gait.

Soon they were on their way. Peder wished he dared whip up the horse, because then it wouldn't take very long to reach the parsonage; but that, of course, wouldn't be polite. Besides, the minister's company was pleasant enough, for he always had so many interesting ideas to talk about—lots of fun to be with him. The two were great pals when they were alone, on which occasions they always talked English. . . . If it only hadn't been for that trip to town this afternoon!

"Pretty fine to have your own coachman!" the minister began chummily. "Not many preachers in Dakota Territory have reached so high a state, I am sure! Tell me, what was it that you were pondering so deeply this morning? I could see you were thinking hard. It wouldn't surprise me in the least if there was a great theologian hiding back of that forehead of yours. . . . No, no, no, not so fast—we are not fetching the doctor!" The minister's ruddy face beamed cheerily. . . . "What did you say the problem was?"

"Well, you see, I was thinking that if God is only spirit, then, well, then ——"

"Then it won't be easy to get hold of Him," the minister finished decisively. "No, that I'll grant you, my good Peder. But that's exactly where we must begin if we are to *reason* about God." The minister began stroking his beard upward. Soon he had his mouth full, and sat holding it thus between his teeth, a habit of his whenever he had a knotty problem confronting him.

Perceiving him in deep thought, Peder made use of the opportunity to get the horse into a trot—he knew a mean trick with the right rein. . . . Going pretty good now!

"The Catholics do wisely in forbidding the laity the use of the Bible," * the minister continued, releasing his beard and stroking it down again; "thereby they forestall much trouble, though I can't quite agree with them in the practice. There must be other ways of preventing wrong conceptions of God." The minister looked into the distance. "The danger, as I see it, lies exactly in the fact that when we begin to reason about God we immediately resort to figures of speech, and that's fatal, because we cling to the image and forget the meaning behind it. Thus it happens that with most of us God becomes nothing more than a common idol; you see—we have made Him after our own image."

Another pause. Peder watched his chance to give the horse another fillip.

. . . "With the holy men who wrote the Bible it was a different matter altogether; their language consisted of figures; they thought and spoke in figures. But when we phlegmatic Northerners begin to use the picture language of the Orientals we get ourselves into hopeless confusion

* Reverend Gabrielsen having heard a colleague make the statement had never questioned its truth.—The Author.

because our language and temperament are so entirely different!" The minister patted Peder on the shoulder, as if wanting to beat these profundities into the boy.

Peder strained so hard to follow the minister's explanation that his grown boy-face took on an angry look. "But," he objected, "if He isn't anything but spirit, then no one can have seen Him. It says about Moses ——"

"Figuratively speaking, of course! Moses felt the mystery of God until he saw Him—that's what happens to all minds who contemplate the nature of God." The minister stroked his beard slowly. "If only we could get people to understand that God must be *experienced!*"

The boy's face opened wide as he looked into the minister's, his grip on the reins loosening:

"But how can we experience what is only—yes, well, only *air?*"

The ministerial arm stretched out along the back of the seat; the whole face radiated eagerness to explain:

"That question is easy to answer!" he assured Peder. "When you ride fast, you feel the air, don't you? And you experience light and darkness, day and night, isn't that so? And how about color—no, that of course you couldn't understand? But, did you ever see the fragrance in a flower? And don't you experience daily that your mother loves you?" Suddenly the ruddy glow on his face broke into a hearty laugh and he slapped his knee. "Have you ever seen the good taste in the food you eat—heh, heh, heh, well, have you now, Peder?" His right hand clapped the shoulder it rested upon.

In a moment the minister got another idea:

"You must plan on the ministry, Peder. What a privilege to go about helping people to experience the goodness of God! There is nothing the world needs more, I assure you!" They had just passed the Bethel Church. The minister pointed back: "Look at that now! There those misguided souls have gone off by themselves, because they crave only sensuousness in their worship, and so they have made themselves a deity in their own image; him they have taken with them, forgetting that all the heavens cannot contain the glory of God! But," he broke off abruptly, "that is not what we were going to talk about." Clouds had suddenly obscured the sunshine; all brightness was gone; the minister had fallen into deep thought and sat thus for some time, his hand about his beard.

The minister's words had made Peder blush hotly. He gave the horse a slap with the reins; yet the speed did not satisfy him, and so he reached for the whip; his companion continued deep in thought, and neither saw nor heard.

After a while they turned in at the parsonage. Peder wanted to start for home at once. But that the minister wouldn't hear of—Peder must tie up his horse and come in, certainly! He had a book dealing with the nature of God, which he would lend him.

Peder's heart fell. This meant still further delay; the day, bright and big, was calling him to hurry and come on. . . . Still, he would like to borrow that book, and, moreover, how could he say no when the minister himself invited him? Peder tied the horse and followed.

Inside, the parsonage seemed smaller than it actually was because it had to house so many lives. The rooms fairly teemed with children: Children prattled, children sang, children romped about in play—noisily, children whimpered for something to eat; one lay on a pillow over in a corner, sleep painting roses on the upturned cheek; the cat, making use of the opportunity, had stolen up and lain down, its side snuggled up to the face of the child and its tail curled under the chin. Golden-haired, all of them—their skin the color of fresh cream, in their clear eyes dreamt blue spring days. There were eleven all told, counting large and small. Kenneth LeRoy, the youngest, came rowing across the kitchen floor, on his way to the dining room; he thrust his right foot in front of him and pulled himself forward as if by a hook. Else, going on fourteen and the oldest of the flock, was setting the table. The source of all this sunshine and life stood large and smiling by the kitchen stove dishing porridge out of a big kettle—she almost the fairest of them all.

The minister and Peder entered the house by the back way.

"Peace be unto this house, Eline!" the minister said as he came in. "I thought I would bring my coachman with me, so that we might have an even dozen. First of all, he needs enlightenment about the nature of God, and that he shall get from me; but if you have a bowl of porridge to spare, I think it will be fine, for his body also needs sustenance."

The bright smile which the minister got in reply assured Peder that he was welcome. Yet he felt so bashful that he could have sunk through the floor. . . . And now he would be delayed still more!

"We'll go into the study while the porridge is cooling," the minister suggested. "I see you are in a hurry."

The kitchen was large; the dining room larger. From it one entered the largest of the three rooms downstairs. An atmosphere of order and peacefulness greeted one as soon as he opened the door. Peder had never been in the room before and was so astonished by what he saw that he could only stare up and down the walls. He had never thought there could be so many books in the world. And the minister had studied them all!

Reverend Gabrielsen asked him to sit down, went over to a shelf, and pulled out a small volume, which he began paging.

"Now we shall hear what the old Latin church fathers have thought on these matters. They have divested the concept of God of its picture dress and have regarbed it in the cold cloak of logic. They have, so it appears to me, succeeded only moderately, for they themselves have been compelled to resort to images. . . . Here we are!" The minister leaned his back against the edge of the study table and began reading slowly and sonorously, stopping often and looking up at each pause:

Whosoever will be saved, before all things it is neccessary that he hold the true Christian faith.
Which faith except every one do keep whole and undefiled, without doubt he shall perish everlastingly.
And the true Christian faith is this: that we worship one God in Trinity, and Trinity in Unity,
Neither confounding the persons, nor dividing the substance.
For there is one person of the Father, another of the Son, and another of the Holy Ghost.

*But the Godhead of the Father, of the Son, and of the
Holy Ghost, is one; the Glory equal, the Majesty
coeternal.*

*Such as the Father is, such is the Son, and such is the
Holy Ghost.*

*The Father uncreate, the Son uncreate, and the Holy
Ghost uncreate.*

Here the minister was interrupted by Else, who came
and asked them if they would not please come.

"In a minute, in a minute, Else dear—just a moment
and we'll be there!" Now that he had to hurry, the
minister raised his voice in order to bring out the meaning
still more clearly:

*The Father incomprehensible, the Son incomprehen-
sible, the Holy Ghost incomprehensible.*

*The Father eternal, the Son eternal, and the Holy
Ghost eternal;*

And yet they are not three Eternals, but one Eternal.

*So also there are not three Incomprehensibles, nor
three*

*Uncreated, but one Eternal, and one Incomprehen-
sible.*

*So likewise the Father is almighty, the Son almighty,
and the Holy Ghost almighty;*

*And yet they are not three almighties: but one Al-
mighty.*

*So the Father is God, the Son is God, and the Holy
Ghost is God.*

And yet they are not three Gods, but one God.

*So likewise the Father is Lord, the Son Lord, and the
Holy Ghost Lord;*

And yet not three Lords, but one Lord.

*For like as we are compelled by the Christian truth to
acknowledge every person by himself to be God
and Lord, so are we forbidden by the Christian
religion to say, there be three Gods, or three Lords.*

The door was opened quietly, this time revealing Mrs.
Gabrielsen's buxom person.

"The porridge will get cold, Johan!"

Peder had to notice that she said Johan. Never having

heard anyone pronounce the name in that way he had to look at her again, and the look made him feel that it was pleasant to be here.

But the minister did not stop; he merely raised his hand just as when pronouncing the benediction in church; and, pressed for time, read still faster and more sonorously, his whole body fairly trembling under the sound:

The Father is made of none; neither created, nor begotten. The Son is of the Father alone; not made, nor created, but begotten.

The Holy Ghost is of the Father and of the Son; neither made, nor created, nor begotten, but proceeding.

So there is one Father, not three Fathers; one Son, not three Sons; one Holy Ghost, not three Holy Ghosts.

And in this Trinity none is before, or after the other; none is greater, or less than another;

But the whole three persons are coeternal and coequal.

So that in all things, as aforesaid, the Unity in Trinity, and the Trinity in Unity is to be worshipped.

He, therefore, that will be saved must thus think of the Trinity.

Red and breathless the minister laid the book away: "Now we can stop, Mother, and begin on the porridge!"

Presently all fourteen of them were sitting around the table eating oatmeal porridge and milk, the mother with Kenneth LeRoy on her lap.

Peder, embarrassed and feeling very much out of place, didn't know what to do with himself. No matter where he turned he seemed to get in his own way. He didn't know what to do with his hands and arms. He had been given a place next to Else, who sat at the lower end of the table, supervising the whole troop down there. The fact that the minister constantly kept asking him questions only made matters worse for him. . . . What a Goldenlocks this girl! Two heavy braids of yellow hair fell down her back; her face of the same hue, except that it was a tone lighter, only sunshine radiating from it. Most remarkable of all was her arm—his eyes could simply not let go of it; it was fuzzy, covered with a golden gossamer. Fortunately, she was so busy helping the two nearest her on the other side (they were eating from the same bowl) that she didn't have time to look at him. Since porridge was the only dish they had, the meal didn't last very long. The moment they were through eating, the minister took Peder back to the study.

"Take this book home with you and study the portion about the nature of God; then we'll take it up and discuss it Saturday."

Peder's attention had been attracted to a stack of books piled up on the floor, all of them red-edged, of the same size, and bound in limp leather, a broad rubber band encircling each one. He had picked up the one on top and was looking at it. . . . So that's how an English Bible looks! How small it was—why, this one couldn't possibly contain all that was in his own big one at home . . . that he had read through.

The minister, noticing Peder's puzzled look, smiled: "Don't you have one like that?"

"No, not like this."

"Would you like to have one?"

"Yes, I would!"

"You have a Bible in your home, haven't you?"

"Not an English one!"

"That's a mistake," said the minister, positively, "for you will be preaching the Word of God in English. Twenty years from now not a word of Norwegian will be spoken in this country. . . . Well, I think I can pay my coachman that much. Let me have the book and I'll write your name in it." The minister sat down to write, and looking up asked:

"What is your middle name?"

"Victorious."

"Victorious? That's a peculiar name; very beautiful, too bad it doesn't fit in English."

The minister got up and handed Peder the book. "Now I'll tell you something: You prepare to read the twelfth chapter of the Book of Ecclesiastes at the meeting tomorrow. Look it over carefully so that you can read it well; then I'll use it for my text. I think you will find it the most beautiful thing you have ever read."

"Shall I read it in English?"

"Certainly."

Peder didn't move.

The minister looked at him:

"Don't you want to?"

"I'd like to!"

Peder had turned red as a beet. He took the book, mumbled, "Thank you," and hurried out.

He left the house by the kitchen way. Just then Else came along, dangling a pail on her arm, going to the pump for water. She seemed to be in a great hurry, and because she came so close behind, Peder had to turn around—it simply would look ridiculous to run away from her. Else understood that perfectly; she returned the look, assuring him that he need pay no attention to her, because she was in a hurry. Peder didn't know how to answer that smile. Just a little while ago he had been sitting beside her at the table and now she was looking at him chummily as though they had played together all their lives. Perhaps he ought to offer to fetch that pail of water? Anna Marie was always wanting him to do that at home. Mustering his courage, Peder took hold of the handle:

"Let me do it for you!"

But Else didn't let go, and so both trotted off with the pail between them, she laughing, with a teasing look in her eye. . . . What eyes that girl had! Their walking this way became very embarrassing to Peder but he couldn't let go—then it might look as though he hadn't meant to help her. He gave the handle a jerk and said boastfully:

"I'll carry the water for you!"

"Is that so?"

To all that teasing he couldn't possibly give in, and so they walked along swinging the pail between them.

At the pump they had to set the pail down, which brought their heads very close together, and caused one of her braids to fall down on his arm. In the same instant both grabbed for the pump handle, and because he got there first, she must try to shove him aside; which only made Peder laugh, for now he was already pumping! Feeling himself the stronger and absolutely master of the situation, he dared to look right into her face and to talk to her.

—Did they like it out here in the West?

—My, yes, lots of fun here!

—How so?

—Look at all the room to play in! She had put her

hands on her hips just like a grown person, and was looking out across the prairie.

—You bet! Peder assured her enthusiastically, room enough here all right!

The pail was full and so he carried it up to the kitchen porch and set it down.

"Much obliged for the help!" Peder tried to make his voice sound gruff but the laughter gurgling in it betrayed him.

"Oh you smarty!"

"What did you say?" He looked at her innocently.

"You'll be a funny minister, you will!"

"Minister?"

"Father says you are—then you'll have to behave!"

"Uh huh," nodded Peder, "here you'll see a minister!"

Thereupon he left her and walked down to the buggy. He ought to run—he knew he ought to because he had wasted so much time already; but it didn't look just right for a grown man, especially when there were people watching. . . .

V

The sun had just closed his eye. A dreamy silence followed. The landscape rose and listened. A meadow lark, becoming curious, struck a note through which it discovered its sweetheart, perching on a fence post a little way beyond. The two of them made ready to rejoice for a while but before they were aware of it the drowsy twilight had cast its spell over them, and so they forgot their song.

The dusk deepened imperceptibly. Through it, from one skyline to another, quivered soft tones. Inaudible they were, yet exerting a peculiar power. A dream only, all of it, full of strange pictures. . . . All the noises of the day the gloaming had lulled asleep. The prairie seemed to be adrift. Had at last no weight at all. Only floated in a vast sea of impenetrable violet and purple. Became unreal . . . of no substance, but felt vaster now than in the flood of sunlight which deluged the sky at high noon. . . . Here and there drowsy lights awoke. No life in them yet. Only embers half asleep.

Over in the dusk a wagon, loaded with shingle, was

rumbling heavily and thoughtfully along. Peder rode on
top. He had stood a bundle on end, placed against it a
sack of hay which he used as a pillow for his back. He
was hauling an enormous load and let the horses take
their time.

No need to hurry either! On his way out he had tried
to drown the rattle of the empty wagon by singing, and
had succeeded fairly well, for he had a strong, clear voice
when he really wanted to use it. Now he only sat fooling
with senseless thoughts so as to keep himself from going
to sleep. Silken and balmy the feel of the night air about
him. The shirt opened wide at the throat; the sleeves were
rolled up over the elbows; even the trousers had been
unbuttoned—the silky air felt so pleasant against the
body.

Peder was staring straight ahead. . . . Full of living
mystery the dusk round about him. Though it uttered no
sound it called to him with a thousand voices. It was close
and livingly real; yet he could never get ahold of it. . . .
Almost like God. . . . Strange this, about the nature of
God. If He were only spirit and present everywhere He
must be in the twilight too. For He dwelt in the sunshine
and in the rain; in the storm as well as in the fair weather;
the flowers and grass in the meadows manifested His
glory, so the minister had said today. Only living presence,
and everywhere! . . . Feeling a bit uneasy Peder buttoned
up his trousers.

He sat up and listened. Somewhere, a dog had bayed
—a sleepy sound, dying quickly . . . must have been
very far off.

Peder's thoughts were adrift. Floating aimlessly. Found
a problem and lingered for a moment, left it, and passed
on.

. . . A dance tonight in the hayloft at Doheny's.
Susie was a good dancer, they said. Charley, too. . . .
Peder cracked his whip at the horses. Why not get a move
on you! . . . For young people, Satan had no more
cunning snare than the dance, Mother said. . . . Yes,
well—he knew several who danced. Charley, for example.
A mighty fine fellow, Charley—in many ways better than
himself. Pluck in that kid! Peder doubted there was a
thing that Charley wouldn't dare to do. . . . Peder lashed
the horses hard, getting them into a lively gait which

lasted for some time. . . . If God was only spirit and everywhere present He would be in the hayloft at Doheny's tonight, wouldn't He? How could it be so wrong if He were there? . . . What did Mother know about real fun? Had she ever dared to have any? . . . Always that way with old folks—they were afraid of anything they hadn't tried. Easy enough to call it sin when one was afraid! . . . Peder stood up, and from his position on top of the load began to laugh at the idea which he now saw. Wonderful to go about in the world granting people the remission of their sins.—"The gracious forgiveness of all thy sins!" . . . To be able to pronounce these words in such a way that people really believed them and got up and went away rejoicing—well, he would just like to try that job! . . . But they didn't believe them. Never were their faces more downcast and solemn than after Communion. . . . Peder glanced about him in the dusk. The lights had a brighter glow now. Yonder lay the parsonage. He saw it and laughed aloud . . . he knew where the minister's wife lived!

. . . "Get a move on there, you lazy plugs!" He struck the horses, but only just enough to make them swish their tails a couple of times and then amble on, leisurely as before.

Daylight was gone entirely when Peder drove into the yard at home. He unhitched the horses in a hurry, watered them, and put them in. Before going to the house he had to see how far they had progressed with the work on the new barn this afternoon. The framework loomed silent through the dark; way up at the top it disappeared altogether; here an arm reached out, there another—all mysterious and quiet like some living being withdrawing itself into secrecy, not wanting to be disturbed. . . . Monday they'd be shingling. Man, what excitement they'd have then!

A little later he was sitting by the kitchen table eating supper. Mother, near the stove, was busily hanging clothes over the back of a chair, shirts to be ironed for tomorrow. The living room lay in darkness but the door stood open; his sister was playing the organ—a soft, plaintive melody. . . . The boys must be out somewhere. He didn't care to ask his mother about it, for he knew how strongly she disliked this chasing about on Saturday nights. She seemed thoughtful and low-spirited again. . . . They were dancing at Doheny's tonight!

Beret, having finished her work, came and sat down opposite him at the table.

"You got the load home all right?"

"Oh I guess so!" Peder ate and ate, every bite he swallowed only seeming to make him the more hungry. He felt dead tired and so drowsy.

"Did you have money enough?"

Peder handed her the pocket book.

She took it and counted the money which was left. Tapping the table with the pocket book she said, "I see that the minister has given you a present."

Peder came to. One glance at her told him that there was trouble in the air. What on earth could it be? Her face seemed careworn and worried.

"I tell you Gabrielsen is a fine man!" Peder assured her.

His mother did not answer for some time. When she did her voice choked with indignation:

"It seems to me that if he really wanted to make you a present of a Bible, he might have given you a Norwegian one. You'd expect a man so well educated to have better sense!"

"Aw, you!" Peder grabbed a slice of bread, and was about to reach for the butter.

"You needn't 'aw you' me! It's bad enough now without the minister helping to make matters worse."

"Is it wrong to read the Bible?" Peder's voice was thin, his eyes fixed narrow and gleaming upon his mother.

"That you know I don't mean!" she retorted sharply.

Words which he must spit out, get said instantly, sprang to the tip of Peder's tongue.

But then she spoke again:

"Pretty soon there'll be nothing but English here—it's English at home, only English wherever one turns. The language we have spoken time out of mind, we cast away as if it were a worn-out garment. . . . And now our own minister comes along saying *yea* and *amen* to the act. Oh, it's shameful—shameful, I say!" She pounded the table with the pocket book, as if thereby to give greater weight to her words.

Her lunacy infuriated him. Not for one minute need

she think he'd give in to such nonsense! A sneer had
come into his voice; he heard it himself, but had no time
to think of that now:

"You are a queer one, that I must say'"

"What are you saying, Permand?" she asked, leaning
farther in on the table.

"I say you're *crazy!*" he shouted—he had to defend himself against her.

Without a word Beret rose hastily, and went over to
the stove. There in the dim light she stood, motionless.
After a little she began puttering about. She stirred up
the fire, put the flatiron on the stove, picked up one shirt
after another, examining each collar band carefully. Finally she folded the shirts and piled them on the chair.

Peder sat waiting, certain that more would be coming.
And he intended to answer—he would not stand for
her saying such things even if she were his mother.

But she said nothing more. She brought out the
ironing board; set it up; seemed to be done and went into
her bedroom, closing the door behind her.

Peder got up from the table and looked for his cap.
. . . He had better look after the horses for the night.
Before going out he went to the living room, where his
sister sat playing, now very softly.

—Where were the boys?

—She didn't know.

—Hadn't they told Mother where they were going?

—She didn't think so. The sister reached the end of the
melody she was playing, and after resting a moment on a
couple of chords, glided over into "O Bread of Life from
Heaven."

—Had Mother put the iron on? his sister was asking
from somewhere within the music.

But Peder had already left. Out on the porch he had
stopped. . . . A hand had clutched his throat and was
choking him. He could have shrieked out in despair.
As he calmed down he began to listen to the noises of the
night. . . . From down on the road the sound of a vehicle,
driving fast, came floating up to him. . . . There came
another. Now they were racing! A shout rent the air.
Loud laughter followed. Then silence. . . . They were
dancing at Doheny's tonight. Nothing but youth and
laughter and merrymaking. All sorts of fun going on over

there. . . . On such evenings his sister sat pumping hymn
tunes out of a wheezy old organ, and he himself must not
stir lest there be too much English—by golly, if the world
wasn't queer! . . .
    Peder took plenty of time about caring for the horses.
Having finished, he went to the windmill and sat down,
staying there a long time.

VI

    Beret got little sleep that night, but took no notice of
it because that happened so often. At times when those
spells came on she might lie awake night after night, get
up to her tasks in the morning without having slept a
wink. So at least she thought.
    She had discovered a remedy against sleeplessness,
which, if she only caught herself before her thoughts
became too restive, would work very well. She would get
up and light the lamp. On her bedroom table lay the old
Bible ready for her. Finding the place where she had left
off last night she would begin to read, little by little losing
herself in the scenes until pleasant drowsiness enveloped
her mind. If she then succeeded in keeping her thoughts
fixed upon the portion of God's Word just read until
she got back into bed, she would usually drop off to sleep
at once. But the remedy did not always work. For days
at a time she might walk about in a half stupor, not
knowing clearly whether she was living in dream or in
reality.
    Beret's bedroom was large and spacious. The fall Per
Hansa built the house, he had mentioned jokingly that
this room was to be theirs; when Permand had married
and filled the other rooms with children, the grandparents
would live in here and sort of keep an eye on things. . . .
Perhaps he had been serious? One thing, anyway, was
certain—in this room she had Per Hansa more livingly
present than in any other place on the farm. Sometimes
she actually heard him talk.
    The bed occupied one corner of the room; a small
bureau, always having a white runner on it, stood just
inside the door, and near the bed an old table they had
used in the sod hut—also with a white cover. Anna Marie

often nagged at her on account of that table. . . . Did they need to keep such rubbish? Looked as though they were too stingy to live like decent folk! . . . And the table wasn't exactly an ornament either; Per Hansa had made it himself, out of parts of an old homemade wagon they had brought with them the time they moved out here; the boards in the top yawned so wide apart that one could stick his whole finger down between them—in those days Per Hansa had had to be saving on the material! . . . It would do her as long as she lived; after she was gone, they might do with it as they liked.

In the corner beyond the bed a huge immigrant chest devoured all the space. That piece of furniture, too, Anna Marie looked at with an evil eye, despite the fact that it was solidity personified—massive and substantially constructed, reinforced with heavy iron bands. Nevertheless, the tooth of time had marked it: The iron bands were eaten rough; the paint, in many places, must have worn off long ago; but on the front side one could yet make out traces of a date *Anno 16* . . .

After lighting the lamp Beret went to the chest, and lifting the lid, sat down on the edge. There she remained for a while as if she had forgotten why she had come, her face dejected by many cares.

Bending down, she brought out a curious old casket, shaped like a chest, with a rounded cover. On a black background were glued yellow figures of straw; those on the cover representing a church and a whole populace on its way thither; those on the sides, garlands. The casket had been given her by her father on the day of her confirmation, to remind her, he had said, of the promise she had that day made the Lord. Her grandfather had brought it from Finmark one spring when they had been fishing off the Russian coast. Because Beret didn't trust the banks in this country she was now using it as a money box. Whenever produce of any kind was sold, and the money brought home, she would put it in the casket. This summer when they began building the new barn, she had had a little better than four thousand dollars lying here.

Beret opened the box and took out a twenty-dollar bill for the next trip to town. She paid cash for every load she bought, in order to have no account charged against her. . . . Beret, returning the casket to its place in the chest and closing the lid, seemed to forget what she was about. She still held the bill and looked absentmindedly about. . . . What had she done with the pocket book? Oh, there it was! She put the bill into it, stood with her back against the bureau, listening. . . . Was Permand going out? . . . He couldn't have taken time to tend the horses before he came in!

From sheer force of habit her eyes sought the place where the Bible lay. Picking it up, she pulled out the chair and sat down to read. She had set herself the task of memorizing the New Testament, hoping thereby both to find greater peace for herself and to please God. Now she was already far into the Gospel of St. John. But tonight she could not fix her thoughts on the holy words; her mind wandered elsewhere. Every now and then, as she tried to repeat a verse, she would be looking up and listening. She heard Anna Marie finish the ironing and go upstairs to bed. . . . Not much trouble with that child! . . . Then Peder came in. He stopped in the kitchen to get a drink. Involuntarily she made a move as if to get up, raising herself halfway from the chair . . . no, she had better let it go until some other time! She heard him go up to his room, his step was heavy on the stair tonight. A faint smile brightened her face. . . . Soon it was quiet above. Only the occasional scraping of a foot against the floor as it swung back and forth. . . . He was sitting up late. . . . Must be the gift of the preacher which he was so taken up with. They had become fast friends, it seemed! . . . An expression of bitterness crossed her grave countenance.

God's Word was no longer good enough in Norwegian! Oh no—long since had she foreseen that if they were to get along in this country, they would have to cast away all that they had brought with them from Norway. . . . After all had been taken and there was nothing but the body left, what then? What kind of creatures would they be? What would the country use them for? . . . That people could have eyes and yet not see . . . and he an educated man! He knew well enough that Permand was never at a loss in Norwegian—how could he do this thing? . . . And now the boy, having the minister on his side, came home and threw it right in her face that she was out of her mind! All life went out of Beret's face. . . . There probably were others in the house thinking the same thing—she heard strange utterances at times! . . . Where were they tonight? The book dropped into her lap, her muscles having gradually relaxed under the long strain. . . . Store-Hans was taken up with Sofie. . . . God help them to restrain themselves so that they didn't get too intimate before the time came! A brighter look stole over her face, lightening its soberness. . . . The boy was beginning early—but so had others in the family!

Beret shifted to another position and pulled herself together, determined to make her thoughts fasten themselves on the reading:

Jesus went unto ye Mount of Olibes:

And early in the morning hee came againe into the Temple, and all the people came unto him, and he sate downe, and taught them.

And the Scribes and Pharisees brought unto him a woman taken in adultery, and when they had set her in the midst.

They say unto him, Master, this woman was taken in adultery, in the very act.

Now Moses in the Law commanded us, that such should be stoned: but what sayest thou?

This they said, tempting him, that they might habe to accuse him. But Jesus stouped downe, and with his finger wrote on the ground, as though he heard them not.

So when they continued asking him, he lift up him= selfe and saide unto them, Hee that is without sinne among you, let him first cast a stone at her.

And againe hee stouped downe and wrote on the ground.

And they which heard it, being conbicted by their own conscience, went out one by one, beginning at the eldest, eben unto the last: and Jesus was left alone, and the woman standing in the midst.

When Jesus had lift up himselfe, and saw none but the woman, hee said unto her, Woman, where are those thine accusers? Hath no man accused thee?

She saide, No man, Lord. And Jesus saide unto her, Neither doe J condemne thee: Goe, and sinne no more.

So frequently had she felt the need of seeking consolation in this simple narrative that she already knew the story by heart. But in order to connect it to the portion that followed, she repeated it now. And in no other place did the Saviour speak with greater sweetness—it was as though she could feel His benign hand touching her. . . . Again the book fell into her lap, and again her mind wandered. Many memories crowded in upon her. . . . Beret sighed, wistfully . . . how inexplicable, how utterly unsolvable the riddle of one's life!

After midnight a buggy turned into the yard. The boys came quietly in. She scarcely heard them. Beret couldn't help being amused; tonight they had even removed their shoes outside! . . . Presently all was quiet upstairs.

By and by she felt drowsiness overtaking her. Getting up, she put the book away, took the lamp and set it on the kitchen table, leaving it there while she went on her nightly round of the barns to make sure that no beast was uncomfortable. When she returned she removed her shoes in the kitchen. From a box on the stove shelf she took a stump of candle, which she lit, then went to the stairway and listened before tiptoeing up to Peder's room. . . . The boy lay fast asleep, face toward her. There was a faint trace of a smile on it. Shading the light, she approached the bed. God be praised—he is seeing beautiful things now! He must have been in good spirits when he went to bed. Beret seemed greatly relieved, walked to the table and looked at the objects lying there. . . . Had he been reading from his new Bible tonight? Her face clouded—the one she gave him two years ago had been put underneath . . . to be discarded, she supposed! . . . She exchanged the books, smiling as she did so. But just as she was putting the Norwegian Bible in the place where the other had lain, she discovered a paper with some writing on it. . . . What could this be? The word *Else* was written all over the sheet. And down below, at the very botton of the page, was printed in bold letters: "The gracious forgiveness of all thy sins!" . . . Could anyone imagine what the boy had been up to tonight? Beret looked long at the paper. Finally she replaced it, walked quietly down the stairs and went to bed.

But no sleep came to her eyes. . . . Where in the world could one imagine that the boy had got that name?

VII

Reverend Gabrielsen had come to St. Luke's at the end of the winter, and though it was now midsummer, his parishioners had not yet ceased to wonder about him. From the very first Sunday Tönseten had had his misgivings. The moment he saw the new pastor enter the church, wife and numerous progeny trooping up behind, he had whispered a word or two to the man beside him: Huh—if we are to feed all of that crew, we'll soon land in the poorhouse, that's sure! I thought it was a minister we'd called and not a whole congregation. The deacons should have looked into these matters beforehand.

The ways of Reverend Gabrielsen differed widely from those of his predecessors. Some of his ideas were so curious that the discussion concerning him would not die down. Soon after his coming he had startled them by proposing that Bethel should join with St. Luke's. Why have two congregations here—the people were of one nationality, all professing the same faith? Here stood two churches, the one shaming the other. Why not use Bethel for a parochial school? How could they have made this blunder? Did they think that God looked with favor upon their having two churches in the neighborhood? He clasped his beard and beamed upon the men with whom he was talking. The men only smiled and shrugged their shoulders. Presently it was noised abroad that he had called on Nils Nilsen and on several others of the Bethel people. What answer he had got, no one knew. For some time now he had not mentioned the matter.

The gossip about him continued. Without consulting either the deacons or the trustees he abolished the churching of mothers. A medieval custom, he explained. In reality barbarism! She who had journeyed to death's door in order to bring a new life into the world, ought not be punished by being pilloried before the whole congregation —they could understand that, could they not? Thereupon he launched into a talk on the glory of motherhood, which was so touching that even the deacons forgot to object.

But afterward people talked. Could this man really be

orthodox? . . . He had queer notions, that's sure! . . .
Time would, of course, tell. . . . No doubt about his
good intentions, anyway.

Had conditions been different Reverend Gabrielsen
might have been a reformer; as he found them here, however, he could only make slight improvements. Before
very long he conducted, every other Sunday afternoon,
Bible hours for the young people of the congregation.
Partly because these meetings were new and partly because he held them in the homes, they gained in popularity until both young and old attended. After reading a
portion of Scripture and discoursing on it for a while, he
turned the meeting into a social hour—the young people
playing games, the older women visiting while the men
smoked their pipes and discussed crops and politics.

The first two meetings had been held at the parsonage.
In spite of the size of the crowd Mrs. Gabrielsen had had
enough coffee and cake to go around. All had marveled at
her; why, it was just like the feeding of the multitude in
the desert! How could she manage with so many? . . .
But when the minister announced the third meeting, that
too at the parsonage, Tönseten got up and protested.
They'd better try his place next; someone else would have
to invite the meeting after that—in the long run, this arrangement would be cheaper for them all! he added laughingly. And Reverend Gabrielsen took no offense whatever;
he simply nodded, "Thank you," and went on to say that
there wasn't so much neighborliness among them but
that, at times, it might be wise to come together and taste
each others' coffee. Didn't they agree with him? The
minister smiled benevolently at Tönseten.

These meetings Reverend Gabrielsen conducted in English, which innovation caused several of the elders to
shake their heads. They all understood Norwegian, so
why change the language? To that objection the minister
smiled good-naturedly, like one seeing a complicated matter in all its ramifications, and knowing that he must be
patient with good people who in understanding are as yet
only children. . . . Not for the elders did he hold these
meetings! The young people needed English, they would
have to defend their faith in the language of the country.
English was their language as assuredly as America was
their home. In twenty years from now not one word of

Norwegian would be heard in America, no doubt about that! In the minds of some this prophecy took root. Twenty-five years later when the language question became acute and threatened schism and reorganization, there were many who recalled Reverend Gabrielsen's words—the English camp adopting them as their battle cry.

Beret had attended the first two meetings. After that she hadn't cared to go. Thirsting, she had come to the fountain, had begged to have her thirst slaked, and had received nothing but a few drops of lukewarm water.

Afterward she had gone about silent, and in a bitter mood, reflecting upon what was taking place among them. . . . Was the minister right? Would his predictions come true? Was it possible for Norwegian hearts to beat in so alien a medium? Must it not eventually mean death to them? . . . She understood nothing any more, it seemed. . . . But could a common sparrow take the meadow lark's song? Would the cow ever forget she was a cow and begin to grunt? . . . The horses were grazing in the same pasture with the cattle; though few in numbers compared with the others, they did not begin to bellow! . . . Ceaselessly her mind struggled with the problem. . . . This spring she had sent for some duck eggs and had put them under a hen. In due time both ducklings and chicks appeared. At first they had looked almost alike; but with each passing day, despite the fact that she fed them the same food, the difference grew more marked, the chicks gradually developed into chickens and the ducklings becoming more ducklike. It had seemed a great wonder to Beret and she had derived much comfort from it. Wasn't this sufficient proof that God's law was still operating? . . . But according to the minister it signified nothing—in twenty years, he said! . . .

Today the meeting was being held at Gjermund Dahl's. Beret wanted to have Gjermund superintend the shingling tomorrow, for then she could feel sure that the job would be well done; so she made herself ready to go with the children to the meeting.

They were rather late in getting started. Though Peder had kept to his room all day, he was not ready when the others called to him. The brothers had lost all patience

and did not mince words in telling him so. And Anna
Marie, that everlasting tease of a girl, couldn't leave him
alone! She always had a very mean way about her teasing
—in a quiet voice and very innocently, she would ask him
a question, pause a bit to hear what he was going to say,
whereupon she would answer the question herself.

Peder climbed into the wagon and invited her to shut up,
saying it in such a way that anyone who saw fit might
take the hint. His mood got no better because Mother was
going along, which he had not figured on at all. He had
not even mentioned to her that he was to be on the program. What would she say when she found it out, the
way she had carried on last night? He didn't know what
to do now; the book he held under his arm inside his coat
where no one could see it.

At Dahl's every room in the house was packed full of
people. And more continued to come. In one corner of
the kitchen stood a group of girls, whispering and gig-
gling, whom Anna Marie joined as soon as she saw them.
Mrs. Dahl herself came and escorted Beret into the bedroom, where she cleared a place for her on the bed by removing a number of hats.

The boys joined the crowd on the front porch. This
too was filled, mostly with younger men and boys, now
betting and joking in a low tone—the meeting had not
yet begun.

Peder took a position near the door. He would have
liked to sit down. . . . Too conspicuous to stand. They
must be wondering what was the matter with him? Peder
was in a cold sweat from embarrassment. . . . Now Store-
Hans was looking at him . . . had he better go in? The
minister might be wondering if he had come. But there
was no room inside. . . . To make sure that his book was
safe, he thrust his hand inside his coat. . . . Then Ole
hemmed. Peder could tell it was meant for him. Presently
the minister stood in the doorway looking out, saw him
and nodded encouragingly, which made Peder feel more
comfortable.

The meeting began by the minister's announcing a
stanza from a Norwegian hymn which he felt certain they
all knew. After the singing he arose and told them what
text he had chosen for today; and thereupon he sprang a
great surprise by adding that he had asked one of his

catechumens to read the chapter. That he had done with a purpose, he explained; the Lord had endowed the boy with most unusual gifts; he ought to study for the ministry and consecrate his life to the service of the Lord. And in order that God's plan might not be frustrated, he enjoined the congregation to be watchful: Those who had the gift of encouragement must encourage; those who prayed must include the boy in their prayers. Especially would he commend to the young people that they, in their associations with him, be considerate. He who had been consecrated to the Lord was beset with temptations and might most easily be led astray sometimes. The minister delivered a whole discourse on the subject, concluding by reminding them of how blessed it would be if St. Luke's could send out a real apostle. Everyone in the audience craned his neck—of whom was the minister talking anyway?

As he stepped into the crowded room to read, Peder was all confusion. He would have liked to know where his mother sat, but dared not look up. The thought of their set-to last night sickened him . . . and he had not told her that he was to read here. . . . If only the minister had not talked that way!

He managed to get his book out and begin the reading. His fresh young voice, now trembling with conflicting emotions, rang sweet and clear throughout the rooms. The content of what he was reading was familiar to him, the minister having recently discussed it in class. And Peder had read the chapter over so many times that he knew it by heart. Yet he used the book, reading slowly and distinctly in order to make the audience see how beautiful the picture really was. The strange majesty of it gripped him, made him experience a sweet sadness—almost like that Killdeer-song of Tambur-Ola's. And the more lovingly he treated it, the richer it got.

People listened wide-eyed and marveling. . . . That that youngster of Beret Holm's could read God's Word so edifyingly!

Beret, sitting on the bed with Kjersti, listened intently to the minister's remarks. She fell to wondering what boy it might be. The moment she realized that the minister was talking about Peder she wanted to get up and protest —Permand was not going to read the Word of God to her

in English! . . . But there he had started already and in
a moment she was listening so eagerly that she was oblivious to all else. . . . Now he is afraid—I can tell it by
his voice. I hope the boy isn't going to break down and
disgrace himself! . . . He surely has studied his lesson?
. . . She felt herself trembling and dared hardly breathe
till Peder had finished.

Not before the meeting was over was Beret able to collect herself; but then people who wanted to talk to her
began crowding into the room. Some took her by the hand
and congratulated her. How proud she must be to have a
boy like that! Kjersti, her eyes full of tears, chatted beamingly with anyone who would listen . . . yes, indeed, Per
Hansa would have rejoiced today could he have been here
and heard Peder speak! . . . And hadn't she seen it all
the time? Clear as day that the Lord intended that boy
for something more than ordinary! Didn't she remember
the night he was born—what had she said then? Her head
wagged in motherly pride.

The many felicitations made Beret reserved and cautious. . . . Now I had better look out or I might say too
much. If I speak my mind they won't understand . . .
they will think I'm vain, and that I'm trying to show
better judgment than they. . . . Beret was standing in
the midst of the group, her cheeks flushed, there was a
smile on her face. . . . Her neighbors looked at her—
what a comely woman Beret Holm was! . . . Small wonder, the way things prospered for her!

Beret started for the kitchen to help Mrs. Dahl with
the serving. The minister seeing her came over and shook
hands.

"I suppose you are proud of your boy today, Mrs.
Holm?"

"That hasn't occurred to me," she answered slowly.

"But you are thankful to God, I am sure!"

Beret did not answer, and so he added:

"I do not think I have ever had so gifted a catechumen.
You must urge him to become a minister."

"To whom should he preach?" asked Beret quietly.

The minister looked at her in amazement, repeating
her question:

"To whom should he preach?"

"Yes?" Now there was a faint smile on her face.

"I don't think I understand what you mean, Mrs. Holm." The minister's kind face actually looked troubled. "If your predictions come true, twenty years from now our people will not be found in America."

"Oh I see!" he laughed heartily, "you're thinking of us as Norwegians. But, strictly speaking, are there any Norwegians now? Take yourself, for instance: You came into a wilderness and have ever since been building America— aren't you an American? And your children ——"

"Oh I don't know . . . I am first of all a human being. The moment I cease being that, I can't be of much use to any country."

The minister, putting all his natural kindness into the question, asked, "You don't cease being a human being just because you change language?"

"Are you so sure about that?" Beret's excitement was mounting, yet she had to go on: "The Bible tells about Ten Tribes which were lost and have never been heard from since."

"On account of their sins of course, because ——"

"That they had so little regard for their language must have been part of their sin," she interrupted him.

"Not necessarily, my good woman, no—not necessarily!" Suddenly his face beamed: "Do you think I was committing a sin by speaking English here today?"

"Yes," said Beret very quietly, "I do."

The minister scrutinized her questioningly. She was about his own height; today she wore a black dress, neat fitting and prettily made; her cheeks were tinted by a warm glow of animation; her eyes, clear and bright, looked straight into his. The conviction that had grown out of many years of silent wrestling with a problem, the issue of which, to her, must mean either life or death, dominated her personality.

Reverend Gabrielsen forgot himself, and began stroking his beard upward. His mouth being unable to hold any more he smoothed the beard down, asking as he did so:

"Do you mean to say that we ought to go on talking Norwegian in America?" He couldn't keep from laughing a bit because the idea seemed so ridiculous.

Beret noticed the laugh and the flush in her face heightened perceptibly. She fingered her handkerchief nervously, folding and unfolding it—one of the corners wouldn't lie right; she had much trouble with that corner.

"Yes," she said guilelessly, "because I cannot understand why the acquiring of a new language must crowd out our own!"

"But history shows us that such has always been the case; we have no reason, absolutely none whatever, to believe that it will be different in America. Take, for example, the Norwegians who immigrated to——"

A nervous agitation was upon Beret, she could not wait for him to finish; her voice had an impatient note:

"A great many things are taking place in America which have never happened before! Here we are building, as you said; a people who have eyes and can see may do wonderful things!" . . .

Beret had more to say. But just then Gjermund Dahl came and hurried the minister away—if he didn't come quick, the coffee would get cold! Where had he been keeping himself all this time? They had been scouring the whole farm for him, and Mrs. Gabrielsen—well, Gjermund dared not think of what she might do to him! As the two men walked off together, Beret heard the minister confide to Gjermund that Mrs. Holm was a most extraordinary woman, really . . . their voices trailed off and were soon lost.

The silence about her made Beret discover that the room was deserted. . . . Had she done something wrong again? An odd sense of well-being filled her. . . . What had happened? What had she said to him?

In the kitchen was great stir and bustle, many women being busily at work serving the refreshments. Beret went out to help them. But seeing that she would only be in the way, and preferring not to talk to anyone just now, she walked out on the porch to cool off.

Bright, beautiful day. The yard teemed with people. A little distance away stood a long table, covered with a white cloth, and on it veritable mounds of sandwiches, cakes, and doughnuts; the aroma of strong, freshly made coffee floated upon the air; small groups, having helped themselves at the table, were now standing and sitting about on the lawn. Friendly talk and good spirits prevailed everywhere; the mood was festive as at a wedding.

A little farther down the yard a crowd of young people, all of them in their teens, were shouting and laughing in a game. Beret looked at the crowd to see if any of hers might be there . . . they were making a terrible racket. "Last couple out!" a boy's voice sang out, deep and bubbling over with uncontrollable merriment.

—Can that be Permand again? wondered Beret. A mad race for a fair-complexioned girl started in the yard. Quickly she darted out from the nearer side of the line, ran for dear life to avoid her pursuer's hand—stalling, laughing, and making unexpected turns; her partner tried just as desperately to save her; the ranks kept shouting encouragingly. After a long chase Peder caught the girl, and from all appearances the capture must have proved exceedingly agreeable, for the two of them laughed right into each other's faces and the girl did not withdraw her hand until they had reached their places in the line.

Beret stared hard . . . what in the world? . . .

Sörine had come up beside her and was laughing:

"Did you see Permand nab the minister's daughter? You just trust him to pick the right one!"

"Was that one of the minister's children?" Beret had lowered her voice.

"Sure it was, her name is Else."

"*Else*, did you say?" Beret stepped closer as she asked.

"Yes, that's the oldest one. Have you had your coffee yet?"

Beret was sober and taciturn. While eating her lunch she looked from group to group, and had little to say to people who came up and spoke to her. All seemed gay and not a bit concerned over the prospect that in twenty years the Norwegians would have disappeared in America! And their own minister turned the hearts of the children away from their parents. . . . The shepherd being like that, what could one expect from the flock? . . . Beret's hand shook violently; she had to set her plate down.

Presently she began to search for Gjermund. As she walked about she stopped here and there to exchange greetings. People smiled at her and seemed pleased by her wanting to shake hands with them, and so she lingered a little longer each time. But try as she might, she could not put real heartiness into her talk—the feeling of being a total stranger among her own people would not leave her. When at length she found Gjermund and told him what she wanted he laughed good-naturedly. He would certainly have come anyway even though she hadn't asked him, he assured her, greatly pleased, as though she had conferred a real honor upon him. Several came up and inquired how she was getting on with the building . . . and didn't she need more help? . . . they weren't very busy just now. She felt thoroughly disgusted with herself because she couldn't respond more heartily.

Seeing Tönseten make ready to leave, she went over and asked if he and Kjersti wouldn't stop in on their way home; there was a matter she would like to talk to them about. Immediately Tönseten proposed that she go with them and let the young folks look out for themselves; anyhow, she might be sure those fellows wouldn't quit for a while yet—the sun was too high in the heavens for that! Tönseten was undoubtedly right; the game was going more merrily than ever. Many more had joined in the play. Having told one of the boys not to look for her she left with the Tönsetens.

At Beret's, as soon as Tönseten had tied up his horses, all three strolled off to the new barn. The windmill Tönseten passed by because he had marveled at it so often that he knew every detail of it by heart; before the snow flew he would have one himself—no mistake about it! But in the barn he hobbled around inspecting things closely. Every now and then he would thump the floor with his stick, clear his throat and stop to exclaim: "Well, well, I never saw the beat!" After looking around for a while he frankly offered the opinion that this barn was altogether too large and much too fine for just beasts. Too much style here—she shouldn't have thrown away so much money on an old barn! . . . Per Hansa himself could certainly not have done much better, no, not as far as he could see.

Beret looked at him. Others had expressed the same opinion, and though she knew it wasn't true, the neighbor's kind words soothed her, like a warm bandage on a painful wound.

After a while a buggy turned into the yard. It was

Sörine who came to ask if she might not help tomorrow.
Beret's eyes blurred:

"I intended to ask you today but I didn't have the
heart . . . you have plenty of work at home, I am sure!"
Sörine looked the other way, replying slowly:

"No lack of work—'tisn't that. But there is so little fun
these days . . . we are glad of all we can get."

The lowering sun shed a deep glow on the boards of the
new barn, deepening their color to rich amber; the air in
here was laden with the fresh smell of resinous pine. Beret
picked up pieces of sawed-off boards which she placed on
nail kegs, and invited her neighbors to sit down. She herself rested her back against the wall.

"Things are certainly turning out fine for you, Beret,"
Sörine spoke up; "I don't see how you could wish for
much better."

"No indeed not," nodded Kjersti. "I say as I have said
before—Per Hansa would have rejoiced could he have
been here to see how well you have managed."

Beret interrupted their chatting, speaking slowly as if
debating the matter in her own mind:

"Time will tell how well I have done. . . . But I
think I can truthfully say that my only concern has been
how he would have done it." Beret paused before going
on. The others sat remembering scenes from their first
years out here in this new world when the three families
had shared everything in common and life had been like
a game they were playing. . . . "I am glad you came,"
Beret continued a little embarrassed, "for I need your
advice; had he been here tomorrow, he would have passed
the bottle at the shingling. And now I don't know
whether it would be proper or even right for me ——"

"My good woman," cried Tönseten emphatically, slapping his knee, "don't talk about *right!* Everything is right
just so it's done with decency; and don't we all know
that to make the barn leak-proof the ridgepole's got to
have a little soaking during the shingling." *

* The custom to which Tönseten refers was an old one in
the part of Norway from which he came. The thatching of
a house was a festive occasion and celebrated accordingly.
The drinks served were known as *tækkingskande*—literally:
the thatching bottle.

A smile illumined Beret's thoughtful face. Without answering him she turned to the two others: "What do you women think about it?"

"You just treat 'em a drop, if you have it," advised Kjersti heartily, "that'll only make 'em step all the livelier . . . yes, why not?" Sörine said never a word. But her eyes were fixed admiringly on Beret. . . . How could she think of all these things—and in such a kind way? That woman was a marvel!

"No, that I will not do," smiled Beret in answer to Kjersti. "Liquor I have hated as long as I can remember. But I'll tell you what I have thought of: I want you, Syvert, to go to town tomorrow and get what's needed for a glass of punch, and then I want you to make it for me. What do you say, women, tell me honestly—am I crazy to think of such a thing?"

Tönseten jumped up and pounded the floor with his stick.

"Crazy?" he shouted enthusiastically. "Don't talk blasphemy, Beret! Haven't I been saying all the time, and Kjersti knows it's true, that your equal is not to be found in the whole Territory! Who should have sense if you haven't got it? . . . I'll gladly undertake that job—never you fear! I'll mix you a punch so fine that you can invite the minister himself if you wish." . . . Suddenly Tönseten's eyes lit up with a bright idea: "But I must have just a wee bit of ground cinnamon, just a teeny, weeny bit, you understand, because that brings out the flavor much better."

Kjersti and Sörine both laughed. But Beret looked serious.

"I'm doing this for Per Hansa's sake," she said. "He talked a good deal about the barn the winter he was lost. That's eight years ago now, and this is as far as I've got, so you can see how well I have done."

"I don't want to hear you talk that way," admonished Tönseten sternly. "Just so Per Hansa knows how well and wisely you have managed since he left you, he'll now be resting easy—no doubt about that!"

The young people returned earlier than Beret had expected. Tonight Peder was in a fine humor, all obliging eagerness to help Mother. The moment she set out for the barn to feed the calves he was at her side to carry the pail for her. As she bent over the edge of the stall to let them drink, Peder asked in a low, chummy voice if he might not ride to Doheny's and ask Charley over for the shingling tomorrow.

"Tonight?"

"Yes, right now!" The boy threw a lot of kind eagerness into the answer.

"Isn't it too late tonight?" asked his mother persuasively. Emboldened by her friendly tone Peder hastened to set her mind at ease on that point. He would be back before she could wink an eye. "You see," he went on, "I can't very well get out of inviting him because he keeps asking me all the time. He is such a fine boy, too! . . . The best friend I have, really!" It was almost dark in here and very easy to confide secrets.

Beret waited a moment:

"If it's a matter of honor with you to have him, you better go, though we don't need to ask the Irish for help. . . . They are strangers to us."

"Aw, I understand that!" Peder agreed amiably. "But you have no idea what a fine fellow Charley is. You never saw him do anything wrong. . . . Well—I'll be back in a jiffy!"

In a little while he was on his way to Doheny's. But he didn't return home before very late. When he rode into the yard at Doheny's the place looked quiet and deserted. Shep wasn't there to greet him. Charley didn't come out, which Peder had expected. But there must be people at home because light shone from both the kitchen and the living room windows. He waited awhile outside, then tied his horse down by the barn, and went in.

Peder stepped out of the dark and right into a room full of company, which made him feel exceedingly embarrassed. His wretchedness increased when he learned that Charley wasn't at home, for now he didn't know what to do. Neither Doheny nor anyone else among the Irish was being asked to help with the shingling tomorrow, and so he couldn't very well explain what he wanted of Charley. . . . How idiotic of the Norwegians to shut themselves off from other people! Doheny, who himself

had built such a fine barn, was the very man they ought
to have asked!

Ill at ease and not knowing what to do, Peder sat listening to the talk. He could not join in the conversation because he saw nothing to say that would sound natural; yet
it seemed worse to keep still. What was he to do? He
couldn't very well stay on indefinitely and wait for Charley, and somehow, he didn't like to leave either. . . .
There were others here whom it would be pleasant to see.
The kitchen door stood open; Susie was busy out there,
making lemonade. He knew it was lemonade because he
heard her cut the lemon and squeeze out the juice. Peder
twirled the cap on his finger nervously. . . . If he left
now, it would look as though he felt ashamed and didn't
dare tell why he had come; if he stayed, it must look as
though he were waiting for the lemonade to be ready—
plain as day, all could hear what Susie was doing in the
kitchen!

The conversation moved desultorily, from one subject to
another; at times it died down altogether. The silence con-
centrated around Peder and asked loudly what he was waiting for. . . . Can it be that they are embarrassed on my
account? That's too bad!—His face was set with determination as he resolutely got up to go.

—What? He didn't intend to go yet? Doheny spoke up
kindly. Now he must wait a bit and see what Susie was
about in the kitchen—*he* surely wasn't afraid of the Irish?

This remark brought a laugh, the weight of which forced
Peder to sit down again.

Directly across the room from him sat a young woman, a
stranger to him, rocking a baby on her lap—her face so
pleasant and full of intelligent brightness that he had to
look at her again. He found her eyes and smiled unconsciously. The woman asked good-naturedly if it really was
true that the Norwegians were afraid of the Irish?

The question made them laugh again, all looking at him
inquiringly.

Peder reddened noticeably. . . . Terrible how these people laughed! thought Peder, and straightened up. Suddenly
he heard a fine answer ringing in his ear and all the
puckers in his face smoothed themselves out—did he dare
fling it at them?

"I guess you've asked the right fellow all right!" laughed Murphy, nodding in the direction of Peder. The note of scorn in his laugh, the woman seemed to take as a challenge.

"I shouldn't say that he looks scared exactly!" The woman beamed on Peder as she spoke.

"Perhaps not. But he had to be taken out of our school and be put in with his own clan, whatever the reason might've been. Those Norskies are a queer lot—that's sure. Must have everything by themselves except politics; then they want us along, and begorry if they don't scrap like devils!"

"Just like us!" the woman flung back. "Seems to me more sensible to stick together than to be flaying the hide off one another the way we Irish be doing."

Mrs. Murphy decidedly disliked the tone of finality which this inexperienced young snip of a woman used against her husband, and now hurried to his assistance, speaking in a voice shrill with indignation: The Irish did at least talk English; no one need suspect them of saying horrid things about others in a jabber no one else could understand! She certainly would never forget the time that she and Mrs. McBride had attended Ladies' Aid at Mrs. Tönseten's. There they had sat the whole day without understanding so much as ten words of all that was said—a terrible experience that was! She knew they were only talking about her and Mrs. McBride; she could see it on their faces—there should be a law against such things, indeed there should! Mrs. Murphy looked at Peder while she spoke, as though he was to blame for the tribulations she had suffered that fatal day.

All of a sudden a heated discussion had arisen concerning whether it was right for the Norwegians to talk their native language in America.

Two persons in the room defended them—Michael Doheny himself who joked so much that it was hard to tell just what he meant, and the fair-complexioned woman. She argued joyfully, with eager enthusiasm; and because of the challenging phrases and the striking similes she used the debate grew heated.

Peder sat by the door, facing the whole room and taking it all in. No one took the slightest notice of him. His cheeks were burning hot; his fingers twitched. For it was him they discussed. . . . No, not now could he leave. He'd have to show them *one* Norwegian who wasn't afraid of the Irish! . . . His eyes wandered defiantly from one to another . . . well—here he was!

Peder sat on doggedly. At last Susie came into the room, bringing a tray of cakes and lemonade and stopping at each one as she made the round. She wore a rose-pink gingham dress over which she had a white apron; her hair she had done up in the manner of grown-up girls. She moved easily from place to place and seemed full of a bewitching deviltry; wherever she stopped laughter pealed forth, occasioned by some funny remark she made. Finally reaching Peder she had nothing to say, and then the laughing died down entirely. She was standing with her back to the others. Not a word did she utter, only offering him what was on the tray. Peder looked at her, imploring her to say something which might break the silence that was gathering around them. Susie never lifted her eyes once; her face had a peculiar expression—it might be a grin. Peder's hand shook violently as he took the only glass left. The silence about the two was terrible. Every soul in the room must hear it. . . . Susie went back to the kitchen again.

Peder gulped down the lemonade, waited a moment, got up and forced out a loud, "Thank you!" then stopped and looked about the room—if they had more grievances against him, he would, of course, have to face it! A strange calm was upon him.

Just how he got out of the room he didn't know because his knees shook so badly that he had all he could do to stand up. As soon as he was outside an overwhelming sense of shame over having fled seized him . . . how they must be laughing at him now!

Peder managed to get his horse untied and to mount. Just as he rode across the yard the kitchen door opened and Susie came out. There she was standing in the full light of the opening. Glancing in that direction Peder gave his horse a sharp crack with the reins and passed close to the porch, but without looking at her . . . she came down the steps . . . did she call to him? . . . She could call as long as she pleased for all he cared!

VIII

The new barn Beret Holm was building seemed to her like an old friend who had been absent for an interminably long time, one nevertheless whose every feature she remembered clearly. For many years she had been planning and changing details, only to tear down again and begin anew. Though it was still unfinished she knew exactly how the barn would look when completed. Not at any time since she came to America had she felt so much at home as during this summer. She walked about with a feeling of quiet satisfaction. Day by day she would go out and watch the work. Each board that was being nailed on brought out more clearly the picture which she with so much care had constructed.

Ever since the spring she laid Per Hansa away she had had the barn in mind. At first the undertaking had seemed hopelessly impossible. How could she, helpless and foolish as she was, plan and execute a task which had baffled some of the ablest farmers around here? She didn't have the means either. And how was she to plan it? But the need for better shelter for the cattle grew more insistently imperative every year, and so the idea that she must get a barn no matter at what cost, wouldn't leave her in peace. Every structure of the kind which was being raised in the neighborhood she would go and look at. After coming home she would go to work and make alterations in her own plans, trying to embody some practical feature she had seen. Thus she would keep on until the season had advanced so far that she could not start building that year.

Had she only known how Per Hansa would have wanted it! Not often while he lived had the project been talked of; the only thing she recalled having heard him say, was that he would have both cow barn and horse barn under one roof. And on that point she had made up her mind long ago, because a building scheme like that would be less costly and make more pleasant quarters for both cattle and horses.

Two years ago this spring she had enough money saved up, and though she didn't mention it to the boys she was

fully decided to build that summer. The cattle suffered terribly during the winter; every fall the same story, the old
straw barns had to be patched up, which meant no end of
toil for all of them. Her decision came abruptly to naught.
One evening while Ole was reading his farm paper he came
upon a drawing which arrested his attention. After studying it for a while he showed it to his mother: Now look—
there was the very barn father would have built! Without
listening to her he called excitedly to his brother to come
and see—wasn't this the identical barn Father had described to them the day he left? Store-Hans looked at the
drawing. Why, here were the very things Father had mentioned: A ridgepole equipped with track and carrier so
that the hay could be hauled into the loft and dumped
wherever one wished! The device had sounded so easy and
novel to the boys that they remembered it the minute they
saw the picture.

Beret said nothing about it. She cut out the picture and
studied it often. The scheme seemed exceedingly practical.
And thus it might be with other things, too. Had she gone
to work now the barn wouldn't have been at all the way
Per Hansa would have wanted it!—There was no building
started that year either.

A year ago last spring Store-Hans, coming home from
town one day, had a remarkable story to tell. He had been
to the lumberyard for a few pieces of board. The man
there had given him a leaflet, advertising a wonderful invention: On one page a windmill, pumping water to an
immense herd of cattle; on the opposite page the same mill
grinding corn for the hogs. The reading matter gave an
enthusiastic account of how farmers in the East had long
been using the windmills and could not now do without
them, the Dutch being the first to introduce them. The
mills were built near the barns with the water tank usually
outside; where the winters were severe it was advisable to
place them inside in order to prevent too much freezing.

"This isn't possible!" cried Beret, incredulous, and asked
Store-Hans to explain the description to her once more.
After the children had gone to bed she sat far into the
night trying to understand how the mill worked. It was the
most marvelous thing she had ever seen; the idea fascinated her so that she couldn't let go of it. If it were really
true that the wind could be harnessed to pump all the

water they needed right up to the barn, then she would
have to study the matter a little closer. Her thoughts,
conjuring up a picture of a new, large barn with a windmill and all, standing just across the yard, brought a
pleased smile to her face . . . wonder if Per Hansa would
ever have thought of that? It would be fun if she could add
just a little to what he had planned!

After the windmill came into the picture Beret thought
of little else than how she might get it and the barn built.
Some evenings she even forgot her reading.

One afternoon in the early part of the summer, just as
she was carrying water to the hogs, a Norwegian peddler
who always stopped in whenever he visited the settlement,
drove into the yard. Seeing her slave so hard with the
water, the man began telling her of a remarkable structure
he had seen over near Brookings, owned by a real farmer
who was a Norwegian—a huge barn, having a windmill
right outside, and a dairy nearby where the milk was being
kept in cool water all the time. A real marvel, that barn,
he assured her. These days farming was getting to be what
it ought to be because people were learning how to apply
intelligence to it. Beret forgot her work and asked many
questions.

For days and weeks afterward she went about thinking
of what the man had told her, but didn't mention it to the
boys. When the haying was done she took Store-Hans
with her one Saturday and drove to Brookings, found the
man the peddler had told her about, and stayed there until
Monday, asking many questions and getting much good
advice from him.

And this spring, as soon as the plowing and seeding were
done, she had gone to work. The windmill she had built
first, the dairy next, and now the barn was ready for the
shingling.

If it had been made to order the day couldn't possibly
have been finer. Still, clear transparency, reaching far back
into the spaces beyond the sun; nothing else. Coming out
into it made one stretch and laugh.

As soon as Beret got through with the morning's work
she went into her bedroom to wash and to tidy herself.
During the winter she had had made a new gingham dress,
a shepherd's plaid in deep green and black. She was fond

of the dress because it gave her face a better color. Today she put it on. And a new *Hardanger* apron over it, a pretty garment, neatly made, with embroidery and crocheted lace. The apron was a gift to her and had come from far away. Summer before last a girlhood friend in Norway had sent her a letter. Beret had answered it, and so, many letters had followed. And now a few weeks ago the apron had come—Beret had not worn it before. . . . She looked at herself in the mirror and broke into a smile—how had she put on her clothes anyway! Under the left ear a bit of the lace on her collar was turned under the band, making her neck look abnormally long on that side. Carefully she straightened it out, taking plenty of time, and looking often into the mirror.

At nine o'clock she brought out lunch to the men—sandwiches of various kinds, some spread with cheese, some sprinkled with brown sugar, and a large pitcher of fresh milk which she had mixed with sweet cream. The constant *tik-a-tak-tak* up on the roof deafened her. Men's voices rang through the fusillade of hammering. Now and then a laugh broke out in which they all joined. . . . Must be easy to laugh up there—there was a merry ring in it. From the rest Beret singled out that of Tambur-Ola. . . . Had he seen her come? He is in high spirits today, she thought, her cheeks flushing a deep red; in her eyes shone a soft clearness. . . . She set down her trays and stood looking up. Peder and Charley (the boy was standing on the porch this morning when she came out) scurried hither and thither across the roof like two weasels, working as handymen to the eight who were shingling. She waited in the barn until the men had come down from the roof; then she gave Peder instructions about the dishes, and went back to the house to begin preparing the dinner—through the door she had seen Sörine coming.

Today Beret sang as she and her neighbor went about the work. Strains of an old love song she had often sung when a young girl popped up in her consciousness and kept ringing in her ear. Before she was aware of it she was humming the melody, mumbling the words to herself. Realizing what she was doing she laughed, a bit embarrassed. In order to pass it off she asked Sörine whether she could remember the words to the ditty, and straightway she began singing it. Beret was a little surprised at herself, because, once started, she remembered the whole song and sang it clear to the end. Anna Marie laughed at her mother and made teasing remarks. . . . Two old women, acting silly like that, must surely be a bad sign!

Doors and windows stood open. Through the clear transparency out of doors the rhythmic *tik-a-tak-tak* of the hammers came floating into the kitchen. Often Beret walked to the window, and standing there, looked over at the barn. . . . Dangerous the way the boys were running up and down the steep roof. Would they had sense enough to be careful . . . and the others too! . . . Her eyes sought out one of the men . . . a wistful expression came into them—she sighed as she went back to the work.

Just as dinner was ready and Beret was about to go out and call the men to come in, a buggy drove into the yard. Reverend Gabrielsen, having made a sick call down in this part of the settlement and coming by here on his way home, dropped in to see the building project which he had heard so much about.

Sörine was the first to notice him. "I declare if we aren't getting company—here comes the minister! You just ask him in, we've plenty prepared."

Beret looked out into the yard and said nothing. Removing the big kitchen apron she was wearing over the other one, she went out to receive him.

The minister had stepped out of the buggy when Beret came.

"Here you have me, Mrs. Holm!" he greeted her cheerily. "Today you have no time for argument, and so I'll declare a truce. I was passing this way going home, and had to stop in to have a look at what you are doing." The minister shook her hand heartily.

Beret paid no attention to him, but called to Peder, to come down and put up the horse. She turned to her visitor, a cool aloofness in her manner. If he would be satisfied to share with them what they had, she said calmly, he was welcome to stay to dinner; if not, he'd have to go elsewhere.

—Oh no, no, no, she mustn't mind him! He had only dropped in to shake hands. There were many here today . . . some other time!

—Many? Beret said. Were they so few at his house?
In her voice was a note of contempt.

—So few? He should hope not! he laughed confiden-
tially. But with them the increase had come gradually—
they hardly knew how many they were now!

Beret surveyed him coolly; her face puckered because
she was trying to conceal her disgust.

Peder came down to put up the horse. Leaving them,
Beret told him to hurry, and to call the men for dinner
right away.

The minister walked about in the yard, inspecting the
new buildings—greatly surprised at how efficiently and
how conveniently all had been planned. Mrs. Holm must
indeed be a remarkable woman! . . . As the men came
down from the roof he shook hands with each one. Charley he didn't know, but the moment he looked into the
face of the boy he was attracted to it and wouldn't let
him go before he had found out all Charley cared to tell.

The men came into the house. The large table in the
kitchen fairly groaned under its burden of food. The minister was given the place of honor at the head of the table.
As soon as all were seated he folded his hands and offered
a lengthy blessing in English. Meanwhile the women,
their heads bowed, stood over by the stove. Beret's face
had turned pale. . . . The brazen effrontery of that man!
This he dared to do—right in her own house!

When he had finished, the women began serving,
Sörine bringing the potatoes and the gravy, Beret following with the meat and the preserves; her hand shook as
she handed the platter to the minister.

"I don't s'pose you can eat our food . . . it's prepared
in Norwegian fashion!" Her voice sounded leaden, as in
one who, having suffered a bitter disappointment, must
talk aloud to herself.

All glanced up at her. Store-Hans turned crimson. Seizing a cup and jumping up from the table he went to the
water pail for a drink; there he stood watching his mother,
trying to catch her eye.

"We must beware lest we give offense to others," the
minister said peaceably.

"Aye, aye—on that we're agreed. And when I come to
the parsonage on a visit I shall try to accommodate myself
to the ways of your house!"

"Provided, however, you don't consider our ways ethically wrong," he retaliated amiably, secure in the feeling that he had the better of the argument.

By now Beret had reached the lower end of the table. From here she could look straight at the minister, which, at the moment, she felt she must do lest she choke.

"In your opinion then it is wrong to say grace in the Norwegian language when you are in a Norwegian home where everyone in the household understands the language, just because there happens to be a child present who doesn't understand it?" Beret spoke fast, and seemed out of breath.

Tambur-Ola took the platter she was offering him, remarking soberly:

"It might contaminate him, you know, which would be terrible. . . . If the Irish, too, should begin saying grace in Norwegian, we'd sure have an awful condition in the Territory!"

The tenseness of the atmosphere around the table lifted; most of the men broke into a loud laugh; but the minister, plainly annoyed, looking right down into his plate, waiting for the guffawing to stop.

"The precious gifts which the Lord has bestowed upon us He surely doesn't want us to keep to ourselves; that would be selfishness. Better human relations are not brought about by that spirit."

Over by the stove Beret was refilling the platter; all so seated that they could see her were looking at her. She hesitated before answering:

"But supposing that what is precious to me is worthless to others? . . . It might also be that I cannot make any use of what I am getting in return." Now she spoke slowly; her indignation seemed gone. To the others she looked like one who has lost her way and doesn't know whither to turn.

"It can hardly be as bad as all that," the minister smiled affably.

"No, then we sure would be in a hell of a fix!" Tambur-Ola remarked dryly.

Silence followed; none of the men laughed out loud; all looked at the minister . . . how did he take that thrust? But he returned their look serenely and ate on. Obviously, he had decided to drop the argument.

After a while Gjermund Dahl engaged the minister in conversation about the cemetery. The place was growing up into weeds and looked like a pig pen . . . a disgrace to the whole congregation . . . something ought to be done about it . . . hadn't he seen it? Several got the impression that Gjermund laid the blame on him for the condition of the graveyard because his remarks were made in a cutting tone.

The minister agreed with Gjermund. Perhaps something ought to be done. He would talk to the Board of Trustees about it. Their greatest concern was, however, not with the dead—they were now being taken care of by a higher power; he would have to render account for how well he had looked after the living!—Gjermund and the minister had quite an argument over the matter.

Aside from their talk and now and then a terse remark from Tambur-Ola, not much was said at the table. The tenseness lying in the air would not allow itself to be dispelled. None of Beret's boys uttered a word. Peder, hot with shame, kept his eyes to himself. Ole was the first to finish. He got up, leaving the house immediately, and was not seen until the others had begun shingling—then he came out of the old cow barn.

Tönseten was faithful to his promise of last night. About two o'clock he and Kjersti drove up to the house. Despite having left his stick at home he bustled about as spryly and officiously as though his body had never known a rheumatic pain. First he put up his horse; then he came back to the buggy where he took out a bundle—something heavy, wrapped securely in a gunnysack, which he tucked under his arm and carried up to the house. With his hat shoved as far back as it would go and an air of officiousness about him, he would have looked tremendously important were it not for the mischievous gleam in his eye. Bustling into the kitchen he demanded peremptorily to see the mistress of the house—at once and without delay. "My dear woman," he brushed Sörine aside, "I can't see you, you won't understand it at all! . . . Here," he told Beret, "you take this little sweetheart of mine and keep her in a cool place until I call for her . . . you have the cinnamon on hand, I hope?"

But he had no time to spend on the women. Right now he must be off to see how the boys were getting on with the shingling. On his way across the yard he stopped at the buggy, turning his back to the house. In the corner of the seat lay his coat, which he removed with great care. Tucked securely into the corner nestled a pint bottle of whisky, peering indolently up at him. A slight chuckle escaped him as he pushed the bottle down into his hip pocket.

Near the barn he stopped, and thrusting his thumbs under the band of his trousers he called to the men: Weren't they ever to get done? What had they been doing all day? . . . Did they have a rope?—yes, *a rope?*

Tönseten simply had to get up on the roof. But not wishing to risk climbing the ladder unaided he called for help. Two men stepped down into the gutter and threw a rope to him, the loop of which he fastened under his arms; and so the ascent began.

And it didn't stop until he sat straddling the ridgepole. While recovering his breath he surveyed, with an important mien, the faces of the men, who had all gathered about him. "You fellows must be crazy! Are you shingling the roof without as much as giving the ridgepole a single sprinkling? A fine job you're doing for a poor widow who can't look after things herself! And you, Gjermund, have the reputation of being a sensible man . . . about time I got here!" Ceremoniously Tönseten removed his hat. "Now you, youngsters," he commanded Peder and Charley sternly, "get yourselves away while the old veterans hold a council of war—clear out, I say!"

Sober as a deacon, he pulled out of his pocket a small tin cup; thereupon, the bottle. "Now, Gjermund, drink this drop, and promise me never to betray a poor widow again. If you weren't so damned obstinate in politics, you'd get by St. Peter all right . . . well—never mind that now!" . . . Tönseten kept on treating until the bottle was empty; then he had to get down at once. . . . No, indeed, he had other things to do than to be wasting his time up here! Now he would trust no one but Gjermund himself to help him down.

Day was waning fast. The sun hung blowzy on the rim of the western horizon. By and by the prairie, having lost all substance, lay floating in a purple sea. No stir. No sound.

At last the hammering on the roof had ceased. Up on the porch the men were washing for supper, their talk merry and full of witty remarks despite the long day's work. No one seemed the least bit tired. The sight of Tönseten bringing a large pitcher brimful of punch heightened the mood perceptibly. . . . This was a little treat from the mistress herself, he explained as he poured each one a glass. Now they were to go in and thank her fittingly. . . . "Hold on there, fellows—don't run off before we've got the tank empty! Here is one last drop . . . and now you hurry—the women will be fainting on me unless I get to 'em quick!"

Presently he stood in the kitchen, treating the women-folks. Beret thought the punch tasted a bit sweet but drank her glass nevertheless. The other two did likewise. Sörine laughed gaily, and in thanking Tönseten, had to pat him on the cheek, for never had she tasted finer drink, not even at a wedding. The merriment increased greatly at his insisting on returning the pat, and by his wife's slapping him on the ear with a dish rag, telling him to behave himself. She was getting hysterical with laughter.

At supper Anna Marie and Kjersti waited on the table, the other two women eating with the men. There was much good talk and cheerful laughter tonight. Bright memories from the early days came back to them. Each recalled some experience of which he must remind the others. All had heard the stories often, which fact didn't seem to detract from the interest. Charley, almost forgetting to eat, kept looking from one to the other. Every time a laugh broke out he would nudge Peder in the ribs, wanting to know what it was all about. But Peder only laughed so uproariously that Charley was forced to join in. . . . Jollier people than these Norskies he'd never seen!

The meal finished, Tönseten got up and slipped out of the room, only to return with the pitcher filled once more. The men stared at him in utter amazement. Where had he discovered that spring, they'd like to know? Did the mill pump it out of the ground? . . . If so, they were going home to erect one right now!

Tönseten didn't utter a word. His face wore an ominous expression. Filling Beret's glass first and his own last, he took a position at the lower end of the table, there waiting solemnly until he had all eyes looking at him. After clearing his throat noisily, he launched into a eulogy on the greatest farmer in the town of Spring Creek, who, though only a woman, had outdistanced the others by many leagues. His emotions soon got the better of him; before he could stop it tears were rolling down his cheeks; but then he grew so eloquent that all agreed he was making a wonderful speech; and as to that, there wasn't the least doubt in his own mind. . . . "Well," he concluded, "if you now will promise me to be real good, I'll just squeeze the bottle for the last drop!" When he returned he filled the glasses with brew that was considerably stronger.

They remained sitting around the table. No one cared to get up. By and by, emanations which immediately kindled laughter began sparkling from Tambur-Ola. After a little he was relating incidents from the war. Sörine, desirous of proving what a wonderful man he really was, begged him to continue. He didn't seem to pay any attention to her, but went on. Deep, mysterious dusk filled the room, and was gradually sinking into the consciousness of the occupants. The man continued talking. Now he was drawing pictures for them of his experiences in the prison camp at Andersonville, which not even Sörine had ever persuaded him to do. Imperceptibly his habitual manner of reticence dropped off him; his narrative became more quiet; into his tone had crept a note of awe, constantly recurring; his voice had a catch in it which occasionally caused him to stop; in his mood—all could sense it clearly—lapped choppy billows of pain. At last the words came flowing across his lips like some song laden with the burden of a great sorrow, but which he nevertheless now must sing.

Kjersti broke the spell. She had never heard the like. The narrative had depressed her, worse than the most dismal fall night up by the Polar Circle where she had been brought up. Unable to endure it any longer, she got up, found the lamp, lit it and placed it in the middle of the table.

Tambur-Ola broke off abruptly. Jumping up he shaded his eyes. "Much obliged for the entertainment!" he shouted sardonically, his face awry with a mawkish grin. In the next instant he had found the door and was gone.

Beret arose as if to follow him, but caught herself and remained standing in the middle of the floor, dazed. . . . Oh, no, no, no—he must not go yet . . . not before she had had a chance to talk to him! The others were still sitting at the table; Sörine with wet, beaming eyes, which kept asking: There now—isn't that what I've been saying all the time? Isn't he a fine man?

But Tönseten paid no attention to any of the rest; his mouth felt dry; and moreover, he had to blow his nose, after which he remarked huskily, "There you can see what this country has cost us!"

IX

All save Sörine had gone; Beret's own boys too. Peder was taking Charley home, the mother having consented to his taking the buggy, because then he could convey Sörine home at the same time.

But tonight Sörine would rather not ride.

"You'd better come with me for a little walk," she said to Beret. "A little airing will be good for us, after all this feasting."

The two women crossed the yard. Before them, over in the dark, the prairie receded into deep mystery and could only be felt. A thin, frail shell of a moon, not over three nights old, hung in the western sky, promising a spell of dry weather. "Not many tears on the prairie this month!" joked Sörine as she looked at the new moon. Her remark made both of them laugh. Having reached the windmill, they sat down on the first rung.

"I'm glad to have you alone," Sörine began. "I need your advice in a serious matter—your judgment is so much better than mine."

"How you talk! . . . What is it?" asked Beret, surprised.

Not heeding her, Sörine repeated, "I don't think I've ever been up against anything more serious."

"Then I am the wrong person to consult," smiled Beret, her answer belying the pleasure she felt over the other's unfeigned confidence.

"No, you are not. And now you must give me your honest opinion."

"You frighten me!"

"Do I?" Sörine hesitated a moment before blurting out: "I'm thinking of getting married!"

"What are you saying?" gasped Beret, clutching Sörine's arm.

"I knew it would surprise you. . . . But, you see, I am not able to manage the way you can, so I'd better get someone to help me. . . . Tell me honestly, what do you think of it?"

Beret did not answer.

And so Sörine went on:

"Hans Olsa was always very kind to me . . . during all the years we lived together he never wished me aught but good. I'm sure he would have no objection to my marrying again."

Still Beret was silent, which greatly surprised Sörine; she had confided in her friend because she wished her to rejoice with her, and here she sat mum and distant!

"Who is it?" Beret asked finally, her voice so low that Sörine could hardly catch the words.

Eagerly Sörine hastened to explain:

"That's just the point! People think he is queer, you see, and so I don't quite know if I'd better. . . . But if they only knew him, they wouldn't think so. . . . There isn't a kinder hearted person in the world—I know there isn't!"

"Has he asked you?"

Sörine resented the distinctly hostile tone in her friend's voice, and had to defend herself:

"You don't suppose that I've been proposing to him?"

"How can I tell? I don't even know whom you are talking about!" Beret laughed bitterly.

The remark mollified Sörine. Here she had been so intent upon her own self that she had forgotten to explain decently. "Of course, you don't!" she exclaimed. "Well, it's Tambur-Ola. He's been asking me so long that now I must give him an answer."

Not a syllable from Beret. With the prolonged silence Sörine's spirits sank lower and lower. Expectantly, she had longed for the moment when she could tell her friend her great secret, not altogether because she wanted advice, but because tonight she felt such a deep need of sharing her happiness with someone whom she loved—and this was the response she got!

When Beret finally spoke, her answer stung because of the malicious taunt in it. "He gets some queer notions, that fellow!"

"That you would never have said had you known him as well as I," Sörine protested sadly.

"What about your children?"

The unkindness of the question cut Sörine deeply. Now it was her turn to delay answering:

"Sofie is already grown up. What may come of the affair between her and Store-Hans, I don't know. . . . To the little boy, Ola has been like a father ever since he came to us."

Beret rose with startling suddenness: "Better look before you leap, that's all I can say! . . . I hear a calf over in the barn. Guess I'd better go and see what the trouble is." She started to walk off, but stopped: "If you wait till I get back, I'll go with you a little way."

When Beret returned to the windmill she found no one there. She had taken her time about looking after the calf—a great deal of time, as a matter of fact; but now that she found Sörine gone, she felt badly about it. . . . Sörine ought to have waited. Beret had an important question to ask her, one that Sörine ought to weigh carefully—she might as well tell her since Sörine had asked for advice. . . . Perplexed, Beret stood there. . . . Sörine couldn't have gone so very far yet. Perhaps she could overtake her if she hurried? She must speak to her before she had a chance to see Tambur-Ola again . . . most likely Sörine had never considered *that* side of the question!

Beret started to walk, hesitatingly at first, but then faster and faster until she almost broke into a run and had to stop to catch her breath. . . . She must avert this tragedy . . . Sörine was so common and straightforward, and Tambur-Ola had to be handled with a light touch. How could she imagine herself a fit mate for that man? . . . Oh, no—she was hardly the woman to give him the care he needed! . . . Too bad for Sörine herself! Of the two it would be harder on her . . . she didn't realize

what it meant to satisfy one like Tambur-Ola! . . . Again
she quickened her steps.

After having walked some distance, she was arrested by
the sound of a buggy coming toward her. She stopped to
listen . . . if people should find her traveling here alone
at this hour, they must think something was wrong with
her. She stepped aside quickly and crouched low in the
grass. . . . The buggy was not coming very fast . . .
was it standing still? No, there she heard it more distinctly. She held her breath . . . what, did she hear
young voices? Merciful heavens, wasn't that Permand—
were those boys out riding yet?

The horse came nearer, barely shuffling along. Now
and then it halted, snatching a mouthful of grass from the
roadside, which it crunched before ambling on again. . . .
A *girl's* voice? No, her senses must be fooling her—the
boy wasn't out with girls at this time of the night! . . .
There was the voice again. Beret squatted still lower, her
body shaking so violently that she had to hold on to the
grass in order to steady herself. . . . A girl's voice,
now and then bursting with joyous laughter, was chatting
in the dark; the clear deep voice of Peder seemed to be
winding itself in and out of it. . . . It could hardly be the
minister's daughter? The boy must be out of his senses!
Her impulse was to jump up and reprimand him severely
right then and there—bid him pack himself home instantly; but she was rooted to the ground and couldn't
stir. The buggy rolled by, directly in front of her. . . .
What was that they were saying? Now they were talking
so low that she couldn't catch the words. . . . Surely the
girl wasn't sitting in his lap? . . . The buggy had rolled
past, and on into the dark night where it soon disappeared. Now they were driving faster, she could tell it
by the hoofbeats . . . could he be bringing company
home? With great difficulty Beret pulled herself together
and hurried after.

No sign of life in the yard . . . everywhere, only intense stillness. She went straight to the outhouses. The
buggy was not standing in its accustomed place between
the corncribs; she hurried to the horse barn; the stall
yawned empty. She ran down the yard to the main road.
Stood there for some time, listening breathlessly. Not a

sound—only the night, and her own heart pounding as though it would break through her breast.

Beside herself, because of the nameless fear which was tormenting her, she turned and went back. In the middle of the yard she again stopped to listen. A gust of wind sweeping out of the darkness struck the windmill squarely; the whir of the big wheel as it swung around, resembled the wing-stroke of some prodigious bird. The noise increased her fear. Detecting no other sound, she hurried into the house, tore off her shoes, lit a candle and ran upstairs . . . perhaps her senses had deceived her—the boy might be in bed, sound asleep. . . . In Peder's room she sank down on the empty bed. The pain she felt seemed insufferable. In her ear spoke a voice, loudly and with great distinctness, "Now you have lost your boy, Beret Holm!" . . . It isn't true, oh—it can't be true! she sobbed and sprang up to hunt for him further. The door to the boys' room stood ajar; pushing it open, she found Ole fast asleep; Store-Hans, to whom she hadn't given a thought, had not come home yet. . . . "Now things are going fine here!" she heard a voice cry derisively. Beret could have shrieked the words out herself!

In a moment she descended the stairs and went into her own room, where she lit the lamp. She reached for the Bible, but her hand dropped limply into her lap. What did it avail when no one heard her supplication? . . . The light hurting her eyes, she turned the flame down. After a while Store-Hans came in; she arose halfway from the chair but sank down—no, she'd have to try to bear it alone!

Time passed; yet did not pass at all. The night dragged on endlessly. When the clock struck one Beret would not believe she had heard right—it must have struck wrong. In order to make certain she went into the kitchen to see. But both hands showed one o'clock.

Unable to go to bed, she went out on the porch. There she sat down and stared aimlessly out into the night. Her fear had now changed into a dull, gnawing ache, right below her heart. Her thoughts, ranging restlessly about, would persistently return to one idea: She had only herself to blame for what had happened—as the tree, so the fruit thereof! At last she saw herself stripped naked, stand-

ing in a glaring light . . . aye, aye, as the tree is, so must
the fruit be! . . . The soughing of the wind had caught
the words and was using them as a refrain—Beret could
hear them distinctly.

About two o'clock a buggy drove up the yard, the horse
blowing a prolonged snort as it came to a halt. At once
Beret knew who it was, waited one instant, and slipped
quickly into the house, blew out the light and lay down.
. . . No, she could not speak to him now—not tonight,
anyway! Shortly she heard Peder enter the house, mounting the stairs so stealthily that she could hardly detect his
steps.

Beret lay with her eyes closed. Back of her eyelids her
thoughts worked ceaselessly, torturing her until the balls
seemed to be afire. Dawn came. She heard the songbirds
commence their morning concert. Above the chorus rose
the glorious solo of the meadow lark. . . . Another day
of bright sunshine must be coming. . . . Beret felt it so
good to relax a bit that she didn't get up immediately.

Having dressed as usual, she took the Bible, paging a
long while before she found what she was looking for:

**And it was so, when the dayes of their feasting were
gone about, that Job sent and sanctified them, and rose
up early in the morning, and offered burnt offerings
according to the number of them all: for Job said, It
may be that my sonnes have sinned, and cursed God in
their hearts: Thus did Job continually.**

She let the boys sleep a good half hour longer than
usual, awakened Anna Marie and set her to getting the
breakfast. By the time the boys came out Beret herself
was hard at work, seemingly in a great hurry to get the
chores done. She didn't take time to skim the milk. Telling Store-Hans that she had to go away for a little while,
she went in, washed carefully, and changed her dress.
Presently Store-Hans saw her walking down the road.

Beret's early appearance at the Waags' that morning
and her request to have a word alone with Sörine, greatly
discomfited the other woman. . . . What was up today?
she wondered. Beret looked as though she had just come
from some strenuous work, her face was blowzy and
puffed. Sörine asked her to be seated.

No, Beret could not stay. "I was going to see you on

your way last night, and could not. Now you better come with me."

Her voice sounded peculiarly strained. Sörine looked at her bewildered. In silence the two women left the house . . . walked down the yard.

Down the road a little way, Beret stopped:

"I only wanted to say that I think you better say *yes*."

. . . Bending low, she sorted out and pulled up a long grass, which she began drawing through her fingers. "But I warn you to be careful—not all can handle Tambur-Ola . . . I'm convinced of that!" she added, her voice unusually soft and kind.

Sörine was crying, not knowing that she did so. . . . How fine of Beret to come and tell her this!

X

During the week immediately preceding confirmation, Reverend Gabrielsen held private conferences at the vestry with each catechumen, in order, as he explained to the parents, to give a word of counsel to each just as he was about to set out on life's journey.

The innovation caused much favorable comment among the parishioners. Commendable indeed that he took such interest in the young people! Before the week was over, however, ominous mutterings arose, because with some of the youngsters it didn't take long to tell them what they ought to know about life, while with the others the minister would need a whole hour, or even more. Why didn't he portion out his good counsel equally? He wasn't showing partiality, was he? They weren't used to such— America was a land of equal opportunity . . . they would stand for no caste system here! But the festivities over, that kind of talk soon died down. The exercises went off in fine shape, the church was packed full, and the catechumens acquitted themselves in a most creditable manner. Two boys were catechized in the English language, which procedure the most up-to-date in the congregation hailed with much satisfaction.

Peder was to be at the vestry at nine o'clock Thursday morning. So far Beret had kept silent concerning what had happened the night after the shingling. Since then, she had gone about her work low-spirited and taciturn, weighing many sober thoughts. But Wednesday evening, all their work done, she asked Peder to go with her up to the Indian Hill—she hadn't seen the place all summer, she said, and tonight the weather was so beautiful. The boy gave her a look, and went with her.

"I must have forgotten how lovely it is up here," she remarked soberly and sat down on the bench.

Peder, hands in his pockets, stood a little way off, gazing out into the dreamy prairie evening.

The mother spoke again, her voice low and very grave: Tomorrow morning he was to meet the minister. And on Sunday next he would meet One still higher . . . on that day he was to stand in the presence of God—there to renew his baptismal covenant! * Had he given proper thought to what that meant? Did he feel himself prepared for the solemn hour? The awful holiness of it was terrible to face, yet it would be the sweetest experience of his life.

Peder was trying not to pay more attention to her talk than he had to. Over against the skyline to the east, the landscape was fast being enveloped in a haze of purpling dusk. The gray unpainted church spire could no longer be seen. The edifice itself lay there like a huge white boulder; looking long and hard he thought he could distinguish the tower too!

He had not answered his mother. Now she resumed her admonitions, and in the same restrained and deeply serious manner:

—For none of her other children had she borne so much anxiety. His father had early been taken away. . . . In many ways she might have acted unwisely, though she never had had aught but his own welfare in mind.

Peder began to feel the effect of her mood. Wanting to wrench himself loose from it, he called her attention to

---

* The three questions which at confirmation in this particular Lutheran synod were asked of each catechumen:

"*Dost thou renounce the devil, and all his works, and all his ways?*

"*Dost thou believe in God the Father, Son, and Holy Ghost?*

"*Wilt thou, by the grace of God, continue steadfast in this covenant of thy Baptism, even unto the end?*"

how strikingly the wheel of the windmill resembled a
white wreath against the sky of the evening.

—What? she cried out in dismay—how could he be so
worldly minded! Her seriousness deepened, took on a still
more somber tone: He mustn't mind these things now,
but come and sit down by her in order that they might
prepare themselves!

Peder came closer but remained standing.

—Was he ready to make that sacred covenant with
God?

—Aw, 's much as the rest of 'em, he s'posed. Her dis-
quieting sadness was hard to resist, despite his efforts.

—She was concerned about him now; the others must
answer for themselves. Sunday he would partake of the
Lord's Supper . . . eat the true Body of Christ and drink
of His Holy Blood. He remembered, did he not, God's
condemnation upon those who ate and drank unworthily?
. . . After a pause she continued: He had been away
from home a good deal of late, and had been experiencing
many things. If for any reason he felt that he could not
give God his promise and partake of Holy Communion,
they had better postpone his confirmation another year.

Beret, getting up and coming close to him, did what she
had not done for years—she put her arm about his shoulder, and for the first time realized that he was much
taller than herself . . . here she was standing beside a
grown man!

Peder turned his face away from her.

Her voice sank very low, because pitifully entreating.
Peder could hear how hard she strove to keep back the
tears:

"What you were up to the night you were out with
that Doheny girl, I don't know. . . . It certainly looked
strange to me. Pray God you kept yourself away from
wickedness! Never since the time your father disappeared
have I felt such anguish." Beret had to pause in order to
steady herself. . . . "Little did I dream that any of mine
would take to fooling with the Irish—in that way! . . . I
had to speak to you about it before you meet the minister
tomorrow. If you have anything on your conscience you
must confess it before it is too late!"

Peder stood there, burning with shame . . . how could
she have found it out?

When his mother spoke again it was about another matter, and now she could no longer hold back the tears:

"You are a grown man, Permand . . . I want you to think seriously about what I have said. If the day should come that you get yourself mixed up with the Irish, then you will have lost your mother—that I could not live through!"

Peder started to walk away, but stopped . . . it wouldn't do to leave her thus.

"Promise me to remember what I have told you!" she pleaded beseechingly.

Peder walked on, saying nothing, his mother following. To him the distance down to the house seemed endless.

When Peder the next morning appeared in the vestry, the minister's face looked more sober than usual, but his voice had its habitual cheerfulness:

"About you, my good Peder, I am sure I need have no fear," the minister began as Peder stood before him. "You are, without exception, the brightest young man I have ever confirmed. I want you to realize what extraordinary gifts God has given you. Remember to thank Him for them when on Sunday you come into His presence!"

Peder dropped into the chair standing by the table.

The minister, regarding him affectionately, went on:

"I have mentioned the idea before, and I want to take this occasion to speak to you about it again: You must consecrate your life to the Lord! Nothing is more beautiful. If you want an abundant life, you will find it in His service. The Israelites used to set aside their most gifted sons for the priesthood while they were as yet only little children. Your father could not do that for you—now I want to do it in his stead!" Reverend Gabrielsen came around the table and laid his hand paternally on Peder's head.

The boy had crossed his arms on the table; at the touch of the minister's hand he buried his head in the fold of his arms and broke into a paroxysm of crying.

The outburst was so unexpected that Reverend Gabrielsen had to blow his nose violently.

"Don't cry about that, my young friend! It may indeed be that at first God's call seems dismal, but once you, out of a willing heart, are heeding it, you will understand that

by surrendering your life you regain it tenfold. Would
that my pastor, on the day of my confirmation, had done
as much for me! Then I should have been spared much
sin and much sorrow. . . . Until Sunday, try to live in
these thoughts." As he spoke these words he patted Peder
lovingly.

Upon his return both Anna Marie and his mother
wanted to know how he had got along today, what he had
been quizzed on, and what the minister had said . . .
he had been gone a long time!

But Peder would give them no satisfaction, either then
or later. He kept himself out of their way as much as he
could, and had little to say; most of all he took care not
to be left alone with his mother. The following two
nights he sat up very late; Beret felt certain he was reading—the occasional scraping of his foot told her so. Saturday night he was sitting up even later than usual; the
mother finally got so tired of waiting for him to go to bed
that she dozed off. Sunday morning when she came upstairs to wake him and wish him God's blessing on the
day, she found him lying on the bed, wide awake and
fully dressed. She gained the impression that he hadn't
slept at all, and felt quite alarmed.

—Wasn't he feeling well?

—Yes. Peder turned his face to the wall.

—Couldn't he sleep nights? She came over to the bed
and patted him on the cheek.

Peder did not answer—only lay there immovable. Beret
left the room, quite assured that now a Higher Power was
grappling with her boy!

Bright, beautiful day. The church proved altogether too
small to hold all who flocked to services that Sunday
morning. This was Reverend Gabrielsen's first confirmation in St. Luke's; people came from far and wide, both
to hear him and to visit friends who had children that
were being confirmed. Several of the Bethel people were
here also; they had come early and had takn seats in the
rear in order not to deprive any member of the congregation of his place—they wouldn't think of such a thing
. . . not for all the world would they get in the way of
anyone seeking God's House! But after all the pews were
packed and people jammed the aisles down the whole

length of the church, they continued to sit, not wanting to cause disturbance by getting up and leaving.

The catechizing went off like a pleasant game. The minister's beaming countenance, his friendliness and easy manner, inspired such confidence in the catechumens that they couldn't help answering his questions. As the questions proceeded, the listeners marveled more and more at the unusual cleverness of that boy of Mrs. Holm's. Whenever someone got stuck on some intricate problem in theology, the minister, smiling confidently, would turn to Peder, and straightway the answer came in a clear, deep voice that could be heard throughout the whole church. . . . But then, of course, Mrs. Holm had waited until he was grown up—they must not forget that! Some were actually embarrassed at seeing a grown man stand there among the children.

But when Peder stood before the altar and the minister put the three questions to him, the boy never uttered a sound. His failure to answer didn't, however, seem to disturb the minister in the least; merely shortening the pause between each question, he went on with the ceremony. He had had similar experiences before, and this particular confirmand he knew he could vouch for.

But people in the front pews had noticed what was happening. . . . This certainly was queer procedure both on the part of the minister and the boy! In one of the front pews sat Beret, eagerly awaiting this solemn moment. She had rejoiced at the thought of hearing Peder's clear voice in the answers, because that would give her the assurance she so sorely needed—and now not a word came from him! The room went black before her eyes, and the church began to heave like a boat in a heavy sea.

Suddenly her attention was arrested by the expression in his face. Peder, getting up from his knees before the altar, was staggering and had to grab hold of the rail to steady himself. His features, drawn and haggard, looked like those of one in terrible pain. The instant he reached his seat he collapsed in a faint. Store-Hans hurried to get water for him. Considerable commotion arose on account of it. The minister had to wait awhile before he could go on.

As soon as they had reached home after the long services, Peder went right to bed. His mother came up, and sitting down on the edge of the bed, began talking to him long and earnestly. But she could elicit no other answer than that there was nothing the matter with him . . . just a little dizzy, that was all. . . . When supper time came he got up and ate with the rest of them, afterward helping with the chores. These done, he went straight up to his room.

Tonight, as usual whenever the boys were out late, Beret was lying awake waiting for them. Ole came home early. But Store-Hans didn't return until midnight, the clock striking twelve just as he entered the house. Then she dozed off at once . . . Beret had lost much sleep of late.

She had not been asleep long before she began struggling back to consciousness, without reaching it at once. A dream would not release her. . . . A great bird kept circling over her head, flapping its wings. She couldn't see it, only heard the beating in the air. It was the effort to account for the strange phenomenon which brought her to. And then she heard footsteps . . . someone came stealing down the stairs—descending so quietly that she had to strain her ears to catch the sound of the steps.

—That's Permand, I can tell it by his walk, she said to herself.

She heard him stop for a moment in the kitchen and then hurry out. In a twinkling she got out of bed, slipped on a dress and was out on the porch—stood there listening, looking out into the quiet night. The moonlight almost blinded her. Judging by the position of the moon it must be long past midnight. . . . Where could he have gone? There . . . she caught sounds coming from the barn. . . . What could the boy be doing there now? A terrible fear clutching at her heart, she hurried across the yard, stopped in front of the barn door . . . peering in through the dark. Someone was within. The next instant Peder emerged from one of the stalls, leading a horse which he had bridled after him. The boy was dressed in his working clothes—the first thing she noticed about him —and carried a bundle under his arm. The moonlight falling upon him revealed to Beret the palest face she had ever seen.

"Permand!" she called hoarsely.

The boy stood still a moment, facing her, his features contorted. Muttering something which to her sounded like a curse, he led the horse back into the barn.

His mother came after him into the stall, got hold of his arm and shook him:

"What in the world are you up to, I ask?"

Peder gave her a shove that sent her reeling.

"I was only going for a little ride!" he said huskily, passed her, and walked out.

IV. The Song of the Shulamite

I

The air was electric with stir and excitement of many kinds! Even the incredible happened: God tempered the minds and bended the hearts of men in three different synods until they flowed together like brooklets, and the United Norwegian Lutheran Church of America was established.* The most important event in the history of the Norwegian people in this country, declared the large majority of those who became its members. Press and pulpit alike proclaimed it; and upright men thanked God with fervent hearts for the great good He had let come to pass among His people.

St. Luke's and Bethel were now members of the same church body. Still they stubbornly continued apart. But Reverend Gabrielsen was not dismayed; he beamed with satisfaction over the happy outcome of events, rubbing his hands in anticipation of all the good to come. Here they could see, he said, what happened when people earnestly wanted that which was right in the sight of the Lord. 'Twouldn't be long now before the other synods also would fall in line . . . no, not very long. For who could resist the visitation of the Lord? Just wait until the new synod adopted the English language and became a truly American church. . . . And give the Bethel people time, my good folks, give them time; we shall, by the Grace of God, rejoice in a victory here too!

Stirring times politically, as well. The year of Peder's confirmation saw the admission of South Dakota, North

* The three synods referred to were: The Anti-Missourian Brotherhood, The Norwegian-Danish Conference, and The Norwegian Augustana Synod.

Dakota, Montana, and Washington to the Union. The year following, that of Wyoming and Idaho. No less than six new states now lay beckoning 'neath the western sky! Contrary to expectation, the division of Dakota Territory caused no great excitement. Why oppose it? It would have to come sooner or later anyway—that had long been apparent. People had already talked themselves weary of the subject; besides, there were more interesting matters in the air.

Joyous tidings kept floating in from the vast empires to the west. Montana was altogether a more beautiful country than either of the Dakotas. Who had ever heard of such fertility? The merest whiff of the soil out there would send the seed wheat sprouting in the sacks! And no winter to speak of; nor as much as a sign of tornadoes in summer. Just beyond Montana lay Washington. If one didn't find Montana to his liking, he could move on to that Eden . . . a veritable Norway with ocean, mountains, and fishing. And all manner of *fruit*—man alive, you never saw the beat! The Dakotas were full of nothing but ignorant old cranks anyway, who simply could not see farther than their own noses. People here had no idea of progress. Plague take it, why slave and never get anywhere? . . . There were many—young people mostly— who, when spring came, would rig up a schooner and hold the course on sunset land. Occasionally there were old-timers, disgruntled, sucking comfortless pipes, unhappy because no amount of liniment, applied externally or taken internally, availed against rheumatism, who would begin to sniff the air and stare into the west until they caught enchanted visions . . . especially on evenings when the twilight fell clear and dreaming. Before you knew it, they too had found company and were off . . . what would a poor devil stay on here for?

No, topics for conversation were not wanting when neighbor met neighbor. During the spring of the year following South Dakota's admission to statehood, an epidemic of matrimony began to break out among the settlers in the Spring Creek district. One of the first to succumb was Ole Holm. That winter a sister of Mrs. Sam Solum's had come out from Minnesota, eager to see the wonders of the West. Her name was Randi. She was a lighthearted, fun-loving lass, liking best to be where people laughed, because then she could join in. At a social in the Tallaksen Schoolhouse one evening it happened that Ole Holm bought her basket. Thereby the madness started. Before the summer was very far spent Ole and Randi went to the minister and got married.

Only their two witnesses had been present at the ceremony. Because they had had no wedding celebration, the young men in the neighborhood had been greatly disappointed, feeling themselves cheated of the fun to which they were by right entitled. After dark on the wedding evening a boisterous crowd gathered in front of the bridal house to serenade the couple, using old boilers, tin cans, dishpans, rolling pins, and what not for instruments. The racket was so fiendish that the bridegroom was forced to hand them enough money for a keg of beer—after that there was peace again.

The gossips were much concerned about how Beret Holm would take this blow; her son's marriage had certainly come off in a hurry. Nor did Ole's going to his brother-in-law's to live lessen their curiosity. Some laid the blame to Randi. On the day after the marriage she paid her mother-in-law a visit, and on that occasion used her eyes well. The place gave her the impression of boredom; nobody laughed and no one seemed to have much to say. The welcome she got was considerably less cordial than a daughter had a right to expect. Nor had the son been received any more warmly. Beret scarcely spoke ten words to them all the while they were there. But what offended Randi most of all was that her mother-in-law had not so much as congratulated them. She had been downright rude! On the way home Randi cried a great deal and vowed that never again would she set foot in that house. Ole put his arm around her and tried to laugh it away, assuring her that she didn't know his mother. The marriage had come upon her too suddenly, that was all. Mother would be all right as soon as she had had a little time to think the matter over. . . . They mustn't let her attitude mar their happiness . . . even a sod hut would look good to him as long as he had her at his side! Ole pretended a good deal more happiness than he actually felt.

Ole continued living at his brother-in-law's. That fall the two men, in the hope of making big money, went partners in a threshing machine and were out threshing as long as the season lasted. But in the spring they rigged up a covered wagon, filled it with household goods, bade their wives climb in, and bidding Dakota good-bye, took a westerly course and were gone.

The following Christmas Sörine and Tambur-Ola were married. The wedding was a quiet affair, only the nearest neighbors being invited. Beret Holm came and helped with the dinner; but she left early. Her health had not been good all year, though not alarming. She had managed her work as usual. As a wedding gift she took Sörine a beautiful hand-knit bedspread. She had wrought it herself and it had taken her a whole year. The sight of the gift made Sörine speechless. At the time Beret had started hers Sörine had begun one of her own just like it. To start with they had competed, but after a while Sörine had given up because she was not equal to sitting up at night. If she hadn't known Beret so well, she would have believed that she was trying to humiliate her.

The following May Store-Hans and Sofie were married. People whose habit it is to keep tabs on such matters looked wise and marked the month—an unusual time to get married! Hans might at least have waited until the spring work was done . . . one didn't marry in May except for very good reasons.

The wedding was held at Sörine's place. Many guests were present, but cheer seemed to be wanting. Efforts to enliven the crowd only provoked forced laughter; the men sat around moody and out of sorts. It had never happened before at any wedding in this neighborhood that the guests were not offered so much as a glass of beer. That was the doing of the groom, so it was whispered. Tönseten felt so mortally offended at the treatment that he went straight home to bed. Never could he have believed it possible that any boy of Per Hansa's would turn out to be such a stingy gut—no sir, that he couldn't! The mothers-in-law, who knew what was proper among decent folk, weren't one whit better. . . . What will become of us anyway? . . . Toward evening Tönseten got up again and went back. He had happened to remember a bottle he had standing in the barn—one that Kjersti knew nothing about. He took the bottle with him. Perhaps he, for Per Hansa's sake, had better play the good host at this wedding feast!

During the summer the new couple lived at Beret's, but that fall, as soon as the harvest was done, they moved to Sam Solum's farm. An intimate friendship had sprung up between Store-Hans and Sam in the early part of the spring. Sam had proposed to Store-Hans that he take his farm. He might have it all—buildings, implements, stock, everything just as it stood, provided he would run it for three years exactly as though it were his own; every cent he made he could have, except that he must pay the taxes and keep the place in repairs. If Sam didn't return before the end of three years, Store-Hans was to have an option on the place at twenty dollars an acre. This offer was so exceptional that Store-Hans felt he could not afford to turn it down. Before Sam left, the two went to an attorney and a contract was drawn up.

Beret knew nothing about the transaction until some time after it had been made. One drear day in March before the marriage she went into the granary where Store-Hans was winnowing seed wheat. Their wheat last summer had been more weedy than usual, which she laid to the boys' not having taken time enough with the fanning the previous spring; today she herself intended to make sure that the mill was working right. Her coming on that errand didn't please Store-Hans exactly—she might have had that much confidence in him! For a while little was said. Leaning against the edge of the bin, he told her about his contract with Sam. His words came slowly and hesitatingly as was always the case whenever he had anything serious on his mind. Beret, having removed one of the screens from the mill, held it up to the light to examine it, after which she replaced it carefully, without looking at Store-Hans. She said not a word.

She is taking it ill, he concluded, just as I feared she would. . . . She ought to understand that a fellow has to set up for himself some time. Ole would hardly have played that trick if she had given him more tether from the start. Now he has struck out for himself, the devil only knows where! . . . Why need she feel so hurt over this? He had negotiated an important transaction all by himself and had made an exceptionally fine deal. Why should that make her angry? . . . He went over to the mill and poured wheat into it, but waited awhile before setting it in motion.

Beret had gone to the doorway and stood looking out across the yard. After a while she spoke in a quiet voice, difficult to hear above the hum of the mill:

—Did he intend to get married this year?

—He guessed so. He and Sofie had been talking about it.

—When? Beret continued to stare out upon the gloomy day.

—In May sometime. Store-Hans pulled hard at the mill.

—In May!

—So they had thought.

Beret's next question came from far away:

—Why such hurry?

—Oh, nothing particular.

—Couldn't they wait until fall?

—No! Store-Hans was turning as fast as the mill would go.

Beret waited until the mill was empty, and then asked, in a voice still hollower and more colorless:

—Did they intend to move over to Sam's place right away?

—He couldn't say just yet, they'd have to see. Store-Hans replied quietly, and came back to the bin after more grain. He had decided to hire a man for the summer. One would hardly be enough for the harvest, but they'd have to manage somehow. . . . She must not think that he didn't intend to help with the work at home even though he was starting up for himself!—This last remark he wasn't sure she had heard, for when he glanced up from the bin, she was gone.

That fall when Store-Hans moved to the other farm rumor had it that his wife and her mother-in-law couldn't get along together.

However that may have been, in the early part of November Sofie gave birth to a fine boy, who was given the name Henry Percival, after the grandfathers. At the christening party Tönseten remarked gloomily that weddings and christenings were coming so thick and fast these days that he and his wife would land in the poorhouse if they had to attend them all. . . . What a terrible mistake he had made by giving up his office! If he had had that job

now he could have become rich just by marrying people!
. . . "Now, Sörine, you listen to me—if yours is a boy,
you've got to name him for me . . . the kid won't regret
it, I don't think!"

Beret had witnessed the christening in church but to
the party at Hans', afterward, she would not go. She left
as soon as the services were over, and went straight home.

At dinner she was unusually talkative and loud-voiced,
touching now upon one subject, now upon another, and
laughing nervously. She couldn't bear a moment's quiet
in the room, it seemed. Peder and his sister exchanged
looks, wondering what could be wrong again. Upon leaving the table she asked what the child's second name was
. . . she didn't hear very well . . . did they remember it?
Anna Marie told her the name, which only excited her
the more, her voice growing louder, her thoughts seeming
to move in a circle, like one who sees the incredible, sees
it unmistakably, but refuses to believe his own eyes. . . .
Percival? What sort of name was that? What might it
mean? Surely that wasn't a name for human beings. . . .
For whom could it be, anyway?

"Can't you understand that it's for Father?" said Peder
disgustedly.

"For Father? Don't talk nonsense—you know very well
your brother wouldn't make fun of a dead man! What
do you think your father would have thought of it? . . .
I can't understand what Hans is thinking of!"

Without answering, Peder left the room in anger and
went to the barn to tend the horses. Beret kept on talking
about the name . . . was Anna Marie sure she had heard
right? . . . Sofie's doings, of course—Hans would never
have ridiculed his father's name!

After that, Beret never mentioned the matter. Whenever Peder and his sister went to visit at Hans' she would
always remain at home. . . . "I can go some other time,"
she would say . . . "we had better not all leave the farm
. . . greet them for me." . . . Upon their return she
would question them closely about how they all were, and
most of all about the little boy, but she never called him
by name.

II

The people of St. Luke's had to admit that the few dollars they had subscribed toward the purchase of a new horse and buggy for the minister was money well spent. Unlike his predecessor, who like Jacob of old had stayed quietly by the tent, Reverend Gabrielsen could be found on the road at almost any time. A housewife could never know, except on Sunday mornings, when his beaming countenance might not appear in her doorway. And yet no one really minded his coming, because one could treat him to what there happened to be on hand—a piece of cake and a glass of milk for himself, a quart of cream or a jar of butter to take home for the family—and his face would shine with a pleasure as warm as sunshine.

It was a matter of conviction with Reverend Gabrielsen that if a minister of the Gospel is to win people, he must go out into the highways and the byways, meet them on their own level, and let them feel how sincerely he wished them well. The preaching was only secondary. And no one could deny that the man had been endowed with a most extraordinary gift for talking to people. His tolerance and patience were unusual. If one opposed his measures or gave him a malicious dig, he would ordinarily let it pass unnoticed. Easy nowadays to be a servant of the Lord—the prophets of old had been stoned! . . . Somehow, no matter how cheerless the place, he succeeded in leaving a ray of sunshine.

Whenever he passed that way and could spare the time, he would stop in at Beret Holm's. And he never came away empty-handed. No one knew better than he what a generous woman Mrs. Holm was. Her early aloofness had not disquieted him much; he knew the cause, and so he never mentioned the subject again . . . in time, that matter would take care of itself—he knew the younger generation! All the same it was a bit provoking to see sensible people display so little intelligence. Had the Norwegians, from the first, had the foresight to found a church in the language of the country the work for the Kingdom of God would have prospered far more, and all the lamentable schism could have been avoided. . . .

Just so they didn't continue the Norwegian until they alienated their own children from the church—the language of the older people was no longer that of the young!

A striking example of that was in this very house. The two children always spoke English to him. And yet there was not a more intelligent woman in the whole congregation than Beret Holm. The better he learned to know her the more he admired her uncommon astuteness. In her quiet manner she might say only a few words, yet the homely figure contained in them would shed a white light on the subject under discussion. The way she was managing her farm was the marvel of the community. He often heard it said that she was the most prosperous member of the congregation; whether that was true or not, he knew that she was contributing more to the different activities of the church than anyone else.

Beret's knowledge of the Word of God was nothing short of phenomenal. Her habitual sadness, therefore, Reverend Gabrielsen was at a loss to explain, and he tried in many ways to make her realize the sweet joyousness of being a child of God. But he might have spared himself the effort; the moment he began on that subject, Beret would grow strangely reticent. At such times, though she said very little, he would somehow get the impression that she was listening to him with forbearance, just as one does to a person who talks about matters he doesn't understand, and whom, on that account, it is idle to gainsay. Once during a conversation she had remarked quietly, as though reflecting aloud to herself, that he who wished to find out about a certain road, had better inquire of one who had traveled it often. . . . She had noticed that the lamb must go down on its knees when it wanted to suck! For a while the minister had sat clutching his beard, utterly baffled, and then had asked, in a kindly voice, if she hadn't also noticed how the lamb would skip and play afterward. Indeed she had! she answered in a voice as even and gentle as his own, but did he think it was the skipping, or was it the milk which was making it strong? Thereupon she had left him. To the minister it almost seemed that she actually called his Christianity in question.

Aside from wishing to speak a comforting word to Mrs.

Holm and perhaps get a little butter and cream wherewith to help feed the many hungry mouths he had at home, Reverend Gabrielsen had another purpose for these visits. Never before had the Church seen such golden opportunity; now came the problem of finding suitable workers; and in this house lived the young man whom he had chosen to fill his place in the ministry. The mother could well afford to give him the necessary education; God willing—his hopes would be realized!

Notwithstanding his optimism, during the past year his hopes had often been darkened by ominous clouds. Since Peder's confirmation the minister had found it increasingly difficult to keep his hold on the boy; every time he dropped in to see the family the boy studiously avoided him. If the minister stayed for a meal, Peder either did not come in at all, or else maintained a dogged silence throughout, eating hurriedly, and leaving as soon as he was through; when the minister was ready to leave, Peder was nowhere to be seen.

At first the boy's peculiar behavior hadn't particularly worried Reverend Gabrielsen . . . only natural for a boy to act that way, we must give him time to find himself . . . of his ultimate decision there can be no doubt.

But the boy's attendance at Sunday Bible hours had grown more and more irregular; finally he had stopped coming altogether. One Sunday the minister had invited Beret and the two children to dinner, but Peder did not come—he had promised to go elsewhere, the mother explained.

Above all else it alarmed Reverend Gabrielsen that Peder was often the subject of much gossip. Some said he was developing into a reckless sort of fellow, both in speech and in actions; others reported having seen him in a saloon. At a beer party at Tallaksen's he had drunk more than he could stand; the party had become rowdyish, a brawl had threatened, and Peder was said to have been the cause.

This incident in particular gave Reverend Gabrielsen much concern. As the pastor of the Holm family he could not let the matter pass, and made up his mind to speak to both mother and son about it. It ended, however, by his saying nothing to either of them. If Mrs. Holm did

not know about it, then why grieve her by telling her?
And Peder he didn't find at home when he called.
But Tönseten had been mentioned in connection with
the affair. Why not find out from him just what had
taken place? This the minister set out to do. And to his
great relief it wasn't so bad after all. Peder came, indeed,
to appear almost heroic.

. . . Yes, you see, related Tönseten dramatically, 'twas
all the fault of one of them blamed, loose-tongued Tallaksen boys, who got Peder mad by twitting him on account of being such a good friend of the minister, and
wanting to know if it was true that he knew the Bible
by heart and was going to be a preacher. . . . Well, you
see, Peder had got a bit riled, and had just up and defended his faith, kinda! . . . That was about the way it
had begun. Peder maintained that he had a perfect right
to become whatever he pleased without asking anybody
about it. One word had led to another, but certainly no
one could call it a fight. And they certainly hadn't been
drunk—far from it. Sakes alive! how in the world could a
dozen men have got drunk on one measly little pony
keg? he exclaimed heatedly. Shameful of people to talk
that way! . . . Tönseten forgot to mention the fact that
there had been a stout portion of whisky mixed with the
beer; but that didn't worry the minister since he hadn't
heard about it. He concluded that the story had been
grossly exaggerated and went on talking companionably
to Tönseten about the disgrace of such parties, in which
view the other concurred most earnestly. . . . The minister had gone away greatly relieved.

That had happened the previous fall. This spring other
troubles had arisen to worry him. Without conferring
either with him or with anyone else the Bethel congregation had called a minister from another synod. Michael
Bakken was a very handsome young man just out of the
seminary; his personality was so winning that people liked
him the moment he shook hands with them. Being unmarried, he had plenty of time to visit his parishioners;
before long he was to be seen on the road quite as frequently as Reverend Gabrielsen himself.

Reverend Bakken was especially zealous in his work for
the young people. It was really amazing what interest and

enthusiasm he could stir up. Within a short time he had a young people's society going, the time of whose meeting coincided exactly with Reverend Gabrielsen's Bible hour. The young people themselves furnished the programs: some would sing or read selections, others would give declamations they remembered from their school days, while the minister himself would give a short talk, in Norwegian, on "Great Men and Notable Events in American History." After the program light refreshments were served, and then the members, in accordance with the Constitution, were permitted to play "godly games." In addition, a choir was started, whose appearance on every program greatly increased the popularity of the meetings . . . perfectly amazing the amount of latent talent among the young people!

These affairs soon drew large crowds. That other young people besides those in Bethel enjoyed them, Reverend Gabrielsen did not need to be told, it being altogether too apparent from the size of the crowd which now attended his own gatherings. The older people came as before, but fewer and fewer of the young. Tired and discouraged he would go home, not knowing how to attack the evil. . . . New brooms always sweep clean in the beginning, he reflected, trying to comfort himself. . . . It won't be long before the glamor of this thing will be gone—it's too superficial to last!

Not that he wasn't being kept informed about what was going on! Only the other day a woman had come to him greatly concerned because sin was getting the upper hand among the young people. Had the minister heard that that boy of Mrs. Holm's who was supposed to become a minister, had actually joined the Bethel choir? . . . It could hardly be his eagerness for religion which was prompting him. More likely that Miriam of Nils Nilsen's! Perhaps he hadn't heard that Peder was out with her both night and day? . . . Hard to tell how the affair would turn out, but if one listened to what people said, the preacher over there was in love with the girl himself. . . . The woman talked long and was much disturbed about the irresponsible behavior of the young.

Reverend Gabrielsen felt it his pastoral duty to try to console her: It was only natural for young people to become interested in each other, such was the law of Life.

And certainly the Lord could make a fine minister's wife out of a daughter of Nils Nilsen. He had shown Himself capable of doing things much more difficult than that! . . . This attitude in one who was supposed to be the shepherd of a flock struck the woman as being extremely light-minded.

But the cheerfulness Reverend Gabrielsen affected greatly belied his feelings. Not for anything in the world, he felt, must Peder become interested in girls at this critical time of his life. How unpardonably stupid of him not to have insisted that Mrs. Holm send the boy to school last fall. . . . Least of all would he have suspected the Holms of disloyalty! . . .

On the very next afternoon he was on his way to Mrs. Holm's. Before leaving, he told his family not to expect him home to supper.

The minister found Beret alone in the dairy skimming cream. Greeting her pleasantly, he went straight to his errand: What had she decided about sending Peder away to school next fall? They really ought to settle the matter now, for he would like to write to the school at once and have Peder enrolled. . . . What did she say to it?

At first Beret didn't say very much. Reaching up on the shelf for an empty gallon pail, she filled it with cream and handing it to him bade him take it home.

The minister smiled and thanked her. But that wasn't his errand today! . . . Had she discussed seriously with Peder the matter of going to school?

—No, she couldn't say that she had exactly.

—But didn't she feel it her duty to do so, he inquired kindly. These were dangerous years for the boy; associating with the young people he had grown up with might easily sidetrack him.

—Would the danger be less away from home?

—Certainly! The minister waxed eager. There could be no doubt about it! Remarkable what influence Christian teachers exerted upon young minds; it was precisely that influence which would make Peder surrender to the call.

Beret walked over to the water tank and sat down on the edge of it, her face looking worn and very tired; a strong light, falling on it, revealed to the minister that she had aged perceptibly during the last couple of years. At once he felt impelled to say something comforting to her, but the right words wouldn't come, as had happened many times before whenever she looked at him thus.

—Her will did not count for much in the matter, she supposed. A strange bitterness was in her voice; when she continued she looked straight into the minister's eyes:

—If it was God's will that Peder be a minister, He would, she supposed, find a way. She had noticed that the chick would always find its way out even though the shell was ever so solid—when the time came. The boy was now grown up, and would have to decide the question for himself.

Beret lapsed into silence, pressing plaits in her apron. She has more to say, the minister reflected, and waited for her. The plaits properly straightened out again, she began to speak, but now about a different matter:

—She had seen in the papers that the Church was now establishing homes for the aged. . . . Possible, perhaps, for old, worn-out men and women to wear away their last days in an institution like that . . . yes, it might be; though a big barn full of old decrepit cows would hardly give one much of either "joy" or "beauty"! Beret put marked emphasis on the two words he had so often used in speaking to her. . . . Queer sort of charity, it seemed to her. When people got too old to work and were only in the way, they were to be torn loose from everything they had grown attached to, and carted off to some institution for safe-keeping! . . . The members of the Church need only give a few pennies yearly to such institutions; thereby they'd fulfil the commandment of Love . . . easy nowadays to be a Christian! Could that be what Christ had meant by charity? Beret relapsed into silence while she worked with the folds of her apron.

The minister, much perturbed by her unreasonableness, explained earnestly and kindly to her: That wasn't what he had meant at all; she wouldn't need to sell the farm in order to send Peder to school; Hans could move back on the home farm; and what about her other son out in Montana? . . . They must not forget Christ's parable about the marriage of the king's son!

Beret rose hurriedly, began stacking the pails together, and was about to go out. Stopping in the doorway she turned on him agitatedly: "You ministers have a mania for meddling in things you don't understand . . . seems to me," there was a catch in her voice, "if you really loved mankind you'd hardly act the way you do!"

Beret left the dairy; but after a little while she reappeared in the door, and then she seemed quite calm: "You had better come into the house and wait; Peder will soon be home and you'll have a chance to speak to him yourself." Thereupon she left him.

Utterly bewildered, the minister could only stare after her, and stroke his beard upward till his mouth was full. . . . Mrs. Holm was attempting to reason about matters she did not in the least understand! He would have to do his duty by her better than he had in the past—that was quite evident. He must guide and instruct her, show her the way. . . . She was too old-fashioned in her views. The minister paced up and down in the yard. But how to handle her? . . . She was immovable, like a stone wall. . . . These old Norwegians were sometimes very difficult to deal with! . . . What could a farm matter in comparison with having her son ordained for the holy ministry? . . . So little, seemingly, did she understand God's will, despite her great intelligence!

Peder stretched his day in the field. Beret and Anna Marie had already done the milking and all the other evening chores, except tending the horses. The sun was making ready to slip below the rim of the prairie; over the farm twilight was fast deepening.

Blithely humming a tune, Peder rode into the yard, leading the other horse by the bridle. He suspected nothing of the presence of company until he caught sight of the new buggy over by the machine shed; on the instant his humming stopped, and with a sudden jerk, he pulled his straw hat farther down over his forehead.

The minister crossed the yard and greeted him warmly, inquired if he was busy with the corn these days, and whether he could make use of a first-class hired man.

Peder answered curtly, his voice friendly but evasive, as if wanting to prevent too many questions. He took the horses to water, led them into the barn and unharnessed them, the minister following and talking all the while. As soon as Peder was through, he came out into the passageway, ready to leave. The minister confronted him, and putting all his natural kindliness into his words, stated the errand on which he had come:

"Tonight, Peder, I am here to talk to you about a serious matter."

"All right." Peder avoided the minister's face, and waited for what would follow.

"We'd better leave it until after supper; your mother has asked me to stay."

"I'm going out this evening," Peder said reticently, and continued to wait.

"Are you out many evenings?" the minister inquired kindly, coming a little closer.

The boy only gave a wry smile.

"It is just this, you see, that now I want to write the president of the school and apply for your admission; you ought to get started next fall."

"Any particular hurry?" Peder forgot himself and spoke Norwegian.

"There certainly is!" the minister assured him, continuing in English; "the sooner you go the better. The longer you put it off, the more uncertain you become, that I can see clearly, and the harder it will be for you to break away. You are forming ties of one kind or another which make it increasingly difficult for you to get loose. You remember the warning, 'No man, having put his hand to the plow, and looking back, is fit for the kingdom of God' . . . Jesus knew whereof He spoke!"

Peder remembered that he must feed the horses before he left, and went up into the hayloft. While he was about it he might as well give them their oats too, then that job wouldn't delay him later on. When he returned, he found the minister still in the doorway waiting for him.

"We'd better go in," said Peder, "Mother will have supper waiting."

"Let supper wait. I have had this matter on my mind since the day of your confirmation—now I must speak to you about it!" The minister spoke with kind eagerness: "I think I can understand your difficulties; other interests are holding you back; and you don't seem to feel the call. Well, you see, that comes from your not understanding the true greatness of being a minister. But think of the blessed privilege of going about helping sinful human beings to become good! Perfect Goodness is the aim and the end of all life, because Goodness is the very essence of God. I want you to think on these things, Peder! Have you forgotten our many talks about the nature of God? Those were happy hours for me . . . you were so far ahead of all the others in understanding, could see right through the most difficult problems—oh, I know that God has chosen you for His holy calling!" . . . The minister waxed warm with eloquence over the divine beauty of Perfect Goodness. "Man must be taught to understand that Goodness and God are one—then man will find it easy to serve Him. Take your own mother, for example: If she could only understand that God is good, she would be infinitely more happy and she would bear the cares of this life with a cheerful heart."

Peder, having removed his broad-brimmed hat from his head, was slapping his leg with it.

"Guess I got to hurry," he said quietly; "we'd better be going in!" Again he was speaking Norwegian, which astonished the minister.

"All right, then I'll write and say you're coming. The president is a good friend of mine—I know you will like him!"

"We'll see about that later. I can't leave Mother now!" Peder stepped aside, so that he could pass by the minister, and walked out of the barn; but in the yard he stopped to wait for him.

The minister resumed the conversation, now more deadly in earnest:

"I have already had a long talk with your mother about it, and she said I would have to speak to you."

Peder walked on silently, the minister keeping step with him.

"I don't get the impression that she is against your becoming a minister—in fact, I know she isn't. And now I'm going to see your brother right way and ask him to move back here as soon as you leave."

"You better not!" said Peder, his voice very low.

"Why not? No one is nearer to it than he. You go about the business to which God has called you; your brother takes charge of the home farm and cares for your mother in her old age; thereby we are doing good all around."

"I ask you not to meddle in this affair!" said Peder

doggedly, immediately quickening his steps so that the minister found it difficult to keep up with him.

Beret was on the porch looking for them.

Peder told them not to wait for him, went directly upstairs, and was gone a long time. When he came down he was dressed in his Sunday clothes.

Beret looked up at him:

"Are you going out this evening?"

"Guess so." Peder sat down and began to eat.

Looking from one to the other the minister was struck by the strong family resemblance in the little group. All three had the same fine, clear-cut features, the highly intelligent look; but in the faces of both mother and son there was an expression of reserve, almost of secretiveness—something that one couldn't get at, which was entirely lacking in the girl. Peder had matured considerably of late, that also the minister observed.

No one seemed to have much to say after Peder had sat down; he felt it himself and began conversing with the minister—rather self-possessed and casually about everyday affairs, inquiring what people round about in the settlement were doing these days.

The minister having finished his meal sat playing with his knife. . . . A good deal going on. . . . That Bethel preacher had a remarkable gift for making things hum. The minister chuckled good-naturedly, in his voice was a teasing note:

"I hear you are singing in his choir; don't know that I like it exactly, seems to me I ought to have the first claim on you; not that I think there is anything wrong in what you are doing—don't misunderstand me! . . . Sooner or later the people in these two congregations will have to begin working themselves into one . . . that will be your task when you take up your work as a minister here. After you are a student and come back here to teach our parochial school you can take charge of our choir and assist me in preaching, then we two will make things hum! . . . I had no opportunities for choir work in my student days; that's because I got started too late."

The color in Peder's face deepened perceptibly.

"That'll hardly be *here!*" he said; his voice had an odd ring in it, his eyes were fixed on his plate.

"Why not?" asked the minister, unruffled. "I've been

told that your father was one of the leaders in the land-taking out here; could anything be more appropriate than that his son should become a spiritual pioneer in the great Commonwealth of Love, which is only another name for God's Church on earth? Never, I tell you, has the outlook been as bright as now; hence, the importance of calling and preparing the right kind of leaders—that, too, I am confident will be possible!" The minister's face beamed with enthusiasm.

Beret observed him quizzically. . . . Was the man joking? He couldn't actually be that stupid? An amused smile crossed her face, she was about to speak, but thought better of it.

Excusing himself, Peder got up from the table, and prepared to leave.

The minister also rose at once, went over to him, and grasped his hand:

"I won't let you escape! . . . I too resisted once. It has been the greatest regret of my life, and now I wish to spare you a similar mistake!" He shook the hand he held heartily, but did not release it.

"Looks that way all right!" said Peder, who was now laughing.

III

Peder had a young filly, Dolly by name, a beautiful animal that he loved dearly, having had her as his special pet ever since she was born. So attached were they to each other that the moment she heard his whistle she would come running to meet him and would rub her head against his cheek, begging to be fondled. This spring, he had broken her for driving, but she was still so high-spirited that neither his mother nor Anna Marie had dared risk her life in a buggy behind the filly.

Tonight he flung the harness on Dolly and got her hitched in a hurry, keeping an eye on the house meanwhile, determined not to permit any further delay. Nevertheless, he took time to fold the buggy top clear down. Pleasant to feel the wash of the air flooding him like a bath . . . tonight he was in need of some form of exhilaration.

Peder jumped in and drove off. A peculiar state of excite-

ment was upon him. Mysterious restlessness and vague,
nebulous thoughts played in his mood. Waves of strange
emotions came and went. Up ahead of him in the road
rattled a wagon; the noise jarred him. Cracking his whip
he sped by. . . . Whoa, whoa—not so fast there, Dolly,
we'll get there on time, don't worry! She won't have gone
off and left us—hardly. The horse fell into a canter. Peder
stretched himself. . . . Queer that they never could leave
him alone! What did they want of him anyway? . . . He
a "pioneer in the great Commonwealth of Love"! The
thought amused him: Ya, sure, you wait and see, he
laughed to himself; by and by, I'll turn out to be a pretty
decent sort of fellow! . . . In order that he might get a
chance to think better, he forced the horse into a walk.
. . . How stupid people are—and that Gabrielsen! When
it comes right down to it, he has less brains than the rest!
How much does he sense of all that lies round about here
dreaming and wanting to be awakened—he, a man with
eleven kids and red whiskers! Peder laughed aloud to himself. . . . Sheer twaddle his talk about God, it simply
didn't hang together at all; bet he could stick him on it—
hadn't he done so many times already? . . . "To teach
people to be good," how disgustingly sweet and sickening!
Just what did he mean by being *good?* People sitting prettily at home folding their hands? . . . To stand there year
in and year out, preaching to people on a subject he didn't
know the first thing about—huh, was that a man's job?
Just suppose that all should become like Gabrielsen? What
would life be worth then? . . . A little faster there, Dolly,
old girl! Only a low whistle from Peder, and immediately
the horse broke into a run. The speed tugged at his spirits
and roused them. . . . No, sir, rather would he like to
turn the whole prairie topsy-turvy . . . take people by the
neck and compel them to sing—by Jove, that would be a
man's job! . . . Because God was Power . . . yes, and
then that other thing too! . . . Peder lost himself in
revery. . . . People were talking about him, eh? And they
had gone to the minister? And now Gabrielsen was wanting to get him off to school and make a preacher of him—
just let him try it! "A free country for a free people!" Tönseten always insisted.

Becoming aware that the horse was barely ambling along
brought Peder to. He cracked his whip, and Dolly started

off at a gallop, which put an end to his musings. On and
on through the dark he sped, the vigor of the life bearing
him forward filled him with strength . . . his courage
seemed to soar on wings. . . .

A while later he drove up to the door at Nils Nilsen's,
ran up on the porch, the reins still in his hands, and rapped
on the door. The door opened, and a half-grown boy stood
full in the light from within. Seeing who it was, the boy
came out and closed the door after him.

"Miriam gone yet?"

"No, not yet."

"Say, Gabriel, you go in and tell her I'm here, and then
I'll hire you for a whole season's threshing when I get a
rig!"

"Are you going to get one?"

"Maybe. Hustle up now!" Peder patted the boy on the
shoulder, and then sprang up into the buggy again; over in
the yard a little way, he stopped and waited.

After a few minutes Miriam came out. In a low voice
she said good evening and stepped into the buggy.

Peder put the robe around her knees, taking great pains
to tuck it in snugly, and made use of the opportunity to
pat her a little. Miriam pushed his hand aside. "What's
the matter?" Peder laughed jokingly, and quit.

"You are late tonight."

"Yes, so I am!" His words rang self-assurance. "I've
got a lot to 'tend to, I want you to know."

"You ought to get yourself a hired man."

"Oh, ought I, now?" he asked teasingly. "I'd much
rather have a hired girl!" He tried to put his arm around
her neck, a tussle ensued; Miriam was strong, but this time
he was determined to have his way. Dolly hearing the disturbance in the dark became nervous; if Peder hadn't got
hold of the reins and talked soothingly to her, she would
have run away.

When he had succeeded in calming the horse, Miriam
resumed the conversation as though nothing had happened:

"Then you wouldn't have to work so hard."

"The deuce with the work!"

Miriam could tell from the tone that he was out of
humor and turning to him and putting her hand on his
arm, she said in a low, friendly voice:

"Now you are mad again!"

"Mad—who said I was mad?" And as if to convince her that she couldn't make him mad, he added indifferently: "To run a farm isn't any trick!"

"What made you so late then?"

"What made me late?"

"Yes?" Miriam was looking straight into his eyes, and Peder could feel how earnestly she was trying to make up again.

"Huh—I'm going to be a minister, if you've got to know it!"

She held back a moment:

"You ought not to joke about such things." Her voice was very serious.

"Should I weep, perhaps?"

For some time Miriam did not answer him.

"Now, *you* are mad!"

"When you talk so frivolously."

"Is it frivolous to be a minister?" Peder was fast recovering his good humor.

"You are joking, and that isn't nice . . . about such things!" There lay a deep seriousness in Miriam's words. Peder, feeling how strongly she disapproved of what he had said, bristled instantly:

"Let me tell you something," he announced, with assumed indifference:

"Preachers are fools!"

In spite of herself, Miriam had to laugh:

"You mean Gabrielsen!"

"No sir; I mean that fellow of yours!"

"He's a fine man!" retaliated Miriam warmly.

"Huh, fine! Perhaps he has been over to see you again?"

"Yes," she replied wistfully . . . the thought seemed to be lingering.

"Next thing I know, you'll have married him!"

"You're perfectly horrid tonight!"

"Horrid?—you just wait till I get my hands on him!"

"If you aren't good, I'll have him take me home." Her words sounded dreamy, had more of earnest than of jest in them.

"Suit yourself about that!"

Peder lashed the horse, and drove so fast that Miriam had to hold on to her hat.

On their arrival at John Baardsen's, choir practice was in full swing. Four-part singing and strains of organ music came floating out through the open windows. Every now and then the singing would cease, and Reverend Bakken's animated voice could be heard directing; occasionally he sang a few measures to demonstrate the tempo. Out in the yard stood a group of youths who were not taking part in the singing, some having brought a sister, others someone else's sister.

Peder assisted Miriam to alight. For a moment she waited, expecting him to say something, but he straightway began unhitching his horse.

"Are you going to take me home?" she ventured timidly as if speech were difficult.

"Unless I find someone I like better!"

The moment he had uttered the words, he felt sorry. But, never mind . . . he certainly wasn't going begging!

Miriam left him.

From near the house came the squeak, squeak of an ice-cream freezer. John Baardsen and one of the boys were taking turn about at the crank, pulling for all they were worth, the perspiration pouring from them. Peder joined them and started talking to John about work and crops and the happenings in the settlement. John was glad to see Peder because he wanted to ask questions about their windmill; this fall he planned to put up one of his own. Peder offered to turn awhile; the two kept up a steady talk while they worked. Mrs. Baardsen came out to inquire if the ice cream wasn't nearly frozen, and when they investigated they found that it was just right; the coffee being ready, the serving began at once.

The members of the choir stayed on in the parlor while the refreshments were being served; the minister was in there, too, occupying the chair next to Miriam, but conversing with everybody.

Those of the boys who did not sing had taken possession of the porch, most of them sitting, a few standing. Peder was leaning against the window sill, occasionally looking into the room; after a while he too sat down. He was very quiet this evening and had little to contribute to the conversation. The interest seemed centered on the Fourth of July celebration the following week, the boys joking and teasing one another about the girl each was taking; there was much laughter and noisy protest because each swore up and down that he didn't care for girls, least of all for the one he was being teased about.

When the choir again resumed practicing, Tom Hove asked Peder why he wasn't singing tonight; he answered that he was hoarse and didn't care to use his voice, and the teasing broke out anew. Tom would like to know the cause of that hoarseness . . . had they heard that the minister was a frequent caller at Nils Nilsen's? They knew of course that he had a brand-new horse and buggy, some style to that chap! . . . There certainly had been a lot of beautiful moonlight lately. . . . Miriam, poor girl, was exactly cut out for a minister's wife—she might not care to wait until Peder had been ordained!

Tom's raillery exasperated Peder, but he managed to laugh with the others. "You're an ass, Tom, but I suppose you can't help it, so there's nothing to do about it!" Peder got up and left the porch—a moment longer and he would have to give Tom a licking.

Just then John Baardsen came along looking for Peder; he had a couple of questions he'd like to ask him about the windmill. Would he come and see the place where he had thought of putting it?

A steady stream of talk was flowing from John: This is where he had decided to put it . . . did Peder think the place was all right? And he was thinking of rigging up a contrivance whereby he could get the windmill to turn the grindstone for him . . . what did Peder think of it? . . . Must be possible to utilize the mill for many things . . . he had also thought of using it for sawing . . . a terrible chore with the wood all the time, only he didn't know just what to do with all the sawdust. . . . Why not throw it to the pigs, Peder suggested, and he wouldn't have to haul straw. The idea dumbfounded John—well, sir, that he hadn't thought of!

John talked and asked questions. Choir practice was over; Peder heard the first buggy start off, but old John was showing him so much attention that he couldn't very well leave. And now he asked Peder what he thought of Reverend Bakken . . . well, now, wasn't that a real minister for you? The Lord had certainly been good to them this time. So kind and friendly always, nothing stuck-up about him. And so fond of the Norwegian—a remarkable young man indeed! . . . From the porch came loud laughter; one buggy after the other was rolling away. . . . John had now embarked on his favorite subject, the comparison of Reverend Bakken and Reverend Isaksen; which reminded him of the time he went to Reverend Isaksen to resign from the congregation. This topic was inexhaustible. Peder was desperately anxious to break away, but John was hardly in the middle of his story.

On the porch the girls were standing in a knot, their arms about each other's waists; a buggy drove up, and in a moment there was one less in the group; another came, one more gone—it looked like the picking of grapes from a cluster.

At last there was only Miriam left.

No more buggies came. She had taken hold of one of the pillars. . . . Where could he be? Had he actually left her? . . .

Then a buggy came out of the dark and stopped right in front of her. Reverend Bakken, having looked in vain for the host before he went out to hitch up, now came back to say good-bye. Recognizing Miriam, he took her hand, which he held: Would she do him the honor of letting him take her home? . . . She need not walk, he was going by her place anyway. . . . The minister talked in a low, eager voice.

Miriam's eyes searched the yard, and then without saying a word she went with him.

When they had gone only a little way down the road they heard a horse coming up behind them at a furious speed; the voice of a man called in the dark; the buggy whizzed by, in an instant it had disappeared in the dark— not even the rumbling could be heard.

—Who could that be driving so recklessly? the minister wondered.

Miriam had retreated into the far corner of the buggy, and ventured no information.

IV

Every day that week Peder was in the cornfield cultivating. Shortly after five in the morning he would be at work, change horses in the middle of the forenoon, and take no more time off for dinner than he absolutely had to. To his mother it seemed senseless to carry on this way; she offered to take the other plow and help him. . . . Why not? They were two grown women in the house with little to do; the horses stood idle in the barn; she need not stretch the hours longer than she could stand—why work himself to death when it wasn't necessary?

Peder wouldn't hear of it. He didn't see other women working in the field . . . no more necessary here than elsewhere! . . . He was silent and moody these days, and very difficult to talk to. At mealtime they could hardly get a word out of him, and in the evenings he would sit up in his own room far into the night. . . . It must be this matter between him and Gabrielsen that is on his mind, Beret concluded.

On Saturday night Peder didn't stop work until it was too dark to see the rows. During the afternoon the sky had become overcast with threatening clouds, but no rain came until nightfall, then it began to mizzle.

At home they had waited supper for him a long while. Unable to understand what could be keeping him so late, Beret went out to look for him. She found him in the yard unhitching, and apparently in excellent spirits. He thought he would be able to finish the corn next week, he said, even if he did take Wednesday off for the Fourth.

—Is that why he has been working so hard? Immediately her anxiety left her . . . that I call being thoughtful for one so young!

He took plenty of time with the meal. When he had finished, he tilted his chair back, and began discussing with his mother the advisability of hiring a man a little later on. There was a lot to be done here; besides they ought to be breaking more land. He had heard that there was a newcomer over at Joe Lund's who was supposed to be a splendid worker; perhaps he would see him Wednesday. They might hire him; if they liked him they could keep him until they were through husking this fall. Hans would have enough to do at his own place. Peder talked about it at length. Beret agreed that he should try to see the man.

Finally he got up; asked his sister to find him a clean shirt; and taking the clothes and a towel, he left the house.

Utter blackness outside. The rain was still falling quietly, but more secretively. As he crossed the yard he held out his hand to feel the drizzle.

Peder went into the cow barn. Just inside the door stood a large barrel, which he had filled with water during the noon hour. After stripping off his clothes, he let himself slide down in, *ughing* and gasping for breath as the water rose higher about his body. He stayed in the barrel a long time, splashing, and scrubbing himself.

Getting out of the water, he went to the doorway where he stood rubbing his body briskly until the skin glowed with a pleasant warmth. A strange sense of well-being, infusing new vigor into every muscle, began trickling through him. He thrust his arm out to see how hard it was raining; the drops felt warm and soft, like a lukewarm ointment. Flinging the towel away, he drew a deep breath, and ran out into the wet darkness. Round and round the yard he trotted, all the while slapping his body with the flat of his hand; pretty soon he felt the blood tingling. The rain seemed warmer than the water in the barrel—if only it would beat down on him a little harder! He stopped a moment to peer up into the sky. The darkness overhead was a solid wall; underneath it were drifting black mists from which dripped warm, tiny drops.

Back in the barn again, Peder rubbed himself long. He threw a dry garment about his shoulders, and seated himself on a milk stool, right in the doorway. Outside, the drops fell with gentle tip-taps. Those dropping down from the eaves were bigger and struck the ground with loud splashes. The others were coming secretively, stealing down as cautiously as though they were afraid of disturbing the dark. . . . Where did they come from? Peder smiled . . . yes, where were they coming from anyway? Did they have life? What was their errand? . . . Of course, they had life—he was aware of a living presence all around him.

Whiffs of cold found the doorway and struck his body. Having got into his clothes again, Peder sat down once more to listen to the rain.

. . . If it should pour down tomorrow, he wouldn't have to go to church. . . . Perhaps he would escape the minister after all! Peder sat and chuckled to himself: He s'posed he couldn't get out of it this time by giving as an excuse that he had been invited to his sister-in-law's. . . .

Couldn't have been so terrible to say that—she had told him to come over whenever he found the time.

Peder, listening to all the whispering voices, continued to gaze into the dark. . . . Funny they could never leave him alone! Well, they'd better look out! Tomorow he would tell Gabrielsen frankly that this was a matter for himself to settle when the time came. . . . Later on he'd see about *that!* . . . Farming wasn't such a bad business. He'd hire that newcomer and break a lot of land, and make a great haul in flax next summer . . . he'd show 'em a boy that could farm!

The water guggled good-naturedly . . . got chummy and intimate with him . . . told him of his future . . . whispered strange, mysterious thoughts about great achievements.

Peder was looking at the different ideas as they came and went: The Norwegians had begun to make themselves felt in politics. About time they were waking up! What had they accomplished since they came here? Nothing! . . . Only wrangled about false doctrine. . . . Their uniting three church bodies, what was that to crow about? And now this new Church would keep right on fighting with the others—fine business!

. . . That Knute Nelson over in Minnesota must be a real man; he seemed to have ideas. . . . What he had done, others could do, too—Lincoln grew up in a log cabin! . . .

. . . Minister? No, thank you! Preachers weren't one whit better than other people. What did they do but wrangle and stir up trouble? Just look at the situation here —two of 'em chasing around the prairie all day long! Was life getting any better on account of it? They didn't even seem to know what they were trying to do! . . .

Peder no longer heard the rain. . . . Everything had gone wrong lately! The gloom deepened and was closing in upon him like the solid darkness without. . . . There was that Bakken, smooth and slick, talking Norwegian just to ingratiate himself with the old folks. . . . Miriam would regret *that* trick, all right! . . . Not that he cared . . . but she might have waited, she knew very well he was coming. Why hadn't she come to look for him? She certainly must have heard him and John talking—they hadn't been very far away. . . . More stuff for Gabrielsen to gossip with the women about!

Peder shuddered and sprang to his feet. Must be getting colder outside. Perhaps it would begin to rain in real earnest. . . .

When he came in, his mother, sitting at the table reading, looked up.

"Took you a long time tonight."

"Am I not going to the minister's tomorrow?"

A smile crossed her face:

"Looks like we're going to have a heavy rain."

"Suits me all right!"

"You mustn't talk that way; the minister wishes you naught but well. Now you must go right to bed—you need the rest, I'm sure."

Up in Peder's room stood a bookcase with a number of books in it. Since his confirmation he had been reading a good deal, often staying up far into the night. This winter he had fairly devoured books.

From the case he took out a huge tome containing Shakespeare's complete works. The winter before, after procuring the volume, he had begun to read the plays he knew by title, taking *Hamlet* first. But he didn't get very far into it before he gave up in disappointment: the action was slow, the play full of strange words and expressions, the scenes were gloomy; and the tone was so melancholy that it gave him the blues. Next he had tried the comedies, which he had found easier; in their coarse jests laughter sat waiting for him. . . . Must be I didn't take time enough with the other, he concluded. He returned to *Hamlet,* and kept on reading the tragedies. Remarkable pictures indeed! Here people abandoned themselves to love and lust, hated and sinned recklessly, murdering each other right and left; the sword always sat loose in the scabbard; pools of warm blood on every hand. And up out of the pictures rose a deep sadness, hopeless always, reminding him of that Killdeer-song of Tambur-Ola's. . . . This evening he turned to *Hamlet,* and selected the soliloquies, most of which he knew by heart. The studied indifference of a soul crying in despair lightened his own depressed spirits. After a while he put the book aside and reached for his English Bible; there was a certain selection in the Old Testament he felt the need of reading just now.

It got to be very late before he went to bed. Outside, the rain was still falling; he lay listening to the patter of the drops on the roof until he dozed off. . . . Perhaps he wouldn't have to go to Gabrielsen's after all!

An endless expanse of azure sky. Dazzling sunshine. Sky could never be burnished more brightly. Over in the northwest still hung a couple of woolly rags, left there from last night's polishing.

At the parsonage Peder had just put his horse in the barn and was standing in the doorway looking about. His mother and sister had gone in; the minister was in the study conferring with two men from the other congregation who had come to see him on business.

—What a fool I was not to stay home, Peder thought. What do I want here anyway? Am I not my own boss? I could have told him straight out I wouldn't come and have avoided this!

Seeing a small boy at play up by the wall of the woodshed, he walked over.

—What was his name? Peder inquired.

—Kenneth LeRoy Gabrielsen!

The boy, four years old, golden-haired and of fair complexion like the rest of the family, was deeply engrossed in his play, yet seemed pleased to have someone to talk to. . . . Would the man please look at all his horses?

Sticks of wood had been stood aslant against the wall; between them had been placed shoes of all sizes and descriptions, each tied by a piece of twine to a nail in the wall. Peder counted the shoes and found thirteen in all.

"My, but you have many horses!"

"Oh yes," the boy agreed joyously, "I have lots!" He was squatting on his haunches and pouring dirt into the shoes.

—What was he doing now?

—Feeding them oats!

—Did he have names for all of them?

—Sure he had! The boy got up and began pointing: "King," "Dan," "Prince," "Fox," "Jim," "Maggy," "Jumbo," "Dick," but moving his finger faster than he could say the names, he became confused and had to start all over again. At the left end of the row stood the largest shoe of all, brown with age, and run down at the heel.

Peder didn't quite catch the name, and bent down asking in a low voice what he had called it.

"Victorious."

"What's that you say?" Peder had grabbed the boy by the shoulder.

"Victorious," repeated the boy, who had begun feeding it oats, and looked up. "My papa knows a man by that name, he's a Norwegian; the horse's the biggest I got, he's strong too, 'nd he c'n pull the whole house . . . he eats lots of oats, I c'n tell you."

"You call him Victorious?"

"Sure!" Suddenly the boy sprang to his feet, and took Peder's hand:

"Come on, let's water 'em, then we c'n ride 'nd have fun; Else can't today!"

"Else?—Did she give him that name?" Peder asked in a low voice, glancing at the house, which stood close by.

"No, papa knows a man, 'nd Else she likes it, she said for us to use it, don't you think it's nice?"

But Peder had no time to think about it because at that instant the kitchen door opened, and Else stepped out on the porch to look for them. The moment the boy caught sight of his sister, he wanted to run to her and tried to drag Peder with him, but finding him too slow, deserted him: The man wouldn't believe that they called the big horse Victorious!

Peder didn't know where to turn, and Else, horrified, threw up her hands and exclaimed, "Well, I never ——!"

She came hurriedly down the steps and gave Peder her hand, her whole person begging forgiveness. She could not let go his hand until she had explained how it all had happened: Would he please not be offended—it was all her fault! Kenneth was so wrapped up in horses that he could think of nothing else, and then they had run out of names, and Papa had said they'd have to name the horse for someone they liked . . . they had tried several and then . . . well! . . . A few wayward hairs having strayed down over her ears, Else let go of the hand; she straightened up and looked at Peder as she pushed them back. The blue dress set off her golden richness, as a frame a lovely picture. . . . The name, she confessed with naïve admiration, was so beautiful—he wouldn't take it ill, would he? It was all her fault!

Peder's resentment was entirely gone. . . . Well, if that was the way! Glad they'd found a name they could use . . . was she, too, fond of horses?

Indeed she was, she assured him. She meant to buy a horse of her own some day, the very finest to be had . . . when she got rich, of course; and then she'd ride—ride—ride—

"Where to?" Peder wanted to know.

"Oh . . . to the end of the world!"

"Why, then you might as well ride with me," Peder laughed joyously. "I intend making that trip myself!" And the two stood beaming into each other's eyes.

Dinner went off easier than Peder had expected. The children ate in the kitchen, the grown-ups in the dining room. The two strangers had also been invited, and since they had so much to talk to the minister about, Peder was left in peace.

Else helped serve in both rooms, Peder watching her and thinking many thoughts.

After dinner he took a turn about the yard, enjoying himself as best he could; Kenneth LeRoy was napping and wouldn't be out for a while yet. Peder fell to wondering if his mother would soon be ready to leave . . . perhaps he ought to begin hitching up. Still, there wasn't any particular hurry—not yet.

Else came out and went into the woodshed; Peder sauntered after, and began talking to her while she squatted piling sticks on her arm. . . . He wondered if he shouldn't offer to carry the wood in for her, but before he could make up his mind Else was ready to leave. . . . Well, never mind—Anna Marie was most likely helping with the dishes, and then he'd never hear the last of it.

In a few moments, Else returned, this time with a pail on her arm. Immediately, he was reminded of the day they had fought about the pail; she, too, must have thought of the same thing, for she stopped and laughed teasingly, waiting for him to come.

When he had filled the pail Peder set it to one side where she couldn't reach it, and inquired if she was going to the celebration next Wednesday.

—She guessed not . . . Papa never cared about going to such affairs.

—S'posing someone came and asked her?

—That would hardly happen! Else looked away from him.

—But just s'posing it did? His voice low and entreating.

Blushing hotly, Else turned to him:

"Do you mean yourself?"

"Exactly!" nodded Peder.

"Then I'm sure Papa will let me go," she said so flustered that he felt sorry for her. Straightway he picked up the pail and carried it up to the porch. When she took it she didn't dare look at him, which Peder couldn't understand. . . . There was something else he should have spoken to her about. . . .

Presently his mother came out and asked him to get the horse ready . . . they had better be going.

V

The minister was walking up and down in the yard, waiting for Peder. No smile today, only preoccupied seriousness and a thoughtful tugging at his beard. . . . This was the first time, he confided to Peder, in a worried tone, that he had let his little Else fly out of the nest alone. Queer about that child . . . she had never cared for other entertainment than her little brothers and sisters; they had been her dolls. A good thing for him, for he hadn't been able to afford any other kind . . . a most remarkably good child, that she was! . . . But just then Else appeared and the minister barely had time to add:

"You must take good care of her!"

Peder wasted no time in getting started. Today Else was wearing a dress of deep golden yellow. Her whole figure radiated a light which dazzled him; he scarcely dared look toward her side of the seat. The story about Goldenlocks came to his mind—here she sat by his side! He would have liked to ask Else if she knew that story, but could not . . . too much light for talking.

Instead he'd better show her how swift and light of foot his horse was and how intimately it obeyed him. He gave a low, melodious whistle, cracked the whip ever so slightly, and instantly the air whizzed by their ears. Day, golden, glorious day, stretched out wide open arms to welcome them. They seemed to be floating through yellow and

greenish hazes. On either hand along the road light green
fields danced courtesying toward them. Neither spoke.
Between them lay deep silence, rich in mysterious secrets.
When after a while Dolly decided she had shown them
enough of her tricks and slackened her pace both felt re-
freshed as after a bath.

"Now we're off for the end of the world!" Peder ventured, stealing a shy glance at her.

"And I'm going along!" Else cried in delight.

"So you are!"

For the present there was nothing more to be said about
that, and the silence grew so rich that both had to listen
to it.

The grove in which the celebration was held already
swarmed with people. In an open space under the trees
wide flooring had been laid, with a platform and a speaker's
stand at one end, both of which were profusely decorated
with bunting and flags. On the boughs of the trees round
about there hung gaily colored Chinese lanterns, in readi-
ness for the dance. Even a brass band had been secured for
the occasion! The players, handsome and stately in their
gold-striped, red uniforms, dotted the crowd, like a few
scattered poppies in a field. Near the platform were refresh-
ment stands and various booths, offering for sale cigars,
pop, ice cream, fireworks, and slender canes decorated with
small flags and pennons. Peder bought two canes and gave
Else one.

Jugglers and charlatans had flocked together and found
their way to the spot, as birds of prey discover carrion.
One had set up an ingeniously devised mechanism which
he invited people to strike at with a heavy wooden club,
only ten cents a try; a miraculous contrivance it was. If
one only could hit hard enough, a beautiful little doll with
a dollar bill in her hands would pop out of a hole at the
top. Crowded ranks of men—most of them young—stood
waiting a chance to try their strength; today they were possessed by a reckless courage . . . you just wait until I
smash that infernal outfit to smithereens and dolls will
rain like manna! Next to this attraction was a shooting gallery, where curious animals ran along a wall; but this was
not nearly so interesting and therefore didn't draw much
of a crowd. In a joyous mood Peder and Else walked about,
taking in everything.

Farther off between the trees stood a brown tent, alone and well concealed. "For Men Only" read a warning sign in big, green letters at the top. On a table in front of the tent, a pouchy-faced man proclaimed in a hoarse, wheezy voice that within the tent was the world's greatest wonder, *The Pearl of Abyssinia!* She was endowed with the gift of prophecy and could show any unmarried man his future wife; the King of Assyria had dispatched a ship for the sole purpose of having her come to see the prince; no young man could afford to miss this golden opportunity, because on this very night the Pearl of Abyssinia would be leaving America forever! . . . Occasionally a man would go in, remain for a while, and come out, grinning sheepishly.

The Pearl of Abyssinia was only a fat old hag, deluging her customers with a flood of obscene talk and selling poor whisky at the exorbitant price of a dollar per bottle. The entire furnishing of the tent consisted of a table onto whose top had been nailed the queen of spades and the queen of hearts; on each card was placed a whisky bottle —the purchaser decided, unalterably and forever, his own destiny (the old hag swore to it) according to whether he chose hearts or spades.

But most wonderful of all was the merry-go-round. Not at any previous Fourth of July celebration had such a marvelous attraction been seen. Else, not knowing what it was, looked at it clapping her hands; the gorgeous carriages, traveling at a dazzling speed, almost made her dizzy. Peder was not much better; he bought tickets, and soon they were riding in fairy carriages, drawn by golden-maned horses, and mingling their joy with that of the others. . . . It was all like a dream.

Once more Else and Peder lost themselves in the crowd. They let themselves be carried on the current whithersoever it wished to take them . . . who cared! The carnival mood of the crowd rose joyously and swept them along irresistibly. Else had suddenly been transported to a fairy world. She knew the place must be full of gnomes and witches and hideous troll monsters, but the Prince, too, was here. On bright moonlight nights the elves and the fairies would come out and dance in the meadows by the brook . . . it was all so strangely beautiful.

Peder could no longer keep silent: Had she never been to a Fourth of July celebration before?

—Only once, when she was a little girl; it was so long ago she could hardly remember it. . . . Mother had told her about it; she had been frightened and had given much trouble . . . at last she had fallen asleep.

Peder felt deep sympathy for her. She couldn't have had much fun while she grew up. Yet she always seemed to be happy. He couldn't understand it, and questioned her about it:

—What did she do to have a good time?

The question puzzled Else—what did he mean?

—Well, when she never got a chance to get out and see things?

—Oh that! She had plenty of fun at home . . . indeed she had, he mustn't think otherwise. Else's enthusiasm kindled as she began telling him how she played the part of Watchful Providence over all the little ones at home. There was Kenneth LeRoy and all his horses; sometimes they rode far, far away—clear to the end of the world! . . . And for Mimmie she had to make dolls; no matter how many she had, she would always be teasing for one more— Else sighed, to find time to make dresses for all of them was no small task. . . . But Vernon had been the worst to satisfy, because while he was little he wanted boats and ships; such things she didn't know much about, and Papa never seemed to find time to help her. . . . Suddenly her chatter ceased, a wistful look came into her eyes—she was wondering how things were going at home now when she wasn't there to look after them.

I never heard the beat! thought Peder. This is what her life is like, and still she can be so happy.

—Did she never go anywhere?

—Oh yes, certainly. She went to church every other Sunday, and Papa let her do the driving.

—Didn't she ever go to town?

Else shook her head: How could she go to town? She couldn't do all the buying for the house.

Peder looked and looked at her, and thought he had never heard anything so strange.

Sometimes they were interrupted by people who knew Peder and wanted to shake hands with him. Once they met three girls, acquaintances of Else, who stopped to talk to her. Peder didn't know them, and Else, noticing it, introduced them to him. Peder felt deeply mortified and ashamed of himself—why hadn't he thought of doing that with her!

It was already past noon. And so Peder took her to a food stand and ordered everything that was to be had. But she wasn't hungry . . . no, really . . . yes, perhaps a small piece of pie and some coffee.

Of course she must eat! Hadn't he promised her father to take good care of her? But in spite of his vigorous protest she ate little or nothing, helping herself only to tiny morsels. Peder wondered if it could be because she was accustomed to better things and didn't dare eat this food. . . . He marveled at her still more.

Before they had finished, the program began; the band was already playing. They hurried off, and came in time to get a place on one of the benches farthest back.

Peder took off his hat—why did he want a hat today? Quite unconsciously, his right foot kept time to the music, his mood growing more joyous. The glittering uniforms of the players, the exhilarating rhythm of the music, the gay colors round about him, and the girl sitting by his side in oblivious bliss, made him giddy with strength. He was seized by a desire to embrace people . . . catch them in his arms and toss them up in the air just to play with them. . . . How stupid not to have come earlier so that they might have had a place nearer the front!

The address of the day was given by an attorney from Sioux Falls. The man had a powerful voice and his energy made the perspiration glisten on his face. He spoke in pompous, rhetorical periods about the men of the Revolution who carried through successfully the War of Independence, of those days when a few colonists, scattered along the Atlantic seaboard, bade defiance to a mighty world empire and thereby fought themselves into immortality.

For a time Peder listened enthusiastically, but finally wearied of the speaker because he got no further. Was this all he had to offer people on such an occasion? Didn't the man see the future and all the promises that lay therein? The past must be of small consequence in comparison with that which was to come!

Peder forgot the speaker, lost sight of him entirely because of a vast host of ideas marching before his eyes. A slight tremor passed through him: He himself was standing on that platform; above his head the flags fluttered in the breeze; before him were a thousand eyes looking enraptured into the future, always penetrating further, their happiness constantly mounting because he was explaining to them their innermost hopes. . . . The revolutions which had been could be nothing more than a source of strength to those that must come, he heard himself tell the audience. Wherever progress forged ahead toward a divine goal, revolutions were inescapable. . . . The time would actually come when every big-minded man would be his own lord and master because he had become a freeman and a king. . . . No government, no law—everything accomplished in fellowship with others who dared to will big things and who steadfastly looked to the future. . . . A picture from an old book stood before him . . . a picture of the Millennium—that people would never reach by clinging to the past. "The old is passed away, behold all is new," he mumbled in Norwegian.

Peder was brought to by Else clutching his arm and staring amazed at him.

—What was the matter? he had looked so queer, he had clenched his fists and talked to himself. Her voice was full of anxiety, and he was moved by it.

Peder, flushed with agitation, rose abruptly. "Come, let's go—this isn't worth listening to!"

But Else would not let go of him: What had been the matter? He had looked so angry that it had frightened her.

—Nothing at all, he assured her. . . . "You see," he talked in a low tone, "I was just thinking if *I* had been making that speech!"

Out in the grove they passed other couples. Suddenly Peder made an interesting discovery—there stood Reverend Bakken and Miriam. He was holding a parasol over her; yet there was no sun in here among the trees, and no sign of rain. Peder couldn't resist the temptation of calling their attention to the condition of the weather; as he and Else passed close by them he nodded to Miriam, and remarked carelessly that likely as not it would rain before sundown —didn't they think so?

In great mirth he and Else walked on. Wherever they went they found couples pretending to be listening to the program. Others had hid themselves away in buggies, oblivious to the fact that the sun was still high in the heavens. Peder, noticing them, had to admit to himself that there were people who had more courage than he.

When they had made the rounds of the grove and had come back to the center, Peder stopped at a stand and ordered ice cream. This made Else very happy; but momentarily an uneasiness came upon her and she hesitated about eating. Innocently and helplessly timid she wanted to know if he could afford all this treating.

Peder gave a hearty laugh; and in order to show her how easily he could afford both this and much more, he ordered another dish of ice cream for each of them, and in addition, a bottle of pop for her. Why, she hadn't eaten anything all day, she'd be nothing but skin and bones when they reached the end of the world . . . no telling what would happen when they got there!

Both laughed at this. There were other things he'd have liked to tell her about that journey but he couldn't say them to her because people were constantly coming and going.

And now the program was over and the stream of people grew more turbulent; everywhere one turned, boys were running about shooting firecrackers; the floor beneath the trees was being cleared for the dance; some of the older people prepared to go home; loud voices could be heard here and there, and boisterous, coarse remarks. It was getting to be late afternoon; the sun was already slanting its rays in between the trunks of the trees, but the heat in the grove was very oppressive.

"Let's find a place where we can talk," proposed Peder.

"Don't we have to be going home soon?" sighed Else.

They struck off for the outskirts of the grove. Far, far away from the others, it seemed to them, they went. At last they could hear only the faraway din of the crowd and the distant reports of exploding firecrackers.

Else sat down on a windfall which lay close to another tree. Cool and pleasant here; the evening breeze came sweeping in from the east, piled itself up at the edge of the wood; taking hold of the tree tops, it rustled them.

Else leaned her back against the tree. "I think I'll take off my hat." She looked at him; it sounded as though she were asking his permission.

Peder was standing just a little way from her, giddy with courage and a sense of superhuman strength. . . . He simply couldn't sit down!

"Now we've come to the end of the world, and here I'm King. I command that you never more wear a hat—your hair is so beautiful. I have issued an edict, that henceforth you shall be known by the name of *Goldenlocks*; he who disobeys, shall forfeit his life!"

While he talked, Else closed her eyes. For a while she sat silent. A sweet languorousness had come upon her; but she was smiling:

"Tell me some more."

Peder sat down beside her:

"You mean about how it is at the end of the world?"

"Yes . .   tell me everything!"

"That will only scare you."

"Is it so terrible then?"

"No, glorious. Strong men are fighting for things they really believe!" Peder had pried loose a piece of bark, now he flung it away.

"Are you King here?"

"Uh huh," he nodded, "here I am the King!"

"Then you musn't let your men do such wicked things. . . . It is sin to fight."

"Not if one is trying to reach the Millennium!"

For some time Else sat silent, her eyes still closed. Then she asked dreamily, a veil wrapped about her voice:

"Aren't God's angels at the end of the world?"

Her question made Peder laugh:

"Haven't had time to look for 'em yet!" Tearing off another piece of bark he threw it with all his might. . . . "The Princess looks after them . . . that'll have to be your job!"

Else saw beatific visions in her dream; a smile was on her face; her voice seemed firmer and more full of happiness:

"I want a big hospital, the very biggest in all the world. . . . There I shall gather all the poor and the unfortunate, they who suffer and are in misery, and be good to them . . . to all of them!"

"To me too?" Recklessly Peder took the hand that lay in her lap. It felt cold and lifeless. . . . He clasped it more firmly—was she cold?

"Don't . . . don't do that!"

"Why?"

"Because God's angels . . ."

Else rose abruptly and walked away. But a short distance off she stopped and put on her hat. Without looking back she stood there waiting for him, her head bent, as though in profound meditation.

VI

Peder waited a long time before joining Else. When at length he came strolling over to her, she talked in the same distant, dreamy voice:

"We must be going home. Isn't it getting late?"

Peder, walking silently, and in a preoccupied manner, hands in his pockets, his hat tilted toward her so that only part of his face was visible, didn't seem to have heard her.

In the grove deep dusk had settled. Between the tall trunks only a faint glow of day was discernible. The lanterns, suspended from branches, shed a many-colored light down on the dance. The crowd, now perceptibly thinned out, had grown more youthful in appearance because so many of the older people had already left—also more noisy. Loud talk, coarse laughter, were heard all over the place. Here and there arose bawlings from drunken men. But upon couples strolling about in the outskirts of the grove, mysterious silence had fallen. If one chanced to pass by, they would stand aside, not uttering a sound.

Peder, keeping slightly ahead of his partner, steered straight for the dance floor. Reaching the edge of the platform, without looking at her, he stepped up defiantly. Uncertain, and hesitating for a moment, Else followed him, like a dog who has had a whipping from his master and doesn't know whether he dares disobey. Clutching his arm she whispered, terrified:

"Do you dance?"

"Certainly—of course!" Peder put much emphasis into the words. And feeling that he must punish her still more, added in a careless, haughty tone:

"What about you?"

Else only shook her head, which he didn't notice at all. His feet were keeping time to the rhythm of the music;

into his eyes, intently following the couples before him, had come a warm gleam. He was breathing heavily, like some animal following a scent.

"This is fine," he said jubilantly. "Thank God—there are still folks who dare have fun!"

A couple came dancing toward the corner where Else and Peder stood. Peder saw them, clapped his hands, and called to them. The moment they caught sight of him, they stopped and came over to shake hands—the brown, soft eyes of the girl sought Peder's joyfully:

"Tonight I want a dance with you, Peder Holm . . . now you know it!" she cried before reaching him.

"Who said so?" he asked teasingly.

"I—and don't try to get out of it!" The girl shook his hand heartily as though to assure him that she meant everything she had said.

Peder, not letting go of the hand at once, turned to her partner:

"Must be a great scarcity of girls here tonight, seeing that you have to dance with your own sister."

"Not at all," the other assured him laughingly. "But there is a shortage of men, and Susie, poor thing, nobody seems to want. . . . Why aren't you joining in? Anything the matter with your legs?"

There was an infectious air about the couple, carefree and happy—an urge they gave vent to gladly; the boy was bareheaded; on his well-shaped forehead sparkled beads of perspiration which intensified the luster of his eyes. But the girl didn't seem to feel a bit warm, her whole being only healthy, animated life, asking for more fun.

Peder looked from one to the other. A nervous restlessness had come over him, his foot beating a merry tattoo. . . . "What have you been up to all day? You must have come just now." Grasping the boy's hand he shook it and wouldn't let go of it. Suddenly he was aware of his own partner, standing here so forlorn, and introduced her to Susie Doheny and her brother Charley.

The music struck up again and Charley bowed to Else: "May I have this dance?"

Else only shook her head and looked down.

Susie, catching the feel of the rhythm, couldn't resist it; taking hold of her brother's arm and turning him around, she cried:

"Nobody wants you, come on—I just got to have this polka!" As they swung off, she nodded beamingly to Peder over Charley's shoulder: "See you again!"

"Now I must go!" Else whispered in a low, frantic voice and stepped down from the platform.

For a moment Peder stood looking down at her. Her helplessness and the fear he saw in her eyes touched him. . . . Here was a child who had taken fright at her own shadow and was trying to run away from it!

"I'll get you home all right, never you fear!" He came slowly and deliberately after.

Only a little way from the dance floor they were stopped by a mob of people which surged back and forth, and then broke in huge waves; angry shouts, the bawling of drunken men, curses and obscene cries filled the air; now and then the smash of a fist against a face, and the thud of a heavy body falling prostrate to the ground. A demoniacal fury had suddenly been unleashed, the whole place boiling madly. Else hung desperately on Peder's arm. Before they knew it they had been swallowed up completely by the backwash, were being whirled hither and yon, like chips on a mighty eddy.

The trouble had started around the mysterious slot machine. Throughout the day many young men had tried their strength, but with no other result than to be robbed of one bright dime after another. Because Lloyd Bolgen was a hard loser and never would give up, he soon found himself minus a considerable number of small coins. Forced at last to give up, he had gone about thinking how he might get revenge on the fellow operating the machine. After pondering the problem deeply he made a visit to the Pearl of Abyssinia, where, having paid the dollar, he chose the queen of spades. Searching the crowd with a shrewd eye to find out who were there, he picked out, first of all, Dennis O'Hara, whom he invited to a private conference; next, a light-complexioned giant by the name of Thor Helgeson. During the threshing season last fall, Lloyd had learned what each of them was good for; to the best of his knowledge they were the strongest men in these parts. After treating them to a few rounds, Lloyd confessed openly that he was in doubt as to who was the stronger of the two. He grew quite intimate with the boys and passed the bottle once more. There was this goldarned machine over in the grove; if they didn't mind trying it, he'd gladly pay the cost. Laughing in the chummiest manner, Lloyd looked at the two men.

—That would be a small favor indeed, Dennis spoke up. He had tried his luck twice and would just as soon take a crack at the machine once more!

In spite of his huge bulk and superhuman strength, Thor was only kindness itself. There was, however, this peculiarity about him, that whisky always made him want to sing. If he had had as much as three drinks, he'd insist on singing Norwegian love ditties to anyone whom he could get to listen; and if by chance he took a fourth, which indeed did happen, he didn't care a darn whether anybody listened or not because then his happiness became uncontrollable.

After sampling the bottle once more, the three set out to see about those dolls—Thor in such towering humor that he must get the first try. Spitting on both hands, he swung the club and struck the iron peg a terrific crack, stepping back quickly to watch the result. Seeing nothing happen, he sang out to Lloyd, in Norwegian, that if he'd be so kind as to pay just one more dime for him, he'd smash this infernal deviltry into a thousand pieces; Lloyd complied cheerfully and so Thor struck again. This time he missed the mark, striking the platform just ahead of the peg. Yet the miracle actually happened—a tiny doll, holding a dollar bill in her arms, soared up from the machine. In spite of his great happiness Thor noticed how it had happened.

"Here you are, Dennis," said Thor handing him the sledge, "and now let's see what you Irish are good for!"

Many people had gathered about the place; more came running—the hurrahing and Thor's uproarious laughter were heard all over the grove.

Dennis struck with all his might—once, twice, was seized with a fit of madness and smashed the peg so hard that the earth trembled underneath the feet of the crowd; but no doll designed to come forth and greet him.

Seeing Dennis' bad luck, Thor was filled with the spirit of brotherly love; he threw his arm about him, rushing him off among the trees, all the while laughing and pouring secrets into his ear; and hurrying him back again, Thor paid the dime himself.

Dennis, choosing his position carefully, hit where Thor

had told him to, and, lo and behold, there came the doll! In the same instant Thor was standing beside him, patting his shoulder admiringly:

"Take another while the picking is good—here we've struck gold, boy!"

Dennis tried to do his best, and the next doll popped out, wavering a second in the air before it fell.

But now the owner of the machine understood what was happening. When Thor rushed up for the next try the man shoved him aside and tried to wrest the club out of his hands.

Thor stared at him in blank amazement, at first not understanding what the man meant. . . . What? . . . what was he trying to do? No—really? . . . Thor broke into an uproarious laugh:

"Here, Dennis, you club all the little darlings you can find while I attend to this fellow!"

Then an unforeseen thing happened: The man stuck two fingers into his mouth and gave a shrill, piercing whistle; the next moment he had sprung at Thor.

Thor received him rather kindly; putting his arm about him, he threw the man on his shoulder as though he had been handling a sack of grain. "Now, fellows," he called to the crowd, "if you'll pick up that machine, we'll just chase the whole outfit out of the county!"

The fight was on in real earnest. The minute the man guarding the Pearl of Abyssinia caught the sound of the whistle he left his post of duty and came running; so did the fellow operating the shooting gallery; a third came from one of the stands; two from the merry-go-round followed him. All five of them, fighting with demoniacal fury, were trying to penetrate to the center of the surging mob, men sinking groaningly before their terrible onslaught. But at the very center, Thor, still joyous, with the man on his shoulder, stalked on. Dennis and seven other men followed, carrying the machine. Not even the lantern, which had been hanging above it, had been left behind—that Lloyd had remembered to take along.

When at last Peder succeeded in disentangling himself from the mad swirl Else was on the point of fainting. She had to stop and lean up against him. Her head sank down on his arm, her breath flickering faintly, like a candle in a strong draft. In order to steady her Peder put his arm around her. He did it rudely, it seemed to him, felt exceedingly embarrassed, and tried to console her, "It's only Thor Helgeson and Dennis O'Hara chasing some tramps. . . . Nothing at all to be afraid of!"

His words awakened her:

"Come! Oh, can't you help me out of this terrible place?" she whispered frantically. She seemed beside herself; grabbing hold of his arm she pulled him with her. Fear was making her ghostlike, she glided along like a shadow.

Her fear had contagion in it. Peder had a sickening sensation . . . began to feel dizzy. Not knowing what else to do, he hurried her to the buggy, and got his horse untied. He drove at a furious rate. But having reached the open road and got so far away from the grove that the tumult no longer could be heard, he reined the horse in to see how she was getting along. Huddled as far back into the other corner of the seat as she could get Else was crying hysterically. He held the reins tighter, forcing the horse down to a walk. . . . I can't come home with her in that state, he thought. The spell must surely pass off—no one, as far as I know, has done her any harm. . . . He thought of many things he might talk to her about, but unable to hit upon anything suitable for the occasion, he gave up in despair. To touch her, even with his finger, he wouldn't risk doing for his very life. . . . Peder sat listening to her sobs until he didn't know what to do with himself. . . . Either she is crazy or else I am!

Little by little the sobs grew less violent. The interval between each lengthened. Finally they subsided entirely. No sound came from the other corner of the seat. But the silence seemed worse to endure than her paroxysms had been—now he dared not speak lest they should break out anew. In his great helplessness, which was fast getting impossible to bear, he saw nothing else to do but to whip up the horse. The rumbling of the buggy soothed him. . . . Dolly was a fine horse!

The moment Reverend Gabrielsen heard the buggy drive up he hastened out to receive them, his mood a good deal cheerier than when they left in the morning. The man was fairly bubbling over with bright talk. . . . Aye, aye, and here they were back again! Had they had much fun? Was the dear little Else-girl all right? Kenneth LeRoy and

Vernon had been asking for her all day . . . what would they do without her? Helping her out of the buggy he put his arm lovingly about her.

Else only murmured a tired good night and left them. The door had no sooner closed behind her than the minister turned to Peder:

"And now, my dear Peder, you and I had better talk seminary before you leave. Today I've written the president. Tie up your horse and come in—I want to read the letter to you."

"No," said Peder, a defiant ring in his voice, "I'll not be a minister . . . that's settled!"

Reverend Gabrielsen was so astounded over Peder's flat refusal that he had to let go of the buggy in order to catch his beard. "Don't say that!—No, no, don't thwart God's plans!"

Peder, seizing the opportunity, said a curt good night and, striking the horse a sharp crack, was off instantly. . . . If he were to have a turn with Susie tonight, he'd have to hurry! Peder breathed free and easy; his chest expanded. He had suddenly been relieved of a heavy burden. . . . Stretching himself, he gave a long, entreating whistle to Dolly . . . can't you trot just a bit faster? . . . hah, there now—that's right!

VII

Late autumn and perfect days. Night after night a sleepy harvest moon was drifting across an immeasurable sea, quiet and of greenish color. Evenings more bewilderingly enchanting than the day because they brought dreams to young hearts. But the twilight breeze was at a loss to understand what had happened: Every time it found a cornfield and began flaying the leaves, there would come queer sounds, dry, dead sounds, and very unpleasant. . . . No tender life, swelling with luxuriant fullness, would open up, eager to hear legends about love. And so the breeze would sigh mournfully and search on.

The Murphy Schoolhouse was half full, mostly young people. In the district it had become a tradition that each year the teacher should arrange a program, consisting of readings, dialogues, farces, *etcetera*, to which the whole neighborhood was invited. These programs were commonly known as *Exhibitions*. Most often the persons performing were young people who during their schooldays had gained reputations as declaimers. Yet not infrequently did it happen that older persons also took part. Old Tönseten, for example, was a veteran in the dramatic arts; no exhibition could be counted complete without him. The meeting tonight had been called for the purpose of choosing those who were to take part. Rather early in the season, people thought, but of course the teacher was new and, hence, didn't know the customs.

The name of the teacher was Ted Gilbert. Despite the fact that he hadn't been here many weeks, he had already gained a reputation because of the interest he showed in his work and the energy he put into it.

That he was a Norwegian, the Irish did not know at the time they hired him. The name had fooled them, though he had come by it rightfully enough. His father's name, at the time of landing in America, had been Knut Gilbertson; but prompted by a desire to be a real American from the start he resolutely cut away the last syllable of the surname —easier and much more handy that way, Knut thought. The son had been baptized Theodor, which name the boy bore until he entered school; but the first schoolma'am under whose care he came, meaning to do the boy a real kindness, shortened Theodor to Ted. The rechristening seemed to fit perfectly, for the man was short, rather stocky, wore his hair close-cropped, talked incessantly, and could never stand still for long at a time.

Tonight Ted Gilbert sprang a real surprise. When no more people seemed to be coming he got up and told the audience that he had heard a great deal about these exhibitions they held here every year. Fine idea—a very ingenious invention, he'd call it! He'd advocate it wherever he went; the one who first thought of it ought to have a monument erected to his memory; only give people plenty to do and they won't have any time left for deviltry! But this year they would beat all previous records—wait and see! Now listen: Rather than fool away the time by getting up a hodgepodge program of all kinds of odds and ends, they were going to stage a *whole play*, that's it exactly, a whole play! They would choose one which had been run in the

finest theater in America; now how did that idea strike
them? The plan was a corker. If they made a success of it
—and why shouldn't they make it a success?—they could
stage it in the other schools in the neighborhood and perhaps in the nearby towns as well; they might even get an
invitation to come to Sioux Falls; well, why shouldn't they?
They'd play themselves into fame—such things had been
done before, but no time to consider that now. They'd
start the rehearsals at once; if they finished by Thanksgiving, they'd put the play on then—yes, why not?—and
thereby get ahead of all other schools in the county. And
now he needed five women and nine men, all of different
types—Negroes and white people, tramps as well as real
gentlemen, heroes and villains, for there'd be brawls, yes
—real fights; they'd have to use revolvers, blood would
flow, oh—this was going to be the real thing! Gilbert
stopped to catch his breath before continuing, letting his
sparkling eyes dance over the audience.

—Was there a man present here tonight by the name of
Syvert Tönseten? Ted Gilbert went on. If so, he'd ask him
to stand up.

Down in the middle row Tönseten arose with much
dignity.

The teacher hurried down to shake hands with him.
"Glad you're here! My name's Ted Gilbert. I have a part
that'll fit you exactly; will you please come forward and
help me a minute?" Taking Tönseten by the arm, Ted led
him up to the platform. "Now will you do me the favor of
naming for me those who in your opinion are the best
players? Then we can get started at once."

Much merriment broke out in the audience. Several
held up their hands. From all over the room came shouts,
"Don't forget me!" "And me!" "Say there, Syvert! . . ."

Tönseten, paying not the slightest attention to their
fooling but weighing face by face critically, began to mention names (pausing long after each) which Ted Gilbert
immediately wrote on the blackboard. Out of the whole
crowd he found no more than ten persons who in his opinion possessed histrionic talents—he himself would make
the eleventh.

"Splendid—fine!" Ted Gilbert exclaimed when Tönseten had finished. The remaining three he could easily

pick from among his pupils; in a pinch he'd be glad to play one of the roles himself—he knew the whole play by heart anyway, he added modestly.

Again facing the blackboard, Ted Gilbert began writing another list of names, all the while talking and explaining: —Here are the different characters, all must listen, please! Aunt Charity, a kindhearted Negro woman—no trick at all to transform Irish and Norwegians into Negroes—the right kind of black paint is all you need, such things are done often on the stage; next: Dick Langley, the villain, the finest gentleman you ever saw, but an arch intriguer nevertheless, he's courting two women at the same time—no easy task to play that part well, oh no! But here (Ted Gilbert wrote the name and underscored it) is Louva, the heroine, a real Cinderella character she is, they'd have to comb the whole prairie for the best-looking girl—deucedly difficult to play her well; next: Colonel Farnham, fine Southern gentleman, distinguished-looking, well-mannered, he had played that part himself and would be perfectly willing to do it again—great fun—one learns a lot! And here was Bub Craft, foolish but good-natured, really a good lad, with a poor bringing up, which, of course, he couldn't help—he too is deadly in love with poor Louva! Ted Gilbert wrote another name on the blackboard: Will Spriggs, and paused. Here was the hero—fine man—good looking—courageous, he's willing to go through hell fire for Louva; difficult to interpret him properly—very difficult indeed—he doesn't say much, but his actions count—well, they'd take their time about finding the right man for that part. "And here," Ted Gilbert turned his beaming face to Tönseten as he wrote the name, "is the shrewd peddler, Peleg Pucker, who always talks so funny—just the identical role for you, why, it's made for your particular benefit!" . . . Tönseten nodded condescendingly. No trick for him at all to act the part of a clever peddler!

When at length Ted Gilbert had the names of the *dramatis personæ* on the board and had explained them all, he took out of his desk a package of unbound books; requesting the ten whom Tönseten had chosen to come forward and take the front seats, he gave a copy to each, and so the first reading of the play began.

Louva the Pauper, a short piece in five acts, had real melodramatic qualities. From the opening of the first scene to the last curtain, Virtue and Love locked in a deathly struggle with villains and cunning intrigue! In both the second and the fourth act the hero and the heroine embraced and kissed. But the kissing was done in all propriety, the force of circumstances requiring the deed to be done; hence, the onlookers were not scandalized. In the denouement, the villains caught it where the rooster got the axe, but alas, Virtue was not properly rewarded; just as the curtain went down slowly the last time—a most painfully slow curtain—the heroine breathed her last in the arms of her lover. That the girl had been in perfect health throughout the action, that she hadn't shown the least symptoms of weakness, and that she had suffered no harm, but that she nevertheless gave up the ghost in the arms of her lover just as she had got him, no one gave a thought to because the effect was so profoundly touching.

For once, old Tönseten was unable to express his enthusiasm properly. He waited until all but Ted Gilbert had left. The man wasn't acquainted out here and would need advice . . . he'd tell him whom to pick for hero and heroine, all right!

Peder was included among Tönseten's ten chosen ones. Before retiring that night he read the play through twice. The next day while resting after dinner he went through it again, and by that time he knew almost the whole piece by heart. He liked the play; it would be great fun to take part, yet he couldn't quite make up his mind . . . much depended upon who would play. At the supper table that night he told his mother about the exhibition the teacher this year was planning. . . . He must be a fine teacher. Did she know he was Norwegian?

Beret showed no particular interest in the matter.—Was he taking part this year?

Peder buttered a piece of bread, smiling to himself as he did so. He hadn't made up his mind exactly . . . the teacher had asked him . . . he didn't know if he had time . . . he'd see, perhaps he'd take one of the parts.

Shortly after, he had changed his clothes and was driving over . . . he'd have to bring back the copy he had taken home last night. . . . It was late already; Peder drove fast.

Only a few present tonight. As he entered the room Susie Doheny, a copy of the play in her hand, was stand-

ing in the middle of the floor, reading and laughing, Ted
Gilbert giving her instructions as to how she was to say
the lines. Susie had not been present last night.
The teacher was too taken up with her to give Peder
more than a nod. "Let's see how nicely you can die—
you're dying in the last act you know—you pass away in
the arms of your lover—you couldn't wish for any sweeter
death, could you now?—Someone come and hold her while
she expires!" Ted Gilbert was in a heat of excitement and
had little patience. "Can't one of you fellows come here
and embrace her—you won't get a chance like that every
day!" After getting the necessary support Susie did her best
to part with life artistically, only she couldn't prolong the
process sufficiently; the teacher had considerable difficulty
with her on that point; but finally he rubbed his hands
jubilantly, as pleased as though he had been the manager
of a metropolitan theater who had suddenly discovered a
great star. "There now, that's fine—fine, I say, just take it
a little slower—no hurry; at first you stand—then just sink
—sink—sink, gradually, you understand—like *this*. . . .
Well folks, there's your heroine, no doubt about that!"

In order to find the right hero Ted Gilbert used the
process of elimination. Placing one boy after another of
those who possibly could be considered out on the floor
beside Susie, he stepped a few feet away to judge the effect. Peder had taken a seat back of the others; every time
a new boy was to be called he ducked his head behind the
row in front of him. Tönseten, observing him for some
time, went up and whispered a few words to the teacher,
to which Ted Gilbert only nodded.

At last there was no one but Peder left, and so he also
was called. No sooner had Ted Gilbert got him placed at
Susie's side than his enthusiasm bubbled over.

"Ah, there you've Louva and Will Spriggs! I'll bet my
last dollar that a better hero and heroine never were found
for this play—dandy—great, I tell you! If we aren't going
to stage an exhibition the like of which never has been
seen, I'll be a liar! What do you say, folks?"

Peder blushed furiously. He tried a laugh but couldn't
quite make it. . . . He didn't know if he had time, he
stammered. . . . Why not take Charley? Then he and
Susie could practice at home?

"Never!" shouted Ted Gilbert decisively. "No, indeed,

that wouldn't do—altogether too unnatural between brother and sister; on a crowd knowing their relationship, the illusion would have no power.—Time, did you say? Why, man, you can easily learn those lines after breakfast!"

Peder only grinned foolishly. Here stood Susie right by his side, smiling into his face . . . she might think it was on her account. . . . The grin still on his face, he shambled back to his place.

VIII

Already Peder knew most of the play by heart. And now he had a strange experience: No sooner had they begun to play than the action became reality to him—more real than anything he had heretofore lived. Susie was the Cinderella he had read about, and he the Prince. Time out of mind he had loved her. Inscrutable Destiny had decreed that they should belong to one another. Hostile forces were at work, trying to alienate them. He alone could save them both. His own experiences and the action of the play merged into one . . . all was real . . . a terrible earnestness possessed him.

They reached the love scene in the second act, and the presence of the others made him blush hotly; yet it didn't scare him. He put his arm around Susie, according to the directions in the book. Once his arm was there he drew her to him . . . close . . . protectingly. Blushing shyly, a faint smile puckering her face, Susie yielded. The moment she offered him the kiss, her eyes opened wide, in wonder, and looked into his. There was fathomless mystery in those eyes. Out of the brown specks shone a deep glow, making the blue underneath still richer and more unsearchable. He pressed his lips to hers, and Destiny itself laid its hand upon them and blessed them—Peder sensed it as clearly as though he had heard the words spoken right into his ear. . . . Here he held within his arm her whom his innermost being always had sought. The room, the people present, disappeared in a haze . . . into nothingness . . . didn't exist. A great joy which drove tears to his eyes, filled him. He must do something, give vent to what he felt or he'd faint. The next moment he had thrown himself passionately into the play. Paying not the slightest attention to the teacher's directions, he went on directing himself. Even in the scenes in which he had no part he would find something to do; he couldn't stand still, nor keep quiet—all depended upon him. When they at last reached the closing scene, and Susie lay in his arms, limp, dying, he knew it clearer than a thousand words could have told him—there Susie wished to die. The others laughed and clapped their hands. Peder couldn't understand it . . . why did they laugh? . . . With a half-silly, half-pathetic smile the two stood looking at each other. Not if their lives had been at stake could they have uttered a word. Peder's eyes were moist . . . he rubbed them with his hand . . . then he, too, was able to join in the laugh. But as they were to leave, she came over to him, naturally, as though it had always been thus between them. . . . Peder only nodded gravely, took her arm, and helped her into the buggy.

The verdigris green light of the full harvest moon, flooding all the vast silences of the prairie, took them along on its western course. The one mile between the Murphy Schoolhouse and Doheny's that night lengthened into two . . . got to be three . . . four . . . no one could tell how many. Yet at parting, about three o'clock in the morning, they both sighed distractedly because the ride had been much too short and the leave-taking seemed impossible to bear; it was as though they would never see each other again.

At first both had sat silent, neither of them daring to speak. What they felt seemed beyond expression. Not that they needed words. They had found each other at last— wasn't that enough? . . . But however it had happened, both had become aware of the fact that his arm was about her waist. Peder couldn't understand his own recklessness and feared to withdraw it. And Susie made no effort to remove it. She seemed actually to have been waiting for his arm to settle there; she yielded to the pressure—willingly, gladly. Perceiving how intensely he wanted her she snuggled into the hollow of his arm, resting there, confident that he would shield her from all harm. Out of the depths of her being rose a murmur of happiness. Peder's eyes blurred. He wasn't at all sure that he didn't cry. After an indefinite time he regained sufficient control of his voice to use it—though it was husky and had an odd tremor:

"Never shall anyone take you away from me!" He spoke the words solemnly, as though he were taking an oath.

"No—that you mustn't let happen!" she entreated . . . "it is good to be with you."

No longer able to control the unnamable joyousness which was bewildering all his senses, Peder stopped the horse and drew her to him. . . . Was this eternity? Or could it—could it be life?

On and on they moved westward into the silent mystery of the moon-night. . . . The horse stopped and ate grass from the roadside . . . ambled on . . . stopped again . . . snuffled softly, mouthing fresh tufts by the road's edge. A golden enchantment lay upon the earth . . . and they were alone in it.

By and by reason returned to them; they regained their power of speech. But they never got far beyond the starting point because each would take the word out of the other's mouth, like two children chattering in a happy game. No sooner had Susie begun than Peder would think of something so important that he must say it right away; thus each attempt became only a new starting point. Never before had two human beings experienced the like of what had happened to them. . . . Peder did not get to bed until long after three o'clock, and then he couldn't sleep because of all the things he had forgotten to tell Susie.

During the evenings that followed, until they should meet and have each other again, Peder sat up far into the night, trying to write to her. The efforts ended only in dismal failure. Reading through what he had written he would become gloomy and tear the letter into shreds—it wasn't true enough! The words sounded cold and indifferent . . . if Susie read this she'd think he didn't love her at all! One night, despairing of his helplessness, an idea occurred to him: Taking a new sheet he began to write down what the King sings to the Shulamite. Reading it through slowly, Peder's face broke into a bright smile. Wasn't this exactly what he had experienced that night? . . . The sweetness, the same divinity?

During the day he sang at his work. All living creatures to which he could get near enough, he had to caress.

One day as he was standing in the stall petting Dolly

and singing softly to her, his mother came into the barn and observed him unnoticed. . . . What could be the matter with him? . . . When a young man gets that way you'd better look out!

"You are full of many pranks these days. . . . Must you be singing all the time?"

"Aw—I'm only so glad 'cause we're through cornhusking! Why don't you sing too? It lightens the heart."

Leaving the barn, Peder kept thinking of what his mother had said. Why shouldn't he sing? Wasn't the whole universe song-filled? Out in the yard he stopped to look up into the sky. . . . Hadn't he read somewhere, that the morning stars sang together and all the sons of God shouted for joy? . . . What was it the minister had said once about the goodness of God?

But back of his joyous satisfaction with life he was aware of dark clouds . . . clouds which stood there silently, far back on the horizon. Now and then cold, black shadows swept across his sky. Thoughts would bob up in his consciousness . . . unpleasant memories. He recalled that night before confirmation, what his mother then had said to him. In these thoughts also Susie was present. The moment he saw her image the clouds disappeared. . . . Nothing else in the whole world mattered to him but Susie.

And now—he was a grown man and his own boss! Peder would lay hold of heavy objects out of sheer joy in the sense of his own strength. . . . From now on he intended to steer his own course. Hadn't his brothers done the same? Let the old women around the settlement wag their tongues all they pleased! . . . Phrases from an old hymn which his mother, while he was only a little fellow, had forced him to learn by heart, came drifting into his consciousness:

> And were the world with devils filled,
> All wanting to devour us,
> Our souls to fear we need not yield
> They cannot overpower us ——

Peder sang the lines. . . . Some sense to that!

The next night they were together he asked Susie timidly what she thought her father would say to their engagement.

"I don't know." Susie snuggled closer into his arm as if seeking protection. "Father is kindhearted; he has always been good to me . . . it'll be worse with the priest."

"The priest?" Peder ejaculated. "What are you saying?"

"I am a Catholic."

"So you are—and I a Lutheran!"

"Don't I know it!"

Peder gave a hearty laugh:

"But in the sight of God we're just two human beings."

To Susie this remark seemed so full of good sense and did her so much good that she must thank him for it. Clasping her hands about his neck she pulled his face to her and kissed him.

"What about your mother?" she murmured.

"She? . . . We're going to be good to her!" said Peder soberly.

"I had lots of practice with Grandma," Susie assured him, and began telling him how she had had to care for the old lady the last year she lived. For a while Peder listened without interrupting her. But when she told of how she had even had to light the pipe for Grandma he experienced a strange elation—an omnipotent hand stretched out and swept all his fears away. . . . No trick for a person like that to be good to Mother!

Feeling that he must thank her in some tangible way for having been so kind to the old woman, Peder stroked her hand. Suddenly he broke out:

"Let's get married in the spring!"

"In the spring?" Susie had taken his hand and was patting it. "That'll be a long time to wait!"

"But, you see, that event can only take place in the springtime, 'when the winter is past, the rain is over and gone; when the flowers appear on the earth; the time of the singing of birds is come; and the voice of the turtle is heard in our land,' " he quoted softly.

"How beautiful that is—say it once more!"

"Wait until we get to the end of the world, then I'll tell you all manner of beautiful things!"

"Are we going to the end of the world?"

"Of course we are!"

"I'd rather be here with you!" she begged timidly.

Peder stopped his horse in order to thank her properly. Each night, with a punctuality equal to their own, the moon took her serene way to the west. The night flowed over them in silvery beauty, dreamlike and calm. Peder and Susie stretched the hours as far as they dared. Each time the parting seemed more impossibly difficult. . . . It would be long to wait until spring!

IX

During the evenings of his absence Beret sat alone; first in the kitchen for a while, after which she would retire to her own room; but peace she had not until she heard the buggy drive up the road, and then she was unable to sleep because she could not imagine what he had been about all night.

Now that the work had let up she was fighting a great loneliness. Aside from attending church every other Sunday she never went anywhere. And few people came to the farm this season of the year. At times she would feel herself a shipwrecked person stranded on some lonely island far out at sea. . . . Occasionally there was a sail on the horizon, which drifted across the day and was gone. Nothing more. Dead, everlasting sameness. After Sörine was married she seldom came over. Kjersti complained of her feet troubling her. Over at his place Store-Hans was working early and late. This year he had paid up the farm, and now thought of little else than how he could improve it.

During the cornhusking Anna Marie had gone to Montana to visit her brother. Beret herself had urged the girl to make the trip. Just the other day a letter had come from her, asking if she might not stay over Christmas. Things were going well for Ole, she told her mother. This fall he had harvested a bumper crop. And now Randi had a baby —really, she needed help. It was a baby boy. They had named him Randolph Osborne after Randi and Ole. Next spring Ole intended to build. The country out there was extraordinarly beautiful.

After reading the letter through several times, Beret stuck it in her bosom. In the evening, when Peder had gone, she took it out and read it again; before retiring she hid it in the small treasure chest where she kept the money. She slept little that night. . . . Ole did not intend to come back. . . . And he had no more respect for tradition, for that which ought to be holy to a people, than to give his boy such a name! . . . During the night Beret had occasional spells of crying; it annoyed her so much that she had to get up. The next day she mentioned, in an indifferent way to Peder, that she had a few words from Anna Marie; but she didn't offer to show him the letter.

It happened often that Peder was gone until the small hours of the morning. In the evenings, when Beret saw him go upstairs, preparatory to going out, she would find work and sit down by the kitchen table. As he came down and passed through the room she looked up, always asking the same question, "Will you be gone long ——?" Tired of sitting up she would go into her own room, and without undressing, lie down to wait for his return. When, after weary hours, he had come back and gone upstairs she would get up and undress. Before retiring she always looked at the clock, getting wider awake than ever. . . . What had kept him out all night?

That his mother was worrying over something Peder inferred from many things, and that he himself might be the cause he guessed by her solicitude for him. Every day she prepared dishes of which she knew he was particularly fond. And never before had she been so anxious about his person: Did he remember to change his stockings? He must keep his feet dry now that fall had come! Had he put on heavier underwear? . . . At times she would grow very talkative, sharing her thoughts with him in friendliest fashion; she told him about Norway, about his grandparents, and of how her life had been when she grew up. Sometimes he would be compelled to listen because of an unusual animation in her talk; more often he only affected interest—his mind these days was elsewhere.

But her manner made him watchful of how he treated her. His attention to her became almost paternal; he saw to it that the wood box was always kept full; she must not be allowed to carry in water when he was home; and so with other chores he could do. As the days went by it developed into a contest between them as to who could be the more considerate; it looked as though one were trying to fence the other in by being good.

Peder had often heard her speak of what marvelous, fine silverware the well-to-do people in Norway had. One eve-

ning, returning from town, he spread twelve silver spoons
before her on the table, teaspoons and soup spoons, all imported from the old country. Beret stood speechless at first,
looking from him to the table. . . . What did this mean?
Had he lost his senses? Had he found a gold mine? He
wasn't going to ruin them? . . . It seemed difficult for
her to speak, tears blinked in her eyes.

—No, he intended nothing of the kind! . . . He had
bought the spoons with his own money. . . . Couldn't
they afford to live like decent folk? . . . If she wanted
anything else for the house she need only tell him! he
added boastingly.

Again she gave him a long look. . . . What had come
over him? He seemed filled with prankish joyousness—
was so sure of himself, yet so kind . . . just like his father
in the olden days.

That same evening Peder suggested that she need not
help with the milking. Why should she trudge to the barn;
he could easily do the chores alone—would she please sit
down now and rest herself?

His proposal offended her deeply:

—What was that? Wasn't she to be allowed to tend her
own cattle? . . . Or perhaps he intended going into dairy-
ing? . . . Oh no, looking after the cattle was the only en-
joyment she had left now—that they'd have to let her
have. But if he had other duties, she could easily do the
chores alone! . . . Perhaps he was going out?

Peder deemed it wisest not to answer her. . . . Now
she's lonesome, I can see it in her. That imp of a girl ought
to have more sense than to be staying on out there in Montana! . . . I don't see how I can better things by sticking
around home every night. What would I talk to her about?
The management of the farm I understand better than
she does.

The next Sunday after services he spoke to Store-Hans:
"Why don't you folks ever come over?"

His brother smiled wryly:

"Because you never ask us."

"Then I'm asking you right now! Today you do your
chores early and come over, all of you—be prepared to
stay for supper."

"Has Mother asked you to invite us?"

"No—but you can come anyway. Mother is lonesome

since Sister left; no one comes to see her, and she never goes anyplace."

"And you yourself are out much, I hear." There was a note of accusation in his brother's voice, which Peder resented:

"Not as much as you were at the time you were going it!"

"That was different—then we were all at home."

Peder gave a harsh laugh:

"Am I always to hang around home because it pleased you and Ole to leave?"

For a moment the two brothers looked at each other, neither speaking. But in the afternoon Store-Hans came over, bringing his family with him, and stayed until late evening.

In a pen down in the cowyard Beret kept a herd of yearling cattle which she was feeding for the winter market. On the following Tuesday afternoon, while carrying corn to them, she was interrupted in her work by Reverend Gabrielsen driving into the yard. Beret was startled by his coming, for the minister had not called since the early part of the summer. She had wondered at his absence, had even spoken of it to Peder, who only laughed. Now she was glad to see him because she had a few dollars laid aside which she wanted to give the missions.

The minister drove up to where she was working but didn't step out of the buggy.

—No, thank you, he replied to her invitation, today he couldn't stop; he only wanted to see Peder. Was he home?

—No; he had gone to town with a load of wheat.

The information seemed to trouble him.

—Did he want to see him? Beret asked.

—Yes, indeed. Reverend Gabrielsen looked unusually sober and appeared at a loss what to do.

—Was it something urgent?

The minister cleared his throat before speaking:

"I am told he has taken up acting . . . as his pastor I feel it my duty to warn him against such wickedness."

"What's that you're saying?" Beret's hands clutched the buggy box.

"He is with that ungodly crowd that's carrying on in the schoolhouse every night. . . . Little did I think that Peder would ever stoop that low!"

Beret felt at the verge of tears, and did actually cry; yet she had to smile. Her countenance became odd to look at, like waves ruffled by a sudden gust of wind blowing straight against them. . . . "Every night, you say? I wonder if you aren't paying too close attention to what folks gossip about?" Beret looked at the minister searchingly. "I don't know of anything other than this exhibition—that we've had many years now, both before you came, and since."

The minister was profoundly concerned:

"I'm afraid this is a good deal worse!"

"Is it so awfully bad?" The smile was still upon her face.

"Aye, that it is, Mrs. Holm!" There was firm assurance in the minister's sober tone. "The theater is a most dangerous enemy to godly living; I saw enough of that the time I served in Chicago. The theater deadens all good impulses in us by appealing to our sensuality; no Christian can afford to have anything to do with it. . . . To think that we should get this infamous institution out here in the country!"

As Beret looked into the face of the minister her own seemed to open wide:

"Have you been over to the schoolhouse yourself?"

Instinctively Reverend Gabrielsen drew away from her . . . what did she mean? Did she expect him to attend theatrical performances?

Beret's earnestness made her pursue him. Bending over the box of the buggy she asked:

"Don't you think you ought to go over?"

"That a minister of the Gospel cannot do—no, decidedly not. But I need no further proof. Members of the congregation have come to me with complaints. Only today I received a letter from Reverend Bakken who asks me to stop this iniquity; him I don't pay much attention to— let him sweep his own doorstep! But how bad this business is we know from the fact that it is leading astray one like Peder. Never before have I prepared a young man for confirmation who was dearer to me; his knowledge, his understanding of the Scriptures, was indeed phenomenal. Now the god of this world is getting the better of that boy!" The minister spoke sorrowfully.

Beret stood silent and bent, the wind flapping her skirts.

"I s'pose we must harvest that which we've sown," she said meditatively, a note of bitterness in her voice.

Reverend Gabrielsen felt a bit annoyed. "What do you mean, Mrs. Holm?"

"Breaking down the fences will let the cattle out . . . it takes no great wisdom to understand that!"

The two faced each other, he questioningly, Beret accusingly; she spoke first:

"Both early and late you've dinned it into our ears, that in twenty years we'll all be alike."

"I'm afraid your zeal for a cause makes you judge unjustly—that all speak the same language can hardly necessitate all behaving in the same way!"

Beret's eyes took a firmer hold of his:

"I wonder which of us has given most thought to the problem, you who are hastening the amalgamation, or I who all these years have tried to hold back—it's easy to coast down a hill, one needs only to hang on! The Norwegians are as yet only children in America. Turn children loose to roam where they please, and it's hard to tell what they'll be up to."

"Now you're doing me a great injustice, Mrs. Holm. Do you really mean what you are saying?—No one, nay, not even you, his own mother, has wished your son so well as I have." Reverend Gabrielsen's face was redder than usual from the sober solicitude agitating him. . . . "It is my duty to tell you that your son has taken a road which leadeth to destruction!"

"Then you who understand it must talk to him about it!"

Suddenly, Beret turned and left him. Her eyes were blurred, she couldn't see clearly. . . . The rumbling of the departing carriage jarred a sore spot in her head; it hurt her so . . . she pressed both hands against her temples.

Half dazed she had begun to walk. . . . Had she fed the cattle enough corn? Picking up the pail she had left a while ago she went to the corncrib to carry in some more feed. . . . Evil tongues again had told of the boy. . . . What he was up to now was so bad that people had gone to the minister to complain? Reverend Bakken had written . . . and it led to destruction? . . . Beret forgot to fill the pail, a puzzled look had come into her face. . . . Permand had never been so kind to her as he was these days. . . . Perhaps she had lost her reason . . . others had been more solicitous about him than she! . . . She bent over to pick up the scoop shovel but left it . . . what was it the boy said the other day? "If you want anything else, you need only tell me"—those were his very words. . . . The minister meddled with many things he didn't understand himself. . . . What had she said to him anyway? . . . And she had forgotten to give him the money!

Beret forgot the cattle; she felt tired and sat down on the doorstep of the corncrib. . . . Every night? How could the minister let himself be so easily fooled? . . . She ought to know how often the boy had been out!

X

At the supper table Beret was unusually cheerful—almost lighthearted, Peder thought. She asked him many questions. How had he fared in town? What price had he got today? Had he met anyone from up this way? What did people talk about nowadays?

But all of a sudden she changed the topic of conversation:

—How was the exhibition getting on? Would it be worth while seeing it?

—Oh fine! Peder felt tired and lazy after the long ride on the lumber wagon. He hadn't paid much attention to what she was saying.

—Hadn't they started rather early this year? . . . What kind of program were they getting up?

Peder became wide awake; his voice was full of tranquil enthusiasm:

—Something wonderful this year, all right!

—What was it then? Beret too was getting enthusiastic.

—A *play!*

"What do you call it?" In her eagerness to catch the English term Peder had used, Beret leaned forward.

Pondering a moment, Peder laughed heartily. "I can't tell you what it is called in Norwegian, but it's great fun!"

"Is it *skuespil?*" * Beret spoke the word slowly.

Peder nodded. "We play it all right. . . . It's the same thing that Shakespeare wrote."

* Skuespil, literally: play or playing which one looks at.

Beret watched him closely. . . . No look of guilt on his face. Only happy innocence . . . how could it be so bad then?

For a while they ate in silence, Beret helping herself only to small morsels, just enough to keep him company. She was on the point of asking who was the man he had named, but thought better of it. Instead she wanted to know who was taking part this year. . . . Were there many?

Peder mentioned most of the players by name.

"What are you telling me?" Beret exclaimed. "Is Tönseten in it too?" Beret began to laugh. "No, really?"

"Of course, and he's good too!"

Beret took Tönseten's presence in the cast as a good joke and enjoyed it immensely. . . . "When are you meeting next?"

"Saturday night."

"Not before Saturday night? That will be a whole week?" Beret seemed greatly surprised; she asked the question as though she didn't think it quite right of them not to meet before. But presently she was sober again. "I hope you are not doing anything wrong!"

Peder laughed at her, teasingly. "You always find something to worry about! I wonder when you will give up fretting about me."

Neither that night nor later did she mention the minister's visit. She was much preoccupied these days. Whenever Peder was near she would study him furtively; then her apprehension would quiet down. She had never seen the boy in a happier mood—and he sang continually!

But the longer she thought of what Reverend Gabrielsen had told her the more uneasy she got. He would hardly have come unless something out of the ordinary had prompted him. She had, moreover, done him nothing but good . . . he surely wasn't seeking revenge because the boy refused to study for the ministry? "He has chosen a road which leadeth to destruction" . . . she had never seen him so sober-faced as when he spoke those words . . . an ordained servant of the Lord would hardly say such things unless he had good reasons!

Saturday brought raw, cloudy weather. A low, woolly sky hung right down on the prairie, a cold, howling wind tugging at the clouds. All afternoon Peder was busy grinding corn for the cattle. Off and on Beret came out and helped him carry corn to and from the mill. Today, too, he sang.

After supper he went straight upstairs to his room. Tonight he was a long time about getting ready. All the while he was whistling a merry tune which Beret had not heard before. Occasionally he would break off whistling and hum a strain or two.

When he came downstairs ready to go, Beret was sitting by the kitchen table, mending winter clothes. She looked up at him:

"Did you find a clean shirt?"

Peder nodded, waiting for her to say more.

"That's a becoming necktie—when did you get that?"

"The other day. Do you like it?" He started for the door.

"Wait a moment," Beret rose and came after him, "you have a white thread on the back of your coat." Having picked it off, she turned him around to see if there might be more. "Are you stopping in for Tönseten?"

"He takes his own rig." Peder wanted to be off, yet hesitated . . . what was the matter with her tonight?

"I s'pose it's lonesome for Kjersti, sitting there all alone night after night. Wonder if I ought not to go down to see her?" She asked the question as though wanting his advice.

"Just so it doesn't rain."

"In that case she'd never dare venture up here—no, that I am sure she wouldn't."

Peder took hold of the doorknob.

"They go to bed early at Tönseten's."

"What else is the poor woman to do? . . . Will you be gone long tonight?"

"Not so terribly long!" Peder opened the door and slipped out.

Beret didn't sit down to her work right away. Going over to the window she stood there, peering out into the dark, as if waiting to see him come back. . . . He might have offered to take me down to Kjersti . . . it wouldn't have delayed him much!

Not until she heard the buggy drive down the road did she leave the window and go back to her work. Her hand was unsteady; every now and then she looked up, glancing around the room. . . . So many noises in here tonight. The wind laid hold of the windows, shaking them with a loud rattle. . . . Must be a draft from one of them—Per Hansa's picture wouldn't hang still. She got up and put the locks on both windows. That done, she closed the damper in the stovepipe, from which came a hollow rumbling. A queer uneasiness possessed her. Going over to the door she opened it and looked out. . . It'll hardly rain on this side of midnight. A noise from the barn caught her ears. Now a horse neighed. . . . Were they fighting? Then he must have forgotten to feed them hay before he went.

Among the clothes she had taken down to mend was an old duckcoat of her husband's which she had used every winter. Beret put the coat on, lit the lantern, and went to the barn to see what was wrong. But now all was quiet and peaceful. Two of the horses whinnied the moment they saw her. Having filled the mangers with hay she went into the cow barn to look at a cow which was overdue. She stepped into the stall to feel the animal. . . . It would be more than strange if they didn't have little folks here before morning! . . . She bedded the cow with fresh bedding, and looked after the calf stall; into it, too, she carried straw.

Before leaving the barn she blew out the lantern. Out in the yard she stopped and looked up at the weather. . . . Not so dark but that one could see the road . . . the rain would hardly come yet.

Back in the kitchen again, she looked about the room irresolutely. By the stove hung a black kerchief; she felt it before she tied it on her head. For a moment she seemed to have forgotten what to do next. . . . Aye, there stood the match box, what was the matter with her anyway? She took out a few matches and put them into her coat pocket. Turning the lamp low she waited until it went out. Picking up the lantern, but without lighting it, she left the house.

Upon reaching the main road she stopped, uncertain which way to take. . . . They did retire early at Tönseten's. By this time Kjersti would most likely have gone to bed. Perhaps she'd better not disturb her. . . . Still Beret hesitated. . . . It wasn't very far over to the schoolhouse . . . no, really. . . . The night was dark. As threatening as the weather looked tonight not many people would be on the road. . . . A pent-up sigh escaped her as she started westward. At first she walked slowly, deliberately, but little by little faster—in a moment she was running.

When she had reached a point only half a mile distant from the schoolhouse she took off from the road. Here began a cornfield which continued all the rest of the way. Going into the field so far that she was sure no one could see her from the road, she picked out a row which she began to follow westward. The stalks under her feet broke with loud crashes. The sound frightened her and made her pick her way more cautiously. . . . Her foot stepped on a cob; instinctively she picked it up and took it with her. Here was another cob—they certainly hadn't picked very clean . . . too bad to let all this corn rot in the field! Both cobs she stood up against a root.

Reaching the western edge of the field, she stopped dead still, facing the schoolhouse. From the windows light poured out upon the dark. One window was open; talk and much laughter came floating through it. Seized by a violent shaking, she crouched down, grabbing hold of a stalk in order to steady herself. A little distance back of the schoolhouse ran a fence, to which were tied several horses. No human being in sight.

In an instant Beret was standing close up against the back wall of the schoolhouse, listening intently. The loud voices of men reached her ear . . . could they be quarreling?—one sounded angry. . . . There a girl laughed . . . a voice full of youth and gaiety. Beret's knees were unsteady as she began working up to the nearest window. Reaching the corner of the window so that she could get a peep at the room, she looked right into the faces of two Negroes sitting on the platform by the teacher's desk, grinning. Their jet-black faces arrested her attention.

But only for a minute. . . . What was this? There stood Permand out on the floor, engaged in some silly manner with a girl—a girl . . . who was that girl? . . . God have mercy! . . . His arm was about her, her head resting on his shoulder, his face close to hers. . . . Beret found it difficult to breathe; her neck craned; her eyes had opened unnaturally wide, the pupils seemed to pop out. She couldn't see clearly because of innumerable small sparks dancing before her eyes. A faintness came over her; she had to lean against the wall—a cold hand was clutching her heart. The fierceness of the grip made her groan.

Like a drunken man she staggered away from the wall.
Over in the field she sank down on a bunch of cornstalks.
She groaned like one in unsufferable pain, all the while
whimpering, "Oh, my God, how can You let such things
come to pass?"

She didn't know how long she had sat thus when a
voice, clearly and distinctly, spoke by her side:

**Now goe, and smite Amalek, and utterly destroy all
that they habe, and spare them not; but slay both man
and woman, infant and suckling, oxe and sheepe, camell
and asse.**

Repeating the words carefully, she nodded to him who
spoke them, adding when the voice ceased talking, "Hush,
don't speak so loudly, I can hear you!"

Someone came out of the schoolhouse, took one of the
horses, and drove away. . . . A group of people was standing on the porch, talking and laughing gaily. A boy and a
girl, leaving the group, came around on this side. In the
light from the window Beret recognized them both plainly.
She could see that his arm was about the girl's waist and
that she clung close to him. She heard him speak, in a
low, thrilled voice, the girl only clinging closer to him.
. . . There he goes now, she thought . . . they'll be staying out all night—and me he couldn't even take down to
Kjersti's!

In the schoolhouse, someone blew out the lights. The
last buggy drove out of the yard. Before her in the dark,
the schoolhouse, crouching low and mysteriously alive,
stood waiting for her to come.

Beret arose stealthily. Stealing around to the front she
tried to open the door, which wouldn't budge. Putting her
lantern down she tried to break the door open, throwing
the weight of her body against it.

The resistance infuriated her. Running down the steps
she left the lantern by the corner; the next moment she
was over in the cornfield, snapping off stalks and tearing
leaves which she gathered into her skirt. With demoniacal
fury Beret worked until she had a load.

Carrying it over to the wall she began to hunt along
the sill on the lee side of the house. . . . Here a stone
had come out of the foundation! . . . Beret was on her

knees putting stalks and leaves into the hole. Suddenly her head raised—did she hear steps? . . . steps that walked with a heavy thud? No—it couldn't come from walking feet. The sound seemed more like intermittent snarls of an angry animal . . . didn't it come from the other side? On all fours she crept around the nearest corner, past the back wall, and peered around the other corner. All her senses were taut. Again sparks flared and flickered before her eyes. . . . The farther window must be loose . . . only the wind . . .

"Aren't you going to get done here tonight?" someone cried in her ear. The voice didn't frighten her, nor did she seem surprised. Of course she'd have to get ready—the rain was already commencing to fall, big drops with which the wind pierced the darkness.

Seeing clearly what must be done, she took the matches out of her pocket and got ready. But in striking the first one she broke it because her hand shook so violently. The little mishap with the match increased her excitement. Forcing herself to work calmly she struck another, carefully shading the light until she got it down into the kindling . . . thank God, now it was catching! Small flames —they seemed weak and drowsy—tried to take hold of the damp leaves, but after a few attempts gave up; in the edges tiny embers glowed awhile, curled back, then died, and again all was blackness.

Beret wouldn't believe it. The Lord Himself had commanded her to destroy this place of wickedness—it must burn! . . . Before her eyes drifted layers of mist, dimming her sight; her whole body shook as under an attack of ague. . . . Now I shall have to be careful, she thought; otherwise I shan't be able to carry out the Lord's command. . . . Careful? She felt resentful of the idea. How was one to work in a darkness like this? The wind had increased in violence, and now it was raining hard. . . . You might have fixed things a little easier for me! She protested in the manner of a pouting child. Beret crept close up to the wall; unbuttoning her coat and using it for shelter against the wind, she struck match after match and thrust it down among the damp leaves. Faint flames flickered for a moment, burning cheerfully wherever they found dry spots, then darkness again—blacker than ever. . . .

Now what is this? she sobbed, rising on her knees and hunting frantically for more matches. Suddenly she collapsed in a heap, moaning pitiably, "O God, help me to carry out Thy will!"

XI

No common rain this. The downpour came in torrents. The sluices of the heavens had all burst open. The huge waves racing through the air, encountering an obstruction, broke like surging breakers against a projecting mountainside.

Every time Beret put her foot down there came a sopping sound from her shoes. Her clothing pasted itself to her body. Yet she plodded on, her feet moving with a dull, monotonous regularity. An idea occurred to her—I must have been walking thus since the beginning of time. A stupefying satisfaction came over her because she had been able to keep on walking for so long a time. Nevertheless she couldn't help wishing that it would end pretty soon. Never had the walking been quite so difficult, for that she'd have remembered.

Tonight her mind was befogged, and refused to remember anything clearly. She had come to, sitting up against a wall, soaked through—what wall was it anyway? After getting to her feet she had kept searching for something she had lost . . . some object. What was it she had been searching for?

The weather disturbed her in her thinking. The wind was almost worse than the rain. Out of the raging darkness came solid barn walls falling upon her back—thank God she had the storm with her! Every once in a while she was thrown forward on all fours. Each time she would lose the lantern. And the lantern she couldn't afford to part with because she must look after that cow tonight. . . . The lantern? There you have it—that's what she had been looking for all night!

God be praised, here was home at last! Just as she opened the door the wind tore it out of her hands. Over by the clock Per Hansa was pounding the wall—if she didn't get the door shut this minute, the picture would come tumbling down. With some difficulty Beret got the door closed. . . . Now I'd better see about the lamp. Her thoughts worked sanely and orderly. She knew exactly where the matches were, found one, and got the lamp lit. . . . Awful how she was tracking up the floor! . . . Beret looked at the floor. What was that black cloth? Did you ever see the like—the wind had torn the crepe off Per Hansa! Carefully, lest she soil it, she picked it up and laid it on the table. . . . What was it she had been thinking of all the time? The cow? Yes, certainly she must look after the poor beast—she could change afterward. Before leaving the kitchen she stirred up the fire and put on a kettle of water . . . if the cow didn't need it she would want it herself.

Outside, the storm was so violent that she bent low in order to stand on her feet; still she had difficulty in reaching the barn.

The cow greeted her with prolonged mooings. And sure enough, there was the calf! Beret felt real satisfaction because her predictions had proved true. . . . What a fine little fellow! Beret took plenty of time in caring for the cow. She hurried back to the kitchen for a pail of luke-warm water. From a sack of cornmeal she had standing in the barn she mixed a few handfuls into the water. Later she busied herself with the calf.

When she came out of the barn again the rain had changed into sleet. Sticky flakes of snow were flying before the storm like mad furies.

Entering the house, she felt she was shivering . . . unless she got out of the wet clothes this minute, she'd get a cough. Undressing from top to toe she rubbed herself dry; even so she didn't stop until she felt a warm tingling through her body—then she slipped on a Sunday dress.

In the stove blazed a cheery fire. The kitchen was filled with a pleasing warmth which brought a languorous drowsiness to all her senses. Having wiped up the water on the floor she would have liked to go to bed. But back of her drowsiness an idea was working hard to break through, an idea of something undone which she must not forget. It must be important because the more she thought of it the more uneasy she got. A cold draft came sweeping down the stairway . . . he surely didn't have the window oper on a night like this?

Lighting the candle, which always stood ready on the kitchen shelf, she walked upstairs into Peder's room. She cast an eye on the empty bed, but showed no surprise because he wasn't there. Nor did she have time to ponder the problem where he might be, for through the window, left partly open at the top, the backlash of the wind drove sleet into the room. . . . This is a fine state of affairs! she exclaimed to herself. Water was dripping from the table. The cover of the English Bible, lying on top of a pile of books, had been soaked through. . . . This I must take down to dry on the stove-shelf.

Downstairs again, she wiped the cover with a dry cloth . . . too bad for such a fine book!—Closing the Bible, she saw sheets of paper sticking out. She pulled them out to see if they were dry; there were three of them, all three sheets written in a beautiful hand.

She placed the papers by the lamp while she took care of the Bible, then came back and looked at them. . . . Permand certainly wrote a fine hand when he wasn't in too much of a hurry! . . . Wonder what this can be? . . . English, of course. She held the pages close to the light— certainly, she might have guessed as much! . . . Reading the first words at the top which she understood readily enough, Beret began chuckling softly to herself. "To My Beloved" it said—aye, aye, so it did! . . . She hurried into her own room after her glasses, and returning quickly, sat down close to the lamp, her face wearing the expression of a child who has unexpectedly come upon a deep secret of a grown-up, and, knowing that he is not supposed to see it, gives in to an overmastering temptation. . . . She began to read slowly:

> For, lo, the winter is past,
>   The rain is over and gone;
> The flowers appear on the earth;
>   The time of the singing of birds is come,
>   And the voice of the turtle is heard in our land;
> The fig tree ripeneth her green figs.
>   And the vines are in blossom
>   They give forth their fragrance.
> Arise, my love, my fair one,
>   And come away.

O my dove, that art in the clefts of the rock,
In the covert of the steep place,
Let me see thy countenance,
Let me hear thy voice;
For sweet is thy voice,
And thy countenance is comely.

Beret's face beamed in childlike wonder and was lovely to look at. . . . Has Permand been trying to make poetry! This is nice—I don't care what you say. . . . She read on, making slow progress because she found many words that were strange to her.

Behold, thou art fair, my love; behold, thou art fair;
Thine eyes are as doves behind thy veil:
Thy hair is as a flock of goats
That lie along the side of Mount Gilead.
Thy teeth are like a flock of ewes that are newly shorn,
Which are come up from the washing;
Whereof every one hath twins,
And none is bereaved among them.

Beret's face took on a worried expression . . . I wonder where he can have got all this?

Thy lips are like a thread of scarlet,
And thy mouth is comely.
Thy temples are like a piece of a pomegranate
Behind thy veil.
Thy neck is like the tower of David builded for an armoury,
Whereon there hang a thousand bucklers,
All the shields of the mighty men.
Thy two breasts are like two fawns that are twins of a roe,
Which feed among the lilies.

Beret shook her head, her hand trembling . . . the boy didn't intend to show such nonsense to anyone—because that would never do! . . . Before she was aware of it, she had continued reading, getting at the sense slowly:

Thou art all fair, my love;
And there is no spot in thee.

Come with me from Lebanon, my bride, with me from
 Lebanon:
 Go from the top of Amana,
 From the top of Senir and Hermon,
From the lions' dens,
 From the mountains of the leopards.

Thou hast ravished my heart, my sister, my bride;
 Thou hast ravished my heart
 With one look from thine eyes,
 With one chain of thy neck.
How fair is thy love, my sister, my bride!
 How much better is thy love than wine!
 And the smell of thine ointment than all manner of
  spices!
Thy lips, O my bride, drop as the honeycomb:
 Honey and milk are under thy tongue;
 And the smell of thy garments is like the smell of
  Lebanon.

A garden shut up is my sister, my bride,
 A spring shut up,
 A fountain sealed. . . .

Beret had to read the lines once more. Now her hand
shook so violently that she had to lay the paper down . . .
had the boy lost all reason? Picking up the next page her
eyes scrutinized it absentmindedly before she began reading.

 Thou art beautiful, O my love, as Tirzah,
 Comely as Jerusalem,
  Terrible as an army with banners.
 Turn away thine eyes from me,
  For they have overcome me.
 Thy hair is as a flock of goats
  That lie along the side of Gilead.

While reading these lines the set expression in her face
relaxed. Her eyes shone with a soft brilliance, a dreamy,
faraway look having come into them. But at the conclusion she came to, with a sudden start:

How beautiful are thy feet in sandals, O prince's daughter!
The joints of thy thigh are like jewels,
The work of the hands of a cunning workman.
Thy navel is like a round goblet,
Wherein no mingled wine is wanting:
Thy belly is like a heap of wheat
Set about with lilies.

Beret arose abruptly . . . such wickedness shall get no further—I don't care how angry he gets!

Tearing up the sheets into small bits, she removed a lid from the stove and threw them into the fire, watching them while they were being consumed by the flames.

But the sight of the fire seemed to distract her. Shivers ran up and down her back. . . . It was burning fine now . . . well—didn't it burn? . . . She rubbed her forehead —how helpless she had come to be, here she had forgotten something else! A deep sigh escaped her as she stared into the fire. . . . Mechanically her hand moved, putting the lid back into place. . . . It must be bedtime by now. . . . Perhaps she had better go to bed.

Beret took the lamp to go to her room. From sheer force of habit, she stopped by the wall to see what time it was. The clock was nearing twelve, but she did not see it at all. Her eyes were fastened on her husband. She held the lamp close to the picture. . . . How odd he looked tonight. His whole face smiled roguishly at her . . . was so strangely light and cheerful. . . . I wonder what he can be thinking about. Beret looked at the picture a long time.

Turning down the lamp, she let it burn low . . . she might have to use it later on. A vague idea, hazy and far away, was trying to get her attention. She was waiting for someone who would be coming pretty soon. In the meantime she would only lie down on the bed and rest herself. Pulling off her shoes, she lay down with her clothes on. . . . A languorous bliss came over her—how good it felt to stretch a bit! . . . She had better be careful not to fall asleep before he came.

She didn't sleep either . . . only lay there looking at her own thoughts moving slowly across a faraway horizon. At times she had to strain her senses in order to see them. . . . Wouldn't he be coming pretty soon? . . . How

could he be gone so long on a night like this? . . . He
would be here soon now . . . of course . . . pretty soon.
. . . There he was now! And he didn't go upstairs, but
came into her room! Beret turned her head to look at him
. . . what—of all things! What kind of company was this
tonight! . . . Right by the bed stood Per Hansa, her dead
husband, beaming down upon her. By his eyes, which were
only narrow slits, she could see he was in high spirits. . . .
But how strangely had he dressed himself. She looked
closely at his clothes—a big stocking cap pulled down over
his ears, that old duckcoat of his, and heavy German socks
on his feet. Aye, aye—now she remembered, it was snow-
ing outside! But she found no time to think of how he
was dressed for he was speaking to her:

"It's only this, dear Beret-girl. The last time I was here,
I did what you wanted me to, though I didn't quite like it.
Now you must listen to me, I've set my mind on it: Don't
go against Permand! Let him have the girl he is so fond of.
Don't you recall how mad I was about you? And you
weren't much better yourself as far as I remember; you
never paid any attention to what your parents said about it
—and thank God you didn't!"

Beret was sitting up in bed, looking at him.

"What are you saying, Per Hansa? Go and change your
clothes this minute while I get you a cup of warm coffee!"

"Never mind troubling about that. I have much to attend to and can't stop here. But you talk to Permand right
away. Hard to tell how this business will turn out unless
he gets the girl. . . . Now I've got to be off, the Lord
Himself is standing outside the door waiting for me!"

XII

When Beret awoke the voice of her husband was still
ringing in her ears. He must have left the room this very
minute. Jumping out of bed she hurried to the window,
stood there looking out. A pale, gray light greeted her. The
day seemed asleep yet. The prairie had a soft, white covering on it. Hastening to the kitchen and opening the door
quickly, she peered out, holding her breath. . . . No
sound save the dripping from the roof, the drops falling

with a heavy splash. . . . No sign of footprints in the snow . . . where could they be?—why, he had just gone.

The cold air chilled her. Closing the door she went back into the kitchen and made a fire, put on the coffeepot and the oatmeal; then going to the stairway she called to Peder as she was wont to do every morning. But without waiting for him she took the milk pails and went to the barn—she needed to be alone to work this out before he came.

While Peder was having his breakfast in the kitchen, she kept puttering about in her own room, not being able to recall why she had gone there. She looked at the different objects, sat down, and, getting up again, stood by the window staring out. Her lips moved, but no sound came. Hearing Peder go upstairs, she went back to the kitchen; seeing food on the table she sat down to have her breakfast. As soon as she had done eating she cleared the table and washed the dishes, working very slowly. At times she forgot what she was about.

All through the day she moved as one in a dream, yet omitted nothing from the customary routine. But for dinner she put only bread and butter on the table, and a glass of milk for herself and for Peder.

Peder came down from upstairs whistling softly to himself. By the table he stopped and broke into a laugh—he couldn't help himself. . . . What kind of feast had she prepared today? Was this all she had to feed hungry people?

His mother, her back turned to him, was standing over by the stove.

"We're going away today," she said absentmindedly.

"Are we going away?"

A pause followed.

"I s'pose we'll have to go over to Doheny's and see about the wedding."

Peder turned crimson. He sat down and didn't dare look up. A wave of deep joyousness surged back and forth in him. . . . How good of Mother! He could have gone right over and hugged her.

"We've agreed to wait until spring," he confessed, low-voiced and very bashful.

Again silence.

"Neither your father nor I can agree to that." An odd

note of resentment had come into Beret's voice. She was
still busy by the stove. Peder glanced up at her. . . . Today she is in bad humor. She has been lying awake during
the night, waiting for me. . . . Perhaps she was down at
Kjersti's last night. . . . The tongues are wagging all right.
. . . Well, let 'em talk!

Beret hung up a kettle and turned to him. Her face
seemed flushed; her eyes had a strange expression; they
shone with an unnatural brilliancy, yet had a faraway look.
Peder, finding it hard to meet her eyes, looked down. . . .
She takes it hard all right . . . that I knew beforehand.
. . . Just wait until she gets to know Susie!

"There's no great hurry," he said slowly, trying to calm
her.

"Enough of that, Permand, this time you'll have to mind
me!" Beret spoke in excited determination, like one afraid
of not gaining his point.

Peder got up from the table, uncertain. She seemed so
upset today that he was afraid to talk to her.

Seeing him stand there irresolute, exasperated her beyond the point of endurance:

"Go and get yourself ready—don't you hear me? . . .
Later in the day they may not be home at Doheny's. . . .
I must see him at once!"

Peder couldn't remember having seen his mother thus.
Not knowing what else to do he went upstairs. A mingled
feeling of resentment and depression played in his mood.
He would have liked to smash things up a bit, yet he felt
more like throwing himself upon the bed and bawling for
all he was worth.

But little by little the thought that they were really going to Doheny's to talk over an event which he and Susie
had seen only in dreams, dispelled his anxiety. . . . His
preparations completed, he slowly descended the stairs.
. . . Why worry about it anyway . . . if necessary, he'd
be willing to get married tomorrow . . . then Mother
need no longer be lonesome! . . . The idea cheered him.
. . . Of course Mother will get over it . . . she has always been a bit queer. . . . Let's hurry and be off. . . .
The astonishment to be caused by their unexpected arrival
together at the Dohenys' filled him with laughter; yet he
managed to keep a sober mien. . . . And Susie . . . what

an amazing surprise for her! . . . Peder glanced up to find his mother's eyes upon him with a strange intensity that startled him. Suddenly her face lit up into a bright smile, like that of a child who has fussed long and then unexpectedly gains his point.

THE END

A Biographical Note

Ole Edvart Rölvaag was born on 22 April 1876, in a small fishing settlement on the rocky island of Dønna off the Norwegian coast just south of the Arctic Circle. His paternal ancestors of the family Ravnöy had lived on the Helgeland islands for nearly two centuries and in the eighteenth century had even taken the name of the little cove where they lived, Rölvaag. For several generations the family, once quite prosperous, had been fishermen and cottage-farmers, free but owing allegiance to the landed family Coldevin of Dønnes. Among the Rölvaags there was an unusual amount of native intelligence and ambition, which showed itself from time to time, notably in Rölvaag himself and in his gifted older sister and brother, both of whom died young.

Little is known of Rölvaag's youth, although in the sketches for a projected autobiography, *The Romance of a Life*, he left a number of remarkably graphic descriptions of Dønna and Lofoten and some truly charming reminiscences of his childhood among his hardy, independent family. The Norwegian Sea with its icy fjords and austerely beautiful coastal islands made a profound impression on the child's mind, an impression that was to remain with him forever and to be reflected later in his descriptions of the American prairie. A second and equally profound impression on Rölvaag was his father's conviction that of his seven children Ole Edvart was the stupid one, not worth educating and best suited for fishing. This impression, too, never left him and influenced all that he later felt and did.

321

Largely for this reason young Ole Edvart's formal schooling was slight and generally semireligious. He attended a preconfirmation school at Snekkevik, some fourteen miles from Rölvaag, nine weeks a year for seven years. In 1891, when he reached fifteen years of age, he was confirmed as a Lutheran, and his school days ended. The following winter he sailed as a nonsharing apprentice with the Lofoten fishing boats. It was a hard and demanding life of long hours and exhausting labor, but Rölvaag learned and became one of the best. Nevertheless, he continued to read widely and miscellaneously and to study the Bible. Thus, his early education actually came from books. Once, when he was about ten years old, Rölvaag walked fourteen miles and stayed away two days to read a copy of *Ivanhoe* in translation. This extensive reading was not unusual, for among the Helgeland fisherfolk the principal cultural influence, after the stern, pervasive Protestantism of the state church, was the well-stocked libraries.

In January of 1893 an extraordinary storm swept across the North Atlantic and into the Norwegian coast, and great numbers of fishermen were drowned. Somehow the crew of Rölvaag's boat managed to reach shore, but only with almost superhuman efforts that marked him physically and psychologically for life. It was shortly after this harrowing experience that Rölvaag first thought of emigrating to America and wrote to his uncle Jakob Fredrik in South Dakota asking for passage. No reply was forthcoming, and Rölvaag continued as a fisherman, though now sharing fully in the profits.

Three years later a letter from his uncle arrived unexpectedly with an invitation and a ticket. Rölvaag's captain, a man whom he greatly admired and loved, offered to buy him a fishing boat, making him a skipper at twenty years of age, if he would remain in Norway. The offer was probably without precedent and a great honor; but the aggressive and ambitious Rölvaag saw it only as an end to his dreams of career and sadly refused. Several weeks later he left Dønna for Oslo, then called Christiania, whence he sailed on the steamer *Norge* for New York City. There, without money except an American dime and a Norwegian five-øre copper and speaking no English, he took the train for Elk Point in South Dakota. For some reason his uncle failed to meet him. Rölvaag walked until he found a Norwegian settlement, where he learned how to reach the farm where his uncle worked. Here he began three years of hard work as a hired hand to earn the money to repay his uncle. Many of these experiences are recreated in the book *Amerika-Breve* (*Letters from America*), which he later wrote under the pen name Paal Mørck. Rölvaag found farming in those days as exhausting as fishing, and he liked it less. Finally, after a brief time spent working at odd jobs in Iowa and another stint of farming in the Dakotas, he took the advice of a close friend and enrolled in Augustana Academy, a two-year school in Canton, South Dakota, where "a fisherboy . . . from Nordland" began preparing for college at the age of twenty-three. In the fall of 1901, with his diploma and forty dollars in pocket, he entered St. Olaf College in Northfield, Minnesota. Studying very hard and working as well to maintain himself, Rölvaag obtained the education that he had so long wanted and was graduated with honors in 1905. He then borrowed five hundred dollars and returned to Norway, where he studied literature at the University of Oslo. It was there that he first began to feel the great strain on his health of the hard physical labor and the long hours of study. He was often ill, but managed to complete his work on time and was graduated with the highest mark obtainable.

Afterward he visited his family on Dønna, returning in the fall of 1906 to St. Olaf to accept an instructorship in the department of Norwegian. Here he remained until the last few years of his life, teaching and writing. Here, too, in 1908 he married Jennie Marie Berdahl, the sister of a college friend and herself the descendant of very early Norwegian settlers in America.

During his student days at St. Olaf Rölvaag wrote his first novel, *Nils og Astri* (*Nils and Astri*), which he later tried unsuccessfully to have published in Norway. His first published book was actually a Norwegian-English vocabulary (*Ordforklaring*), brought out in 1909 by the Augsburg Publishing House of Minneapolis. This little book was followed in later years by *The First, Second* and *Third Norwegian Readers,* a series of textbooks. Besides these books, written largely for Norwegian-American students, Rölvaag also had published a collection of essays and articles on Norwegian culture in America entitled *Omkring Fædearven* (*Concerning Our Heritage*). Most of Rölvaag's other writing was fictional, beginning with the semiautobiographical *Amerika-Breve* in 1912 and *Paa Glemte Veie* (*On Forgotten Paths*) two years later. "Paal Mørck" received some small notice in the Norwegian communities of the American Northwest and abroad, but it was not until the publication of *To tullinger* (*Two Fools*) under his own name in 1920 that Rölvaag became fairly well known. This novel was followed in 1922 by *Længselens baat* (*The Boat of Longing*), a poetic novel about a sensitive Norwegian youth who comes to America as the land of his dreams only to find intense disappointment. The various themes arising out of the immigrant's situation recur in Rölvaag's work until they find their greatest expression in *Giants in the Earth*. All of these works were written in Norwegian and published by Augsburg.

With the publication of *I de dage* (*In Those Days*) in 1924 and *Riket grundlægges* (*Founding the Kingdom*) in 1925 in Oslo, Rölvaag's reputation as a writer was made. He returned to Norway as a man of letters. It was the notice that he received in the American press because of these books that first attracted Lincoln Colcord, himself a writer, to him. Colcord wrote to Rölvaag about having these books translated; and Rölvaag, whose book had already been rejected by Knopf, replied. A fast and close friendship developed, and Colcord introduced Rölvaag to Eugene Saxton of Harper & Brothers. Translation proceeded by what Rölvaag later described as "double action," in which Colcord edited a translation by various hands and submitted it to Rölvaag for polishing. In the spring of 1927 Harper & Brothers published *Giants in the Earth*, the one-volume translation of *I de dage*, and *Riket grundlægges*, which soon became a best seller and made Rölvaag's reputation as an American writer as well.

The following year Rölvaag wrote and helped to translate the second volume of his saga of immigration and adaptation, *Peder Seier*. This book was published in Norwegian in Oslo in December of 1928 and in English in New York City the next month. Then, encouraged by Colcord and Saxton, Rölvaag revised *To tullinger* and translated it into English. Published as *Pure Gold* in 1930, it, too, was a best seller.

The third volume of the saga was, like *Peder*, written and translated at the same time and was published in 1931 as *Their Fathers' God* here and as *Den signede dag* (*The Blessed Day*) in Oslo. But Rölvaag, who had long suffered ill health and angina pectoris, did not live to see the bound volumes of this book. A translation of *Længselens baat* was published posthumously in 1933.

Among many projects Rölvaag had intended writing a fourth and final volume of the saga, in which Peder's life would have been described through World War I, as well as his autobiography, which was actually begun. In these later years Rölvaag received much acclaim here and in Norway. He was awarded the Order of St. Olaf by King Haakon of Norway and received an honorary doctorate from the University of Wisconsin. But the greatest honor to Rölvaag has been reserved to those generations of readers who have followed and discovered in these books more than the saga of Norwegian immigrants struggling to make their way; indeed, have found in them one of the most beautiful and powerful expressions of that American national phenomenon—pioneering.